MAIRS TALES

by

Christine
Macintosh

Published by
Northfield Publishing,
54 Main Street,
Longside,
Aberdeenshire

Printed by
P Scrogie,
17 Chapel Street,
Peterhead
AB42 1TH
01779 476373

ISBN No. 0-9545645-0-2

Dedication:

To Sheila

"If my slight Muse do please these curious days,
The pain be mine, but thine shall be the praise."

Shakespeare

LONGSIDE 1920

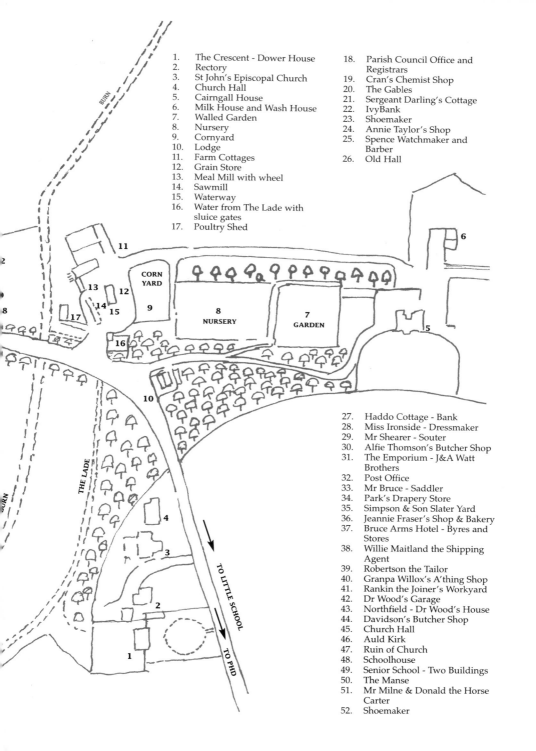

1. The Crescent - Dower House
2. Rectory
3. St John's Episcopal Church
4. Church Hall
5. Cairngall House
6. Milk House and Wash House
7. Walled Garden
8. Nursery
9. Cornyard
10. Lodge
11. Farm Cottages
12. Grain Store
13. Meal Mill with wheel
14. Sawmill
15. Waterway
16. Water from The Lade with sluice gates
17. Poultry Shed
18. Parish Council Office and Registrars
19. Cran's Chemist Shop
20. The Gables
21. Sergeant Darling's Cottage
22. IvyBank
23. Shoemaker
24. Annie Taylor's Shop
25. Spence Watchmaker and Barber
26. Old Hall

27. Haddo Cottage - Bank
28. Miss Ironside - Dressmaker
29. Mr Shearer - Souter
30. Alfie Thomson's Butcher Shop
31. The Emporium - J&A Watt Brothers
32. Post Office
33. Mr Bruce - Saddler
34. Park's Drapery Store
35. Simpson & Son Slater Yard
36. Jeannie Fraser's Shop & Bakery
37. Bruce Arms Hotel - Byres and Stores
38. Willie Maitland the Shipping Agent
39. Robertson the Tailor
40. Granpa Willox's A'thing Shop
41. Rankin the Joiner's Workyard
42. Dr Wood's Garage
43. Northfield - Dr Wood's House
44. Davidson's Butcher Shop
45. Church Hall
46. Auld Kirk
47. Ruin of Church
48. Schoolhouse
49. Senior School - Two Buildings
50. The Manse
51. Mr Milne & Donald the Horse Carter
52. Shoemaker

A personal message to the residents of Longside ... and the rest

Peoples' memories are notoriously inaccurate and despite conscientiously cross-checking my information there are bound to be errors in this book. If I have misrepresented your forefathers in any way I apologise sincerely and assure you that no harm was intended. Also, in these days of "political correctness" some of the old nicknames sound cruelly forthright, but they were given and accepted with the same good nature that I am hoping we all still share today.

CM

Contents

Chapter 1

He That Has Muckle Would Aye Hae Mair

The room was fairly crackling with their animosity as the two siblings argued with each other. Fresh insults had been traded and old grievances resurrected. It seemed that neither party was going to back down. So finally, exasperated beyond anything he had felt before, Sandy drew himself up to his full height, which was an impressive six feet, and delivered his trump card against his sister.

"I'll take no more of your lip! Do you hear?" he demanded imperiously in a tone at complete odds with his previous bitter whining. "Father and mother might be fooled with your constant mealy-mouthing, but I'll not!" he screeched. "And you'd better keep that in mind, Elizabeth," he continued waspishly, "because when they're awa' it'll be up to me to keep you!"

Elizabeth almost shouted back at him after this provocation, but the words died on her lips as she remembered her mother's presence in the next room, and she couldn't bring herself to say anything that would directly cause her to be unhappy. She couldn't talk about her parents' death - especially not in anger.

Sandy mistook his sister's white-faced silence as admittance of her defeat and felt with a thrill, that he had finally got the upper hand. Elated at having at last put his older sister "in her place," he maliciously embarked on expounding the reasons, as he saw them, as to why his spinster sister should show him a sight more respect than she was wont to do up until now. In his triumph he didn't care whom he should offend.

"Aye, Elizabeth. When they're dead and gone, it'll be from me that you'll have to beg for your next pair of shoes! Whoever would be daft enough to take you off my hands?" he sneered contemptuously. And he waggled his index finger at her as he delivered his final threat, as if to some recalcitrant pupil, "You'd better keep a civil tongue in your head when you speak to me in future, for I have a long memory!" He stood towering above his still sedentary sister, flushed with self-righteousness. He looked down on her bowed head and enjoyed this feeling of power over her. "Useless!" he gloated, but not so loud that their mother might hear him say it. Gratified by her continuing silence he took a deep breath ready to berate her further. But he never got started.

"Useless am I?" demanded Elizabeth tersely and jerked her head upwards so that she could look him in the eye. Caught unawares by her retaliation Sandy took a surprised step backwards.

Her eyes flashing with fury, Elizabeth rounded on him.

"Useless?" she asked with slow menace. "I help mother to wash your clothes, starch your collars, mend your socks, cook your food, sweep and dust your room! I have learned father's job back to front and step in when he's tired or sick! On top of that I hold down a man's full-time job at Stephen and Smith's. I may not have had your university education but I do my bit and more for the war effort!" Her anger well and truly ignited, her next words were delivered with the clarity of cold rage. "While it's true that I am a spinster, no-one in this world - especially you Alexander Cormack - has any right to call me useless!" Her eyes were blazing as they swept over her brother with authoritative contempt. She surveyed the soft-jowled, pasty-faced man before her and determined to say not another word. They had had similar arguments to this many times before, but none as bad as this. She knew with absolute certainty that she would sooner wash stairs than ever allow herself to be beholden to her arrogant penny-pinching brother!

"Now, now you two!" their mother scolded sharply as she entered the room. She was vexed by their continual bickering and was especially alarmed at the intensity of this particular argument. "Are you both having words about this soldier again?" she asked them briskly. She looked at the two red faces glaring at each other but didn't get an answer.

"Well that's alright then," she continued crisply. "Sandy, you ask your friend home for a bit supper next Wednesday evening and he'll be made welcome here," she said with forced brightness and glowered at her daughter in a way that allowed no argument. Then her voice softened. "Elizabeth...." she reproached her daughter more gently, "it's not like you to be unkind. I'm pleased that Sandy invites his friends to the house, and this sounds like a nice man he's come across. Not like some of the others we've been introduced to," she added a bit more quietly, outwith her son's hearing. Then, with a conspiratorial wink at her daughter, she attempted to improve the hostile atmosphere in the room by adding lightly, "I expect he'll appreciate a bit of home-baking. It'll be an improvement on army food at any rate. The barracks is no bed of roses.... And I doubt that money comes into it," she whispered even more quietly for Elizabeth's ears only. And before her daughter could object to her platitudes she raised her voice and said plainly, "Let him come by all means."

She knew from the mutinous look that flashed from Elizabeth that there would be no point in pressing for an apology, so she carried on setting the table and ignored the strained atmosphere. "I'll have plenty of Auntie Wyness's home-made cheese, and I'll make sure that there's a fresh batch of oatcakes and scones baked on the griddle and left in the girnal," she continued conversationally. "Now...how will that do Sandy?" she asked confidently.

Her son had almost recovered from his sister's unexpected onslaught - she had never answered back so vehemently before - and he was now looking for a way to show his disapproval of the whole business. So he shrugged ostentatiously and appeared to give serious attention to his mother's suggestion, before replying with a bored drawl and deliberately off-hand manner, "I suppose it will have to do." This response was calculated to leave his mother with the impression that, as usual, her efforts wouldn't really be up to the standard expected of a university-educated graduate. At the same time he hoped his feigned nonchalance would convey to his sister that he found her former outburst merely tiresome.

Unfortunately, a nervous giggle escaped from Elizabeth at this point, whereupon Sandy in a fresh burst of temper, snatched up the newspaper and flounced off to his room.

Neither women moved, and Mrs Cormack waited until she gauged that Elizabeth's colour had returned to normal before saying reproachfully, "What got into you lass? You know better than to argue with Sandy when he's on his high horse. He doesn't really mean it you know." Then she looked keenly at her daughter as a new thought struck her. "Is it that knee of yours?" she asked anxiously. "Is it playing you up again? Here, you sit by the fire while I get the table set."

Elizabeth's thoughts were still deep in the argument she had just had with her brother, but as her mother's concern penetrated her subconscious she snapped back into the present.

"No, no, mother," Elizabeth replied quickly to reassure her. Then her inherent honesty rose to the fore. "Well, it is a bit, but no matter. See now, I'll help you set the tea." And she stood up trying to hide the effort it required. Then rubbing her right knee as unobtrusively as she could, she reached in to the cupboard. But because her thoughts were still immersed in the argument she stopped what she was doing, and couldn't contain the exasperation in her voice. "Can't you see it, mother?" she asked abruptly. And there was pain and indignation in her voice when she continued, "He uses you!"

"Och Elizabeth, dinna start a' that up again!" her mother snapped. "Your father'll be ben in five minutes and I don't want to hear another word on the subject!" And this was said with a finality that brooked no more argument.

*   *   *

The Cormack family lived in the Parish Council House in Bucksburn where Mr William Cormack was Inspector of Poor. The building was situated at 23 Inverurie Road, near its junction with Dyce Road, not far from the fountain. Mr Cormack conducted his work from an office within his home where he lived with his wife Isabella, their three sons William,

Alexander and Edwin, and their daughter Elizabeth. His sister Charlotte, known to the children as Aunt Chat, had also lived with them since the death of their parents.

It was 1915 and William and Edwin were away in the Great War having signed up early on. It was a difficult time for those left "at hame" who had to try and carry on living normally in what was a particularly abnormal situation. They lived in daily fear of the deaths of their loved ones who were facing dangers abroad, but felt unable to voice their private concerns about them on account of their personal and national pride. It was important for everyone's morale during this Great War that they believed a quick and total victory lay "just around the corner."

*   *   *

Elizabeth said no more for the present, but she was still feeling aggrieved. As she saw it, her younger brother Sandy wanted two things in life other than success at his work; and these were to have friends, and to have money. He combined these two ambitions very satisfactorily by getting his mother to provide food and hospitality for the friends he cultivated. Thereby, he earned their gratitude and friendship whilst saving on his expenses.

As a professional man in his twenties it would have been more fashionable for Mr Alexander Cormack to have taken lodgings in Aberdeen, but few establishments would have provided the care and comfort he received from his mother. And few would have done his washing and mending for the pittance he grudgingly handed over to her every month. His salary as Assistant Master at Robert Gordon's Boys' School, plus what he earned teaching at Evening Classes, was more than sufficient for him to live on comfortably, but this wasn't enough for him. Every penny he earned was a prisoner, and he in turn was imprisoned in a very miserly life - or he would have been if he hadn't abused his parents' natural generosity.

He had graduated with an MA at Aberdeen University in 1913. Part of his studies had been done in Rennes in Brittany in Northern France, where he had gained a Higher Diploma in Literature and Languages, and since 1913 he had been Secretary of the Franco-Scottish society. In 1914 he had started teaching French at Robert Gordon's. He was a solitary man and

5

hardworking, but he had an arrogance and a meanness that appealed to very few folk.

It had been taken for granted that their sons' education had had to take priority over Elizabeth Jane's. Although Mr and Mrs Cormack both acknowledged that Elizabeth was certainly as bright as her brothers were, the family finances wouldn't run to putting her through University too. Anyway, there were very few women who got the chance to indulge in further education at that time. So Elizabeth had left school at 16, having studied for two years longer than most girls of her age; and gone on to help her father in his work as Inspector of Poor and Registrar of Births, Deaths and Marriages in the Bucksburn area. Elizabeth had learned every aspect of her father's work, and her beautiful handwriting was a positive asset when writing the certificates. Sadly, a lot of Mr Cormack's work involved overseeing the Poor House at Oldmill where many down-and-outs died nameless.

As part of the War Effort, Elizabeth had accepted a position with "Stephen and Smith Advocates" in Aberdeen, where her youngest brother Edwin, had been serving his apprenticeship. Edwin had enlisted as soon as he was sixteen years old, much against his parents' wishes, and had temporarily given up this post in order to go to war. But he hoped to return soon with a row of medals on his chest, and a plentiful supply of heroic adventures with which to regale the office staff.

With so many men away at war, much of their work fell to the women and Elizabeth had agreed to take over Edwin's post temporarily. And again because of her beautiful copperplate handwriting and experience of keeping complete confidentiality, she was given the special task of hand-writing wills for soldiers keen to put their affairs in order before going off to war. She loved the independence of working, and found it a welcome challenge.

When she was seven years old Elizabeth had jumped off a wall and landed awkwardly damaging her right knee. It had never mended properly, and for the rest of her childhood she had been bedevilled with pain, and endured gruelling appointments with their local doctor who repeatedly removed bits of fractured bone. These surgical procedures had continued until she was around twenty-one, when the condition went into remission. But throughout her childhood it meant that she had had to wear special fur-lined boots to help protect her injured knee. Bad eyesight meant that she had also had to wear glasses. She would never forget wearing her first pair of spectacles when she was re-awakened to the beauty of the world around her, and "deeved" her family by going on about it so much. Having been made aware of the fragility of her sight from such an early age, she would always think of her eyesight as something precious.

She smiled nowadays at the memory of when she was a bairn and the boys in her class used to chant, "Garret windaes and feathery feet!" in the typical way that children ridiculed anyone different from the herd. It had never got her down though, because she was feisty, and gave back as good as she got!

It may have been a consequence of these taunts in her childhood, or perhaps because of her religious upbringing, but Elizabeth was never given to personal vanity. Whatever the reason, if she took time to look in a mirror nowadays she would find nothing in her reflection to be worried by. For there she would see an attractive, slim woman of five feet six inches with straight shiny dark brown hair viewing the world through laughing blue eyes. At 25 years old she had plenty of admirers but no-one special. She wasn't entertaining any notions of marriage meantime.

There were many more men in Aberdeen just now, doing basic training at the Hardgate or at the Harbour, prior to being sent to the front. Times were uncertain and the intense social life that surrounded the soldiers reflected their imminent proximity to death. However, they couldn't really get up to much ill on 1/- a day, and in any case the majority of young women had been imbued with strict Victorian values. Most of the lassies were in service at various houses that entailed having to work long hard days that started very early. They would only have some free time between 2pm and 9pm on a Sunday, with perhaps a day off once a month. Their mothers, landladies and mistresses jealously guarded the morals of these young women, and any attempt at promiscuity meant instant dismissal. If they were ever unfortunate enough to land with a bairn, they would be literally thrown out on to the streets and made outcasts of their families and society in general.

But passions were intense during this war, and marriages could be arranged quickly, which was a respectable way out in many cases. All too often though, this particular solution resulted in widows bringing up fatherless bairns.

Although she was sought after, Elizabeth was too much her own woman to betray her principles, and she steadfastly retained her high moral standards. The Church and its precepts meant a lot to her, and she enjoyed a lot of fun within its doctrine quite naturally. She had grown into a fine woman with great depth of character whose head was not easily turned. A contented quine, she lived at home and spent her leisure hours honing her natural talents in a whole range of domestic capabilities.

Naturally gregarious and full of laughter, she was good company. But for some reason her younger brother Alexander, or Sandy as his friends called him, could hardly thole her - nor for the most part - she him. Some folk thought that he was jealous of her popularity, others blamed her closeness to their father. Whatever the reason, he never missed an opportunity to taunt her about her weak knee and lack of education compared with his own. Over the years Elizabeth had outgrown this imagined rivalry with her brother and nowadays tended not to rise to the bait.

Other than Sandy's constant sniping, there was a new source of disquiet in her life just now that was keeping her on edge, and it cut too deeply for her to share it with her parents since it would only add to their worry about her brothers, William and Edwin. Although the family discussed the war often enough between themselves, Elizabeth could never bring herself to mention what was now troubling her on a daily basis.

Leaving the "Subbie" every morning she saw trains from the south arriving into Aberdeen Station loaded with wounded soldiers taken home from the front. She would watch in horror while these poor young men, who were little more than boys, were given cigarettes and cups of tea by nurses and women from the Red Cross. Then from her office window later in the day she found it impossible to ignore the steady stream of open carts trundling up Bridge Street along Union Terrace, to the Infirmary at Woolmanhill. She had looked closely once, and discovered that these carts were filled with mutilated young casualties. Elizabeth would have liked to talk about it with her brother in an effort to relieve the anguish and distress she felt at these sights, but Sandy would ridicule her and always refused to hear her out. So she kept her own counsel, and kept quiet too when the subject was discussed between her father, the doctor and the minister when they came to visit. She was finding it hard to reconcile the awful spectre of the wounded and bloodied young soldiers, with the government's talk of patriotism, glory and victory. And she was thankful that neither of her two brothers was at the front in Flanders just then.

William and Isabella Cormack were proud of their four offspring. When the children were younger William had been employed like his father before him, as a Ruler at Stoneywood Paper Mill. He had worked on the top floor of the mill under its glass roof and consequently been roasted in the summer and frozen in the winter. They had lived at Lilybank Cottage in Bankhead at that time, and his working day had started at 6am and ended at 6pm. The workers went home for their breakfasts and dinners during the course of their long day, the only two breaks they had. The mill was built alongside the River Don which provided the waterpower needed for the machines. Situated in the valley, it meant that the workers faced a steep climb home in addition to the toil of their work. The children too had to work long hours, and when they fell asleep, as often happened, they were loaded on to a flat horse-drawn wagon, and delivered home to the surrounding areas of Woodside, Bucksburn, Bankhead and Stoneywood.

As the years passed, Mr Cormack had found it increasingly difficult to cope with the arthritic pain brought on by his work. Eventually, ill health had forced him to look for alternative employment where he could use his mind instead of his muscle. Since his family had always been closely involved with the Church, it was no surprise when the local minister took a hand in directing William towards his current occupation.

William's grandfather had been a missionary who sold Bibles and religious literature on behalf of the East Coast Mission, and had distributed his wares in Aberdeen and the various fishing communities on the north-east coast.

William himself was currently an elder of his local church and superintendent of the Sunday School, and had been all his married life. The Cormack family's whole way of life revolved around the Free Church, and when the local vacancy for a Poor Inspector had arisen, the minister had

9

recommended him strongly for the post. Which was how Mr William Cormack had come to be Inspector of Poor and Registrar for Births, Deaths and Marriages in the Parish of Newhills. And as a direct consequence of this, the family had moved from Bankhead into the Parish Council House in Bucksburn.

Isabella Cormack was four years younger than her husband and hailed from Overton of Dyce, about a mile from the village of Dyce, where her father Robert Allan still lived. Mr Allan had been a gravedigger and quarryman and, according to Sandy who later documented his grandfather's achievements in one of his books, "...set off the explosives, and cultivated the fields belonging to the Quarry up to 1912, working from 6am to 6pm in summer, and from dawn to dusk in the winter, earning a maximum of 16/- per week...At work the old man sweated profusely, and consumed large amounts of cool water.... His food consisted of porridge and milk at 5.30am, oatcakes and cheese and milk at noon at the quarry, and at 6.00pm, milk pudding, an egg and oatcakes. He kept black Menorca hens that laid large white eggs, and he cultivated an extensive garden for annual shows at Parkhill and Blackburn. He was the first man in the district to have a honey extractor. As Beadle to Dyce Church - one service on Sunday - he earned £4 per annum, plus fees for interments. A hardworking gentle man, he was loved by his family, and in later years, he liked to have his grandchildren around him. The Cormack children used to help him dust the seats of the church, hoe the walks, and on occasions helped him to blast rock with gunpowder in the opening of a new grave."

Isabella was the eighth of his ten children of which six had survived. She was refined, kind-hearted and deeply religious, with a keen sense of humour that she had passed on to her daughter. She was a neat and tidy kind of woman with a head of wavy white hair. Although Elizabeth had long luxurious brown hair that reached down to her waist, she was envious of her mother's curls. But Isabella wouldn't accept the compliment and instead chided her daughter; "It's better to have thick hair though it's straight and brown." Isabella's tongue was hardly ever at peace and she had something to say about everything that went on in her world. She also knew what she wanted in life, and usually found a way to get it. Her husband knew this only too well, because when he first met her at a local church event he had been too shy to talk to her - until she deliberately stuck a hatpin into him! After that remarkable introduction he had no more trouble talking to her, and indeed must have liked her replies because a year later he had asked her to marry him. They were living proof that "opposites attract" and had happily stayed together for the last thirty years.

Their eldest son, William, or Bill as his family and friends called him, Elizabeth's older brother, had been working in Africa as a manager of a tobacco plantation when war had broken out. He enlisted in the army out there, and was currently fighting against the Germans in South West Africa. 1910 had seen the formation of the Union of South Africa, after the defeat of the Boers. Lord Kitchener had been given the credit for ending the Boer War and at that time was hailed as a hero. It would be a different matter later, when it was realised that he had been responsible for the introduction of concentration camps as a strategy of war.

Back home, this Great War against Germany would be fought under the command of Lord Kitchener, now promoted to Field Marshall, and whatever else he was, he turned out to be a brilliant propagandist. In 1914 when a Taube monoplane dropped a bomb on Dover - the first raid on British soil since the Norman Invasion, everyone realised that it was going to be a very different kind of war, and many feared that Britain was not ready for it. But Kitchener's propaganda left no room for hesitation. Thousands of posters appeared overnight urging the men to go to war, asking of them, "Do You Love Your Country?" Others showed pictures of girlfriends and wives demanding, "Don't I Mean Enough To You?" Or "Wouldn't You Fight For Me?" These posters were designed to bring out protective instincts in the menfolk, and instil an emotional patriotism that would guarantee plenty of aspiring soldiers came forward to fight this war.

When German Cruisers shelled the towns of Hartlepool, Scarborough and Whitby during Christmas 1914, public indignation raised the number of volunteer soldiers even higher. They rushed to Recruitment Offices, which were unprepared for the huge influx of men, and until the war machine got going the new recruits had to train with wooden rifles. Refusing to take up arms was not socially acceptable, even for idealistic conscientious objectors. The disgrace of perhaps being given a white feather as the sign of cowardice ensured that more and more young men joined up. Basically, people were taken in by the clever propaganda that confidently predicted the war would be over and won by Christmas. And if they wanted to be heroes they had better hurry up.

Edwin, the youngest member of the Cormack family, had joined the Navy as soon as he was sixteen. In his youthful idealism he saw himself as "defender" and "protector" of his great country and had been desperate for a bit of glory like his older brother. Despite their most strenuous efforts, his parents had been unable to dissuade him. So he suspended his apprenticeship with Stephen and Smith Advocates and went to sea.

That had been a year ago now, and he was still in the thick of things. News of, and from, him was sporadic. Every so often, heavily censored Government postcards arrived devoid of anything that might have given away his locations. But he had signed them in person showing them that at least he was still alive. With that, like all other families, the Cormacks had to be content.

They knew from the news broadcasts that the Germans were treating the English Channel as a war zone and were attacking every type of ship that passed through. It was likely that Edwin was involved in their defence. In May the Lusitania had been sunk off Kinsale Head in Ireland, and over a thousand lives had been lost, including one hundred and twenty four Americans. President Wilson had been indignant and had declared that such acts of war would be seen as "unfriendly" and, to William and Isabella's relief, the torpedoing had stopped for a while. They were realistic enough to know that this respite couldn't last though, and they were dreading the resumption of hostilities in the Channel when passenger and merchant ships became targets for the enemy again.

Father and mother were praying daily for the safe deliverance of both their sons so far afield and facing dangers quite unimaginable to them.

By the summer of 1915, Britain was thoroughly immersed in her fight against Germany. Respective armies were facing each other in trenches that stretched in long lines roughly parallel to the River Aisne. The First Battle of Ypres (or Flanders as it was called) had been fought and won by British troops with their hand grenades. But in the Second Battle of Ypres the Germans introduced mustard gas bombs, taking a terrible toll on British soldiers. Nevertheless, newspapers were maintaining that the Kaiser was going insane and would soon be "put in his place." The government, a coalition led by Asquith, insisted that all was going well for the allies and hinted again that it would probably all be over by Christmas.

But hints didn't stop the worry that continued to gnaw at William and Isabella. Like many of their neighbours whose children were away at war William and Isabella got a queer kind of consolation from a pamphlet that they kept in the sideboard drawer. It was the reprint of a letter which had been written in the Morning Post earlier that year, and which had proved to be so popular with parents, that thousands of extra copies had been distributed throughout the country. It was entitled, "A Mother's Answer To A Common Soldier," and was signed by "A Little Mother."

It read:

> Sir, - As a mother of an only child - a son who was early and eager to do his duty - may I be permitted to reply to Tommy Atkins, whose letter appeared in your issue of the 9th inst.? Perhaps he will kindly convey to his friends in the trenches, not what the Government thinks, not what the Pacifists think, but what the mothers of the British race think of our fighting men. It is a voice that demands to be heard, seeing that we play the most important part in the history of the world, for it is we who "mother the men" who have to uphold the honour and traditions not only of our Empire but of the whole civilized world.
>
> To the man who pathetically calls himself a "common soldier", may I say that we women, who demand to be heard, will tolerate no such cry as "Peace! Peace!" where there is no peace. The corn that will wave over land watered by the blood of our brave lads shall testify to the future that their blood was not spilt in vain. We need no marble monuments to remind us. We only need that force of character behind all motives to see this monstrous world tragedy brought to a victorious ending. The blood of the dead and dying, the blood of the "common soldier" from his "slight wounds" will not cry to us in vain. They have all done their share, and we, as women, will do ours without murmuring and without complaint. Send the Pacifists to us and we shall very soon show them, and show the world, that in our homes at least there shall be no "sitting at home warm

and cosy in the winter, cool and 'comfy' in the summer". There is only one temperature for the women of the British race, and that is white heat. With those who disgrace their sacred trust of motherhood we have nothing in common. Our ears are not deaf to the cry that is ever ascending from the battlefield from men of flesh and blood whose indomitable courage is borne to us, so to speak, on every blast of the wind. We women pass on the human ammunition of "only sons" to fill up the gaps, so that when the "common soldier" looks back before going "over the top" he may see the women of the British race at his heels, reliable, dependent, uncomplaining."

William and Isabella drew the line at thinking of their sons as "ammunition" and they were both agreed that they did not feel a "white heat" when they thought about the war either. Nevertheless the pamphlet did bring them a kind of peace and reassurance that they had done the right thing in letting their sons go to face such awful dangers so far away.

*   *   *

Sandy was at home because he was medically exempt. No one knew until he enlisted in the Royal Army Medical Corps with his friends, had collapsed on a routine march during training and been subsequently diagnosed as having a weak heart. He didn't advertise that this state of affairs suited him just fine. He was not a "fighting man," and was secretly relieved not to see the war at close quarters, preferring to read about it in the newspapers.

Although his main job was teaching French, Sandy's real passion lay in delving into local history, and he regularly wrote historical articles for several newspapers including The Banffshire Journal. His research often took him into the Banff district where he was becoming well known through his association with the local newspaper.

That evening he had come home raving about "a nice chap" he had recently met in Cullen, where he had gone to corroborate some piece of evidence for his latest treatise.

"Jim is a Master Builder with his own firm at Portessie, and has thirteen employees," he had boasted. "And he's only thirty one! Can you believe that he just closed his yard and signed up for the Royal Engineers! What a money he'll lose by going to this war! We met on the golf course at Cullen yesterday. Man...but he's fit and strong!" Sandy was clearly impressed. But then he gave a delicate cough to remind the women of his own unfortunate indisposition. But he wasn't finished extolling the virtues of his new friend yet. "And Jim's a man of principle," he had continued. "He'll not let the Kaiser do as he pleases just because he thinks he can bully the weaker countries into doing his bidding. 'We must defend the poor creatures in Europe,' he said. 'Might is NOT right.... and it is our clear duty to take up arms for their sakes.'

Fancy him selling up his business tae ging tae war though!" Sandy couldn't help returning to the financial aspect of his friend's decision. He was aghast at the idea of giving up so much money for a principle - no matter how good or great it might be, and in his state of bemusement he temporarily forgot to talk "properly." But not for long, "That's about all he said about the war, now I come to think about it. He doesn't say very much, but what he does say is aye worth listening till." Again Sandy strayed from English to his mither tongue while giving an evaluation of his new friend. "He's not just doing it for a bit of action or glory either - he's just not like that ava'! He's read a lot and is interested in music. He's the church organist at Buckie - or rather ...he was...they'll have to find a replacement while he's at war. But that shouldn't be for long, because we'll have won by Christmas surely. Anyway, he's come down this last week to start training at the Hardgate. What a man eh? He's fair made an impression on me, and I've invited him for a bite to eat wi' us on Wednesday if he's free, and I gave him oor address."

This was how it always started. Sandy would meet some male that he liked, and instead of arranging to meet him at a pub or restaurant where he might have to shell out some money; he invariably invited him home where it wouldn't cost him a penny. And it never occurred to him that his mother's housekeeping was going to have to stretch that bit further again.

But, having been privy to the housekeeping book, Elizabeth knew the draining effect on this week's economy that this man's visit was going to have. Everyone was in the same circumstances during the war.

"Oh." Elizabeth had dropped the word with dry sarcasm into the silence that had followed her brother's eulogy of his latest acquaintance. By leaving her comment for so long, she was deliberately showing that she, for one, was unimpressed by this description of her brother's new friend. It mattered far more to her at that moment, that this was yet another needless imposition upon her mother's strained budget.

"And will this paragon bring something with him for his supper, do you think?" she had asked her brother with exaggerated sweetness.

Whereupon Sandy had lost his temper.

Chapter 2

Charity Begins At Hame

It rained all day Wednesday. It teemed down in bucketfuls and stotted like little fountains off the ground. Children were drawn in delight to the ensuing puddles, and adults were forced to hurry their steps in the all-enveloping wetness. It was cleansing and energising stuff and the farmers loved it even if some town folk weren't fussed for it.

It wasn't often that Elizabeth had time on her hands as she had that afternoon. Her mother and Aunt Chat were busily sewing a new outfit for Chat's singing venue that evening. She had lived with them for the last twenty five years and was one of the family. She had worked at Stoneywood Paper Mills all her life, and had shared a bed with Elizabeth for almost as long as her young niece could remember. Aunt Chat had a good voice and sang with a band that was constantly in demand. She was an attractive woman and liked to be well turned out. Her sister-in-law Isabella was an excellent seamstress since that had been part of her duties as a lady's maid to well-to-do families in Aberdeen before she had married. Between them they were creating a stunning wardrobe of clothes for Charlotte's singing career. There was nothing that Elizabeth could do to help them since the two women had it all in hand.

She couldn't waste her afternoon off though, so Elizabeth went across the road, past the fountain and on to the farm where her friend Mrs Matthews lived. The farmhouse stood opposite the Meal Mill, also owned by the Matthews family. Mr Matthews and his son worked from early in the morning cultivating their cornfields and looking after their livestock. They kept about twenty cows and delivered milk around the neighbourhood. People would bring out pitchers and other assorted containers to be filled up from the urns. Consequently, both men were aye busy, and Mrs Matthews was usually in the farmhouse on her own. Elizabeth knew that she would get a warm welcome, so she packed up her knitting and set off for a comfortable afternoon in front of her friend's fire.

She'd had an enjoyable visit as she'd known she would, but her knee was throbbing by the time she got home. The rain tended to make it worse. She shouted a general "hello" to everyone as she quickly divested herself of her hat and coat. She unlaced her shoes and placed them temporarily by the fire to help them dry out a bit, and later would stuff them with newspaper to keep their shape. Then she spied her dad's slippers, which were far too big for her, lying cosily by the fireside, and the temptation to sink her cold feet into them proved too much for her to ignore. Instant bliss! She would fetch her own later, she decided, before her father came through. Meanwhile she sat down and absorbed the heat from the fire. As she grew warmer the pain in her knee began to subside and she gradually relaxed and looked about her.

Sandy was sitting reading the Evening Express at the other side of the fireplace and it didn't strike her as odd that he hadn't acknowledged her arrival in any way. He had been ignoring her since their last argument and was still put out at his sister. But Elizabeth wasn't going to make an issue of it now because she was in too good a mood with the heat from the fire melting her pain away. She'd had a rare time with Mrs Matthews and was mulling over the conversations they'd shared. The good farmer's wife didn't have an unkind streak in her body and Elizabeth had grown fond of her over the years. Her father was still at work, and Aunt Chat, no doubt dressed to the nines and looking very fashionable, had already left. Her mother was through the house looking out one of her starched tablecloths along with her best dishes - the ones with a broad dark-red band, and edged with gold which she had been told was melted down from a sovereign. Also on the table she saw the "royal" plate as the family called it. Her mother had been working in Deeside House when she met the housekeeper to Queen Victoria, and the pair had got on so well that she had given Isabella a plate from the Queen's own dinner service that had a minute chip on its fancy edge and had been destined for the bucket. Naturally, it was only brought out on high days and holidays.

The sight of all the finery going on display reminded Elizabeth of their visitor due that evening, and she knew a spurt of anger as it rekindled her annoyance at her brother! But she was too cosy to vent her spleen at him. She could hear her father locking up the office and knew she would have to move from his chair, and relinquish his slippers. But she was in no hurry, for by now she felt deliciously warm and mellow. She smiled at her father as he came in. "Hello dad, good day today?"

"Aye lass, not bad," her father answered as he usually did, as he lowered himself onto his chair. Elizabeth's heart lurched as she watched her father. She was sure he wasn't well. He looked pale to her, and his old "perkiness" was gone. But he didn't complain about anything, and had brushed aside Elizabeth's solicitations a few weeks ago. And with that Elizabeth had had to be content. Sandy continued to read his paper very closely and acknowledged his father's arrival by wordlessly handing him the page filled with the prevailing "matches, hatches and dispatches" columns. Elizabeth sat by the table now and stared dreamily at the fire whilst idly rubbing her sore knee. It had been a good day and now she was feeling pleasantly tired.

When the knock came at the door neither of the men stirred, and her mother was so busy in the scullery that she scarcely heard it. So Elizabeth gave a theatrical sigh for the benefit of her uninterested audience and stood up slowly. Then with an exaggerated reluctance she flip-flopped her way comically to the door. Her performance was wasted on the men who remained engrossed in their paper. However as she approached the door, the toe of her dad's slipper caught on the rug and sent her sprawling forwards and downwards, and in an effort to steady herself she grabbed the door handle and hung on. Unfortunately for her, this resulted in the handle being depressed, and it performed its normal task of releasing the catch. Her weight pulled the door open unbidden and almost unbalanced her again. This meant that she was bent almost double and hanging on to the door handle for dear life when she found herself looking at the soaked uniform trousers of a bemused soldier standing tall and dripping wet on the doorstep.

He must have heard the commotion behind the door but his face was inscrutable as he leaned down from his waist so that he could look Elizabeth in the eye.

"Does Sandy Cormack live here, please?" the stranger enquired in a careful even tone. There was a brief pause while Elizabeth and the soldier straightened until they were both upright and facing each other in the normal way. She noted that he was a good six inches taller than she was.

"I have had an invitation to visit him this evening," the soldier continued in a rich bass confident voice, which yet held diffidence. If he saw anything odd about Elizabeth's former posture he wasn't going to bring attention to it she realised. And at the same time she knew that he wasn't looking for an explanation either. She liked this man instantly.

"Yes..yes...come in," answered Elizabeth brightly. Her cheeks were burning with embarrassment but at least her feet were safely back inside the slippers. She motioned for him to go ahead of her while she shuffled behind him taking careful little steppies as she followed him into the kitchen. And it occurred to her that this James Mair was a right handsome chiel, and perhaps the evening wasn't going to be so bad after all.

Mr Cormack and Sandy both rose to greet their visitor while Elizabeth stood behind him feeling very conscious of her feet inside her dad's voluminous slippers. From behind the stranger's back she waggled a foot at her mother who was coming in from the pantry, and both had to stifle a giggle at the sight of her. They were always quick to share a joke.

"Good to see you again, Jim," announced Sandy solemnly as he extended a hand to his new friend. He had witnessed his sister's pantomime act and his whole demeanour was suffused with disapproval of her antics. He was determined to put the proceedings on to a formal level. "This is my father and mother," he continued while they each shook hands. "It's terrible weather to be out in but I'm sure mother's cooking will make your journey worthwhile."

"It's very kind of you to invite me for supper, Mrs Cormack, and you, sir," he nodded at Mr Cormack.

"Let me take your greatcoat and cap," volunteered Mr Cormack. "And by the way, this is Sandy's sister - Elizabeth."

Jim extended a big muscular hand and grasped hers firmly, whilst giving her a searching look that made her blush again. And by the slight twitch of his lips as he glanced at her feet, Elizabeth realised that he was quite aware of the slippers and the havoc they had caused.

"Nice to meet you," she smiled. And as he turned to Sandy she hurried to remove her shoes from the front of the fireside, and scuttle through to the scullery to put them on. Then she started to help her mother boil the tea and put the finishing touches to their supper, while the men sat down and made general observations, sizing one another up as they did so. Sandy's voice sounded strident to the women in the next room as he attempted to take control of the conversation and direct various questions at his guest. It appeared to them though, that after a short reply, somehow the questions were being repeatedly redirected, and they were surprised to hear William Cormack doing most of the talking. This was unusual because Mr Cormack was normally extremely shy in the company of strangers.

While the men conversed, Elizabeth helped her mother to lay out the food and in a short time they were all called to the table. A healthy silence followed while they ate up the delicious if somewhat plain fare, and by the time the teacups were being refilled for the third time the company was feeling relaxed and replete.

Sandy tried again to dominate the conversation, and this time he spoke about the historical biography he was currently working on, that of "William Crammond of Cullen." He had a fanatic's interest in local history and assumed that he was impressing everyone with his knowledge - and what's more, he loved an audience.

While the others listened politely to her son, Isabella tried to quell her mounting frustration. She was intensely interested in folk and had been looking forward to finding out as much as she could learn about this young man. So far, she had discovered very little. And it was only now, while she was taking stock of the evening, that she realised why that was so. Jim would answer direct questions openly and succinctly but would never volunteer extra information. Instead, he would smile and invite someone else at the table, usually her husband William, to answer the question too.

And it was in this way that William had been drawn into talking about his work.

"Oh, there's nae doubt that we Poor Inspectors are needed," Mr Cormack was saying in answer to Jim's enquiry. "Take this example, which is a very common one. Two men apply for "relief." Their circumstances are the same: they're married with a wife and four bairns. There's nae chance of either of them working because they are infirm - either because of a birth defect or the result of an accident at work. Whatever the reason for their disability they are not 'fit for employment,' and as a consequence they've nae money for food, clothes nor rent. Now, in accordance with the 1910 National Health Insurance Act, the welfare system," he said with emphasis, "steps in and awards the same amount of money to both men. That seems fair enough. But having dispensed the same amount of money to both men, the civil servant is under no obligation to check up on how it is spent or where it goes.

The first man is a 'good' man who is out of work through no fault of his own making. He hands the money over to his wife who pays the rent, clothes their children and feeds them all. The second man however, is a lazy drunkard. He has filled in the forms honestly enough, and has come by his allowance in the proper way. But not one penny does he hand over to his wife. Instead he spends it all on drink.

Now, through no fault of their own, his wife and bairns still have no food nor clothes. Is it their fault? Must they go starving and begging on the street as the consequence of a bad marriage? Should the bairns go hungry and be made the objects of ridicule at school? All because no one checks up on where the money goes? And in this society, the money must be paid to the man. Na! It shouldn't happen! I see you agree with me here, Jim."

"I know something about the Poor myself, Mr Cormack. In the fishing villages around Portessie there are widows and children left destitute when their husbands and fathers were drowned at sea," Jim responded earnestly. "But it must be galling for you to give extra financial help to families who are in straitened circumstances because the father drinks too much."

"Aye, lad, but there are times when I feel tremendous pity for their circumstances, and I thank God that I'm not tested in that way," said the older man shaking his head.

Mr Cormack answered the quizzical looks of those at the table by expanding on his last comment. "I'm thinking of when a man suffers a disablement of some kind and is unable to do the work he once enjoyed or took a pride in. He has a lot of difficult adjustments to make. And while I can't condone his drinking, I can understand that his heart is sore, and his pride is suffering. I find that I cannot judge that man."

"Aye," answered Jim thoughtfully. "That must be one of the worst things that can happen to a man - who's healthy in all other respects - but who is denied doing the job he loves because of a cruel infirmity. I think it would be worse than death for me. I love building and making things with my own two hands and I don't know how I would cope if I couldn't make my living working with stone and cement." He shook his head, "Like you sir, I hope I'm never tested in that way."

While she listened to their conversation, Elizabeth gave an involuntary shudder as a cold sensation swept through her and brought her out in goosepimples. A feeling of dread filled her and she found her eyes drawn to Jim whose attention was on her father. What could this mean? The family believed she was fey because she had accurately predicted certain events in the past. Now she was wondering if this feeling was a kind of premonition. She rationalised that it was hardly likely to pertain to a stranger, and concluded that it probably had more to do with her brothers. And with this thought she broke out afresh in a cold sweat. Yet even as she drew her hand across her brow, she reflected that it didn't seem to apply to her brothers somehow. Then as she sat there, her state of absolute terror was gradually infused with strength and reassurance from the same source as her initial dread, and after a while Elizabeth became calm again. No one had noticed anything different about her behaviour and she wasn't on for attracting attention about this, so she shrugged her shoulders in an effort to dismiss all these thoughts as nonsense. And having done so, she wiped her brow one last time, and forced herself to concentrate on her father's next words.

"Nae," continued William Cormack gently. "We need to look after our Poor, but it's difficult." He shook his head sadly. "Very difficult," he added softly almost to himself. "The Church tried for years and failed. And now the government has created a Social Service Department to look after them, and our Prime Minister Herbert Asquith cannot understand why his people hate it so much."

"Do they?" asked Jim surprised.

"If you think about it, lad," nodded William Cormack, "how would you feel if you had to ask for money instead of earning it, even though it wasn't your fault that you hadn't a job? And, on the other side, would you vote for a politician who wanted to raise the amount given to the unemployed? And that money was put on to your tax bill? Aye, I see you take my point." Mr Cormack gave a rueful smile and looked down at the cup he was holding.

"Do you know why this Divinely-inspired Social Service is the best-hated in this world?" he asked Jim.

"I hadn't really thought about it," answered Jim truthfully. "But now that you've raised the subject, I'd like to know."

Isabella twitched in her chair, for she was torn in no less than three ways with the path this conversation was following. Firstly, it was getting too serious a subject for the young man's first ever visit. Also, she had been watching Sandy's growing impatience, and wanted to avert a possible outburst from him. But, on the other hand, it had been a long time since she had seen her husband so animated about his work, and he was obviously flattered by the young man's attention. She knew at that point that she couldn't spoil the evening for him, so she kept quiet.

Meanwhile, upon seeing the obvious interest on Jim's face, Mr Cormack had settled himself more comfortably in his chair. And in doing so, he completely failed to notice the flush of indignation that registered on Sandy's face as his son felt that, once again, he was being overshadowed by a member of his own family. Sandy scanned the other faces at the table hoping for some kind of support against this imagined injustice, but all eyes were on his father.

"The answer lies in its history," Mr Cormack resumed. "In the early Christian days it was the duty of the Church to look after its Poor, and that included old and infirm people. But by the Reformation, there was chaos in the Church and the Relief machinery had broken down completely. So an act was passed in 1574 that made every parish responsible for its own Poor, and that meant that everyone had to go back to their place of birth in order to qualify for assistance. Of course that system was doomed before it started, and, sure enough, in 1592 they had to try some other way. This time the whole administration was put into the hands of the Reformed Church. Its ministers, elders and deacons were empowered to raise funds by taxes and by charging for their services. Do you know," Mr Cormack asked with a chuckle, "that the Church could fine people for swearing?" And as his family dutifully laughed along with Jim, he added sadly, "But however great their endeavour, the clergy could only raise small amounts of revenue that didn't go very far, and then only to the most destitute of souls. And the conditions for receiving relief were so demeaning that a great many people chose to hide their suffering and die with their pride intact." Then he paused and closed his eyes, the better to marshal his thoughts.

And his wife took the opportunity to glower at Sandy and dare him to interrupt his father. Alexander had heard all this before, and throughout his father's talk his high colour had returned to normal - only to be replaced with various expressions of boredom. He had heard it all before, and he was yearning for his new friend's attention. He started fidgeting, which brought another warning glance from his mother. He looked across the room to where the newspaper lay, and deliberated if it would be going too far if he were to surreptitiously slide it across and start reading it. Another glower from his mother scotched that idea. He gave an audible sigh that brought a dig in the ribs from his sister's elbow, and so finally he resigned himself to suffering in silence.

By this time, Elizabeth had shared a knowing glance with her mother, and both were united in their determination that Mr Cormack should finish his talk about his work. William was feeling exhilarated by all the interest that was being shown in his knowledge of Poor Law history, and was blissfully unaware of the warning glances thrown from mother to son.

So he continued affably, "This state of affairs continued for the next two hundred years, and slowly economic conditions started to get better. The Industrial Revolution drew huge numbers of people to the cities and suddenly ordinary men and women had money in their pockets. The Church continued to do its utmost to improve the lot of the Poor both educationally and physically, but the burden wasn't being fairly borne. Some of those who could least afford it would give their best, but were becoming discouraged. Gradually there emerged a demand for some compulsory measure whereby everyone would have to contribute according to his financial ability. This led to the Poor Law Act of 1845 - and a right can of worms it opened I can tell you!"

"Why?" asked Jim. "On the face of it, it seems fair enough."

"So you would think, lad. But I firmly believe that real hatred against the recipients of Poor Relief was born then." William paused thoughtfully, while Isabella continued to glower at Alexander whose fidgeting was really getting on her nerves.

"You see, Jim, when the contributions were given freely in the Church's Offerings, the donors were promised a handsome return in the hereafter. And when a handful of meal was donated to the Poor, it was received with becoming humility and thankfulness. That way, the donor's breast would overflow with self-righteousness, and make him feel superior. And with his donation the donor thought that he had secured a place in the hereafter!

Now all this was changed with the Poor Relief Act. A rich proprietor who was previously lauded to the skies and who felt that he had earned a First Class ticket to Heaven by placing a £5 note on the Communion Plate on a Sunday, was now called upon to pay.... say £40 without any corresponding promise of a reserve ticket in Paradise. Likewise the ordinary householder, instead of getting a 'God Bless you' when he parted with his coppers, was instead presented with a Demand Note, to be paid by a specific time under penalty.

Now do you see why the Act was hated? It is a physiological fact that people in general hate to be parted from their money. And this reluctance is intensified when they seemingly get no return for their money - or - at least, no tangible return for their money. So naturally this Act caused resentment - and that resentment was directed at the cause of this barefaced robbery - namely...the Poor who benefited from it! With the introduction of legalised Relief, private charity dried up of course— and this also increased the rate of resentment. Then, as you would expect, a great deal of friction arose between the Church and the Parish Councils regarding the disposal of many bequests, which had been made on behalf of the Poor.

The courts finally settled the matter and decreed that money or property, which was bequeathed to the Poor of a particular church, was to be administered by that church. And bequests to the 'general' Poor were to be regulated by the Trustees of the Parish Council. So then, by this Act, the Parish Councils were appointed main custodians of the Poor. Politically this meant that votes for the Board went to those members who promised to levy the lowest rates. Consequently, starvation allowances were the order of the day. And pauperism became synonymous with everything that was mean and humiliating.

Aye..." William gave a long sigh. "Truly Robbie Burns knew human nature when he wrote, 'Man's inhumanity to man makes countless thousands mourn.' "

The room fell quiet as they each contemplated William's words.

He roused himself and continued more optimistically. "Asquith took the matter in hand, though, and in 1910 he passed the National Health Insurance Act. With this, large numbers of people were rendered independent of the Poor Law - for a while at least. But none of his schemes are wholly self-sufficient, so some people still need Poor Relief. You see, the Old Age Pension has been set at 5/- per week, and for that the National Health Insurance contributions have to be frequently augmented. Without any other source of income, the pension is simply not enough to live on. Politically though, it wouldn't do our Prime Minister any good to try and raise it meantime, because the money for it must ultimately come from the pockets of his voters. So you see, lad, it'll be a while before Poor Inspectors aren't needed. The Government can only do so much, then the Church must play its part - and then the Poor must have recourse to the Poor Law Code.

No. It's not an easy task being an Inspector of Poor," asserted Mr Cormack. "Sometimes I'm hard-pressed to avoid letting sentiment cloud my judgement. But the rules are there for us to follow and many a person has been richt glad of them!"

Here William sat back breathlessly. Normally a shy man, he was unaccustomed to having so much to say, and indeed he had surprised himself with his fluency. He had found it so easy to talk to this young man who seemed genuinely interested in his work - unlike Sandy who had heard it - or bits of it - before, and had appeared to have been bored by it.

"Of course," he added, looking at Elizabeth and brightening perceptively, for he had become very sombre, "there's the other side to my work as Registrar, which gives me a lot of pleasure. If you could see the proud young fathers, puffed up like peacocks, coming in to register the birth of their newest addition! And it's even better when Elizabeth here joins me at my work. She has the most beautiful handwriting that I've witnessed."

He smiled indulgently at his daughter who turned red. But inwards Elizabeth was still trying to shake off that feeling of dread that was causing her some disquiet. She made a determined effort to ignore it, and grinned at her father. "It's always a pleasure, dad, if only to get out from under mother's feet for a change."

"I admire a good hand," interposed Jim smiling openly at her.

"Oh, Elizabeth's very good with her hands," agreed Mrs Cormack. And her daughter blushed even more deeply as her mother went on to list her daughter's accomplishments as proud mothers are apt to do.

"I think it's time we were away out," interrupted Sandy tired of taking second place in his friend's attention, and certainly not prepared to be outshone by his sister. "I thought we would have a walk before you take the 'Subbie' back to the barracks, Jim. The rain's gone off a bit and I could be doing with some fresh air."

Jim gave Elizabeth a wide smile as he rose for his coat. "Would you like to come with us, Elizabeth?" he asked, looking again intently at her, and causing her to blush even more.

"No, no. She wouldn't," insisted Sandy quickly, not giving her time to answer. And he hustled Jim towards the door, pushing his now-dried greatcoat and cap into his friend's hands. But Jim wasn't to be rushed.

"Goodbye then, Mr and Mrs Cormack," he said politely. "Thank you very much for my tea. And thank you, sir," he nodded to William, "for the interesting insight into your work."

"You're very welcome," William answered surprised at how much he meant it.

"Come again soon," smiled Isabella. "I've heard about army food!"

"Aye, lad," enjoined William. We'll see you again no doubt - and very welcome you'll be!" he added emphatically.

"Good bye, Elizabeth," said the young man shyly.

And with that, they were both gone into the night.

"What a nice young man," opined Mr Cormack after they left.

"He certainly is," assented his wife as they settled down for a quiet chat. Elizabeth sat looking into the fire, with her cheeks still aflame, looking very contemplative.

But their peace was short-lived, for a few minutes later Aunt Charlotte burst through the door.

"Well then," she demanded gaily. "Tell me about Sandy's new friend. What's he like? Is he nice? Is he good-looking? Come on - tell me all!" She was all agog for news, but not so insensitive as not to notice how her niece coloured at her questions. 'Oh,' she thought to herself. 'So this is how the land lies is it?' And she was careful not to ask or say anything that might embarrass her niece.

However, Elizabeth's unusual reticence during their ensuing conversation told her everything she could have wanted to know.

Chapter 3

The Course O' True Love Never Did Run Smooth

After hearing of Jim's fifth visit to the Parish Council House in his absence, Sandy was feeling distinctly peeved. "I can't think what Jim is about," he moaned to his mother. "I keep telling him when I'm away at my Evening Classes and he keeps coming round when I'm out."

Isabella looked at him in surprise, "Haven't you any een in your heid?" laughed his mother. "It's not you he comes to see. It's our Elizabeth. I think he's smitten."

This news was like a slap in the face to Sandy. The shock of it stopped him in his tracks, and his mother watched while he turned a dull red colour, as if indeed he had been physically slapped. He stood in front of her where she could see him reviewing the last few weeks in his mind, and as it all started to fit into place for him he began to tremble with sheer fury. It wasn't long before he gave vent to his wrath.

"How dare she!" he exploded. "She's got no right to take my friend away from me!" But even as he shouted Sandy knew that his anger was impotent, and it was quickly replaced by his familiar feelings of self-pity. He looked at his mother with stricken eyes, "How could he possibly prefer her company to mine?" he whined.

"Wheesht now," reprimanded his mother sharply. She was taken aback by the vehemence of her son's reaction. To her it was obvious that Elizabeth and Jim were attracted to each other. Why - he had even taken to calling her 'Betty.' The wonder was that Sandy had never noticed it.

"It's not that he likes her better than you, Sandy," she pointed out mildly, trying to placate him. "It's just that he likes her in a different way, that's all. In fact, I think he's more than a bit in love with her. You should be pleased for your sister."

"Pleased!" snorted Sandy. "Of all the sleekit, underhand things to do.... To steal my friend! It's not fair..." he added petulantly.

Isabella Cormack looked sorrowfully at her clever son. For all his intelligence he had no sense sometimes, and could be so immature. He hadn't learned yet that love wasn't something you divided out amongst your friends, but was something that grew the more you spread it. And she might have managed to communicate something of this to her son, might have 'worked him round,' - if Elizabeth hadn't chosen that exact moment to come through the door.

"You're a sleekit common thief!" Sandy shouted at her before she had even removed her coat.

"What? What's the matter? What am I supposed to have done?" Elizabeth asked startled.

"What's the matter? What's the matter?" mimicked Sandy nastily. "Look at you standing there all innocence! I'll tell you what's the matter. You're a thief - you stole my friend Jim from me!" he hissed childishly.

"Oh that," replied his sister beginning to blush. A smile started to spread across her face as she looked over at her mother, and obviously embarrassed at being confronted like this, she gave a flustered laugh. But that was the worst thing she could have done, with Sandy in his present mood.

"Yes 'that!'" screeched Sandy, by now almost apoplectic with fury at, what he saw as, his sister's duplicity. He stood tall with self-righteousness and exploded, "How dare you steal my friend!"

Elizabeth tried to hold on to her tongue. She felt sorry for Sandy, because this sort of thing had been happening since they were bairns. Sandy's friends had often ended up preferring Elizabeth's company, and she knew it hurt him. What she couldn't stop herself doing though, was continue getting redder by the minute, for the mention of Jim's name always had this effect on her. Her features had softened into a warm glow when she looked across at her mother, whose half-baked idea of trying to mollify her son was dispelled seconds later, when Sandy gave full vent to his anger. Elizabeth's dreamy countenance was inadvertently adding fuel to the already-burning fire in his breast, and he went all out to hurt his sister as much as possible.

"You don't seriously think that a fine upstanding man like James Mair would get himself inveigled with the likes of you?" he demanded waspishly.

To tell the truth, Elizabeth didn't know. She had been cherishing a tentative hope that Jim just might return her love, for she knew without a doubt that she loved him. She felt vulnerable, but wasn't going to let Sandy provoke her into defending what might be the tender beginnings of a romance.

However, she couldn't help feeling sensitive and insecure where Jim was concerned, and finally, flustered by Sandy's exposé of her innermost thoughts, she defended herself by striking back at his weak spot.

"Why not?" she demanded. "Marie gave you a second glance - and my accomplishments are every bit as good as hers!"

"Oh Elizabeth," moaned her mother despairingly, for Elizabeth had fairly set the cat among the pigeons now. Mrs Cormack braced herself against the storm that was bound to come from her son. Both women looked at Sandy expectantly: Mrs Cormack with exasperation, and Elizabeth with tremulous daring.

Sandy had gone pale at the mention of Marie's name but now his face was puce with suppressed rage and it didn't take long for his anger to erupt.

"You go too far!" he roared. "You will never, and I mean never, mention her name in this house again! Now I'm warning you, Elizabeth. Jim'll be off to France soon and that'll be the end of your silly romantic notion. I'm warning you for the last time, do you hear me?"

He pointed a threatening finger at his sister.

"The day will come when you'll have to depend on me for the clothes on your back, and I have a long memory, Elizabeth. You'll suffer for your insolence today!"

"Och awa' wi' you," said Elizabeth with fearful contempt. She was shaking inside but refused to let her brother see the effect he could still have on her. "That sort of posturing might go down real well wi' the bairns at Robert Gordon's, but it cuts no ice with me. Anyway," she added in a conciliatory tone, knowing that she'd hurt him deeply, and trying to avoid an 'atmosphere' in the house, "I haven't set my cap at Jim, you know. We just happen to get on real well together. That's all."

At the mention of Jim's name, Elizabeth's features had softened and she had resumed her dreamy glow, which was even more infuriating to Sandy than her outburst. He realised there would be no defeating her in this mood and was angry, hurt and powerless to do anything about it.

"I'm off to take my class!" he spat. Then he threw on his coat and hat, picked up his attaché case and slammed the door behind him.

"Whatever made you bring Marie's name into a' this, Elizabeth?" asked her mother reprovingly, after they were both sure that he'd gone.

"Och I don't know, mother," her daughter replied. "I think I just wanted to hurt him back. Why could he not be pleased for me if Jim has taken a fancy to me, instead of getting all huffy? I've done him no ill."

"He's very sensitive, Elizabeth. You know that. He hasn't got your confidence and you know he has had even less since that business with Marie. Just you get on with your own life and leave him be. He'll come round in his own good time, you'll see."

*   *   *

As part of Sandy's degree in French at Aberdeen University he had gone to Rennes in order to study the language at first hand. He had begun writing his doctorate on "The Poor Law" whilst there, and eventually returned to Bucksburn with Marie la Guerne in tow. As usual, he had expected his mother to put her up, and as usual, Mrs Cormack had complied. Marie had been younger than Elizabeth, and with long black curly hair and trim petite figure, was a very attractive young woman. A lively gregarious lass who was exceptionally good at needlework, while she lived with the Cormack family she had spent most of her time preparing a gorgeous hand-sewn trousseau using lawn, a very fine cotton fabric. She had produced lovely nightdresses decorated with inserts of lace and embroidery and exquisite tucking so tiny the stitches were almost impossible to see. They were absolutely beautiful and Elizabeth and her mother had admired her handiwork tremendously. They liked the lass too, and had looked forward to her becoming a part of their family. The two girls had got on famously together, and although Elizabeth couldn't for the life of her imagine what this bright young beauty ever saw in her dull old stick of a brother, she never questioned her about it.

However, as the weeks had gone by, Marie had become ever more impatient to get married - which was, after all, what she had crossed the Channel for. But Sandy having the upper hand so to speak, had refused to be hurried and continued to drag his feet.

Meanwhile, Aberdeen had been rapidly filling up with lots of soldiers who had eyes for a pretty woman. So it wasn't surprising really, when one day Marie announced that she was tired of Sandy's dithering about. She wasn't getting any younger she said, and capped her little speech by telling them that she had accepted a proposal from a very nice Canadian Officer. And that was that!

She vacated the house pretty smartly, which was wise thinking on her part, for it meant that she avoided Sandy's ire - which had been prodigious.

Unluckily for Elizabeth there had been no escaping her brother's wrath, and she had had to bear the brunt of her brother's devastation and rage. Of course he blamed Elizabeth for everything, and thereafter had never missed an opportunity to denigrate his sister.

Elizabeth had held her own in the arguments that had followed, secretly believing that he could have avoided her desertion. In her opinion he had acted too cock-sure of himself and shown his meanness by staying in the family home instead of paying his own way through life. Worst of all he had kept Marie dangling on a string for too long, forcing her to dance to his tune.

But as far as Sandy was concerned, he had done nothing wrong - it was Elizabeth who had put this wild notion into Marie's head and he wouldn't accept that he was in any way to blame.

As time passed, Elizabeth realised that lack of self-confidence had made her brother delay so long, so she'd tried to make allowances for his behaviour and not rub salt into his wound. Tonight's outburst had shocked everyone because it was out of character for her to hurt her brother like that.

If the truth were told, Elizabeth was on tenterhooks. She had recently admitted to herself that she had fallen in love with Jim, but she'd also had to confess that for the life of her she couldn't gauge the strength of his feelings towards her. She had spent five precious evenings with him so far, when he was off-duty. Naturally, his training came first so he had little time left over for them to get to know each other. But all the spare time he did have was given to his "Betty" as he called her. As it happened, this name suited her so well, that the family had taken to calling her Betty too - all that is, except Sandy. He had energetically applied the inappropriate nickname "Lizzie Jane" to his sister when they were young, until their father had put a stop to it, and now he mulishly insisted on calling his sister, Elizabeth.

Jim Mair was a quiet man who was reluctant to talk about himself. He had grown up in the Blantyre Croft at West Bauds where he and his family still lived. The smallholding lay halfway between Binhill and the little fishing village of Findochty, on the site where a battle between the Vikings and the local Scots had taken place centuries before. "The Bauds," as the locals called it, was currently part of the Seafield Estate.

Jim's father, George Mair, had died recently at the age of seventy-one. He had been a Master Builder like his father before him, and had built up his own firm. George Mair had rented land from the Seafield Estate in Banffshire, and built the family croft. A quiet, even dour man, he had been religious, hardworking and honest. His widow, Annie, on the other hand was the opposite in temperament being gregarious, chatty and kindly - if a bit domineering. (This from her son with a rueful smile and shake of his head.) Annie had given birth to twelve children, of whom there were nine surviving, testifying to her ability to bring forth healthy children. She had kept them alive with a good solid diet comprised mainly of fresh vegetables from the garden, milk, and meat from a succession of hens and pigs they had reared on the croft.

Their respective grandparents had been devout members of the Free Kirk, and Mr and Mrs George Mair had inherited strong religious ties to the church. When she was delivered of yet another bairn, Mrs Mair would piously announce it as "God's will." Betty chuckled at the memory of Jim's shocked face when she had ventured an opinion that Grandpa couldn't have always been so quiet - and that she (Mrs Mair) shouldn't blame God for everything! When she'd said it, Jim had stopped walking and stood stock still, causing Betty's heart to miss a beat. Then, to her relief, he had burst out laughing. Betty's sense of humour often took him by surprise.

Anyway, Mrs Mair put her considerable experience of childbirth to good use and became the local midwife. Dark-haired and with snapping brown eyes, sallow-skinned and with a comfortably round figure, Mrs Mair exuded confidence both inside and outside her household. Many a young mother-to-be was relieved to see her portly figure enter their house, because then they could relax - as much as their circumstances allowed - knowing they were in good hands.

Those same hands weren't slow to discipline her own bairns and hurry them along if they were being tardy at some task. She was protective of her brood, and had been so scared of the potential danger of their crossing the railway line to get to Findochty School, that she had refused to let them go to the local primary school there. Instead, her children had been obliged to walk three miles with their peats and pieces, often barefooted, to Rathven.

In retrospect, Jim considered that this was lucky for him, because the headmaster there was a gifted musician who had taught his pupils singing and sight-reading from the tonic sol-fa scale, and had instilled in Jim a deep love for music. One consequence of this was that Jim later sang in the Church Choir, and had learned to play the piano to a high enough standard to be asked to be organist at both Portknockie and Buckie Parish Churches.

Betty had heard him singing at one of the concerts they'd been to, which had ended with the National Anthem as usual, and she had been thrilled by his rich bass voice. She too, could play the piano, but had to concede that she appreciated music far better than she could produce it. She hadn't admitted to Jim yet that as far as singing went she was tone deaf, and could only carry a tune when placed right next to a proficient, and preferably loud, confident singer. She would dreamily imagine standing next to Jim listening to him singing, while she mimed alongside him.

As far as Betty could make out, Jim was a lot like his father in that they were both quietly observant, tall, fair skinned men who were good looking, with soft brown hair.

Jim's eldest sister, Isabella, had married a minister twenty-five years her senior, and despite the difference in their ages, their marriage was nevertheless the source of much pride in the Mair household. Elsie-Jane and Beatrice, his younger sisters, were both "pupil teachers" at Portknockie. And then there was Annie, who was destined to stay at home and be a "comfort" to their mother. Betty learned that Annie had never been encouraged to find work outside the home and instead was expected to remain single and devote her life to looking after their mother and ultimately inherit the family croft. When Betty fully understood Annie's limited career prospects she was astounded, and artlessly asked what would happen if Annie didn't want to fall heir to the family croft? The answer to her question was a silence that lasted so long.... she changed the subject and never referred to it again.

Only Jim and his brother George had followed their father into the building trade and had become "apprentice" then "time served" builders in their father's business. Portknockie and Findochty were centres of the building trade and there was plenty of work for them. Traditionally, fishermen's houses were crammed together, "end-on" for shelter, with small gardens since their men were seldom there to cultivate them. Fishing was one of the main industries in the area and it was undergoing a successful period. Other related businesses were thriving which led to commissions for more distinguished houses as well. There was plenty of work to be had for the Mairs.

Jim's career had taken a slightly different course from that of his brother. He had served his four-year apprenticeship with his father, working ten hours a day and six on Saturdays, like everybody else. Then when he was twenty-one he ventured to Uphill, between Glasgow and Edinburgh, and took part in the building of an asylum there. Jim worked on it for a year and a half, along with friends David Cowie and John Clark. They had lodged with the Watsons, and while staying there Jim had taken the opportunity to practise on their piano. He always put great store by his friends and continued to keep in touch after he left. By then Jim was a Master Builder in his own right, and when he returned home he set up his own business at Portessie. His firm had done well in a short time and he had employed thirteen men.

Betty had had to practically drag this information from him for he was very self-effacing. This reluctance to boast about his achievements was one of the many things she had grown to love about him.

Jim's love of music had never diminished, and when he had saved enough money he'd bought himself a good quality second-hand piano of which he was very proud, and which graced the parlour room at the Bauds. Not content with his expertise on the one instrument, Jim had then gone on to learn the violin as well.

He'd also kept up with his golf and before coming to Aberdeen had usually played once a fortnight at Cullen with Doctor Pirie and William Patterson, his old headmaster's son. Betty was impressed to learn that Jim had recently won a local golf competition, and had been touched when he had shyly shown her the little medal he'd received and had attached to his fob watch.

Betty was full of admiration for this strong, tall, handsome and unassuming, and yet confident young man, and was flattered that he was choosing to spend so much time with her. By now she knew that she was in love with him but however hard she tried, however minutely she dissected his visits, she couldn't find out if her love for him was reciprocated. "The trouble with a quiet man," she mused, "is that you can never tell what he's thinking."

The pair had arranged to meet later that night and when she was ready, Betty settled herself into the armchair to wait for him. But her knitting remained untouched while she pondered their previous meetings. Twice he had taken her to the Playhouse in Aberdeen to see Charlie Chaplin who'd been so funny with his bowler hat and walking stick and his odd little way of walking. She had had a pang of conscience afterwards, because it had given her the perfect opportunity to tell Jim about her knee. But she had baulked at it - not wanting to spoil the mood of the evening. The second time at the Playhouse, after showing her into her seat, Jim's hand had found its way into hers and she had been suffused with happiness.

Another evening they had gone to hear the local church choir sing "Messiah" and that too had been a success. Jim had helped to put on a performance of it at Buckie a few years previously, and knew the score well. Although she had been too happy to be critical of the performance, she had felt him wincing at some of the more discordant notes! They had enjoyed an animated discussion about it all the way home - which had taken about five minutes - and ended with their peals of laughter when they tried to sing the Hallelujah Chorus but couldn't keep time together.

Even the two evenings they had spent with her parents had been enjoyable. Jim could be interesting and funny when speaking about his music and his work, but he never dominated the conversation and was always keen to hear what Betty's mum and dad had to say. It was yet another of the many sides to him that Betty had grown to love. She wondered if he always drew out the best in people - and not just her mum and dad. Mind you, she never knew if this virtue extended to Sandy because her brother never gave Jim a chance. Even tonight Sandy had gone away in the huff when he knew that Jim was due to arrive.

But now Betty was keen to find out if Jim returned her love or not. Tonight was his last night before he travelled down to Irvine for more specialised training. Perhaps after tonight he would move on to new places and new people, and new girlfriends she thought reluctantly. Or maybe he would make some kind of declaration. She hoped he would...but whatever happened she wasn't going to let anything spoil their last night out together. As she looked into the flames, she sent up a silent prayer that Jim would show his feelings tonight - but only if he loved her. If he didn't, then she wanted to be left in ignorance for a wee while longer so that she could enjoy her memories of him without the shadow of disappointment clouding them.

Always punctual, Jim arrived at seven o'clock, and his knock on the door roused Betty from her reverie.

"I'm sorry, Betty," were his first words causing her heart to miss a beat. "I couldn't get tickets for the play, they were all sold out." He stood there making his apology but his face was smiling. She grinned back at him and said lightly, "Never mind, we'll find something else to do instead."

"I was wondering..." Jim's voice was tentative, "if you would fancy a walk along the Howes Road? The night's too beautiful to spend indoors," he added non-committally.

Now this put Betty into a quandary on two accounts. The Howes Road was locally acknowledged as a romantic venue, used mainly by couples who were "walking out" together, and she didn't know if Jim was aware of this fact. Her heart leapt at the possible implications of his invitation. But she also had another problem that she couldn't get around, and that was her footwear.

Like most other people Betty owned two pairs of shoes. Her workaday pair had flattish heels with laces up the front that helped to support her knee; and her "best" pair for Sundays and special occasions, that had a little heel and straps that fastened across the front with a buckle. She could wear those if she knew she wouldn't be walking or standing for very long, because the higher heel hurt her knee after a short time. Until now she had always been able to wear her "best" shoes when out with Jim because she had never had to walk very far.

Also, Jim had remarked upon her "dainty feet" and Betty had flushed with pleasure at his compliment. This particular evening she was already wearing her "best" shoes because the hall was close by. A walk round the Howes would definitely require her workaday ones but she hadn't told Jim about her knee problem. She had been meaning to, especially when he had laughingly referred to her as "his perfect woman" but she had always hesitated when the chance came to tell him about it, and the moment had always passed. She hadn't wanted him to know about her weakness just then, but on the other hand she knew she couldn't keep it a secret forever.

While Betty dithered her mother began to say, "Oh! Betty can't go in those...."

"That'll be fine, Jim," Betty cut in before her mother could let the cat out of the bag. And with a meaningful glower at her mum, Betty put on her coat and hat, all ready to go.

Mrs Cormack sighed as she watched her daughter leave with thon familiar set of her chin that meant she was determined to do something 'come Hell or high water!' Her mother knew fine that Betty was going to suffer for her vanity that evening.

Indeed, it wasn't like Betty to be vain. But then, she thought fondly, her daughter hadn't been in love before.

Minutes later Betty found herself walking along the Howes with her hand in Jim's, and wondering what had come over her.

It didn't bode well that shortly after they'd left the house, the sun had clouded over, and a drizzling rain had begun to fall. Even worse, she'd soon realised that in her haste to stop her mum from blabbing, she had made a big mistake coming out for a walk in high-heeled footwear. 'Vanity, thy name is woman,' she mused despondently. The shoes were a fairly recent purchase and they hadn't even been "broken in" properly, and it seemed to her that every part of her foot had begun to hurt soon after they set out. Although her knee was becoming extremely painful she ploughed doggedly on in silence.

Jim hadn't said a word to her since they left the house, and it was obvious that he was preoccupied about something. He didn't seem to be aware of her presence and was striding on at his usual spanking pace while Betty limped along beside him trying to keep up. She was getting more and more dispirited by the minute, and by the time he did speak she had convinced herself that he was trying to find a kind way of ending their friendship.

To give her her due, Betty had wanted to make this outing a pleasant one, as she had promised to do on their previous meeting together, and she had tried to make light conversation at the beginning of their walk. But Jim had appeared to be distracted and had hardly answered her. This was not going well at all.

When the rain started in earnest, she was close to admitting defeat. Jim didn't appear to be aware of her discomfort and was cracking on with his usual long-legged stride. He didn't even seem to have noticed that Betty had gone unusually quiet either. His brow was furrowed in deep thought and he was oblivious of the elements.

The two of them raced on in this manner, unseeing of the burn or the beautiful hedgerows that flanked parts of the road. Neither noticed the flora around them, nor were they aware of the lichen-covered cliff-face that loomed high on their left. The couple scooted on past the three-part granite boulder where previous lovers had scratched their initials and declared their undying love to each other. Onwards they tramped at a spanking pace till they came to the old large fir tree on the left bend of the road - and Jim finally began to slow down.

By this time, bitter tears of pain and disappointment were escaping Betty's control, but they went unheeded by her "suitor".

'Sandy's been right all along,' Betty thought miserably to herself. 'What would a fine man like him want to get mixed up with the likes of me for?' She was waiting now for him to end their relationship. She knew he would be kind - bless him - but he would be firm too. She was determined to be stoic in the face of her disappointment, and was already building up her resolve to "take it on the chin". Of one thing she was sure - and that was that she wasn't going to make it any harder for him - she loved him too much.

Staring into the space directly above her head, Jim began to speak quietly and haltingly. "I love you, Betty. You're so perfect, and before I go to Irvine I need to know what your feelings are for me. Do you think there's a place for me in your....?" Here his voice faltered and for the first time since he'd begun his speech he looked down at her - and immediately was all concern for her tears. "What's wrong, Betty love? What is it?" he asked in alarm.

It was teeming down and Betty stood with all her weight on her left leg and with rain and tears running down her face. She held her arms out mutely and he caught her close to him. She had dreaded losing him, and had been concentrating so much on surviving his departure, that when her most fervent prayer was answered and he professed his love to her - she was caught unprepared! But this unreal world that she had just stepped into was as good a time as any to tell him about her 'weakness.' Haltingly, at last, she told him about her knee.

"...so you see I'm not perfect," she finished sadly, with all of Sandy's previous taunts ringing in her ears. She hadn't realised till then just how deeply her brother's continual criticising had penetrated her self-confidence. There was silence after she had finished.

Then Jim spoke, "You're perfect to me, Betty. You're perfect for me. Am I good enough for you, though? Will you consent to marry me? I won't care if you wear tackety boots to our wedding - as long as you agree to marry me."

His attempt at humour couldn't take away the awesomeness of what he had just said. He wanted to marry her! "Yes, yes of course you are, Jim. Of course I will," replied Betty, her voice deep with emotion. "Oh Jim..."

And at this avowal, Jim picked her up as if she weighed no more than a feather, and carried her home.

* * *

Mrs Cormack fussed when they entered the house and her immediate concern was for Betty's knee and her tear-stained face. "It's all right, mother," said Betty breathlessly. "It's all right. We're going to be married!"

Her mother's distress turned to surprise. "Well, what are you crying for then?" she asked dazedly.

"I've hurt my knee - but it's all right," laughed Betty wincing as Jim set her down on the settee. "Don't worry, mum, everything's perfect. We're getting married!"

Although she had hoped for some kind of declaration of love to her daughter, Isabella was taken unawares by this formal proposal of marriage after only six weeks. But even when she was lost for words Isabella couldn't let the moment pass without saying something...

"Whatever next?" she smiled faintly.

When Mr Cormack returned from his church meeting a while later, Jim insisted upon asking him for his daughter's hand in marriage. And Isabella was almost rendered speechless again that evening when her husband reacted with a satisfied smile and promptly gave his consent. Then they all spent the rest of the evening together making plans. Since Jim was off to Irvine the next day, he asked Betty to buy an engagement ring of her own choice. "Anything you choose will please me," he added happily. Betty suggested that she would go to her father's cousin Mr Green, who had a Jewellery and Watchmaker's Shop in George Street in Aberdeen, where she knew she would get good value for her fiancé's money. And it was all agreed.

The older couple discreetly disappeared to bed and the young pair continued to sit talking happily till well after the last Subbie had gone. Before he left however, Jim gave "his intended" the kiss that she'd been dreaming of hitherto and quietly told her, "You know, Betty. That first night when I saw you in your dad's huge slippers, with your eyes dancing in merriment, I vowed, 'If this lassie's not married already, I'm going to marry her myself.'"

Betty couldn't help smiling. She had gone through all that soul-searching and pain when, if he'd only given her a hint - she needn't have worried at all!

Chapter 4

The Best Laid Plans O' Mice And Men Gang Aft Agley

Jim went off to Irvine the next day and quickly settled into lodgings with Mr and Mrs Sim who owned a China Shop and turned out to be fellow choristers. Jim was offered temporary membership of their choral society and accepted it with alacrity. Their friendship flourished so well that Jim wrote asking Betty to buy a wedding present from them, and included a cup and saucer whose design they had suggested. Betty immediately sanctioned their choice, and to her delight ended up with a thirteen-piece tea set.

Jim continued to do well and was next sent to undergo a course in poisonous gases in Greenock. After that he was posted to Esher, on the outskirts of London, to learn about bridge building and entanglements. During all this while, he regularly wrote short, factual letters to Betty that always ended with a plea to marry him as soon as possible.

Betty herself had no literary reservations when replying, and wrote her thoughts down on paper as fluently as they occurred to her. She bombarded Jim with questions about his new life, and what the Sim's were like, and how his lodgings were suiting him. She told him her news: how Sandy had come down off his high horse at last, and now wished them well, and pointed out that this was in large part due to his having found a girlfriend of his own, called Jessie Allan. Betty described her as a bonny, timid young girl who'd been a former pupil of Sandy's. And now he was going around confidently stating, "Jessie is young enough to mould to my will." Betty ventured to say that it wouldn't take long because the young lassie was over-eager to please, and doted on every word Sandy said. Still, she wished her brother luck and hoped he would be very happy with her. Then, musing over her own relationship with Jim, Betty concluded that there were all kinds of love in the world, indeed.

No word had come from her elder brother Bill in the meantime, but Edwin, her youngest brother had written to them about the awful assault on Constantinople that he'd recently taken part in. In preparation for the offensive, the Brits and Aussies had landed an expeditionary force on the narrow Galipoli peninsula that forms the shores of the Dardanelles. But the whole enterprise had been a dismal failure and had resulted in heavy casualties. How his letter ever got past the censors was anybody's guess.

By now, poor Edwin had had the misfortune to have been torpedoed no less than three times, and although he'd survived, his health had suffered badly. He wasn't at all well, and in his heartbreaking letter to the family said how bitterly he regretted rushing to join up. Poor Mr Cormack again wished he'd tried harder to dissuade his son at the time, but the family reassured him that he couldn't have done more. The Cormack household lived in daily dread of the telegram boy bringing a black-edged brown envelope bearing the worst news from the front about their sons.

But it hadn't happened yet and Betty declared that she would let herself dwell on it as seldom as possible. In her letters to her beloved she concentrated on happier things and reported all the latest births and marriages which were numerous. She added snippets about the local concerts and films and somehow always made Jim smile at their contents. Also, she would include knitted socks and maybe a fruitcake and other such things to keep her man cheery.

On one thing alone she was adamant, and that was that she refused to marry Jim until the war was over and he was safely home. She had always been a bit fey, and past experiences made her inclined to follow her "hunches." She continued to have a bad feeling about this, and although her love was never in question, she just "knew" that they shouldn't get married while the war raged on. She didn't tell Jim about this dark foreboding, and only voiced the numerous practical objections to their getting married straight away. Where would they live? she asked him. The prices and rents of suitable properties in Aberdeen at that time were sky high. The huge influx of soldiers left very few accommodations available, even if they had wanted to live together somewhere. She pointed out that as well as herself and her brother, Aunt Chat still lodged with them, which left little space for yet another lodger. And on top of that, his would be another mouth for her mother's already-overstretched budget to feed. Then there was the possibility of their having a baby, which would fairly test the nerves of the household! So the answer was always a regretful but firm no, despite her unwillingness to hurt him ever.

Jim never argued with her, but in his own quiet way always repeated his request in his next letter.

*   *   *

Throughout his training period he was granted occasional short leaves and one of these coincided with Christmas. It was decided that he would show his face at the Bauds first, and then visit Betty on his way back down south. Jim's mother had so far shown a reluctance to share her son with another woman and to date had confined her friendship with Betty to only one very polite piece of correspondence, which congratulated Betty on her engagement to her son. Mrs Mair disapproved of "town quines" in general, and would have preferred Jim to settle closer to home with some couthy local girl. But she could see that that was not likely to happen, and so with a little grace and impeccably good manners, she had welcomed Betty into her fold. Since then they had only corresponded once by letter so far, and Betty secretly hoped to win her over and dispel her future mother-in-law's prejudice when they finally met.

Evidence of Annie's power over her son was immediately apparent to Betty when Jim arrived at the Parish House that Christmas.

"What's happened to your mouser, Jim? I thought it was your pride and joy, so why have you shaven it off?" Betty asked when she opened the door to him. They had discussed his moustache in a light-hearted way from time to time, when she'd teased him about his vanity.

"Mother didn't like it," came the stony reply, and that was that. He wouldn't discuss it any further.

Her next question to him as he stood on the doorstep, cap in hand and covered with snow, bringing all their old joyful memories back was, "What's that you've brought with you?"

And Betty pointed at the sack in Jim's other hand, which was twitching and squawking fit to burst.

"Oh this?" said Jim blandly, barely glancing down at it while the noise inside it rose to a crescendo. He looked as if he'd like to disown it on the spot.

Then with a forced laugh he blushed and held up the sack, "My mother thought you'd all like a fresh hen for Christmas."

The smiles of the townsfolk froze temporarily. Mr Cormack's advance to shake Jim's hand was checked momentarily as it dawned on him what the sack contained.

Jim looked abashed and eased it uncertainly down onto the floor, "It was my sister's idea," he added lamely, overcome with embarrassment. "She wanted to be sure it was fresh for you."

"And a very good and thoughtful idea it was too," said Mrs Cormack, the first to recover.

"My word, it's certainly fresh! Please thank your mother for me, Jim." While she was saying this, she was edging cautiously closer to pick up the sack which by now was kicking up a terrific din.

Betty couldn't help it. She tried to stifle the giggle by putting her hand to her mouth. But her eyes still danced until tears started to run and she had to give up the struggle and let her laughter explode into the room. Then they were all laughing together, except Sandy of course; who looked a wee bit silly as he tried to retain his dignity.

"As a 'townser' I suppose I'd better learn about these things if I'm to be your wife," Betty said gaily wiping her laughter-tears away. "Oh Jim, you're always full of surprises!"

Mrs Cormack grasped the sack with both hands and made towards the pantry being jerked this way and that by the apoplectic chicken. And she disappeared from the room shaking her head and asking of no one in particular, "What ever next?" because she was at a loss.

The eventual outcome was that amidst much hilarity, Betty learned how to pluck a chicken and prepare it for the oven. Everyone swore, including Sandy, that they had never tasted better.

By the end of 1916 Jim was in France with the Royal Engineers, and his principal remit was the building of water tanks for the troops. Being so near to the front Jim was unable to send or receive very much mail and only the odd "regulation postcard," always heavily censored, managed to get through to his homeland. Sometimes Betty went for weeks without hearing from Jim and like all the others, she couldn't help worrying despite her best efforts. But she was determined to remain optimistic until told otherwise, so she ignored the lack of correspondence from Jim, and continued to write long 'newsy' letters to him that were sent off regularly in the hope that he would ultimately get them. And she kept sending parcels of foodstuffs and knitted things that she knew he would appreciate. She had now joined the legions of young women throughout the country who lived in daily dread of a telegram from the War Office - on her own account now as well as her brothers'. Although any news of Jim would be sent in the first instance to the Bauds, he had exacted a promise that his mother would contact her immediately there was any news of him.

*   *   *

The year had started badly for the allies when the Crown Prince, the Kaiser's son, launched an attack on Verdun, the key to the French defence. And he had almost succeeded!

 Britain continued to hold Egypt and the Suez Canal, but then suffered heavy casualties in the Dardanelles.

On the thirty-first of May of that year, the British and German fleets engaged in battle off the Danish Coast at the Battle of Jutland. They met in heavy mists in the late afternoon, and the Germans were forced to retreat behind their own minefields. The losses on both sides were heavy, but it was hailed as a glorious victory for the allies since Britain remained in control of the sea. Again Edwin luckily managed to escape with his life, but by now he was very poorly.

The French and British troops then started out on their first big offensive in Europe, beginning with the First Battle of the Somme on the first of July.

They used tanks for the first time and drove the Germans back nine miles along the front.

Lord Kitchener had introduced conscription because the vast pool of volunteer soldiers had drained almost dry. The war generals had hugely underestimated the forces they would be up against. They hadn't expected the war to last into winter and no preparations for the colder climates had been made. This had put the government in a quandary because, they could either rally the folks back home to make warm clothes to help their troops withstand the freezing winters, or they could keep up the pretence that everything was going along fine apart from a few odd casualties.

After many secret debates it was decided that the current propaganda should prevail and that the Press would be kept heavily censored. The country's leaders felt that it was imperative to keep up the high morale of the people who were supplying the "human fodder" for this war that Britain had got itself into.

This decision was to open a huge gulf between people at home whose knowledge of the war was culled from newspaper reports; and soldiers in the field who experienced the war at first hand. Trench warfare was a totally new concept and the soldiers had problems coping with its strategies. And thanks to the successful government propaganda, no one at home could help them with their problems.

Because they were "doing the right thing" morally, the British Generals had assumed that victory was a foregone conclusion. However, it soon became obvious that they should have taken the Kaiser more seriously at the beginning, and not wasted time when they should have been training up staff for command. They had no option but to cull their generals and captains mainly from the young aristocracy, fresh from their private schools. These youths could be relied upon to pull together, stick together and be ready to die for their country as a matter of course. Unfortunately, although they were accustomed to leadership in the sports fields they had had no training in the art of war. The result was that the command structure was shambolic, filled as it was with untrained staff. And because communication was slow, mistakes were commonplace.

The British people continued to believe what they were reading in the newspapers and were unaware of the government's censorship that stripped news items of negative content. They knew about the new "mustard gas" that had been invented by the enemy. What they weren't told about, was what happened to the soldiers who didn't get their gas masks on in time. If they inhaled "the gas" they felt as if their lungs were on fire and knew they would die a slow painful death.

Soldiers were more often than not tired and weary through lack of sleep. Their ill-fitting uniforms dirty and itchy. Their boots didn't fit and the resulting blisters were open to potential infections. Sometimes their feet were numbed with the cold, and gangrene could set in without them being aware of it. The only available medical "cure" was to amputate the foot or the leg, depending on how much dead tissue there was by the time it was noticed. The soldiers were surrounded by dirt in trenches that turned to mud in the rain and were breeding grounds for the rats that infested their dugouts.

Transmission of information was slow and unreliable, food and medical supplies were scarce, and the constant fear-filled waiting underground, listening for sounds of possible attacks from the German lines, all added to the constant fraying of their nerves. The soldiers could barely walk upright, for the enemy was constantly vigilant and at the sight of movement, the Germans would fire off a volley of shells, and massive damage would result. Trench edges had to be shored up again, while the wounded were borne off on stretchers along the narrow paths to the nearest medical station.

Then it was back to nervous waiting again. They had to live with the constant fear of imminent death - of being shot at by men living in the same awful conditions as they were, and who were as close as thirty yards away - across the other side of "no man's land." This was a new and alien type of war being waged. The soldiers could scarcely understand it - how could the folks back home?

Back home "trench coats" adapted for warmth and protection in the trenches had become a "fashion item." Back home families believed that "their boys" were fighting a great and glorious war. Back home everybody believed that the allies were winning. Back home the truth about this war was being suppressed.

The situation was confusing for the soldiers home on leave. They were hailed as heroes but were unable to speak of the horrors that no one could understand. Many soldiers were brain-damaged by the experience of trench-warfare, but their families and friends had no way of empathising with their experiences. At the front, the effect of the nerve gas sometimes manifested as hallucinations or depression or fear of the unknown. These were injuries that couldn't be bandaged; that hadn't ended up being fatal, so in the main were misunderstood. The bizarre and irrational behaviour of soldiers affected in this way, was interpreted as "malingering" or as "attempting to escape from the front," or as "feigning insanity." Not infrequently, after summary trials where no defence was offered, these casualties were shot as deserters. By the winter of 1916, the sheer exhaustion of all the men put an end to active fighting in Europe.

Back in Britain Lloyd George was elected Prime Minister, and he promised to pour more money into helping the troops. And as if this was not enough to rekindle patriotic fever, he stated categorically that he would have no truck with making any "deals" with the Kaiser. Instead, he reiterated fervently that the defeat of Germany was his only resolution to the war! A fresh tide of optimism flooded the country - but conditions scarcely changed for the soldiers at the front.

In other parts of the world though, the allies had been more successful and German troops had been defeated in parts of China and the Pacific. The Cormack family were also proud that their son Bill, under General Botha, was a part of the South African army that had captured German South West Africa.

In December Lloyd George reaffirmed the country's intention to win against "the German aggressor," and again he made it clear, to cheers of approval, that he entertained absolutely no ideas about mediating with the enemy.

*   *   *

Meanwhile, Betty's life was in turmoil. She had been living with an awful sense of foreboding for the last few weeks. Then she had slept badly the night before and was now convinced that something awful had happened to Jim. That morning Aunt Chat had commented on her niece's sleeplessness, and Betty had finally confided her fears to her mother. They had neither of them mentioned her intuitive ability but it was weighing heavily on both their minds. The later events of that day were to be etched in their memories forever.

It was late in the afternoon and darkness was falling on that wet September day. The persistent drizzle seemed to have gradually seeped through the brickwork and into the interior of the house that, to Betty, now felt cold and damp. Inside the kitchen Isabella had built up the fire, but even with the heavy curtains closed against the inhospitable elements there remained a bleakness that couldn't be dispelled by the gas lamps spluttering softly on the walls. Betty couldn't settle to anything. She was tired from her sleepless night, her knee ached with the dampness, and she couldn't throw off the dread that had pervaded her thoughts all that day.

With seeming resignation she rose to answer the knock on the door and it was as if she was taking part in a nightmare. She noticed vaguely that the young lad standing on the doorstep looked about the same age as young Edwin and she tried to avert her eyes from the telegram he held out to her. "Miss Elizabeth Cormack?" he asked again in a neutral voice while Betty stood there blankly staring at him.

He looked uncomfortable and proffered the telegram to her again, this time more earnestly. He was wanting away. He didn't like delivering these telegrams; he didn't like being the bearer of bad news and wanted to disassociate himself from the message as soon as possible. It was just a job to him. He was young and he still felt the invincibility of youth. He wanted no reminder of mortality, nor did he want to take part in another's sorrow. Impatient to be away, he pushed the telegram into Betty's cold hand. And like someone in a trance she automatically opened the envelope and scanned its contents. Bleakly she looked up at the telegram boy and gave an almost imperceptible shake of her head. He understood, and being thus affirmed that there was no reply to take away, he gave a quick nod and with a touch of his cap he was off.

Upon seeing her daughter's anguished face Mrs Cormack felt a fierce wave of protection for her. In that instant she would have borne the hurt herself if she could. She led Betty gently to the chair by the fire and took the telegram from her. Quickly she ascertained that James was seriously wounded and had recently been transferred to Stobhill Hospital in Glasgow. "Thank God he's not dead," said Mrs Cormack gruffly, and took escape in practicalities. "We'll have a cup of tea, lass, and sort this out." And she set about putting on the kettle.

By the time it was ready Betty was more composed. "I must go to him, mother," she said softly. "But what am I going to? How badly is he hurt? It must be bad before he's been sent home. What if he can't work again? What if he doesn't know me? I've heard..." By now Betty was close to losing control. She had heard so many awful stories.

"Now don't fret," her mother urged. "He's not dead and that's the main thing. You've still got your man and that's a lot more than some. Be thankful for that."

"But what if he can't work, mother?" Betty asked in anguish. "Will he still want to marry me?"

"Of course he will," came the short supply. "He'll need your support, and you'll have to work hard to make a go of it...if you still love him?" Isabella asked tentatively.

"Of course I do, mother!" Betty replied, stung. But then she lapsed into her former indecisiveness. "But this might change things, don't you see? Jim's so proud and independent, how will he cope?"

"We don't know how bad it is yet, lass, but that shouldn't affect your love for him surely. You know that he loves you, and you love him in return. Anyway," she added with more asperity, "you've given your word, and you won't be able to live with yourself if you let him down now." Isabella was determined to snap her daughter out of her doubtful worrying and so she added with a forced smile, " I don't know, Betty, but the way I feel about that fine brave young man, if I wasn't married already, I'd...I'd...marry him myself!"

A thin tearful smile broke out on her daughter's face at these words. Then as quickly Betty's thoughts turned inwards again. "But you don't know Jim as I do, mother," she sighed. "This changes everything and I don't know what to do for the best. I really don't."

Isabella shook her head sadly and went to make the tea. They talked away quietly for the rest of the afternoon, and by nightfall the others knew how things stood. Even Sandy didn't have a sour word to say about the tragic situation then. Her father was more practical and suggested that she ask Mr Smith, her employer at "Stephen and Smith Advocates" in Aberdeen, if his wife could possibly help. Mrs Smith was a "high heid yin" in the Red Cross.

And as it turned out, this was good advice since Mrs Smith was only too pleased to be of help to her husband's pleasant employee. She started making arrangements for Betty to go down to Glasgow by train and stay in digs whilst she was there.

Meanwhile, another letter arrived from the Bauds. To Betty's increasing consternation, it revealed that Jim had had his left leg amputated. And then his left arm had turned gangrenous, and it too had had to be amputated. Betty was very worried about the effect this would have on Jim. In her letter, Elsie Jane told Betty how she and her sister Beatrice had gone straight down to Stobhill to see Jim. But he had ignored them completely and had repeatedly asked to speak to "his Betty." Betty was even more alarmed when she heard this. Jim would never be rude, and certainly not to his sisters whom he loved so much. This didn't bode well for his mental state! Betty's nerves were being stretched to breaking point, and this letter made it even more difficult for her to act normally while her mind was in such turmoil. Time seemed to drag for her until she could get down to him.

In contrast to the rest of his family, Sandy was now showing absolutely no sensitivity at all for his sister's feelings, and he was adamant that it would be a waste of time for her to go down to Glasgow. In his opinion, which he voiced loudly and as often as he had an audience, it would be kinder for his sister to end their relationship now rather than wait till later. He purported that he knew Jim better than any of them, and he "knew" that Jim would be too proud to take her on as his wife in his changed circumstances. "What good would she be to a cripple?" he asked contemptuously. Having said his piece once, he insisted on repeating it at every opportunity until it began to undermine Betty's resolve - just as he had meant it to. No one in the family knew if he was being vindictive, or being deliberately cruel to be kind, in order to spare his sister some of the hurt that Sandy was sure was coming her way.

Whatever his motive was, his incessant criticisms of her and her situation multiplied Betty's own doubts as to their future together, and she swung alternately from cautious hope to dark despair every day. On the one hand she wanted to get down there and sort things out - face the devil and get it over with - find out if he still loved her. On the other hand, she was worried that she might not be able to cope with his answer - whichever one he gave. But there was nothing she could do about it until the travel arrangements were confirmed, so she just had to wait.

*   *   *

A week later she found herself in Stobhill Hospital talking to Doctor Simpson who was Jim's Consultant. He was a short stout jolly-looking man who had a "hashed" look about him. His white coat was crumpled with inky smudges around his breast pocket, and the nicotine stains on the fingers of his right hand showed that he subscribed to the prevailing medical notion that smoking was good for you - and that he subscribed to it with a will. The desk before him bore testimony to the huge amount of work he had to get through, and by the looks of his room, today's pile of folders was by no means unusual. He was a very busy man.

"I'm worried about him, Miss Cormack," he confided. "He seems to have given up hope I'm afraid. We've tried everything we can to help but he doesn't respond. It's a common problem with these young men. His physical recovery is going to depend very much on his mental state, and I don't mind telling you that right now I'm getting quite anxious about him. It's not going to be easy for him you know. He's going to have to make a huge effort to adapt to his changed physical state and that will be particularly hard. If only that train had not been left in the siding... Oh now, let me give you some advice, my dear." He paused for a moment and looked intently at Betty. "Studies have been done on cases like these, where our young men have gone off to the war strong and healthy, and have come back crippled in some way - physically and mentally." He paused. Betty shivered involuntarily at the word "crippled" but there was no sign on her face.

Doctor Simpson looked at his fob watch and it appeared that he remembered something. He continued more briskly - after all, Jim's case was one amongst so many, "Where was I? Oh yes. Now the current thinking on the subject is...let me see...Yes. Yes. My dear, no matter how hard it is for you at times, and there are hard times ahead - be in no doubt about that." He paused again and stared at the wall behind Betty's head and there was no way of knowing where his attention had wandered to.

Betty understood that she was in the presence of a man who was overworked and overtired and she tried hard to retain her composure. But what was coming next? Why was every thing so negative? She wanted to shout at him to get on with it.

It seemed an age before he managed to bring his wandering thoughts back to the present.

"Whatever happens," continued the doctor, "never.... And I repeat never... ask him what happened at the front." He was wagging his finger at her throughout this piece of advice, which leant his words, even more force. Betty could only stare at him.

"I know it sounds an odd recommendation, but tests have shown that it's by far and away the best way to go on. He'll probably tell you what happened... Probably....But then again he might not. He might tell you about it today, or tomorrow, or it could be next week or month or year. One never knows. And when that day comes....if it comes....then be ready to listen, for 'They' say it's very important for them to get it off their chests - but only in their own time."

'Time!' thought Betty, almost frantic with anticipation by now. She didn't even know if they were going to have a future together and this doctor was babbling on about 'years' ahead. She didn't know what was going to happen five minutes ahead! But she kept her composure and nodded reassuringly at him.

"I'll get a nurse to take you to him. And then I believe my wife said something about your having taken digs with our neighbour," he continued more conversationally. "I'm hoping to go home about nine o'clock tonight and if you're still here and want a lift, just come along here to my office and wait." He went on to tell Betty of the special privileges she would have whilst there. She would be offered meals along with Jim, and the normal visiting hours wouldn't apply to her. She was to see as much of her fiancé as possible..... And anything else she could think of that his wife might have told him to let her do.

He gave a rueful smile as if to confirm that his wife was the boss, and Betty's smile was also rueful as she wondered if she would still have a fiancé to stay for and visit. They shook hands and he took himself off down the corridor at a surprising speed for a man of his girth, and Betty waited for her guide to arrive.

"You'll find him a good bit changed, no doubt," said the nurse sympathetically, when they stopped at Betty's request, near the open door of Jim's ward.

"No doubt," answered Betty evenly. She shook the nurse's hand and thanked her, then she turned her eyes into the ward and scanned the beds for her man.

The scene before her threatened to undo her resolve. For it seemed to her that the war had provoked Nature into playing a cruel trick on these young men lying in their beds. The nurse had tried to prepare her for this on the way here. She had said that some of them were only young boys of sixteen, yet they all had cadaverous bodies and gaunt skeletal faces, with eyes in them that had seen too much horror and suffering. They all had a frailty about them - a vulnerability, or so it seemed to Betty in this unguarded moment. The beds in this sterile world were crammed close together and extended a long way from where she stood. At nearly every bed there was a medical contraption of some kind that was attached to the patient. Limbs were held in traction by complicated pieces of equipment. Wires attached some men to machines that blinked and emitted strange unsettling noises, while others wore bandages around their various injuries.

Dinner had just finished and everything had been cleared away although the smell of cooking still lingered. The men had been settled down for a rest, and it was quiet inside the ward apart from the murmurings of the three duty nurses who were having a few words with their patients as they went about their business. The rustling of their starched uniforms supplied a soporific background noise.

Betty stood and watched him in the reflection of the window on the door. He had been reading the same page in his book for the last five minutes while she had looked on unnoticed. Betty was filled with pity. "My poor brave man!" she cried within herself.

He seemed diminished somehow. His shrunken frame was enveloped in his blue hospital-issue pyjamas, the left sleeve of which lay empty at his side. A cage covered his legs and hid his deformity. He had lost a lot of weight and his once-ruddy complexion was pale and lifeless. Always thin, now there was no sign of muscle anywhere. His head was skeletal and dark ridges lay under his haunted eyes showing evidence of many, many sleepless nights. He was uninterested in the book he was holding, and it was as if his whole being had retreated from the outer world into one of sadness and pain.

Betty stood outside the door and considered her broken man while her brother's harsh words banged in her ears, "..Useless, useless." Then her mother's strength and resolution would superimpose themselves upon her thoughts. ". You're luckier than most Elizabeth," and she would feel strong enough to enter the ward. But then her heart would tighten and she would falter in her purpose. She prayed desperately for the right words. The thought occurred to her, "He's not expecting me, so I could go home and write instead. There's no hurry. That would give him time to accept it all before I see him." But even as this idea went through her head, she knew that she couldn't delay any longer. "I've wasted enough time over this," she resolved. "I must speak to him now and live with the consequences."

When she approached the bed quietly Jim never moved, nor showed any interest at all in his visitor. He assumed it was another nurse. "Hello Jim," Betty said softly. She felt like crying now.

Startled he glanced at her with ravaged surprise, which he quickly suppressed. He then followed this with another look, which alarmed Betty. She had not expected this reaction! He didn't answer her, and instead he looked away into the room and mentally withdrew from her. He deliberately put a wall of silence between them.

But Betty recognised and intuitively understood his behaviour. He was in despair and had given up hope. Betty sat down with a purposeful air and made ready for a long wait. She was certain that Jim had to make the next move.

When the tea trolley was trundled in Betty accepted a cup of tea from the friendly woman. Jim didn't request a cup of tea, but got one put on his locker just the same. "Jist his usual self, hen," the woman smiled at Betty. "Come on, Maister Mair," she shouted at Jim as if he were deaf. "You's'll no let yer sister jist sit there all day an' no gie her a bit o' news for yer maw!" she urged. Jim didn't respond.

And so they sat, Jim taut and uncommunicative, deep in the recesses of his tortured thoughts, while Betty sat easily beside him, secure in the knowledge of what she had to do - in the knowledge of what she knew now - without any doubt - she wanted to do. She also knew it was important for Jim to make the first move in all this if he was to retain his self-respect. But as the hours went by it was hard for Betty just to sit there and wait without doing anything or saying anything, and at times her resolve would falter and she would come close to speaking her mind. But some stronger instinct restrained her.

The afternoon became dull and the ward lights were switched on. The fine drizzle that had clung to the windows making them steam over, turned to rain, and the wind got up. Before long it was throwing bucketfuls against the windowpanes.

The nurses rustled amongst the patients keeping up a steady murmur of voices in the background, which was broken by an occasional laugh that sounded forced and artificial. A nurse attended to Jim and took his temperature and pulse, saying a few cheery words to them both. Still Jim would not converse, but Betty managed a bright exchange with her. In her heart Betty was very worried now, but she was compelled by some deep emotion to hold her tongue.

Teatime came and went. From the whole ward, only five men were able to sit at the table that was set up for them. The rest, like Jim, had theirs served on a bedside table, which was set in front of them. Betty was given tea then. She ate a little, but she ate alone and Jim's plate and cup remained untouched. Still he would not speak.

The nurses cleared everything away, and those who had sat at the table were instructed to return to bed whilst the ward was given a general tidy-up in anticipation of visiting hour.

The minutes dragged by, but at the appointed hour the bell rang and the visitors arrived. The ward was at once filled with outside noises and smells. People came in shaking the wet off their coats, and divesting themselves of their sodden hats and scarves. All sorts, they came through the doors and squelched their ways to their loved ones and friends. A few gave Betty and Jim a cheery "hello!" to which only she replied. They were obviously accustomed to Jim's lack of acknowledgement and they shrugged their shoulders sympathetically at Betty.

The young pair invited comments like "poor things" whispered just loudly enough for them to hear. Most had noticed Betty's ring which now sat prominently on her left hand which she held conspicuously crossed over her right one lying in her lap. She made no attempt to hide it at all while she kept her quiet vigil by Jim's bedside.

If he was surprised when Betty didn't leave with the others at the end of visiting hour, Jim didn't show it. Betty had been given permission from Doctor Simpson to stay later and get a lift from him at nine o'clock. If Jim didn't speak soon Betty was going to have to come back tomorrow - if she still believed that she was doing the right thing by then.

The nurses settled the other patients but must have been instructed to leave Mr Mair till last, for none approached him. Night time had fallen, and behind the curtains the sky outside was black. The wind kept up its furious assault on the windows.

Finally Jim broke the silence. He kept his eyes on the worktable in the middle of the ward as he said in a strained clipped voice, "You're fey right enough, Betty. It's as well you didn't marry me when I asked." He paused, summoning the emotional and physical strength for what he had to say next. "We can never have the future I promised you, Betty." He paused again and looked at her at last. His eyes were empty and devoid of hope, but he would set her free. At a time when he loved and needed her the most, he put her happiness first. His dignity was intact although all hope was gone. "And I hereby release you from our engagement." Then he looked away and closed his eyes.

Now Betty was free at last to speak her mind! She drew a huge breath and got on with it.

"Now you listen to me, James Mair," she demanded tartly. "You'll not get rid of me that easily! You asked me to marry you and I said 'yes' Jim, and this was for richer or poorer, in sickness and in health, and as far as I'm concerned only death will part us. Do you hear me! I'll not be cast off lightly, Jim. I know you well enough to believe in you, and I know that you'll succeed at anything you'll set your mind to. It's you I love and it's you I'm going to marry - unless you've somebody else waiting in the wings?" she added with a touch of her old mischief. And having said her piece, she waited.

Jim was nonplussed and fairly shaken out of his apathy. And it was a few minutes before he understood what she had just said.

"Oh, Betty," he whispered - his voice full of conflicting emotions, and he reached out for her hand.

Betty finally drew a long breath and started to relax. She had known what she wanted the moment she had seen her man again. She had started off so sure in the knowledge that she was going about it in the right way. But during the last few hours she had begun to harbour doubts that perhaps he hadn't wanted her! Perhaps he had been waiting for her to speak - so that she could end their relationship. She had been in such a state of rising nervousness that this simple happy outcome left her feeling drained. She stroked his hand gently.

The pair of them sat thus for a little while in a new and wholesome silence that was instilled with hope now, their previous despair quite vanquished.

Presently Betty rose, and as she bustled about arranging her outerwear, she explained that she had accepted Doctor Simpson's kind invitation of a lift to her digs. Also, that for the few days she was here she was not to be tied by ward rules, and that she was free to come and go as she pleased within reason. "So," she added in her old way. "I'll expect to be entertained while I'm here."

Her eyes were sparkling when she leaned over to kiss him lightly goodbye, but she whispered for his ears only, "Hurry up and get better, dear. Nothing will part us now."

She then walked briskly to the visitors' waiting room where she broke down and cried. When at last she felt composed, she sought out Doctor Simpson. "I'm ready any time you are, doctor," she informed him steadily.

Chapter 5

Set A Stout Heart To A Steep Hillside

Jim's dark days were over and he had a future again. He fought his way back to good health and was fitted with an artificial leg, then he rose to meet the challenge of his infirmities. His stump was now covered with a woollen sock and fitted into a bucket attached to straps that went round his shoulders. The flesh around the site of the amputation was still swollen and raw but he was assured that this would settle down. It would tighten up he was told, and the skin eventually harden to the extent that it would stop causing pain. From now on he would have to make periodic visits to "Hangers" in McVie House at the far end of North Street in Aberdeen. Although it sounded fancy, Betty described it as "a lot of glorified sheds." However, its purpose was to make continuing adjustments to the fitting of the bucket and allow Jim reasonable comfort. He wasn't in any hurry to be fitted with an artificial arm in the meantime, and preferred to wait until the swelling had gone down more.

The most important thing on his mind at the time was to find himself a job. A return to the building trade would be impossible so he was forced to consider alternative work. He enlisted on a course to become a Sanitary Inspector where his knowledge of building would be useful. The written examinations presented no problems for him and his training as a Master Builder was certainly an advantage. But when it came to actually going underground into narrow and restricted areas to inspect foundations, or climbing up into attics to assess their conditions; he was forced to concede defeat. So he was compelled to cast around for another way to make his living.

This was easier said than done. There was plenty of work available but the jobs were going to fully able survivors of the war. There was no legal or moral compulsion for employers to take on any of the country's large contingent of disabled men who were left to fend for themselves or live off the state. Jim was determined not to do the latter despite his discouraging start, and if anything, the disappointment fuelled his resolve to find a job and be the breadwinner in his family.

When he heard of the vacancy in Mr Cormack's line of work, Jim was immediately interested. The idea of becoming a Poor Inspector was a definite possibility. His intellectual competence was unimpaired, and his physical circumstances wouldn't get in the way of his duties.

The vacancy was in a village called Longside and not even Sandy knew anything about the place. So Mr Cormack and Jim decided to take the train out to the village one afternoon and have a look around. Then, if he still thought it was a good idea Jim would put in his application to Aberdeen County Council. They took the train from Aberdeen and continued on the Peterhead line as far as Longside. They didn't know anybody in the village, but that one visit was enough to persuade Jim that he liked the look of the place.

"It's up to you, lad," advised Mr Cormack that evening. "If you want the position of Inspector of Poor in Longside, then go for it. It's an honourable profession and an interesting and rewarding one, and I can personally recommend it." Then he added with satisfaction, as Jim continued to nod his head in agreement, "I'll be happy to help you all I can. Send away for an application form and then see about getting in touch with two referees who'll speak up for you."

Jim applied for his references to Mr J. Wesley McKee who was the Free Church Minister and Provost of Findochty; and also to his former leader, Captain A.R.Gray of the Royal Engineers. The testimonials he received from those two men helped enormously because they both knew him well and their references did him proud.

Mr McKee testified to Jim's "exceptionally fine character," saying that "All work done by him (Jim) was honest work, and that, "He could survey a field - or plough it, build a church and play the organ in it afterwards!" The good cleric went on to say that: "Mr Mair is a pious man in the very best sense. He is truly religious, but in his religion there is nothing sour or bigoted. Genial in temperament, he is shrewd and clear-sighted...He would take up a cause with enthusiasm, but he would not be readily taken in by appearances." He ended by saying that: "He (Jim) has a good head and a good heart, he has been well educated by study and well disciplined by suffering, he has a good knowledge of business and a good knowledge of men." He recommended Jim unreservedly for the position of Inspector of Poor.

"My, my, but I don't know if I'm good enough to marry this paragon," remarked Betty dryly when she'd read it. But her eyes were dancing as she said it, and she was fairly bursting with pride for her matrimonial choice. After all, Mr McKee was merely confirming what she herself had known for a long while now - that Jim was an exceptional man.

"And what does the good Captain Gray have to say about you, my dear?" she asked lightly, reaching for Jim's second testimonial which had arrived that morning. Jim was staying with the Cormacks meantime in the hope of being called for interview.

Betty read the letter with mounting pleasure and surprise. She gasped, "I didn't know you were going to be made a Lieutenant!"

Then she continued to read aloud: "Of his character and influence I cannot speak too highly. He was a man whom any Commanding Officer would be fortunate to have, and his value was recognised not only by his own Company but by Headquarters, who detailed him for important and confidential duties on several occasions, and his work was always favourably commented upon." By now Betty's eyes were fairly shining. "Confidential work! What a position of trust, Jim! And you never said a word to me!" she accused him, shaking her head with a mixture of feigned disapproval and pride. She read on in silence till the last bit which she just had to read aloud: "...and with the other merits which he possesses in such a marked degree I feel he cannot but be a success."

Betty flourished the piece of paper. "I knew it. I told you you would get good references. They'll be hard-pressed to find better testimonials than these, Jim. The job's as good as yours I'm sure," she asserted with bright confidence.

And she was right. Following a lengthy interview and a series of training sessions, Jim was formally appointed Registrar and Inspector of Poor of the Parish of Longside. With his new certificate in his pocket and canny optimism in his heart, his next intention was to settle quickly into his work and look around for a house there, so that he could marry Betty and set up home together.

But he came up against an unexpected problem - because Longside had filled up with airmen from nearby Lenabo.

The War Office had recognised the need for its north east coastline to be patrolled and had commissioned an airship base at Lenabo, officially called RNAS Longside. A vast area of scrubland and bog two miles south of the village had been cleared for the base and most of the hard preparation had been done by itinerant Scots and Irish navvies. It comprised three huge airship sheds, a gas plant, gasholders, workshops and living quarters for the servicemen.

Although most of the ordinary soldiers lived at the barracks, the officers with their wives and families had snapped up nearly all the available accommodation in Longside and were paying inflated prices for the privilege.

The servicemen increased their popularity by organising concerts and dances in the church halls that were well received by the villagers.

A poet local to Longside called John Imray, wrote poems and articles for various papers in the north east, and spoke for the locals when he described the airship base in this way:

Lenabo- Then, and Now

In East Aberdeenshire, there once was a place,
  Devoid of all beauty or natural grace;
"Creation's backyard" might have well been its name,
  Although now it is justly entitled to fame.

Lenabo is its name, if the truth I must tell.
  Which, for bleak desolation, there's few could excel;
Far away from the city's vain glory and strife,
  Its populace dwelt there, contented with life.

Surrounded by heathery hills and moss bogs,
   Happy land to the sportsman, his game an' his dogs;
The "rest home" of hares, muircock, widgeon and teal,
   After which, in the gloaming, the poacher would steal.

The old-fashioned tenants, aye kindly at heart,
   Ever met friend or foe in true neighbourly part;
And, in tilling their acres, those sons of the soil
   Deemed their labours a pleasure and pleasures a toil.

Right frugal their lives were, in clothes, drink, and meat,
   But sturdier fellows ne'er travelled on feet;
While plodding around on their crofts and their farms,
   Unthinking of danger, or warfare's alarms.

But, suddenly changes occur in the world,
   When war's devastation 'mongst nations are hurled;
And in this one respect, Lenabo has its share,
   Transforming its landscape to scenes bright and fair.

The farmers and crofters evicted have been,
   And their tidy-kept homesteads will no more be seen,
As our law-makers thought it their right to demand
   For national needs those broad acres of land.

Aerodromes have been built for airship and 'plane,
   With a "city" of huts for homes to the men,
Where hundreds of aircraftsmen pass to and fro,
   Protecting our shores from assault by the foe.

Airships now glide o'er us, betwixt earth and sky,
   Well manned by brave lads, who with vigilant eye
Keep watch that no direful invasion is made
   By Hun submarine, or through Zeppelin raid.

A party of fine hearty fellows they are,
   Much alike in their ways to the breezy "Jack Tar";

In music and stage-craft they are equalled by few,
  Ungrudgingly giving their services too.

A new railway branch, it is worthy of note,
  Has of late been commenced to this now famous spot,
Which will bear all the traffic direct to the base,
  And be a memento of war's needy ways.

The "Battle-Bag," also, comes next to my mind,
  With its sharp wit and humour in language refined;
While the "Beauty of Truth," which adorns every page,
  Is an elixir soothing to youth and old age.

This brilliant press medium, so piquantly rare,
  Compiled by a staff of the "sons of the air,"
Is now spreading its wings, with excusable boast,
  From inland Old Deer, right round by the coast.

Such, then, is a picture, concise, brief, but true,
  Though I cannot foretell what the future may brew;
So in closing these verses, my heart proudly swells,
  In wishing all Godspeed, and breathing farewells.

As John Imray said, a branch line was built during the war that went directly from Longside Station to the airship base. The railway line had to cross the main road between Flushing and Longside, and the very first train to use the route collided with a car at the crossing, and an old couple travelling home to Longside were killed. The line was immediately dismantled and sadly never became the "memento of war's needy ways".

The airship base itself did thrive throughout the war though, and its existence caused a continual influx of soldiers and airmen willing to pay a premium to live in the village. This meant that Jim and Betty's plan to get a house together had to be postponed for the meantime, because Jim had a better chance of finding lodgings on his own.

That year of 1917 had started well for the allies and the Germans were driven back to the Hindenberg Line. Then America had declared war on Germany in April and mobilised its army to fight in France. Both incidents helped to revive the troops' belief in ultimate victory.

But the fervour of the people back home was waning and they were no longer so easily roused by proud patriotic speeches. Widows and orphans proliferated, and their numbers couldn't be ignored. After such a long time, the pride in their sons' deaths was giving way to sadness across the nation.

John Imray knew he spoke for the whole country when he described the bleakness that had descended on the inhabitants of Longside.

War-time Reflections

Dedicated to our gallant Soldiers, Sailors, and Air Service Men

There's sorrow on the mountainside, and mourning in the glen,
    All hearts are moved with sadness through the loss of valiant men;
For Britain's just and sacred rights, who've fallen in the war,
    Along with brave Colonials who are aiding us from far.

In the city muffl'd anguish mingles with its busy life,
    For noble heroes, brave and true, now freed from earthly strife,
Who made the sacrifice supreme and shed their precious blood
    Upon the gory battlefield, for country, King and God.

From Britain's fair ancestral halls, down to the humblest cot,
    Brave sons responded to the call who ne'er shall be forgot,
And willingly laid down their lives, in air, on land, and sea,
    While fighting 'gainst the German hordes to keep our homeland free.

Men such as these with Allies brave, who nobly fought and fell
    Shall ever live in history and cast a brilliant spell
On mem'ries which shall never die, until the end of Time,
    Examples to the coming race of patriots sublime.

Beyond the deep blue sea they rest, upon a foreign strand,
    With thousands of their comrades true, far from their native land;
Their warfare o'er, they've crossed the bourne with pure unsullied
    fame,
Their last roll call'd, they sleep in death, with honour to their name.

Tread gently on their hallow'd graves, ye wand'rers from afar
  Each one contains a sadd'ning tale of devastating war;
Yet though their mangled forms lie still, their spirits hence have fled,
  To mingle with the glorious band of the heroic dead.

To wounded, sick, and missing ones our thoughts are thoughts of love,
  For these our heartfelt prayers ascend unto the Throne above,
That health and freedom yet be theirs, where'er their lot is cast,
  To follow on their gallant stand in warfare's savage blast.

When shall these agonising times with all their horrors cease;
  And bring to this sad war-worn world contentment, joy, and peace;
When shall the clash of hostile arms be heard on earth no more?
  And brotherhood, love, harmony, extend from shore to shore.

'Tis hard to tell; though from our hearts we fondly hope and pray
  That aided by the Powers divine soon dawns the blissful day
When humbl'd to the very dust, we've crush'd the brutal foe,
  And sav'd the world from serfdom vile, from misery and woe.

Jim read about the current events in the newspapers but did not discuss them much. Such scant attention as Jim gave to the war reports, and his apparent disinterest in the progress of the war, puzzled Betty. But since Doctor Simpson had warned her never to question him closely about his part in it, she never asked about it, nor voiced her concern for him.

What mattered more to Jim at that time was that he had a pressing need to find somewhere to stay in the village. And at last he struck lucky! Mr and Mrs Robertson who owned and ran one of the tailor shops on Main Street, suggested that Jim could lodge with them, in their house next to the shop. With huge relief Jim accepted their kind offer. Nothing was too much trouble as far as Mrs Robertson was concerned and she helped him settle in.

By now Jim had acquired a specially adapted tricycle, and it improved his mobility greatly. He daily rode to work in the Parish Council buildings next to Mr Cran's Chemist Shop, at the east end of the main street. He quickly mastered the job and was soon becoming accepted and respected as a trustworthy man who would give advice in a clear and concise way. At the same time folk were discovering that Jim Mair wasn't a man to be trifled with, nor was he disposed to suffer fools gladly. But they recognised that he was basically a kind and Christian man who could be depended on for help - insofar as the rules allowed.

Jim continued his ties with the Church, but with a slight difference. The Free Church in Longside at that time was at the top of the hill, on the right off Church Lane. To get to the church and its hall meant climbing a steep brae, which Jim found almost impossible. So, although he got along fine with Mr Carmichael its minister, he was forced to admit defeat when it came to attending his services, and it became necessary for Jim to cast around for an alternative church.

Although the Church of Scotland in Longside was also on a hill, it was on a better-made road, and Jim found the building more accessible. So he became a member of that church instead. His conversion was made easier because he foresaw that due to the dwindling number of its members in the area, the Free Kirk would eventually amalgamate with the Church of Scotland.

The minister of the Auld Kirk, Mr Henderson, was also the Chairman of the School Board whose meetings were held in the Parish Council buildings where Jim worked, and where he had agreed to be their Secretary and Treasurer. Jim also became a member of the Parish Council, along with Mr Younie the Headmaster of the Senior School at the top of the brae. Dean McKay of the Episcopalian Church, Mr Henderson of the Auld Kirk and Mr Carmichael of the Free Kirk represented their respective churches in the Parish Council, and Major Hutchison of Cairngall and Dr Wood completed its professional contingent.

The majority of members sitting on the Parish Council were culled from the surrounding farming community, who tended to be shy and reticent in the presence of the other "learned" folk at the meetings, and consequently were disinclined to take an independent stance in local matters. They preferred to leave the decision-making to the professional bodies who attended, but Jim saw that they could be vociferous about matters that they were expert in - and very generous when it came to making land available for social affairs and outings and money-raising functions.

Altogether they formed a very agreeable committee where each gave generously of his time and experience. Jim, in particular, knew he had to be very circumspect when dealing in these matters. In his privileged position as Inspector of Poor he knew a great deal about the financial situations of many folk, and as a member of the Parish Committee he had to advise on the distribution of the finances of the parish, which was required to look after its "indigent poor." He found himself walking a tightrope sometimes, since nobody liked his financial status to be made local knowledge, and "each man had his pride." On the other hand, it was imperative that Jim helped the deserving people get what financial help was available to them. It seemed that he must have been managing this well enough for no complaint was ever made against him.

Jim missed his Betty though, and would take the train from Longside Station down to Aberdeen most weekends. He hated being separated from his fiancee, especially since her precious commitment to him in Stobhill Hospital. And so he redoubled his efforts to find a house where they could set up together. After all, he had vowed to marry Betty in September - and time was getting short!

The Mair Family

Family Portrait:
MIDDLE (seated): Annie (Grandma), George (Grandpa), Elsie Jane
BACK ROW (standing): James, Annie, Isabella, George, Beatrice
FRONT (seated): Robert, William (Billy), Thomas John (Tom).

The Bauds Croft (1905): James, Beatrice, Annie, Grandma, Grandpa, Billy, Tom.

The Cormack Family

TOP: *Mr & Mrs Cormack.*   CENTRE: *Elizabeth.*
BOTTOM LEFT: *Aunt Chat*   BOTTOM RIGHT: *Sandy & Edwin.*
(Bill was away in Africa).

Hospitals

Wimereux Field Hospital.

Jim on the mend at Stobhill Hospital.

Longside (c 1920)

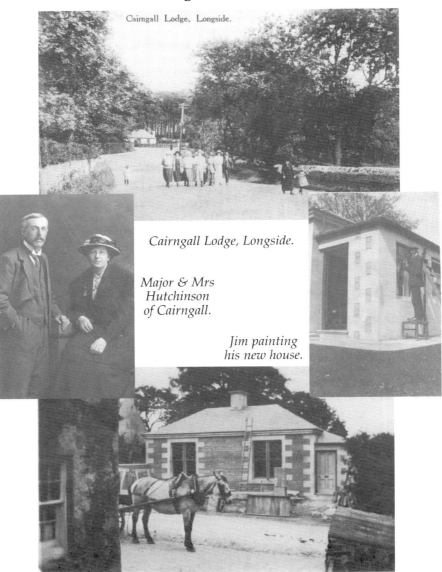

Cairngall Lodge, Longside.

Cairngall Lodge, Longside.

Major & Mrs
Hutchinson
of Cairngall.

Jim painting
his new house.

Donald the Horse.

Chapter 6

Guid Folks Mak' A Guid Village

Jim had fairly taken a liking to Longside. Here was a small thriving leafy village lying six miles inland from the fishing port of Peterhead. A stark bleak road wended its way northwest towards Longside, and on to the smaller settlement of Mintlaw two miles beyond. From there it snaked on to New Pitsligo and eventually to Banff on the Moray Firth. Precious few trees grew successfully against the wild winds blowing hard and cold off the North Sea, and those that survived were gnarled and stunted, destined to remain permanently silhouetted against the expansive sky that covered Buchan's coastal plain.

On descending Thunderton Brae the land was more fertile and the trees around the houses of Faichfield and Monyruy grew taller and straighter. Here the road was lined with hawthorns as it ran past a row of small houses at Flushing where the quarry workers lived. Huge blocks of the finest granite were being hacked out of the nearby quarry and sent to London.

The smithy at Flushing was the workplace of John Kane, an expert farrier who could turn his hand to most jobs that came his way, including mending farm equipment and sharpening tools. Continuing west, the road became flanked with sycamores as far its intersection with two farm roads; the right leading to Cairngall, and the left one to Tiffery. At this time, the newly completed spur railway line to the airship base at Lenabo was being dismantled.

On the left of the main road, before entering Longside, a small plantation of sycamore and beech trees, "Craws' Widdie," was a roosting place for families of raucous messy crows. Beyond was the Infant School and a little farther on, "The Crescent," a dower house built by the current Laird of Cairngall, Major Hutchison, for his mother and sister.

Next door, the Rectory was occupied by Dean McKay, and alongside was the Episcopal Church with its distinctive packsaddle tower, a well known landmark. Built by William Hay in 1853, Saint John's Church was famous for having been ministered by Reverend Skinner, known also as Tullochgorum. The Reverend Skinner had played a significant part in church politics during the Jacobite Rebellion.

A little farther on, on the other side of the road, The Lodge stood beside pillared gates guarding the entrance to Cairngall House. In springtime the grassy borders of the avenue leading up to the mansion were adorned with aconites and wood anemones, and later they would be aglow with pink and purple blossom of the rhododendrons. There was a spacious lawn with a flower border in front of the big house, and a short distance away on the west side, a big walled garden and greenhouse provided lots of fruit and vegetables.

 Past the Lodge, were the mealmill and sawmill. The power for these industries was supplied by The Lade, a small stream diverted from the Ludquharn Burn. It ran round the back of The Crescent, the Rectory and the church and flowed under the main road to the Mill Dam before turning the big wheel of the mealmill and going on to power the sawmill.

Along the main road was a row of buildings belonging to Mr Chivas. The first of these was used as a chemist store and to reach it you had to climb a slatted staircase. Next door were the Parish Offices where Jim worked. His office was in the front right-hand side of the building, and the room on the left was where they discussed Parish business. There was an old cast iron range for heat, and paraffin lamps supplied light. His workplace was kept spotless by Mrs Russell, who also cleaned the "little school" and whose son worked at the local grocer's. Her brother, Willie, mended shoes at the Coop in Aberdeen. Below Jim's offices, in the basement beneath the level of the main road, lived the widowed Mrs Souter and her children Willie and Violet.

Mr Cran, the Druggist, used the building next door and his dispensary protruded on stilts out the back, over Mrs Souter's apartments.

At the end of this row of buildings was Ivybank, a fairly large two-storey granite house where Mr Chivas himself, and his sister, Bella, lived. Mr Chivas was one of the pillars of the Episcopal Church of which he was Secretary and Treasurer rolled into one. His frugal inclination equipped him well for the management of church affairs, because he would never pay a halfpenny for a herring that he could buy two days later for a farthing. Bella was a timid woman who would hop, hop hop down the brae to get going on her bike. She did this for years until the day some Irish navvies shouted encouragement at her, and poor Bella was so mortified by their attention that she became a pedestrian from that day on.

Facing Jim's workplace, across the main road, stood a little red-roofed hoosie with its front path flanked by two huge oak trees, where old Sergeant Darling lived. He was a veteran of the Crimean War who sported a long white beard and, in keeping with his military bearing, kept his back ram-rod straight at all times!

Farther up, on the corner was the Jeweller's shop owned by Mr Spence. He cut folks' hair as a sideline, which he found was a much more convivial occupation than peering myopically at the intimmers of a clock.

Back across the road again, past the water pump outside Ivybank was Annie Taylor's grocery shop. Her front window was filled with big colourful jars of gobstoppers, lucky-tatties, and all kinds of tooth-rotting fine things. Auntie Annie's was a magnet for the local bairns and promised them the best bargains for their pennies on a Saturday morning. Inside the shop she sold more mundane goods like bread, groceries and paraffin.

Round the corner Main Street straightened out and you came to a sizeable granite building. Old Hall had been a private school for girls during the previous century, and daughters of the local lairds were educated there. Nowadays Charlie Bruce lived in the upper part; while Annie Taylor, owner of the afore-mentioned grocery shop, lived with her husband and five children in the rooms on the ground floor.

Between here and the village Bank farther down was a cottage where the Cheynes lived. Peter Cheyne was the local postie and his wife was a teacher at Rora. She was very fond of music, but, as an old village worthy explained, "Oor Maggie disna sing on the fite notes nor the black notes - but on the cracks in between!" She also tapped her toes loudly to the rhythm - two beats behind everyone else- and each hymn in the Auld Kirk ended in a race.

In the Bank that later became Haddo Cottage, lived George Smith, the bank manager. He oversaw the business of The North of Scotland Town and County Bank and must have served the needs of the local farmers and businessmen to their satisfaction, because he was often invited to join their family celebrations.

Across the road lived the Misses Milne, and farther on was the home of Mr and Mrs Simpson, John and Edith, who lived on the ground floor, and upstairs was Mrs Gray, teacher at the Infant School.

Miss Ironside was reputed to be the best dressmaker in the area, and she shared the large premises next to here with Mr Shearer, the souter, and Alfie Thomson, the butcher. Alfie had his own separate shop entrance, and he and his family lived in the apartments above the shop that they accessed by a stairway from Beechie Lane. He had a shed farther up the lane where he slaughtered pigs and boiled up fine mealie puddings. And feathers would fly there on the run up to Christmas, when he employed extra women to pluck the hens.

On the other side of Beechie Lane were Mr Bruce the saddler, then Park's Drapery Store that stocked wool, socks, flannel drawers, and stays, as well as linen tea towels and tablecloths and assorted ribbons and things. Their daughter wasn't keen on being a shop assistant, and so trained as a Music Teacher instead.

Opposite here was a fair-sized grocer's and general merchant's shop, called The Emporium. J and A Watt Brothers ran this busy store that had a small Post Office stuck onto its left side. The brothers, Jamie and Alec, were both profoundly deaf, and Alec ran the shop in conjunction with his sisters, while Jamie ran the Post Office. The brothers were great walkers, and on Sunday afternoons would think nothing of strolling out to Mintlaw, taking the Aberdeen road as far as Yokieshill, and returning home by Inverquhomery and Greenbrae - all done in silence!

Simpson and Son Slater's yard lay farther on and the son had his own band - Simpson's Band that was very popular.

Next door was Jeanie Fraser's Sweetie shop, which also had its own bakery on the premises run by her brother Jamie. They sold groceries as well, that were delivered locally by their brother Sandy who got the nickname "farty Fraser." It must have been a relief for the siblings when he went out on his rounds!

Directly opposite the shop, across the main road, stood The Bruce Arms Hotel with outbuildings that included byres, a garage and a store. The hotelier, "Sinkit Smith," got his name because he prefaced everything he said with the words, "sinkit tae Hell!" He also ran a taxi service and road haulage business. Despite his pessimistic demeanour, Sinkit embraced technology and acquired new-fangled steam carriers for transportation of goods. He was seen as a visionary by some, and a fool by others, and only time would tell.

At the crossroads, Station Road on the right, led over to the Terrace and the railway station half a mile away. It passed through the Haughs, where local people grazed their sheep and cattle, and used to be the flood plain for the River Ugie when it was waterlogged for much of the year. But after the Coble Stank was constructed the drainage was much improved. Jean Watt's auntie, Kirsten Lamb, lived on this road and had the annual task of feeding the workmen when the "steam mull" was in operation. This machine was for "threshing" the corn and was pulled by a traction engine that belched out thick black smoke. It was hard work and gave the men hearty appetites, but if they were inclined to be picky about the food Kirsten would shout, "There's nae a travis in yer stomach!" And heap more on their plates.

Station Road continued across the River Ugie, then climbed up and over the steep railway bridge before descending to the recently built station. Parallel to the railway line and overlooking the village was Station Terrace, a row of substantial granite houses mainly occupied by professional people who took the train to and from their work in Peterhead.

Opposite the crossroads on Main Street, was Inn Brae with the Auld Kirk at the top, and the "big school" for the older children. The Auld Kirk, built in 1835, replaced its predecessor, which had become too small to contain Longside's growing population. The Lych Gate, at the entrance to the original building was still there with hollows chiselled out on either side where coffins could be rested until ready to be carried in.

Back at the crossroads, and continuing west along Main Street, was Willie Maitland, the shipping agent. He arranged passages to Australia and Canada and other far-flung places under the "Assisted Fares Scheme." This programme encouraged farmhands and tradesmen to go to the colonies to boost their working populations, and was seen as a golden opportunity for enterprising hard working men to make a new start after the war. The government saw it as a way of easing the problem of unemployment for the returning soldiers.

Next door was Robbie Robertson, the tailor, where Jim had his first lodgings. His neighbour was Grandpa Willox who sold "everything," and his store was known as "Willox's a' thing shop." Sandy Willox had been a giant of a man before the war, but had returned with both legs amputated below the knee and now had to wear special boots. Some folk said he looked like a genial teddybear as he rode round Longside on his small float, using two long poles to reach over and get at the groceries in the middle of the wagon.

On the far left corner of the crossroads, was Rankin the Joiner's workyard, and after some thatched cottages, Church Lane led up to the Free Church.

Doctor Wood lived across the main road in Northfield and was considered fortunate to have the services of Georgina Chalmers, his maid, who put up with his various idiosyncrasies. Like many others in the village he kept a puckle hennies out the back and distinguished himself by keeping a pig there too. And not to be upside down with Johnny Beattie, the vet, Doctor Wood had a chauffeur too, John Mair from Church Lane.

The 18th Century house next door was made of granite and had a round turret on the front of it, with doorways on either side. Young Mrs Simpson had recently been widowed by the war and was left to bring up their baby daughter on her own. Mr Davidson, "Dites," owned and ran a small butcher's shop that was tacked on to its left side.

Opposite Dites' butcher shop was the Smiddy, an untidy but very busy place run by Johnny Brown. And behind it lived Miss Forest, whose brother farmed at Mains of Ludquharn and was called "tittin' Tammie" because he was continually "tit, tit, tittin'" at his horse as he rode about in his gig pulling at the reins.

Next to the smiddy was Willie Whyte's Garage, behind which was a wooden hall used by the local volunteers in the Territorial Army, and farther along Main Street was Whyte's Hygenic Bakery, a large concern employing over twenty staff and four vansmen. On the hill between here and the old manse was Markethill where travelling fayres were held with hoopla stalls and chowdy boats.

Across the road from Whyte's Hygenic Bakery, was Rose Cottage where Johnny Beattie, the vet, lived who was reputed to be even better at mending folk than he was at sorting out the beasts. However, Johnny had an over fondness for the bottle, ("the drunker the better" folk said,) so as a precaution he hired Sandy Ross from the Toll House two doors up, to do the driving for him. It was generally agreed that "vetinary" must have been a richt scunner to his wife, a refined gentlewoman.

There were three ministers in the village: Mr Carmichael of the Free Kirk, Mr Richard (Dickie) Henderson of the Auld Kirk, and Dean McKay of the Episcopal Church. They saw to the spiritual needs of their flocks, and allowed their church halls to be used for various social activities, including annual productions by the Longside Amateur Dramatic Society.

Major Hutchison lived in Cairngall House, a stone-built mansion situated "a stone's throw" from the granite quarry, but it was reckoned to be very pretty all the same. When the Major bought the estate he said that the grounds were, "little better than waste moorland." He had already spent a lot of money on the house and grounds, and now most of it was in some kind of order, and the gardens were once again productive.

West of the village lay the Inverquhomery Estate, or "Innerfummery" as the locals called it, owned for generations by the Bruce family. The villagers paid a feu to the Bruce family and had to obtain their permission before commencing any building work. The late Doctor Bruce had been a famous surgeon based at Edinburgh University and had won worldwide recognition in the field of medicine. He had died in 1911 but the locals still remembered him fondly for he had been without airs and graces and had been a genial and generous laird. His elder son, Vincent Connell, had succeeded him, but when the Great War had broken out the young man had eagerly joined up and gained a commission in the 13th Royal Scots Guards. Soon afterwards he was granted a transfer to the 5th Battalion Gordon Highlanders, the regiment of Longside and the County. Sadly, he was killed in 1916 while serving in France, and his distraught mother, Annie Louise Connell, was still trying to come to terms with her second bereavement. In the meantime she was running the estate as best she could until her younger son, Walter, could return from Madagascar and take up his duties as Laird.

Not far from Bridgend Farm was the haunted house of Boodie Brae. It was said that in1824 James Wyllie, the occupier, "was sadly and sorely tormented by apparitions that rose out of the floor and stalked across the room during the night; by mischievous spirits that snatched the very staff from his hand, and tried to smother him in bed; and by sudden weird, unearthly sounds, by night and day, here there and everywhere in his house, which at last, so unnerved him that he had to leave his house in despair." The story went on to say that various doctors and ministers had tried to put an end to the hauntings - but to no avail.

Yokieshill Farm on the north bank of the River Ugie belonged to Miss Buchan of Auchmacoy Farm, and Mr William Stephen currently tenanted it. Long ago this farm acquired notoriety amongst farm servants on account of the high standards "adhered to therein." To have served a term there was considered the highest recommendation a servant could have - "so great was the quantity of work to be done there, and so rigorously was it demanded." The farm was immortalised in a bothy ballad:

> "I took a term at Yokieshill
> The teuchest placee I e're gaed till."

Few of Longside's inhabitants had any reason to leave the village, and a train journey into Aberdeen was a big adventure. Their ponies and traps served them well enough locally, and cars were a rarity. The ministers, doctor, and vet each owned a motor vehicle, as did some of the bigger farmers, but nobody else.

Jim was once told that "the residents (of Longside) believe that the world is divided into two parts - Longside....and the rest!" And they speak of London (where the farmers sold their stock, and the quarry sent its granite) as "a nice little place....but somewhat remote!" Jim was told that the people of Longside weren't for the most part rich - but they were extremely hard working and sociable, and their interest and concern for one another formed a community spirit he felt privileged to be part of.

They were a self-sufficient community and this was brought home to Jim in many ways - never more so than when he chanced to speak to Dod Noble one day. Dod was a young lad working with McKenzie the joiner in his workshop at Glenugie at the time. When a death occurred in the village Dod was told to be ready for eight o'clock the following morning and go along with his boss to Ardlaw, (sometimes called Artlaw,) a wooded area to the north of Longside. They would fell a suitable tree and haul it back to Glenugie, where they sawed it up and made it into a coffin to be delivered to the household concerned by nightfall. It was a rough box no doubt, without varnish or fancy bits, but it did the job at reasonable cost - and without the need for the undertaker in Peterhead.

Again, a lot of what Jim felt about Longside was summed up for him by the local poet, John Imray, who sometimes wrote in his native tongue, and sometimes in the King's English - depending on the importance of what he had to say. In this poem Imray celebrated his love for Longside, and gave his memories full sway as he fondly reminisced about the village that hadn't changed much since his youth.

Longside

On Buchan's lowly, fertile plains
   There lies a village bonnie,
Embower'd amang its shady trees,
   Mair dear to me than ony.

O! sweet Longside, a gem thou'rt set
   By Ugie's wimplin' burnie,
Whaur fragrant blooms the meadow queen
   Roon ilka crook an' turnie.

Thy meadows green, wi' dew-drap clear,
   Upon ilk leaflet clingin',
I've wanner't o'er in early morn-
   Aboon the lav'rock singin'.

An' aft, frae Ardlaw's woody hill,
   I've watched in summer's mornin'
The gowden sun rise frae the east,
   Dame Nature's face adornin'.

Upon thy slopin' westrin hill,
   In autumn's dusky gloamin'
The startled hare bounds nimbly by,
   Across thy pastures roamin'.

Frae aff thy fields, the frugal swain
   Tak's hame earth's gowden treasures;
While stalwart youths, an' maidens fair,
   Enjoy life's healthy pleasures.

Near thee, the burnie o' Cairnga'
   Glides by wi' ripplin' motion,
An' joins the Ugie, in its coorse,
   To mingle wi' the ocean.

Thy venerable auld "lych gate,"
   Whaur aft we play'd at "doorie,"
Brings back to mem'ry boyhood's days,
   Like some romantic story.

Aft times, o'er to the Chapel Well
   Our schoolboy's footsteps wandered,
An' rompin' roon its shimmerin' brink
   Youth's happy hoors we squandered.

Methinks I hear the shuttles click
   O' han' leem wrocht by "Tollie,"
While in the haughs wi' mem'ry's e'e
   I see the "dookin' holie."

Thy Pairish Squeel stood on the brae,
   An antiquated biggin',

Wi'ts maister's seat an' dooble desk,
　An laigh pavilion'd riggin'.

Yet tho' a new ane fills its place,
　I min' wi' veneration
Upon the hoary hoosie whaur
　I got my education.

Aroon thine ancient sacred pile
　The tombstanes rise fu' clearly;
Remindin' us o' vanish'd forms
　O' those we cherish dearly.

Auld Tullochgorum's dust lies there,
　In kirkyard kept sae neatly,
Altho' his spirit's taen its flicht,
　He still to us sings sweetly.

An' mony mair, baith great an' sma',
　Aneath the sod lie sleepin',
They ance waur wi's, but noo hae gane
　To Heav'n's eternal keepin.

Jim knew that he, like many others who had settled here up to forty years ago, would always be seen as an "incomer," but he didn't mind. He was accepted and tolerated by these kindly folk and that was sufficient for him. He felt he could put down roots here.

And soon afterwards his tenacity was rewarded thanks to the generosity of old Joseph Penny from Auchlee Farm. Mr Penny was a kindly man with long white hair and a long white beard. He had recently retired and left the running of his farm to his family, while he went to live in Ardlaw, one of the big houses on the Terrace. Apprised of Jim's circumstances by the local grapevine, he decided to take pity on the young couple and offered them two rooms: one at the front and one at the back, on the right hand side of his house.

This meant that Jim and Betty could be together at last - which was just as well - because their wedding was set for September!

Chapter 7

Ne're Speak Ill O' Them Whose Bread Ye Eat

By July 1918 the allies had signalled their counter-attack and were currently using new small "whippet" tanks that could climb across trenches and break up enemy machine-gun nests. The tide had turned, and the Germans were being forced into full retreat on a front of over a hundred and forty miles.

It seemed that the war was nearly over at last, and our victorious troops would soon come home. In this atmosphere of general euphoria the young couple were married at the Imperial Hotel in Aberdeen on the fourteenth of September. Mr Crystal the minister at Bucksburn conducted the service and his daughter played the organ for the ceremony.

For the first time ever - and it was to be his last - Jim wore an artificial arm. While he was happy to tie it on for his wedding, his skin was so chafed by the umpteen straps keeping it in position, that he vowed he would never wear it again. He looked very handsome in his "civvies" and had quite recovered his old confidence. There was no facial trace of his past suffering as he smiled into Betty's eyes and took her for his wife.

Betty herself was most charming, and very lovely in a fashionable mid-blue dress with beautiful silvery beads round the neck and down the front. To complement her ensemble she wore a large matching blue chiffon hat in the current Georgian style, and the whole effect was very chic.

It was a day for celebrations on all fronts, and although it was a modest reception, it was hugely successful. Two of Jim's sisters - Annie and Elsie Jane, represented their mother who was "too unwell" to attend, and amidst all the laughter and gaiety, Annie alone shed tears - and she cried inconsolably throughout the whole proceedings.

"I wish Annie would stop her blubbering," Betty hissed to her new husband as they prepared to cut the wedding cake. "It's not as if I'm going to do you any real harm!" And the bride and groom enjoyed a conspiratorial smile.

It was just as well for them that they shared a strong sense of humour, for it was going to be sorely tested in many ways during their honeymoon up at Findochty.

*   *   *

Old Mrs Mair had been saddened by the misfortunes that had befallen her son, but she was also grateful that the good Lord had seen fit to spare him. She still remembered the anguish of the black-edged telegram that had acquainted her in dry terms of the death of her son Robert, "killed in action." At least James was still alive. When she'd got over the shock of his infirmities she'd thanked the Lord for having shown mercy on her son. Then with the passage of time she had assumed that James would come home and live with her and Annie. Between William's contributions and James' pension, which would be the full amount because of the extent of his injuries, she had thought that life would continue much as before on the croft - except that James wouldn't be going out to work. As to the "townser" he had got engaged to, she never gave her a second thought. She assumed that the girl would soon be out of the picture once she realised that James could never keep her in the luxury expected from his business profits.

So she was shocked again when she heard that this woman was determined to stand by her son. And not only that - but they had plans to set up house together and live on Jim's new wage plus his pension - like an ordinary couple! Mrs Mair had serious doubts about her son's marriage. She didn't know any "town quines" personally, but had heard about them - and what she had heard didn't bode well for James! She could have told him a thing or two about them, if she had been asked - but her advice had never been sought.

According to Annie, her mother only once admitted to her approval of James' final choice of occupation, and thought that being an Inspector of Poor was quite in keeping with his religious upbringing. But at the time, she was very reluctant to praise her son for anything, because this marriage to a "townser" fairly stuck in her craw and she wished that he'd sought her advice first. She would snort that there was nothing she could do about it now anyway. And she couldn't help feeling peeved about his not having asked her advice - before he had proposed to his wife. Well, she would think indignantly - and say as much to Annie - she would soon find out for herself the kind of stuff her new daughter-in-law was made of!

The graceful woman on her sofa took her by surprise. Betty's sense of humour and her obvious poise were making the old woman feel uneasy. Mrs Mair had begun to feel that she was on trial here and not her daughter-in-law, and that was getting her dander up. She "called the shots " in this household and Betty would have to learn that! She looked shrewdly at her new daughter-in-law sitting there so self-assured in her modern fashionable wedding attire and was almost bowled over by her presence. Almost - but not quite, because her resentment towards the girl quickly reasserted itself and her comfortable cynicism returned. At least the woman wore sensible footwear, she admitted grudgingly as her eyes came to rest on Betty's shoes. At that point she realised that Betty was looking at her and she checked herself.

"Now drink up," she demanded sharply. "There's always plenty tea in this house, and always a pot on the stove!"

That explains the dreadful taste, thought Betty ruefully, while she tried to disguise her disgust with a grateful smile. The tea was simply awful. It was thick and nearly coal-black, and try as she might Betty couldn't bring herself to sip one more mouthful of the strong tar-like liquid that clung to her cup and left dark brown stains around its insides. And what was worse from Betty's point of view, was that she was fast running out of ideas as to how to avoid drinking any more of the vile stuff without causing offence.

Mrs Mair sat ramrod straight against the back of her chair with a glint of triumph as she surveyed her new daughter-in-law with sharp defensive eyes. Betty's reluctance to drink her tea was not going unnoticed. Here was tangible evidence that her son's "townser" wife with her fancy hair-do and modern clothes was too "refined" to drink ordinary tea. Theirs obviously wasn't good enough.

Betty was immediately sensitive to this latest reproach from Mrs Mair and grew even more ill at ease. She had known within minutes of meeting her mother-in-law that they would always "wear their Sunday hats" with each other. When Jim had proudly announced his bride to his mother, Mrs Mair had touched Betty's outstretched hand with her fingertips and said "How do you do?" while staring vacantly at the wall somewhere behind Betty's right ear. Betty's heart had sunk to the depths of her "sensible" shoes, and she had mentally acknowledged that she would never have a friend in Mrs Mair. But she would give it a fair try for her husband's sake! She also knew that she had chattered on far too much out of nervousness, and she wished fervently that Annie wasn't so gormless as to just sit there and let her babble on. Annie could have joined in the conversation many a time, but instead she just sat there like a child who had been told not to open its mouth. It was all very frustrating for Betty. Jim at least could have tried to join in the conversation! They all didn't have to make it so obvious that she was being "summed up" and found wanting.

Her dislike of the tea was being blown out of all proportion and Betty had little patience with this kind of situation that was fast developing into some kind of stand-off. She usually liked tea and wasn't all that fussy about how it came, but in all honesty, between the taste of this black tar and her growing nervousness, she knew that she couldn't put another mouthful of the stuff down her throat without being sick. She grew even more edgy as the silence continued - and even more determined not to take another sip. The time had come too, to stop babbling. In desperation she turned to Jim to help her out - and got a shock.

It had registered dully in the back of her mind that she hadn't heard him speak for the last five minutes anyway, since they had sat down to tea in fact. Now that she looked at him more closely she saw how pale and drawn he looked. His white face was haggard and his jaw was set. His lips were pursed into a thin line of ....what? She examined him keenly, and realised with a jolt that it was distress and anger that held him so rigidly beside her! Had she done or said anything wrong? she wondered with dismay. Surely nothing so bad as to produce such anguish! She looked straight into his eyes with concern - the pain wasn't merely physical, that she could tell. He wouldn't respond to her questioning look and instead fixed his eyes on the rug in front of the fireplace.

Betty noticed only then that Mrs Mair kept glancing uneasily at her son, and that Annie's hand was shaking as she lifted her cup to her mouth. Something was very definitely wrong here - and she had no idea as to what it could be. The protracted silence continued to unnerve her.

"What a lovely room this is," she ventured to say eventually, in the desperate hope of starting up some kind of conversation and getting back to normality, even if it was only a veneer.

Indeed it was a nice room. As was usual in the parlour of a Victorian-styled house, the mantelpiece was covered with a rich wine-coloured velvet cloth edged with braid and tassels which hung down about six to eight inches. In the middle of the mantle shelf was a marble clock with a vase on each side of it, and a selection of knicknacks around it. A brass coal box and fire irons lay within the well-polished brass fender and a "clicked" rug lay in front of the fire on top of the shining linoleum that covered the floor. The backs of the red plush armchairs were covered with lace antimacassars and the mahogany armless chairs shone with polish. Sepia photographs of severe grandparents stared unblinkingly from heavy ornate frames on either end of the sideboard.

Betty's comment fell on deaf ears however.

She looked around the room desperately hoping to find something that would force a conversation, and put an end to the awful silence. Her eyes fell upon the red geraniums on the windowsill and on the low table nearby that gave a splash of colour against their background of plain dark brown curtains.

"Someone here's got green fingers," she ventured. "Your geraniums are really beautiful."

This observation, too, did nothing to break the oppressive silence until Mrs Mair remarked absently that that was "Annie's doing." And at this point something seemed to break in Annie, because she stood up and in a strained voice announced that she was going to get more scones. Then she fled to the kitchen.

This left the three of them now in the continuing silence while the clatter of crockery could be heard as Annie noisily saw to her scones. Mrs Mair's face was as white as Jim's by now and her mouth worked silently as she stared ahead at the wall opposite her.

Betty's earlier dismay was beginning to turn to anger. What could possibly be the cause of so much tension? She couldn't have made that bad an impression, for goodness sake! And if she had, then surely she had the right to know what she'd done wrong. Jim had been brought up to put great store by good manners, and here he was along with his mother, making Betty more uncomfortable than she'd ever felt before in her life. Just what was going on here?

Finally, it was Jim who broke the silence but it didn't make things any easier. Instead it made the atmosphere worse and Betty hadn't a clue as to what was coming.

"Where is it?" Jim asked tersely. "What have you done with it?"

Mrs Mair's mouth continued to move soundlessly as she tried to frame her answer, and she took her time before replying. Annie could be heard still clattering clumsily in the kitchen. Meanwhile, Jim's frown deepened and his jaw tightened.

Betty's nerves were so frayed by now that she was in imminent danger of saying or doing something entirely inappropriate - like giggling. Sometimes while at school, if the teacher was furiously reprimanding the whole class, Betty would get into such a state that she would grin or laugh - not because she felt like it - but because her nervous system couldn't cope with the tension. It had been a long time since she had been at the mercy of her nerves, but she was now.

She looked around the room. Where was what?

Mrs Mair shook her head and took up a defiant pose. "George has got it," she stated firmly and quietly. "He didn't think you'd....need it again," she added lamely, for the first time faltering with her words.

In the ensuing silence realisation burst in on Betty. They were talking about Jim's piano! His beloved piano that he'd told her about with modest pride. It wasn't here! It was gone. It must have been like a physical blow to him who had missed it as soon as he'd entered the room. And now he also knew that his mother had sanctioned its disappearance. His brother George had taken it with his mother's blessing and without Jim's permission - as if - because of his infirmities, he didn't have a say in things any more. They hadn't even bothered to consult him!

"And my violin?" he whispered almost menacingly.

His mother nodded. "He took that too," she asserted, her voice growing stronger. "And your tools." She hurried on in a voice that was fully under control now. "Be sensible, James. You'll never use them again anyway."

To Betty's ears the old woman's voice sounded strident and callous. Her heart flooded with sympathy for this, Jim's fresh pain. He was stung and hurt by his mother's blunt brutality. Slowly and painfully he stood up and with great dignity he walked out of the room.

"Oh me," sighed his mother when he'd gone. But she sounded more annoyed than upset to Betty's prejudiced ears. "You'll have to excuse me, Elizabeth," she referred to Betty. "I'll have to see to him." Then she too left the room shaking her head from side to side, though whether that was in sorrow or exasperation Betty couldn't tell.

Bewildered, relieved of the tension, and full of anguish as she was, Betty had the presence of mind to seize the opportunity to get rid of her tea. Quickly she divided it among the pots of geraniums on the windowsill, and had just got sat down again when Annie came fluttering in wailing "Oh dear, oh dear, oh…"

"Your geraniums are very lovely you know," Betty interrupted, trying hard to regain some semblance of normality.

But Annie carried on as if she hadn't heard. "I knew there'd be trouble. I told mother she should have asked James. It's not as if his head was affected you know. Of course you know. But mother would have none of it. I don't think she ever liked that piano. She always complained about it being a dust trap and always went on about it being in her way. I think she just used this as an excuse to get more space in here. But you never know with mother. She might have been trying to protect James by getting rid of it before he came back. But then George always was her favourite and he was always jealous of Jim's piano. And for George to take all Jim's tools too! I don't know what mother was thinking of, I just don't know. And what George will do with Jim's piano? Well I don't know. I just don't know." She was clearly upset and in a dither. "Oh, the geraniums," she harked back to Betty's compliment suddenly.

"Thank you," she said, at once lucid and polite, all trace of her former ramblings gone, causing Betty to blink in amazement yet again. "Thank you, yes, they are lovely. Do you know?" she suddenly fixed her eyes on Betty's. "I treat all the geraniums in the house in exactly the same way. I feed them all every morning, and once a week I give them a little tea from the pot. I treat them all the same, and yet year after year it's only the ones in this room that flourish. Can you think why that is?" She looked earnestly towards Betty with clear unblinking eyes.

"I've been rumbled," thought Betty guiltily, wondering if she should admit to tipping the dregs of her tea in them. She felt emotionally drained but was trying to summon up a wan smile, when a movement in the garden caught her eye. She turned and watched unashamedly through the window at Jim and his mother clearly having an argument, and felt a growing alarm.

From the old woman's aggressive pose it was obvious that she thought she had the upper hand, and was berating her son angrily. She was talking rapidly and gesticulating in a forthright manner that reminded Betty of Sandy when he was on his high horse. Jim stood there; a picture of controlled belligerence and neither interrupted nor contradicted his mother. He stood there steadfast and mute, barely managing to conceal his anger.

Without thinking of the implications Betty moved to be by his side; and when she appeared at the front porch, Mrs Mair threw up her hands in what appeared to be annoyance and stomped off to the water pump. There she energetically pulled and pushed the handle up and down and rapidly filled the waiting bucket with water. Then without another word she completely ignored the couple and carried it into the house.

Betty waited silently until Jim composed himself and then they began to walk round the garden. They were oblivious of the surrounding beauty of the balmy afternoon in this late Indian summer, and strolled wordlessly together, each trying to come to terms with what had just happened. And, eventually, soothed by the soporific murmurings of Nature, and his wife's sympathetic presence, Jim began to cool down enough to talk about it.

"The spoils of war! The spoils of war, Betty," he echoed bitterly. "By my own brother!"

The explanation of the situation was cruel and tragic. Motivated by jealousy and fuelled by his own greed, both sanctioned by his mother, George had helped himself to Jim's piano and violin. But what hurt Jim the most was George's taking all his tools - and seemingly with his mother's blessing.

His mother had also callously informed Jim that she had always secretly resented having the big clumsy piece of furniture in her front room. It had been of no use to anyone except Jim - and she had bluntly pointed out that even he could have no use for it now - with only one arm. She had never appreciated its so-called "resonant tone" and frankly had been glad to see the back of it. What did it matter that George couldn't play the piano? That was his problem! As to George helping himself to Jim's working tools she made no mention.

Annie had suggested that perhaps Mrs Mair had been being cruel to be kind and Betty tried hard to give the old woman the benefit of the doubt. But somehow it didn't ring true, and she couldn't persuade herself even, of the validity of this explanation.

Annie's insipid attempt at a protest had been perfunctorily ignored as was usual in the household.

"George took my tools, Betty - my tools! The spoils of war taken by my own brother as if I was dead," Jim continued sadly, his anger abating. "I'll never see them again - and don't you go asking George for them either," he warned his wife. He shook his head wearily.

Then as she watched, Jim's body stiffened, and he pulled himself up to his full height. He took a deep breath, raised his fist to the sky and intoned with powerful yet contained anger: "I will never forgive you for this, George Mair!"

*   *   *

It wasn't the best of starts for their honeymoon, but they made what they could of it and it didn't turn out so badly. Since the death of old Mr Mair there was no business being run now from the Bauds, and the only people living there were old Mrs Mair and Annie, Tom being away at the war meantime. Isobel was widowed and living in Cullen and E.J. was in Portknockie. Beatrice was married and living with John Jack in Banff, Lizzie was away, and Bill was overseas. George, of course, was married and living in Portknockie.

Designed and built by his great grandfather, the Bauds had been the family home to three generations of Mairs, and Jim showed Betty around the policies with pride. The main building looked southwards towards the Hill of Bin, standing a thousand feet above the surrounding, mainly flat countryside. The croft had a half- house attached to it on its west side occupied by Mrs Lorimer and her daughter. On its east side the stable, byre and hen house were all joined under one red-tiled roof.

Between the house and the road was a walled garden and a stonebuilt wash-house with a fireplace. All the water used in the houses had to be carried from the outside water pump. The door of the wash-house was in line with one of the high dykes that enclosed this garden, abundant with Annie's favourite flowers: standing roses growing tall and strong; rambling roses cascading down walls; Canterbury bells showering their beautiful flower heads, and Sweet Williams spreading their lovely perfumes. This was also the perfect sheltered spot for growing more practical fruits such as blackcurrants, redcurrants and gooseberries. Fine-tasting "mealy" tatties thrived there too, as did cabbage, carrots, neeps and parsley.

In the lea of the east garden wall stood a charabanc owned by Jim's brother, Tom. And, another of Jim's brothers, Bill, used a big black shed in the grounds to garage a car that he drove around in when on leave from the Merchant Navy.

To the right of the main house stood a tall building with a wooden staircase leading to its upper floor where hay used to be stored. Grandfather Mair had depended on his Clydesdale horses for moving huge granite boulders around, and transferring heavy building equipment at his work. There were no working animals left now, because after the death of Jim's father, the business had run down.

Milk was bought from the nearby farm occupied by the Sutherlands and taken to the house in a pail. Jim told Betty that when he was young they had had a cow called Betsy, and swore that no milk had ever tasted as fine as hers. He had then gone noticeably quiet, as if something had sparked off a memory, and his thoughts had turned inwards. The furrow on his brow signified that those thoughts were not happy ones, and she felt a frisson of fear as it came to her that this memory was about his war experience. But even as she went cold, she knew that Doctor Simpson's advice should prevail and she wouldn't ask him about it. So she held her tongue, and consoled herself that these episodes were happening less often now.

Meanwhile, they continued their walk around the Bauds and Jim roused himself to tell her that the Sutherlands who sold them milk had a daughter called Peggy who was a friend of his niece, Marguerrita, and that Betty would probably meet them both while she was there.

A second road approached the house past the water pump. This meant that the visiting grocer's and fish vans could turn right, drive in and pass the front door with its wooden porch; and drive out by the second opening. However, this exit road was little more than a rough track with two deep wheel ruts and a band of greenery in the middle that threatened ruin to their undercarriages. And it was the job of the youngest members of the family to gather little stones from the moor and fill up the potholes, never a favourite chore!

Getting round the croft wasn't too difficult for Jim because thick grass was gradually covering the stony ground surrounding it. And the land was even softer on the twisted grassy paths through the moors, sweetly scented with broom and gorse that reached the main road to Findochty and stretched for miles towards the sea. There were outcrops of rock with grassy patches where little vidas, ragged robins, and special "sundews" flowered, that he'd never seen growing anywhere else. Other wild plants grew in favoured spots, and village children ran barefooted and free across the moor that offered both excitement and solitude.

During the summer, village lads would sometimes camp on the moor at weekends, and as was their wont, would re-enact the Battle of the Vikings, and the Scots ALWAYS won of course!

Due west from the Bauds was a kind of roadway only suitable for a horse and cart that stretched to Rathven three miles away where each of the Mair children had gone to school.

Jim's return home with his new bride triggered many bittersweet memories from his childhood right up to his most recent past, when his energy had known no bounds and his curiosity of the world had still been as fresh as a child's. He had loved to play golf, and had often gone out onto the course with an old school friend. With a gentle rueful smile he reminded his new bride that it was whilst he'd been playing golf at Cullen that he had had that fateful meeting with her brother! While on that golf course Jim had discussed with Sandy his intention of closing his building business temporarily and joining up against the Kaiser. That was when Sandy had issued his "fateful" invitation to have tea with his family, while Jim was training at Aberdeen Barracks. Jim shook his head in mock sorrow at this memory, but his broad smile belied his words while Betty's face had remained radiant with happiness throughout Jim's metaphorical walk down memory lane. Of course, she had always "known" that Fate arranged that meeting on the golf course, because it had led ultimately to their marriage and this new wonderful happiness!

Betty wasn't completely blinded by her love though, and admitted that she was appalled by the dry lavatory arrangements of country living, and was especially irked by the ignominy of having to run past the hens and cock to get there. The skittery little beasts didn't seem to bother anyone else, but the cockerel in particular would scurry over to peck at her heels every time she appeared. Once she had negotiated her way past this versatile and sneaky little hurdle, that could be deceptively fleet of foot, she would sit there and read the torn-up strips of newspaper to take her mind off her circumstances. Then she would have to summon up her resources and run the gauntlet with the cock again as she made her dash to the water pump to wash her hands afterwards. In the evenings Jim had to make use of his chamber pot which was, as was their way in those days, a pail with a lid on the top, that was placed on the shelf under the wash stand in their bedroom. Any "result" was covered with the lid and taken downstairs and thrown onto the midden next day.

During all this time Betty waged her private war with the household tea, and designed all kinds of ruses to avoid drinking it as strong and black as the family preferred. As often as was in her power, Betty managed to dilute it with boiling water without causing offence. At other times Annie's geraniums benefited from her stratagems. Whenever she was called upon to wash the residue from their cups, she would shudder at what stains had also been left in her new family's innards.

Betty's relationship with her mother-in-law never improved during their stay. Mrs Mair had made her mind up about her daughter-in-law long before she met her and there was never anything that Betty could have said or done to "win her over" as she had initially hoped. The young bride felt a brief sadness for what might have been, then resigned herself to the fact that she would never be accepted by the old woman - but she wasn't going to let it worry her. At the same time she was quickly developing a soft spot for Annie - even if she could be a bit gumptionless at times. After all, reasoned Betty, Annie had been bossed around by her mother all her life, so what chance had she had to assert herself? Annie was naturally shy and kind, innocent - and unfortunately - awkward. All the children adored her!

The two bore their honeymoon with as much grace as they could, but there was no denying their relief upon returning to Bucksburn, prior to their setting up house in Longside.

Chapter 8

A Man's A Man For A' That

Jim and Betty knew they were going to have to work hard to make a success of their marriage. He was a disabled young man stuck in a sedentary job unsuited to his nature, having to deal with people all the time instead of being creative with bricks and mortar. He was still trying to come to terms with wearing an artificial leg, and getting used to not having a left arm. Ordinary everyday tasks - like getting dressed, presented difficulties that he had to surmount. He had to learn how to tie a boot lace with one hand, put on his tie, fasten buttons and pull on his socks - all these things had to be learned the hard way. Gradually he was mastering most of these manoeuvres - but he couldn't ever work out how to put in his cufflink and always had to turn to Betty for help.

His new wife was not a robust woman. She hailed from Aberdeen and knew practically nothing about village life. She was going to have to show her mettle and learn how to cook on an old open fire, use paraffin lamps, and carry water in a pail, as well as cope with a newly disabled husband.

Many people were sceptical about the success of this marriage and predicted that it wouldn't last. They included Sandy, who aired his views openly and said it was doomed to failure. And it was generally known that in doing so, he was voicing the fears of a great many people who loved the young couple. The pessimists among them said that they were relying an awful lot on their love for each other. The optimists argued, and sent up many prayers on their behalf.

Then, as if all these changes were not enough for the young pair to cope with, the government delivered a horrible blow that affected the foundation of all their plans. They received an official letter advising Jim that since he was now in full-time employment, he would "hereafter receive only one half of his agreed Pension." This meant that when everything else was added up, he would only receive £2 per week instead of £5, and that was a sizeable reduction.

Not unnaturally, Jim was outraged at this and immediately set about contesting the decision. He gathered as much evidence as he could to justify his right to the full amount. He even included a newspaper cutting that quoted the government's promise not to interfere with any Pension arrangement that had been "previously-agreed" Jim was so affronted by the government's betrayal that he also hired a solicitor from Aberdeen, Mr Reid, to help him fight his case, and prepare it for debate in the House of Commons.

Jim did everything in his power to preserve his full pension, then finally, having sent away his last piece of correspondence to Parliament, he settled himself to await the final verdict with as calm a mind as possible. He had done all that was humanly possible, and from there on was determined not to let the matter spoil their first happy months of marriage together in their new home.

As far as his work was concerned, Jim was faring a lot better. The workload seemed much lighter now that he had Betty at home with him in Longside. Each day brought new and interesting challenges for him that he relished solving. If some of the able-bodied men with whom he dealt saw nothing amiss about their holding out their palms to be filled by a man missing an arm and a leg, the irony of the situation was not lost on Jim, who could be forgiven the odd wry smile. But whatever his feelings, Jim was always scrupulously fair in his dealings with his clients, and wherever possible applied a Christian interpretation to the Poor Laws.

Meanwhile Betty set to feathering their nest. A stickler for cleanliness, she kept their house neat and shining. The furniture belonged to Mr Penny, and was old and grand. Under Betty's clever hands, it was soon decorated with appropriate antimacassars and runners and tray cloths and lace doilies and such, that gave the place a more homely touch. Having been brought up to "improve the shining hour," she was always on the go. If she wasn't cleaning and polishing, there was always baking and cooking, sewing and mending to be done.

Since the village was a half a mile away, various vans brought their different goods up to the Terrace. The men who drove these vans were always very knowledgeable about the latest gossip and they loved to share it with their customers. While Betty was disinclined to gossip herself, she reasoned that it didn't do her any harm to listen. And anyway, these men were such master storytellers; she loved to hear their tales.

"Donald the Horse" for example was the collective name for a white cob owned and driven by Jimmy Milne from Laburnum Lane. When he met Betty, his first words to her were: "I doot, Mistress Mair, that you'll have heard that the new boiler in the church hall blew up yesterday?" He nodded his head slowly up and down while he stroked his horse's mane.

This could have been a rhetorical question affirming that she must have heard about it. Or it could have been a bona fide question that he expected her to answer positively. Betty would never know, because without waiting for a reply, Jimmy abruptly changed from nodding his head to shaking it slowly from side to side, and it gave her the impression the whole calamity had been pre-determined.

"But dinna you worry, Mistress Mair, (he'd already found out all there was to know about the new couple) because the only casualty was Peter Cheyne. He was officiating at something or other and got his mouser singed. Richt annoyed he is ana." He continued without pausing, still shaking his head lugubriously, "For Peter was richt proud o' his mouser. But apart from that, there's nae harm done. Now we," he said nodding at his horse, "usually deliver parcels from the station. We have our ain homegrown carrots for sale as well, and we can usually pick up other things for our customers depending on what requires to be done. And if there's any need for transportation of any kind - we're your men. Just you let us know when you want us. We're usually somewhere about the station."

As Betty was about to thank him for his kind offer he introduced another topic. "You'll be coming to see the Longside Amateur Society tomorrow night in the church hall?" he asked expectantly. As Betty nodded in the affirmative, he added darkly, "I doot you'll have heard aboot the last time?"

And again without waiting for a response, he resumed shaking his head lugubriously, while Betty tried to hide her obvious delight at having met such a wonderful character.

"Well," he said sombrely, although Betty thought she caught a glimpse of a twinkle in his eye as he settled himself more comfortably on the end of his cart the better to tell his tale. "They decided to put on a production of 'Mains' Wooin' by Gavin Greig from New Deer. The twa main characters were excellent, jist excellent. Jake Spence was 'Mains' and Mrs Constance Forman was his ladyfriend, 'Mrs Anderson.' Oh what good they were in their pairts! They were a' good, afa good." He paused, reminiscing and continuing to shake his head. "Well then, the Mains' man was called 'Peter' and he was played by young Sandy. He was supposed to open the door and say, 'Welcome ane and a' to Mains o' Bungry.' But come the performance, Sandy got afa nervous and when the traditional pint was passed roon backstage before the start of the show, Sandy took mair than was good for him. Before long he'd a fair skite in him and when the play started, he kicked open the door and shouted, 'Come in ye shoo'er o' buggers!'"

Mr Milne continued to shake his head in affected sorrow that would have done the Longside Amateur Society proud, and Betty was holding her sides with mirth. He went on to describe how the audience went hysterical with enjoyment.

*   *   *

"But there'll be nane o' that the morn," he added gloomily, waggling a finger at Betty, "for Sandy didna volunteer his services this year. They're going to be doing 'Little Old Lady' this time, and Cissie Carmichael, the Free Kirk minister's daughter, is playing the lead part. Aye, and she's tailor-made for it," he finished smiling enigmatically into the middle distance.

As Betty was getting to know the village's characters, Jim began to acquaint himself of its historical celebrities. His new friends and professional colleagues had loaned him books on the topic, and Jim was happy to dip into some local history.

His research showed that in the year of our Lord twelve hundred and twenty six, (1226) the Abbot of Deir and two of his associates travelled round the Peterugie Estate collecting taxes. William Comyn, the Earl of Buchan, had recently bequeathed this land to the Cistercian Monks in their abbey at Old Deir. He did this in order to stop the monks and the surrounding peasants from helping Robert the Bruce in his quest to be king.

Whilst following the road from the abbey to Peterhead, Walter, the head abbot, came to a cross-roads with a pathway running from the Ludquharn direction, towards the River Ugie. The good abbot sat down here and very soon fell into a trance. He was recorded as saying: "...there are many houses and many people, and the country on every side is laden with crops of grain and....the spring at my feet, which sparkles and flows into the river below..." This vision was qualified by the prediction that all this would only happen "after much blood had flowed."

Sure enough, in 1308 that spot was the scene where Robert the Bruce, who was the new king then, avenged the treachery of William Comyn, Earl of Buchan, and routed the last of that man's armies. Not a tree was left standing, and more than half of the local inhabitants there were slaughtered. Thereby he confirmed the abbot's vision of blood running through the area before it would become prosperous. The inhabitants were consoled by the old prophecy, and convinced that they were "doing the Lord's work."

In the early 16thCentury, a writer described the place as a "worthless bog" where two pathways crossed. Many travellers used it as a resting-place, and in time a hotel of sorts was built that proved to be very lucrative for its proprietors, because of its popular location. They could even justify buying a still for the manufacturing of spirits.

Gradually other small dwellings were built there, but the land was still wet. An innovative drainage system was required to dry the mossy land, and a brilliant feat of engineering culminated in the making of the "Cobble Stank". By the time that great task was completed, Longside was ready to take its place amongst the great villages in this part of the country.

In 1801 the Fergusons of the nearby Pitfour Estate employed a designer called Mr McWhite to plan a rough layout for the village. He came up with a road through the village which was to run irregularly downhill from the Old Church. In time, it was only natural that the main road leading out from Peterhead in the east, should cross this road, as it headed straight on towards Mintlaw and the other small hamlets to the west.

At this time, the inhabitants of Longside lived a hard life with indifferent food and no entertainment. They were a "sturdy race unafraid of rheumatism or the ague," and they worked very very hard. Consequently the village continued to grow rapidly, and several small communities sprang up in the vicinity as a result of the trade from Longside.

Knapps, for example, grew to the north of Longside, and got its supplies of sugar and whale oil from the "Longside Emporiums," as they were referred to then. Mintlaw to the west, sprang up and was supplied with butcher's meat from the abattoirs in Longside. Kinmundy to the south, was founded on a steady trade in shoeing horses, for the people of Longside to cart peats from the neighbouring moss. Also, Flushing, to the east, was built to accommodate the men working at Cairngall Quarry.

Local employment in Longside itself, was concentrated on the Wool Mill at nearby Millbank until it closed in 1828. Longside's semi-industrial tradition continued with a distillery, which was later converted into a sawmill. There was also a Whalebone Crushing Mill that offered employment to the locals.

As the years passed, more and more Longside folk discarded their but-and-bens with their thatched roofs, for fancier, or sometimes more austere houses of substance, perhaps with two storeys, and slate roofs. They grew roses and ivy and clematis up their walls, and that changed the very rugged look that they once had. Surprisingly, according to the historians, beneath the skins of these hardy souls were beautiful and idyllic ideas and plans awaiting their escape.

With the coming of the Great Northern Railway many handsome granite houses were added, like the dowery house and Haddo Cottage, where the bank operated. The Whytes built their Steam Bakery that caused jealousy from the other villages nearby. And the introduction of macadamised roads also contributed to the village's growth and wealth.

Jim was also delighted to discover that although it was a relatively small place, Longside had had "a disproportionate number of famous inhabitants."

Jamie Fleeman, for example, was "the Laird of Udny's Fool" but he was not as foolish as he would have at first appeared. He was indeed, possessed of mother wit. James Fleming, son of James Fleming, was born at

Ludquharn on the seventh of April 1713, and in his boyhood he was the "fool" or "jester" of Sir Alexander Guthrie, the Knight of Ludquharn. When Sir Alexander moved house, a place was found for Jamie Fleeman with the Lord of Udny, where it was agreed that Jamie should be given a peck of meal and sixpence a week. There was talk of shoes too, but Jamie rarely availed himself of these.

Hatless and shoeless, Jamie was free to roam the countryside, and was made welcome in the mansions and estates of the local gentry by virtue of his reputation. He elected to sleep in the barns and kennels with their dogs. Jamie was always faithful to his benefactors, including the Laird of Waterton. But this loyalty did not necessarily extend to the Lord's friends. For example, one day while Jamie was lolling on the bank of the River Ythan, a visitor to the Laird of Waterton approached on the other side, and asked Jamie where the safest crossing point was for himself and his horse. Recognising the man who had previously made some ill-natured remarks about him, Jamie pointed to the deepest pool in the river. And in attempting to cross there, the visitor almost drowned. He demanded to know why Jamie had deliberately directed him there, and was told innocently, "Gosh be here! I've seen the geese and the dyeuks hunners o' times crossin' there; and I'm sure your horse has longer legs than the dyeuks or the geese either."

The Countess of Errol was well aware of Jamie's faithfulness, and she often employed him to carry messages to her fellow gentry folk who had helped in the unsuccessful Jacobite Rebellion. She trusted Jamie to carry secret messages and goods from Slains to many indigent lairds who were her friends, and who had had to go into hiding.

Among these friends she included Lord Pitsligo who at that time was sheltering at the house of Auchiries, in the parish of Rathen, and who went under the name, "Mr Brown." To take a message there from Slains meant passing through the land of a rich proprietor who was a Hanovarian, and who was a fierce enemy of the Prince and all who followed him. "Where are you going, Jamie?" he asked suspiciously one time. "I'm gaun to Hell, Sir!" replied Fleeman drily. And in the absence of further conversation, he proceeded on his way. That evening, on his return from his dangerous mission, Jamie and the gentleman met again. "What are they doing in Hell then, Jamie?" he roared. "Just what they're deein' here, sir," answered Fleeman, "lattin' in the rich fouk, an' keepin' oot the peer." "What said the

Devil to you, Jamie?" he demanded to know. "Ou, he said na muckle to me sir; but he was speirin' sare aboot you!"

Such audacity was the Fool's province and many people flinched at his wit, as well as laughed at it.

Jamie was very strong, fearless and loyal. When staying over at the castle at Knockhall one night, the place caught fire and Jamie rescued the family. They kept their valuables in a huge heavy box, and Jamie braved the flames one last time to hurl this massive chest to safety.

But his superlative strength couldn't last forever, and once weakened with a fever, his health worsened with jaundice. Jamie sought a bed in the straw behind the barn door at Johnson's farm at Cruden. The following morning, the farmhands used force to enter the barn and did not realise that they had wounded Jamie who crawled into a corner where he lay bleeding badly. By the time he was found and taken into the kitchen he knew that he was dying. He begged of Mr Johnson, "When I am gane, ye winna lay me at Cruden; but tak' me to Langside, and bury me among my friends? Please, Maister Johnson!" But Mr Johnson failed to appreciate the extent of Jamie's terrible injuries, and so Jamie made the slow painful return to Longside on his own two feet, stopping to rest wearily and often.

On his deathbed he roused himself to say in a firm tone, "I am one of the Gentle Persuasion (a Christian), dinna bury me like a beast." With these last words then, he exhorted his friends to bury him in the Churchyard of the Auld Kirk.

The good people of Longside rallied together with Messrs Kilgour who employed a number of wool combers and weavers at Kinmundy, all of whom were sent to assist carrying Jamie to his grave. They also supplied porter and cakes at his funeral, so that in the end, he had a decent burial.

His remains lie near the north dyke of the Churchyard of Longside, and in 1861, an Aberdeen gentleman was to provide a plain tombstone that was sculpted by George Donaldson of Aberdeen, a former resident of the parish of Longside. The tombstone was, and still is, inscribed to the effect that this was Jamie Fleeman's grave, "In Answer To His Prayer - Dinna Bury Me Like A Beast."

That Aberdeen gentleman had in fact come to see the grave of another famous man and scholar of Longside - that of Tullochgorum, the Reverend

John Skinner, who was Longside's greatest genius and rector of Longside. The east window of Saint John's Episcopal Church was dedicated to Dean John Skinner who was born on the third of October 1721 and died in January of 1807. Born at Balfour, in the parish of Birse in Aberdeenshire, he was the son of a schoolmaster, and a prodigy who won a bursary competition to study for a degree at Marischal College in Aberdeen, when he was only thirteen years old. There he "passed with honour through all the stages of a Classical education." He began as a teacher in Kemnay and then in Monymusk. Then he accepted a post as a private tutor in Shetland, before completing his studies for the Ministry in 1741.

Although he was brought up as a Presbyterian, he connected himself with the Scottish Episcopal Communion, who were a "small, despised, and persecuted people" hounded by the followers of the king for having allied themselves to the Jacobite Cause. In 1741, Bishop Dunbar ordained him a Presbyter of the Episcopal Church in a ceremony in Peterhead. Reverend Skinner went on to become the pastor of the congregation at Longside when he was only twenty-one. During the Uprising he was imprisoned for six months for refusing to denounce his Episcopal faith. Like his fellow ministers, he was not allowed by law to preach to more than four parishioners at one time. So he held "services" through his window at Linshart for his flock that gathered in his garden. He and his family were evicted and his house burned by "King's men with fixed bayonets," but his piety and faith remained firm.

Dean John Skinner gained not only parochial fame, but became renowned worldwide. He was a "learned divine who wrote theological works in Latin and English."

During his lifetime he also attained eminence as a scholar, and at one time he assisted Doctor Greig of Stirling who was working on the Encyclopaedia Britannica, by compiling several articles for that great work.

Poetry also ran in his veins and he was the composer of many famous songs, one of which was "Tullochgorum" which became his pseudonym in the village. By 1787 John Skinner was Bishop John Skinner, when he met the famous poet, Robert Burns, in the office of "The Daily Journal" in Aberdeen. The owner of the newspaper, James Chalmers 11, had invited both men there. The two poets got on famously together and a friendship arose which resulted in a continual correspondence between them for the rest of their lives. Rabbie Burns professed a lot of admiration for Tullochgorum's work.

With regard to Reverend Skinner's "Tullochgorum," Burns himself said that it was; "the best Scotch song ever Scotland saw." It was written after Tullochgorum had taken part in a political dispute while visiting Mrs Montgomery at Ellon in Aberdeenshire.

The music for this piece was composed first, and Reverend Skinner, who was by then a famous poet, put the words to it by popular request whilst at Ellon. In its time, the song was seen to encapsulate all that was best and liked about the Scots' character. It was sung in a lively and pleasant way, and was seen as a testament to the generosity and vigour of the true Scot. This song then, along with another famous one entitled "The Ewie wi' the Crookit Horn," became one of the best-known ballads of its time. Reverend John Skinner called it simply, "Tullochgorum" .

Tullochgorum

Come gie's a sang, Montgomery cry'd,
    And lay your disputes all aside,
What signifies't for folks to chide
    For what was done before them:
Let Whig and Tory all agree,
    Whig and Tory, Whig and Tory,
Whig and Tory all agree,
    To drop their Whig-mig-morum:
Let Whig and Tory all agree
    To spend the night wi' mirth and glee,
And cheerfu' sing alang wi' me
    The Reel o' Tullochgorum.

O' Tullochgorum's my delight,
    It gars us a' in ane unite,
And ony sumph that keeps a spite,
    In conscience I abhor him:

For blyth and cheerie we'll be a',
　Blyth and cheery, blyth and cheerie,
Blyth and cheerie we'll be a'
　And mak' a happy quorum:
For blyth and cheerie we'll be a'
　As lang as we hae breath to draw,
And dance till we be like to fa'
　The Reel o' Tullochgorum.

What needs there be sae great a fraise
　Wi' dringing dull Italian lays,
I wadna gie our ain Strathspeys
　For half a hunder score o' them:
They're dowf and dowie at the best,
　Dowf and dowie, dowf and dowie,
Dowf and dowie at the best,
　Wi' a' their variorum;
They're dowf and dowie at the best,
　Their ALLEGROS and a' the rest,
They canna' please a Scottish taste
　Compar'd wi' Tullochgorum.

Let wardly worms their minds oppress
　Wi' fears o' want and double cess,
And sullen sots themsells distress
　Wi' keeping up decorum:
Shall we sae sour and sulky sit,
　Sour and sulky, sour and sulky,
　Sour and sulky shall we sit
　Like old philosophorum!
Shall we sae sour and sulky sit,
　Wi' neither sense, nor mirth, nor wit,
Nor ever try to shake a fit
　To th' Reel o' Tullochgorum?

May choicest blessings aye attend
　Each honest, open-hearted friend,

And calm and quiet be his end,
    And a' that's good watch o'er him;
May peace and plenty be his lot,
    Peace and plenty, peace and plenty,
Peace and plenty be his lot,
    And dainties a great store o' them;
May peace and plenty be his lot
    Unstain'd by any vicious spot,
And may he never want a groat,
    That's fond o' Tullochgorum!

But for the sullen frumpish fool,
    That loves to be oppression's tool,
May envy gnaw his rotten soul,
    And discontent devour him;
May dool and sorrow be his chance,
    Dool and sorrow, dool and sorrow,
Dool and sorrow be his chance,
    And nane say, wae's me for him.
May dool and sorrow be his chance,
    Wi' a' the ills that come frae France,
Wha e'er he be that winna dance
    The Reel o' Tullochgorum.

Dean Skinner was a kind, open-hearted pastor. His theological genius never got in the way of his friendship with his flock, and he was sorely missed after he died in his eighty-sixth year. His epitaph in the Auld Kirkyard reads: "Lived so justly respected, and died so sincerely lamented."

Jim also discovered that Longside had not only produced poets, but also had "politicians, authors and painters, musicians and vocalists...a Free Trade champion, two suffragettes, several worshipful Grand Masters, a goalkeeper, a referee and two half-backs." John Imray was a living addition to that list and lived in his hoosie in Armoury Lane with his dog "Lady." Jim would wonder with a wry smile if he would ever be worthy of acceptance into such an elite society, and it never occurred to him that he might leave his own mark on the little village.

Chapter 9

There's Naething Got By Delay, But Dirt An' Lang Nails

Living on the Terrace was enjoyable for Betty. Her neighbours were friendly towards her without being intrusive. Most of them were retired, although some had chosen to live on the Terrace because of its proximity to the railway station. Only a few children lived there, and the area was apt to be quiet - except on Sunday afternoons.

Miss Low and her maid lived in "The Kyles," the house situated opposite the railway bridge. She was the daughter of a former minister, a pillar of the Episcopalian Church and captain of the "Scottish Girls' Friendly Society." Miss Low had a large shed in her front garden where the girls met and had great fun. Nearly all the girls in the village joined, mainly because there was little else for them to do on a Sunday afternoon. Whether they learned anything useful was a matter of debate in the village. Some parents criticised her apparent lack of control, with some justification, judging by the racket that came from the shed. But every girl that passed through her hands defended her idiosyncratic teaching methods, with the result that the Sunday afternoon classes survived for years.

To the right of "Ardlaw" where Jim and Betty were residing with Mr Penny, lived Mr and Mrs Forbes. "Dinty Forbes," a rotund man with ruddy cheeks was the dentist in Peterhead, and his wife, a tall and statuesque lady was always very kind to Betty. A smaller house, known locally as "The Doocot" stood next door to them, wherein lived Miss Lawrence and her daughter Julia. "Julia" in those days was considered an outlandish name, and she won sympathy from the villagers purely on that account! Then at the end of the Terrace lay "Airlie Lodge," a beautiful granite house owned by Captain Calder who had retired from the Navy.

At the other end of the Terrace, next to Bridge End Farm, was a big imposing house where Dr Lawrence lived, and next to him was "Auchingale," owned by Mrs Greig. She had a maid called Mary Jean Ritchie who had been with her for years, and who took special pride in buffing up the shine on her floors. Although she was repeatedly asked not to polish under the rugs, she couldn't restrain herself, with the result that the household and its guests were apt to go flying when they left the comparative safety of the linoleum.

Next door lived Mr and Mrs McBean. He was a lawyer in Peterhead, and she was the daughter of Smith the butcher in Broad Street in Peterhead. Mrs McBean was kept in a perpetual state of anxiety by their three daughters: Irene (Bunty), Shona and Eva. The most recent household drama concerned their dog, Binky, who had been sick on the rug. Helpfully, Bunty had taken a pair of scissors and cut around the offending mess then thrown the whole lot onto the fire. The resultant smell can only be imagined!

On a daily basis, these neighbours kept largely to themselves and observed the usual social courtesies upon meeting outside their homes. There was no inclination towards gossip and that suited Betty fine, for it had never been encouraged in her home. But it did appear to be a major pastime of the village women and vansmen. Betty would listen politely and repeat some of it to Jim in the evenings after his work - and that was as far as it ever went. Betty's discretion was soon acknowledged and seen as a continuation of that quality which was so essential in her husband's work. This shared characteristic, as well as their open and friendly natures, no doubt expedited their acceptance into the village.

The quiet ambience of the Terrace would be broken from time to time by the bustling activities at the station. The station consisted of a booking office, an inside waiting room in which a fire was lit on very cold days, a store room and a Ladies' and a Gents' toilet. The outside wall sported a

"Fry's Chocolate" machine, and a drinking basin with a metal cup attached by a chain. A weighing machine and a few benches stood against the station wall. Over the metal footbridge, and on the platform on the other side of the line, was a small shelter for passengers waiting to go to Aberdeen.

The station master was Mr Duncan, and the clerk was Mr Thomson, and between them they nearly always managed to ferret out the reason for your journey. The porters, Misters Gunn and Barron, were both short wiry men whose statures belied their strength. Their portering duties alternated with solitary hours spent in manning the signal box at the east end of the main platform.

Mr Duncan lived in the station house, a small abode beside the line, below the McBean's house, and situated beside the loading bay where farmers could offload their sacks without having to negotiate the steep bridge. Most passengers used this entrance at the station house and walked alongside the railway line to the platform, avoiding the arduous climb up and over the bridge.

At the back of the station building itself was a small branch line with a huge shed big enough to house a railway engine. This was the destination for wares bound for local firms and shops that had arrived there on the "goods" trains. At the very back of the station yard were the storehouses belonging to Mitchell and Rae, beside which was a coal mountain. All kinds of feeding stuffs and other farming requisites were unloaded there too. At the back of every passenger train there was a "goods' van" where parcels, mail, papers, bicycles and commodities of every description were stacked. Farmers came with their own wagons to collect their effects, and "Donald the Horse" was always at hand to fill up his cart with goods to be delivered to folks in the village and surrounding area.

On one occasion a consignment of barrels and sacks and things arrived at the station to be transported to Whyte's Bakery by horse and cart. The load included a barrel of butter, and a barrel of syrup. Everything was loaded on to the flat cart with the barrels up front. Unfortunately, the driver didn't negotiate the bridge very well and the whole shipment started to slide backwards and everything sprawled onto the road. Inevitably the barrels fell too and split open on landing. The ensuing gooey mess was the "sweet talk" of the village, and it was a long time before the driver was allowed to forget his awful sticky experience.

On occasions the railway was used to deliver livestock to a local farm after it had been bought at the weekly mart in Maud. This was one of the few jobs that Donald the Horse couldn't take on, so the schoolboys vied with each other to make some pocket money. A bemused bull calf would be set down from the train and ushered to its new home by a young lad wielding a stick.

*   *   *

When the weather grew colder, signifying the approach of their second winter in Ardlaw, Jim started to fill his evenings in a new way. Firstly, he established with Mr Penny that he could use the shed out the back, beside the water well, then he began to accumulate second-hand building tools. Betty's surprise turned to fascination as she watched Jim begin to adapt them for his own use. It didn't all go smoothly in the beginning, and sometimes he got very frustrated. But this only served to make her husband more determined, and over the following months he built up a comprehensive set of tools, all adapted for use by a man with only one arm.

He devised a series of clamps to hold small things like nails steady, while he hammered or screwed them into place. For larger and longer implements he made stools of varying heights, so that he could secure a block of wood against them with the weight of his right foot in order to work on them. To move around heavier and bigger pieces of wood or whatever, Jim made boxes of differing sizes and attached pieces of leather from his unused artificial arm to them, so that he could carry them round his neck. He also made a small cart with wheels that he could pull by putting the leather straps round his shoulders.

As time went on Jim discovered an aptitude for working with wood and learned how to do dovetail joints and such - in his own way. And he was never satisfied until his project was perfectly finished off. He was finding fulfilment, and since this was on top of enjoying his daytime work better, he was a happy man.

Betty was gladdened to see her husband enjoying life so much, although she sometimes wondered how long his enthusiasm would last. After all, there were only so many cupboards and tables her husband could make before they ran out of room. But she saw no point in worrying about the future, so she never asked Jim what he planned to do with all his newly acquired skills.

She was keeping herself busy and continued to "fill the unforgiving minute/with sixty seconds' worth of distance run,". She quietly worked away at making their house into a home, and steadfastly persevered with her avowal to adapt to the pleasures and pressures of village life. Now and then she missed her mother and felt weepy, especially during the dark cold afternoons alone at her sewing. But she would stave off her impending tears with a fresh burst of activity. For some reason she felt the cold terribly these days, and would have no appetite for the nourishing meals she prepared so painstakingly on the old-fashioned range. She put it down to homesickness and deemed it unsuitable for mentioning to Jim.

What she definitely couldn't tell her husband about, was that during the worst of the winter weather she was sometimes fearful of his safety when she bade him goodbye and he left for work. He would throw on his old greatcoat, cap and glove to protect himself against the biting winds, and then battle his way down the road to the village on his tricycle every morning and then again at dinnertime. The tricycle was dangerous and hard going on the icy roads, and balance was everything.

Betty would watch with apprehension as Jim pedalled laboriously towards the bridge, and see his progress impeded by whirls of snow that must have nearly blinded him. The projecting stones in the hardcore road kept jerking his front wheel in all directions and yanking the handlebar from his hand. He had to push hard to keep going and drive even harder to get up and over the bridge while the mud sucked his tyres. The descent on the other side was just as bad because then the tricycle had a tendency to slip sideways and Jim could only apply force to the one pedal. At the same time he had to steer grimly with his one strong hand because the weight of the machine would now be propelling him forwards and pushing him off balance. It took a lot of strength and skill and sheer determination.

Betty would stand shivering at the window imagining the rest of his journey after Jim had disappeared into the blizzard. On he would have to go, past the Pot and labour on for half a mile, being blasted by the winds that blew unchecked over the open fields.

Then, having passed the Haugh and the Coble Stank he would reach the junction at Fraser's shop where he would turn left on to Main Street. His journey here became only slightly easier, for the surface on this road could also be rough with snow and ice. But whatever the conditions, he had to plough on for half the distance again to get to the Parish offices. During the morning he hoped to become sufficiently rested to make the gruelling journey home for dinner - and back again for his afternoon's work.

Betty couldn't understand why she was so worried about him, for he had already survived one winter, and it wasn't even as if he'd ever complained or moaned about the journey. She hoped she wasn't being fey again. But she had to admit that there was a good side to it, because after an evening's reading by the fireside, Jim would sleep like a log at nights, and not lie awake with pain from his arm.

While her husband got on with his work, Betty continued her campaign against the old open fire upon which she cooked and baked for the household. She learned how to gauge its heat, and the various recipes it was suited to, and she would wail with frustration as her scones and pancakes got covered in soot that showered down upon them when it snowed or rained. As a "toon quine" she was accustomed to running water and gaslight, but in her new abode she had to fetch water from the well in the back garden. And she had to get used to cleaning and filling paraffin lamps, not the most pleasant of chores. But in her own way she was as brave and determined as her husband, and together their strong wills and determination made them cope against the odds.

*   *   *

The winter was passing in much this way when, in March, an invitation from Mr Penny broke the pattern by formally asking them to join him "for a bittie supper." Until now he had always been very civil when dealing with them, but hadn't encouraged intimacy beyond that. He was known locally as a "canny man" and Betty was touched as much by this show of generosity, as she was propelled by her own curiosity. Of course they must go!

Promptly, at seven o'clock, they crossed the hallway and presented themselves at his "front door" which was the door to his front living room. They had "dressed" for the occasion, and Betty was wearing her "good" frock, which looked lovely but unfortunately wasn't very warm. She had continued to feel it unusually cold for the past few weeks, and for this engagement had initially thought of wearing something warmer. But she couldn't resist the chance to dress up. As a token practicality, she had draped a shawl around her shoulders, but had to admit that while it added colour to her ensemble, it unfortunately didn't add much more heat. Jim wore his working suit with a fresh collar and tie.

"Come in. Come in," invited Mr Penny warmly. He greeted them in a long red smoking jacket and matching cap with a tassel - just like Father Christmas! His long white beard seemed to glow eerily, for the place was in semi-darkness. One lone candle lit the whole of the huge front room, and a small fire smoked palely up the chimney. Thick heavy curtains covered the huge window, but they failed to keep out the noises of the wind rattling in the windowpanes and the hailstones being hurled against the glass.

The young ones could barely make out the shadows of the furniture at first, but as their eyes grew accustomed to the gloom they established that the candle, their main source of light, was burning in its holder in the middle of a huge table on their right. They ascertained that they were required to approach the fire where three chairs were positioned around it, and had to pass a huge sideboard on the left, adjacent to the door that led into the kitchen. The scatter rugs on the floor presented an unexpected problem for Jim, but Betty automatically grasped his hand to help with his balance. All the furniture was old and grand and bulky, and the wallpaper was of a dark colour, which added to the sombre atmosphere that smelt slightly of damp. Their voices echoed in the large room and their footsteps seemed to clatter on the linoleum. Betty helped Jim to his seat and took hers beside him without mishap; she shivered from the cold and silently berated herself for being so vain as to have worn a light shawl.

They found plenty to talk about however, and their conversation flowed from one topic to another. The Armistice was on everybody's lips, and was the starting point of their evening. They discussed the devastation caused by the war, and pondered on how their cities would be rebuilt. Mr Penny had every confidence in the government's ability to sort everything out in triplicate, while Jim's trust in governmental promises was, understandably, more tenuous.

Betty commented on the huge numbers of families that no longer had a father and wage-earner now, and they ended up discussing women going out to work. Emmeline Pankhurst had newly won the vote for women who were over 30, and Betty was surprised to hear Mr Penny's approval of the bill. They thought it right that the Royal family had renounced their German titles, and were now to be addressed as Windsor. And they were all thankful that they had escaped the Spanish flu epidemic.

In fact, the little party was delighted to find that they agreed on so many subjects, and the time was flying by.

Betty eased herself back in her chair, and surreptitiously rubbed her knee that had grown stiff with the cold. She still felt chilly, and again regretted her vanity. She had discovered that there was no point in trying to draw nearer to the fire because there was no heat to be had from the thin trail of smoke. Then, to her embarrassment her tummy started rumbling, and she hastened to disguise it with a cough. At the same time, she leaned forward and laid her arm across her stomach to stem the noise, and concentrated on looking ahead of her while trying again to take her mind off her hunger.

Over the high mantelpiece was draped a tasselled valance made of some kind of heavy material, probably lined velvet that looked purple in colour. On top of it were sepia photographs, the contents of which were not visible in the poor light. At each end stood a tall, ornate and empty candlestick. And right in the middle, was a black marble clock that had chimed every quarter of an hour since they had entered, and which chimed the hour just then as she was looking at it.

"What a bonny tune," she said repressing an even louder gurgling in her stomach.

"Goodness me," exclaimed Mr Penny. "Is that eight o'clock already?" and coaxed his stiff joints out of his chair.

"I've been enjoying myself so much I've lost track of the time, and you must be hungry. Now you two get yourselves to the table - I have everything set - and I'll fetch our supper." And with that he disappeared into the darkness.

With his departure, a silence descended on the room that made Betty uncomfortable. She stood up and rubbed herself briskly all over in a vain attempt to feel a bit warmer. Then she took Jim's hand the better to help him negotiate his way to the table.

"Goodness me, Betty," said Jim in surprise, "you're frozen!"

"Och it's my own fault for being so vain and just putting on a shawl," replied his wife lightly and she kept her voice low because for some reason she felt the need to speak softly.

"You've been feeling the cold a lot more lately, I've noticed," whispered Jim, who too was reluctant to hear his voice echo throughout the room. "I hope you're not coming down with anything." The pair sounded like conspirators.

Betty shared her husband's concern about her health, but she wasn't going to let on to him. They were both aware that if she couldn't manage to carry her weight they really would be in difficulty. So, despite her inner misgivings she passed the matter off with a joke. "Away with you, Jim," she smiled. "You know what they say - 'Cold hands mean a warm heart.'" And with this quip, she held his hand more tightly and guided him across the room.

As they stepped gingerly towards the candlelight, the wind suddenly hurled a fresh burst of hailstones against the window that made them both jump, and Betty's grip on her husband tightened. The dark strangeness of the room was unnerving. "Be careful, there's a rug here," she whispered as she tried to still her beating heart.

They continued their slow progress towards the light on the table, and found three places set as Mr Penny had said. They took seats opposite one another and waited.

"What do you think the glasses are for?" whispered Betty. They were all three of them members of the Free Kirk so they knew the glasses weren't for an alcoholic beverage. "I'm not sure," replied Jim still speaking as quietly as his wife. "At least I don't have to worry about getting strong tea," she hissed. They hadn't long to ponder over this because Mr Penny reappeared from the gloom holding something in both hands. He shuffled towards them and deposited a tray, gently, on the table with his stiff arthritic hands.

He then transferred a plate of oatcakes and a plate of cheese onto the middle of the table, and followed this with a large jug of milk. He said Grace and sat down.

"Now tuck in the pair of you," he exhorted. "I got these from my daughter yesterday," he said, pointing to the stack of oatcakes. "And I asked her for extra for you young ones."

He beamed at them, and Betty's heart melted afresh at the old man's thoughtfulness and his daughter's generosity. "He really is kind," she thought sentimentally, and to her consternation she felt tears pricking her eyes. She pulled herself up short - this reaction was totally out of character for her! With an effort she blinked the tears away, and determinedly gave Mr Penny her most winning smile. "Shall I pour the milk?" she asked brightly.

Talking stopped while they enjoyed their repast. And after they were finished Betty volunteered to carry the tray back to the kitchen. Her offer was declined, and they continued to sit at the table.

They were so comfortable with one another by now that the conversation flowed easily again, starting with, of all things, their favourite war songs. Betty eagerly joined in, even to singing a few notes of her favourite - "Keep The Home Fires Burning" and wondered ruefully why this couldn't have come up earlier and kept her empty stomach secret. They went on to debate the success of British Summer Time that had been introduced during the war to get the maximum use out of daylight.

They continued to discuss this at length, until Jim announced that it was time to be making tracks as he had an early start the next morning. After the usual civilities had been exchanged, Mr Penny saw them both to the door where they again voiced their thanks to the old man, and took their leave of him.

"Oh Jim," whispered Betty through chattering teeth as she snuggled up to their own fireside. "I don't know when I was last so cold." She put her hands gingerly up to her face and confirmed that her nose had gone numb. She shivered again, and once more the awful thought crept into her mind that there might be something wrong with her. This perpetual coldness and tiredness that kept sneaking up on her were definitely beginning to worry her, despite her protestations. But she refused to alarm Jim.

"Having been a farmer he'll have worked outside in the fresh air for most of his life," replied Jim. "So I expect he doesn't feel the cold all that much," he added charitably. "And what are you still whispering for?" he smiled.

Betty laughed as she stoked up the embers and threw on a log that quickly started crackling, and soon fat flames were licking up the chimney.

"Ah... That's better," she sighed, as she pulled her chair even closer and wiggled her toes towards the comforting heat. "Shall I put on the kettle for a cup of tea? Then I can fill the pig and get our bed nice and cosy."

Once she'd set the water on to heat, she sat back cocooned in the glow from the fire with its warmth seeping throughout her body making her feel pleasantly relaxed. "How nice it would be if I could feel as warm as this all the time," she thought wistfully.

"What are you thinking about that can make you sigh like that?" asked Jim gently.

Startled out of her reverie Betty gave a quick smile, and started preparing their cup of tea. "Nothing of any importance," she answered lightly. "Would you like something to eat with this?"

"Well, I've been doing a lot of thinking as well," replied Jim in a preoccupied voice and ignoring her last question, "and I have a plan in mind. It's a surprise that I've been working on for a while now, and today I got my answer."

"It doesn't sound like a nice surprise when you say it in that solemn voice of yours," said his wife cautiously.

"Well. It's a solemn business this undertaking, Betty, but with your support we'll create the nicest surprise imaginable," said Jim gravely. Looking across at his wife's face he saw her concern and bemusement, and decided that he'd teased her enough. His face split into a grin and he laughed aloud.

"What is it, Jim? Quickly, tell me," she pleaded, by now in an agony of suspense. She loved to hear her husband laugh, but not right this very minute!

Reaching into his inside jacket pocket he pulled out a stiff-looking brown envelope and handed it to her with dancing eyes.

Betty quickly skimmed its contents, and was overwhelmed by the magnitude of what she read there.

"Is this what I think it is?" she faltered.

"It is indeed," announced Jim proudly. "It's permission to take over the feu for the bit of land opposite my workplace that used to belong to old Sergeant Darling! There's a little house on it at present where we can stay until I build our new home. He's sold everything to me and is going to take lodgings with Mrs Thomson above the butcher's shop before the end of the month.

Do you see what this means, Betty?" He took her hand excitedly. "It means that I'm going to build you a house of our own - with a big garden of our own - and I'll design as big a fire as you'll ever need to keep out the cold! Now, what do you think of that, my dear?"

Betty had been struck dumb, and was desperately trying to gather her composure but managed to reply faintly, "Whatever next?" because an answer was expected of her.

She closed her eyes as a myriad of doubts and uncertainties flooded her mind. Surely this plan was far too ambitious for Jim to undertake on his own? They could lose all their money if he failed. They might never get more than half of his pension to live on. They might have to pay doctor's bills.....There were so many difficulties involved in this, and it was all happening too fast! He was looking for her support. And she felt scared.

Betty opened her eyes finally, prepared to tell him - but saw his confident eager face and all her doubts fled. She realised that he wouldn't embark on something as big as this if he didn't think he could do it. She knew she could trust him completely.

She took a deep breath, then grinned broadly, "Whatever next indeed!" she laughed.

Chapter 10

A Guid Wife And Health Is A Man's Best Wealth

Jim started by making arrangements for the feu to be made over to him. The Bruce family at Inverquhomery owned the land, and rent had to be paid annually to them. Then, using his skills as a Master Builder, he drew up plans for his house that he based on the popular style he used to build in Portessie. This meant that the outer part was to be mainly made of cement blocks using moulds that he would design and make himself. Jim submitted his plans and had no difficulty at all in getting permission to build his house.

Instead of facing the main road, his new house was to open on to Cooper's Brae. It would have a small hallway with the living room, a big square room, off to the left. A door from the living room would lead west to another large room, which was to be the main bedroom. And also off to the west, would be a smaller bedroom. To the east of the living room he would build the kitchen or scullery, which was to have running water. This would be innovative in the village, and meant that Betty wouldn't have to fetch water from the pump any more, a great boon for her. And their "dry" lavatory would be outside, beyond the large shed and coal house to be built under the house roof.

His plans included tiled fireplaces with wooden overmantles specially made by his former colleagues in Buckie. The top third of the windows

121

would have alternate gold and clear panes of glass. He also intended finishing off the front of his house with an ornamental concrete wall, and he had already devised the moulds for each of the small pillars.

Sergeant Darling was as good as his word, and by spring he had vacated his little red-tiled "hoosie" and was happily lodging with Mrs Thomson.

Jim's first task was to employ Donald the Horse to clear the area where his new house was to be built. Then, before he proceeded any further, Jim built a large substantial shed in the far corner of the garden where he would keep his tools, store his moulds and leave his cement to dry out. It was big enough for him to continue working in it if the weather turned inclement. He had always been very meticulous about the condition of his tools, and everything was stored methodically. This suited his nature as well as being practical for him, for it was necessary to reduce the danger of him tripping over things.

The making of these wooden moulds represented another important turning point for Jim as he discovered a new outlet for his creativity. He designed beautiful wall and ceiling copings, and his more ambitious moulds produced elaborate shapes and sizes of cement casts to be used for decorative mantelpieces and internal pillar work. His plans included ornate walls for outside and edging for the lawns and paths too.

Mr Rankin the village joiner helped him to build his shed, and was contracted to do the joinery work on the new house. Alex Innes was hired to help with masonry work that required two men. Alex had been invalided out of the army after he lost the sight in one eye, but he was a good and steady worker, although his temper was uncertain at times, and he could be morose. Jim ignored these traits and treated him as he would any assistant - getting on with the work at hand without any unnecessary chit-chat.

By the time the clock moved forward that year, Jim and Betty had moved into the little red-tiled "housie." Sergeant Darling had left some bits and pieces behind, and they were "making do" with them until their new furniture arrived that they'd ordered from Buckie. Perhaps it wasn't Sergeant Darling who had shortened the legs on the bed, but his name tended to come up when Jim struggled to get in and out of it, with his artificial leg. As was often the case though, his sense of humour was his best defence in these awkward situations, and Jim would refer dryly to their "sleeping on the floor meantime," and accompany his words with a wry smile.

There weren't enough hours in the day now for Jim who was back in his element working and building. He was up at five o'clock every morning, mixing the sand and cement and filling the various moulds. Then he would come in and have breakfast before changing his clothes and going to work. He always ate porridge with milk added, followed by bread and marmalade and a mug of tea. Betty joked that he spread his marmalade as liberally as he did his beloved cement - and would probably be better off with a trowel! But Jim's breakfast never varied, and he swore that it was responsible for his tremendous strength. Then, after a full day's work punctuated with lunch at home, Jim would be eager to be out and getting on with his house again in the evenings.

Meanwhile Betty had to get used to yet another old open fire that rained soot all over her pancakes and girdle scones! She had managed to make the transition from having running water in Bucksburn, to fetching her water from the well out the back when she had lived up on the Terrace. Now she had to adapt to using the nearest public water pump that stood on the pavement up past Jim's workplace. However, it wasn't long before she noticed that every time she went for water, James Chivas at Ivybank would be at his downstairs window watching her every move. This managed to irk her so much, one day after she had filled her pails she turned round, looked him in the eye, and executed a beautifully exaggerated curtsy to him. At this astonishing acknowledgement of his prurience he grew bright red, withdrew his face hurriedly and quickly jerked the curtain to rights. Betty took a good laugh, and her report of the incident even made Jim smile when she told him about it later that night.

Now that she lived in the village itself, she was learning more and more about how its people got on. For example, she learned that a strict class system operated here, and those people with money had little to do with those who hadn't - be they sinners or churchgoers! And those who weren't rich would have no truck with "their" airs and graces - and were proud of it. Coming from the city as she did, Betty found this narrow-minded behaviour quite amusing, and refused to subscribe to it. She spoke to everyone - rich and poor alike, and was "neither fish nor fowl nor good red herring" as they used to say.

She still felt the cold all the time, but wasn't worried anymore because she had discovered she was pregnant, and due in October. They were elated to discover that, whatever else the future held for them, they were going to experience the joy of parenthood. Their cup was overflowing, but there was still a fly in the ointment, and quite a big "fly" too, because it concerned the amount of Jim's War Pension they could rely on. After all, there was a huge difference between living on £5 a week, and £2, and they hoped they'd be told soon. They never discussed it with one another, although each dreaded the horrible repercussions there would be if it had to remain at less than half. Instead, they each held their whisht and sent up many silent prayers.

*   *   *

It was springtime in 1919 and the country was in a poor way. A sizeable number of soldiers were still waiting to be formally discharged from service, and needed arrangements made to get them home. Too many of them were worn-down gaunt shadows of what they used to be, and in their depleted health they were targets for the Spanish flu that was devastating families throughout the country. After all that they'd been through, the soldiers had looked forward to being received as heroes, and getting back to work where their self-pride could be regained and reinforced. But things weren't turning out quite as they had imagined it. What with all the muddle about getting them home, the flu epidemic, and their fruitless search for jobs, people were beginning to ask where was this "land fit for heroes" that had been promised to them by Prime Minister Lloyd George.

But the resilience of mankind should never be underestimated, because, by June, the country had turned itself around. The terms for peace had been agreed and the Treaty of Versailles signed, and the Germans started paying reparations. Suddenly, it seemed that almost all of the soldiers were back home at last. The flu virus had burnt itself out, and the country's economy was booming. Cities were being rebuilt and new and exciting products were coming on the market. Industries were prospering and there were plenty jobs for everybody. The soldiers had been given generous demobilisation bonuses and most of them were happy to enjoy spending it on having fun. Those people who were still in mourning disapproved of this unseemly behaviour - but that didn't stop the rest of them from celebrating the sheer bliss of being alive! They were happy and had money and they wanted to spend, spend, and spend!

The women too were caught up in this buoyant economy. Gone were the stiff old stays and dark coloured tight-fitting bombazine, and in came new, colourful, shorter dresses with playful fringes. Not only were ankles now showing, but low necks were now also in fashion, and dresses hung fairly shapelessly from the shoulders, giving them new freedom. These women were called "flappers," who copied the dress-designs from the fashion houses in Paris. And Jazz music was played loud and fast, and stirred them to dance the Charleston and shock their parents. Life had never seemed so good!

Of course, this was how they reacted in London and in the other cities down south. Up north in Longside, village life didn't alter much by and large - with or without a war. Some local men had avoided conscription because their beasts had had to be tended to feed the nation; and their fields had had to yield as much as ever to keep the country going. Fish had still had to be caught and cured. Longside hadn't been a prime target for the Germans despite its Airbase at Lenabo, and all the houses were still intact. The villagers had always lived a canny life and wouldn't have understood the carnival atmosphere down south. Instead they were relieved and grateful for the happy outcome of the war. They gave thanks to God, and went about their business with a lighter heart and readier smile.

*   *   *

However, the state of happiness is seldom absolute, and this was especially true for Betty. Her father was very ill and the family knew that his time with them was limited. Cancer was destroying him, and knowing this, Betty travelled to Bucksburn as often as she could. Some of her trips to Aberdeen were with Jim in order to have his artificial leg refitted or refined. The "bucket" which held the stump had to be replaced as the size of the stump decreased with time and use, and the skin hardened and contracted. The couple would make "a day" of it, and afterwards would go and visit her parents in Bucksburn. There was always news to be caught up with, and they would make a point of cheering up her father.

While their main aim was to visit "Hangers," at the far end of North Silver Street, they approached it by turning off Union Street and walking round Golden Square so that Betty could pop in to John Milne's the Auctioneers and see if she could pick up a bargain. She had a good eye for value and bought some beautiful pieces of furniture for her new house -

and each successful bid formed the basis of a good story to relay to her father that evening before they left.

One thing that she didn't buy at auction, though, was her baby's cradle. Instead, she and Jim picked one up at a local roup. It wasn't in such good condition as the pieces from Aberdeen, but with a bit of work Jim assured her he could get it to look just as acceptable.

One bright September morning while Jim was finishing off his breakfast, he was discussing the cradle with Betty.

"I've sanded it down and given it a layer of wax and it's looking well. However, I'll give it a second waxing this evening when I've finished outside, and that'll be it finished. It's a good piece of wood and I think it'll look very well. We were lucky to get such a good sturdy one."

"Fine," smiled Betty. "I've almost finished the blanket for it. I must confess I'm beginning to get excited about...."

Here she was interrupted by a knock at the door. "Oh that'll be postie," she announced and went to answer it. When they had first moved in, Mr Cheyne used to wander in to the house and discuss their mail before handing it over - just as he was in the habit of doing with everyone else. Jim quickly put a stop to that, for he valued his privacy. Thereafter, Mr Cheyne always knocked and waited to hand over their mail without discussion of it beforehand. He hadn't been offended, and always had a cheery word for Betty.

"Beautiful morning Mistress Mair! There was a red sky last night. 'Red sky at night, shepherds' delight. Red sky in the morning, shepherds' warning,' so we're in for another fine day." And because he regarded himself as somewhat of an authority on the weather he added, 'Fair on September first, fair for the rest o' the month.'" And with a smile he handed Betty a stiff brown envelope.

"Thank you kindly," Betty replied forcing herself to give him her usual smile as she accepted it. At the sight of the envelope her heart had given a jolt, and it was now beating fifteen to the dozen. Today they were going to find out if Jim's pension was to remain reduced or not. The government's final decision now lay in her hand and the verdict was going to make a sizeable difference to their lifestyle. Just leave and let us know our fate, she thought hurriedly. She wanted to bang the door shut and run inside to Jim, but common courtesy dictated she do otherwise.

"Yes, you're right," she replied. "It looks as if I'll get my washing dried outside today." And after a short pause she added, "Well, I'll not keep you, Mr Cheyne."

But he wasn't to be hurried.

"The wife and I were saying just the other day that your hoose is coming on real quickly. You'll be moving in gae soon I suppose," he said, ignoring the hint, and leaning against the doorpost all set for a chat. "Your husband's keeping well is he?" he enquired. Then he continued without waiting for a reply, "How does he get on with oor Alex? He can be a real dour ..."

"Fine, fine," interrupted Betty. "Jim's keeping fine, thank you. And he always says that Alex is a grand worker. Now if you'll excuse me, Mr Cheyne.." She began to close the door again.

"We were jist saying that it's a real unusual style of hoose that your husband's chosen. Nae but what it's nae bonny, mind you. It's jist that it's different."

Drat the man, thought Betty to herself. I wouldn't put it past him to be delaying me on purpose. He must know that an official letter from The House of Commons is important to us. People don't get letters from there every day. Then she took a deep breath and tried not to be so uncharitable.

"Yes, we're very pleased with the way it's turning out. It's based on the style of houses that he used to build in Portessie - with a few adaptations," replied Betty. "Now I'd better be getting..."

"That's richt, your man used to be a builder.."

"Master Builder," corrected Betty. "And he's very happy to be back at his old trade."

"Aye, he's doing well - what with his ..er ..er changed circumstances," nodded Mr Cheyne diplomatically. "It couldna be easy for him, but by jings he's getting on real fast - and him with a full-time job as well. I was jist saying to the wife that Jim Mair ..."

But Betty had had enough. "I'm sorry, but you'll have to excuse me, Mr Cheyne," she interrupted crisply. "I'll have to see to his breakfast. And you'll have more deliveries to make I'm sure. So, if you don't mind, let's both get on with our work. Tell Mistress Cheyne I was asking after her please." And with a short smile she swiftly closed the door.

Then she leaned back against it and sent up a quick prayer, Please God let it be good news.

"Well, it's finally come, Jim," she announced as steadily as she could while she entered the room where Jim was finishing off his breakfast. Now that she was free to learn of its contents she knew a brief momentary panic when she wished the letter hadn't come. She held it out to her husband and tried to give him a reassuring smile - but she couldn't.

Jim stood up, and taking the envelope from her, he put it between his knees and ripped it open with the knife. Before he removed its contents, he paused as if he was sending up a silent prayer of invocation. Then he took out the stiff white paper from within, and read it slowly and deliberately, while Betty watched and waited in an agony of suspense. It took him a good few minutes which seemed to her to last an eternity, and all the while, his face was inscrutable. Finally, Jim looked at her and said tersely, "The pension stays at £2 - until I retire, when they'll resume paying me the full amount."

"Oh Jim, I'm so sorry," whispered Betty in anguish. "I'm so sorry."

There followed a silence while they became fully conscious of the effects of this bitter blow and each tried to hide his dismay.

Jim was the first to recover. His face was pale, and his voice was flat as he spoke. "I want to work, Betty." He paused, and it became increasingly obvious to his wife that he had rehearsed his next words, which he delivered in a quiet monotone. "But as things stand, we can have more money coming in to the household if we live on my full pension. I cannot allow my wife and child to suffer as a consequence of my preference, and so I shall tender my resignation by the end of the week."

Betty looked into her husband's eyes. She too, had anticipated having to deal with this dreaded eventuality. Her problem, as she had listened to her husband's words on the matter, had been to find the best way to deliver her decision. She knew what she wanted the outcome to be. But it was more important that Jim understood why she felt as she did, and that this wasn't just an emotional response.

So there was no feigned anger in her voice, no cajoling, no spirited defence of her choice, and no mock indignation in her voice when she said in measured tones, "Jim, you are a working man. We've been managing fine on your salary and reduced pension up till now, and I don't see any reason as to why that can't continue. There's no question of our ever 'suffering,' through lack of money, for you'll always have an adequate wage. I was raised on a Poor Inspector's salary and I haven't come to any harm." Betty's eyes started to twinkle and she almost dared Jim to deny this, in her usual laughing way. But even as her smile began, she dismissed it. This was no laughing matter and she had to convince her husband of her proposal. "You've been so happy since we moved down here because you've been thriving on all the work you've been doing. You like the routine of work; you like using your head and you like helping people, Jim. But I've never seen you so alive as when you're designing something new for our house. You're eager to get up in the mornings, and you look forward to getting back to your beloved cement at nights. Jim, you love working - and I love to see you so happy. So I don't see any need for change." Giving way to a smile at last, she held his eye and said confidently, "We'll manage fine as we are, Jim."

She watched as her husband digested her view of the future and was gratified by the gradual relaxation of his shoulders. She knew he was coming round to her way of thinking when she saw various arguments chase each other across his face but no sound escaped his lips. Then she saw the dawning of hope in his eyes followed by the shrug of his shoulders as if he'd cast off a really heavy weight. She saw his relief, and knew that she had persuaded him.

"Thank you, Betty," he said simply.

He then placed the piece of paper deliberately on the table with the words, "We'll manage." There was a steely determination in his words. If he felt hurt by the betrayal of his government, or anger at its apparent indifference, Jim gave no sign, and with steady and firm resolution, he put on his cap and left for work

Betty sat down and read the letter. Then she read it again. There was no doubt about it. Jim's pension was reduced until he retired, "wherein it would be reinstated in full." In the meantime they would just have to get on with it. She sat there looking at the words on the page, reading them over and over while dreadful conflicting emotions seared through her. She felt desperately disappointed for Jim, and knew a brief bitterness that they weren't going to be rich. They would always have to be careful with their pennies. She was appalled that her husband had been treated so callously by an ungrateful government, and ultimately she felt very, very angry.

"What a cheek," she fumed out loud. "What an awful way to treat a soldier who has given so much for his country - and who has lost so much!" She thought of his prosperous business, and the building work he had loved. "It's not fair!" she raged. "How could they be so cruel? How could they?"

Then in her mind's eye she saw her husband's quiet stoicism. She pictured the months of his ploughing his way to work on his tricycle through the filthy mud and ice against the wild cold wind and rain. She saw again his pale face set in pain against the stark white pillows on his hospital bed. She saw him grit his teeth as he pulled himself out of bed in the mornings. She saw it all so clearly as she looked at the letter. Then she lay down her head and wept at the gross injustice of it all.

By lunchtime her tears were spent and only her anger remained. She knew that Jim would disapprove if she voiced it, so she simmered quietly. Jim ate his dinner in his usual comparative silence, and only shared desultory chit-chat with his wife. After they'd finished, Betty gave him her piece of news from that morning. She wanted to reassure him that she wasn't going to be defeated by the decision either. Life goes on, and she was getting on with it - despite their ungrateful government.

"I was speaking to Miss Strachan next door, and she was telling me that during the summer months some well-to-do families from Peterhead make arrangements to stay in Longside for their summer holidays. They come with a depleted staff of perhaps a cook, a maid and their butler, and rent a house in the village. She said that for the past few years she has gone to her sister's in Inn Brae and has let her house out to a young couple from Peterhead. He enjoys hunting, shooting and fishing, and without her staff she likes to try her hand at being a housewife! How can you try your hand at being an ordinary housewife?"

"I think that some rich people and their money are easily parted," came the dour comment. "But if that's how they want to spend their siller, then by all means let them come."

"Imagine wanting to 'play at hoosies" when you're grown-up," laughed Betty. "I can't wait to see how she gets on."

"Well it's back to work for us mere mortals," smiled Jim getting up and putting on his jacket. "By the way, Betty, I've been noticing that the growing bairn is putting a lot of strain on that knee of yours. Besides that, you're never at peace, and I think you're doing too much at times. The doctor has told you often enough that you've got to take it easy. We'll be moving into the new house soon and there'll be a lot to be done - and you'll have the bairn to look after as well. I know better than to tell you to slow down so I was thinking about getting you some help in the house."

"But.." was as far as Betty got with her reply because by the time she found her voice again, he'd gone to work. She sat down and automatically rubbed her aching knee. It was just like him, she thought. He notices everything but never says anything until there's something he can do about it. He's right. I am tired, and sometimes the thought of moving house again, especially when I feel like an elephant, has been a bit of a trial. Trust him to come up with a solution - and on the very day we're told that his pension is to stay down. Well, I'll tell him that I'm grateful, but I don't want to share our new house with anyone but him yet, and I'll cut back on anything that I don't have to do. If he says we can afford it I'll not gainsay him, but I don't want anyone else - not yet anyway. I wish the furniture would arrive though, it's taking ages. Why did we have to buy it up at Buckie? And why does there have to be a Railway strike on? Och well, I'll get the dishes out of the way and take myself up to the station to see if there's any word of it coming yet.'

When Jim came home from work that evening Betty was fast asleep in the chair by the fire. She had walked up to the station again, only to be told by Donald the Horse that the strike was still on. But she hadn't to mind because he would look out for it and deliver it straight to her. The journey had exhausted her, and when she had sat down and picked up her knitting, the needles had landed in her lap before she had finished the first row - for she had fallen sound asleep.

Jim smiled down at her. She looked so vulnerable. He knew he was a lucky man to have her by his side. She never doubted him, and her support helped him to push farther and farther against the boundaries of his capabilities. Stoic and cheerful, he loved to hear her laugh. She had had to learn so much. Coming from the town, the conditions she'd had to live in since she had married him would have got the better of most. But not his Betty! She'd had a hard time of it, he knew, but all he could remember of it was her laugh. She had never complained or moaned about her new life. She had a fine eye for a bargain and could negotiate a good price or exchange. She kept meticulous books on the housekeeping and oversaw the spending of every penny they had. She was thrifty and yet he never felt that she was penny- pinching. She included some treats in her budget so that he never felt deprived of anything. She was a wonder with her hands. Most of her clothes she made herself, and they looked as good as any other he saw in town. Nothing was thrown out that she couldn't remake and little was wasted. He was so proud of his clever industrious wife, and he loved her so much.

She must have become aware of his presence for her lashes fluttered and she opened her eyes. And opened them even wider when she saw him standing there!

"Good heavens! Is that the time already?" she cried and immediately started to haul her bulk out of the chair. "I'll have your tea ready in two shakes of a lamb's tail. I'm sorry, Jim. I took a walk up to the station, then when I came home I fell fast asleep. I had meant to do some knitting," she added sheepishly as she bent to retrieve her needles and wool that had fallen to the floor.

"I'll get changed and do a bit on the cradle while I'm waiting," responded Jim in a neutral voice. For despite his tender thoughts of the previous minutes he wasn't a demonstrative man - and besides, he was hungry!

The days continued to fly by and autumn with its crisp cold mornings and beautiful changing leaves on the trees was well and truly with them. The cradle was finished and polished, and Betty had made sheets and blankets for it. An old pram had been purchased and spruced up. Baby clothes and other essentials had been acquired. The Rail strike finally came to an end and their furniture was delivered as promised by Donald the Horse.

That day was a particularly busy one for Betty, for the various pieces of furniture had to be placed, polished and filled. At dinner time, she and Jim managed to join the parts of the bed together and Jim tightened the screws securely. Betty looked out her new linen and clean blankets and finished it off with the beautiful hand-crocheted bedspread which she had laboriously and lovingly made. She stood at the bedroom door and admired the whole effect. Yes! It was definitely worth the waiting for!

She was really tired that evening and virtually collapsed on to her new bed. No sooner had she started to admire it afresh than she fell sound asleep. Around two o'clock in the morning she found herself wide awake lying beside her recumbent man. The pain struck again and she knew without a doubt that it wasn't indigestion that had penetrated her sleep.

"Today with God's grace we'll become a family of three," she thought with quiet satisfaction, and not a little trepidation. Then she nudged her husband awake.

"Jim," she whispered. "Go and fetch Mrs Beaton from Laburnum Lane - you know - the midwife. Tell her she's needed."

"Now?" asked Jim instantly alert. "But you're not due yet."

"Tell that to this bairn!" replied Betty tartly through gritted teeth as another contraction came.

Stopping only to light a lamp and throw more coal on the fire, Jim quickly dressed and left on his errand.

There followed a long sair nicht for Betty, with Dr Wood and Mrs Beaton in attendance.

And on the following morning Mr Spence, the watchmaker from two doors down, did a thing unheard of. He shut up shop during the day, to go and announce to his friend Mr Penny and his other friends on the Terrace, that the Mairs had had a daughter, and that all was well. He then returned home accompanied by kind old Joseph Penny who brought half a crown for the new bairn.

Chapter 11

Dinna Look A Gift Horse In The Moo

"She's a restless wee thing, always gadding about the village newsing to all and sundry," remarked Jim idly to Betty one morning.

"What else can you expect of a bairn that was almost born on bare floorboards!" replied Betty with a giggle, referring to the old low bed they'd used in the little red-tiled hoosie.

They were standing at the window watching their daughter, Sheila Cormack, make her daily inspection of the boundary hedge that enclosed their garden. Sheila was looking for an escape route, while her parents were waiting to see where they would have to build their next barricade to prevent their daughter's disappearance.

Sheila was a bright lively almost-three-year old, who was always wandering away to see what was happening in the village. The neighbours knew her well and would humour her for a little while before taking her home. Mrs Souter who lived under her father's office was a favourite, as was her neighbour, Mrs Barron. Sheila had even made it as far as Mrs Gray's who lived up at the Lodge on the Cairngall Estate.

There was no real danger from traffic because only an occasional pony and trap would come by. And Betty only had to appear at the gate to be asked by someone, "Are ye looking for Sheila again?"

"Well I can't see her breaking out today," decided Betty. "But I won't leave her out for long, so that we can leave in plenty time for the train. I haven't told her we're going to grandma's yet, for once she finds out I'll be deeved until we leave."

While Betty remained watching her daughter, Jim turned to pick up his jacket and get off to work. The next thing, he had crashed to the floor!

"Oh Jim!" screamed Betty and was immediately on her knees beside him. "Are you hurt? Can you move?" she asked alarmed. Her heart was pounding with the fear she'd got.

"It's all right, dinna fret," said Jim testily. "I haven't broken anything." He felt his joints gingerly. "I'll have one or two bruises that's all. Just give me a minute to get my breath back and I'll be fine."

"But what happened?" persisted Betty solicitously, noting her husband's pallor. He has enough pain to contend with without the likes of this added to it, she thought helplessly.

Carefully and awkwardly, and with a pull from Betty, Jim reached for the nearest chair.

"It's just a silly wee accident," he said placatingly. "Look," he added, pointing to his feet. "I left my lace undone and tripped over it. Stop worrying now."

He had indeed neglected to tie his shoelace properly that morning, and hadn't realised that Betty had been standing on the loose end while they'd watched their daughter from the window. Betty was stricken with guilt.

"From now on," she vowed. "I'm going to check you over myself in the mornings."

"There's no need for that," returned Jim quite irritably, but recognising the glint of determination in his wife's eye, he knew there would be no arguing with her, and so he resigned himself to being fussed over for a bit.

Betty still hadn't got over her scare. "Perhaps I shouldn't go to Aberdeen today, Jim."

"Now what would be the point of staying at home?" asked Jim annoyed. Then seeing his wife's white face, he took a deep breath and relaxed. "What would be the point, Betty?" he asked patiently. "There's nothing wrong with me apart from a few bruises. Your mother's expecting you, and she'll worry if you don't turn up. Think how disappointed she'll be if she doesn't get to play with the bairn, and catch up on all your news. Now don't be silly," he added gently. "Away you go, and don't worry about me, I'm a grown man now," he smiled at his own attempt at humour.

"Are you sure?" asked Betty, looking him in the eye. "And you don't mind having your dinner at the Bruce?"

"Well, the hotel food won't be up to your standard, but I'm willing to make the sacrifice." His smile grew wider at his second attempt at humour that morning, and Betty began to relax.

"I think we could both do with a cup of tea, Jim. You've plenty time before you start work," said Betty reaching for the kettle.

Seeing that she wasn't completely convinced, Jim tried his usual ruse of changing the subject. "Have you thought about what we'll call our house?" he asked chattily.

"Well yes and no," answered his unpredictable wife. "I've thought of a few names. But then I've gone off them before I've got round to discussing them with you. Why? Have you thought of something suitable?"

"I might have," Jim replied, thankful to see that he'd got all his wife's attention, which meant that she was getting over the scare of his fall. "It came to me the other day quite by chance."

"Go on then," urged his wife when the pause had lasted too long for her. "What have you come up with?"

"Well," said Jim slowly, teasing her deliberately. "I was looking out the window from my work the other day and I realised that with the red-tiled hoosie gone, I look over to the two gables of this house. And I thought - why not call our house The Gables? What do you think of it?"

"The Gables," murmured Betty, and mused a while. "The Gables," she repeated, obviously deep in thought. Not too swanky? she asked herself. She mulled it over a bit more while she got out the cups. Finally she made up her mind. "Yes, Jim," she concurred. "I think that would be most suitable. The Gables it is."

Eventually Jim left for work well pleased with himself on both counts. His wife wouldn't worry about him any more that day, and the name of their house had been decided to his satisfaction. Would that all their problems could be solved as easily!

Meanwhile, Betty tidied away the breakfast things and got Sheila ready for the journey. As predicted, the child went wild with glee when told where they were going. She loved Grandma Cormack, and she loved going on the train! She was shining with excitement while her mother dressed her in her best clothes. Then Betty put on her own coat and settled her hat on her head. She pulled on her gloves, and pausing only for a cursory check in the mirror and customary pat of her hair, she took her daughter's hand and left for the station.

Betty took her time and set a gentle pace. She never hurried if she could help it because it put too much strain on her knee. On the other hand, Sheila seldom walked if she could run, skip, hop or tear along in a zig-zag fashion as bairns do. However, all it took was a sharp, "Sheila!" and she would be at her mother's side in an instant. Fond as they were of their child, Betty and Jim had no notion of spoiling her, and so although they surrounded her with love, they were very strict too.

Mother and child arrived at the station in good time for the train. Sheila was still too much in awe of its hugeness and assortment of loud noises, to let go of her mother's hand. It seemed like a long way down from the platform to the rails. So she stood quietly by, and watched everything with wide-eyed interest while her mother chatted to a few folk, including Donald the Horse. Eventually Sheila grew bold.

"Where's your horse today?" she asked him.

"He's happy grazing roon' the back," replied Donald.

"Why?" asked Sheila who continually asked that question.

"Well, he's nae very happy when he's at the station," replied Donald patiently. "Ye see, he's feart o' trains."

"That's unfortunate, given your line of work," said Betty.

"Aye it is," responded Donald. "But he'll get used to it in time. He's already better than he was, you know. Mony a time I ended up chasin' him takin' doon the road fan the train came in. Though I tied him up real weel, he aye managed tae break loose. Losh, sometimes he near got as far as the main road afore I caught up wi' him! Then I'd wish that I'd stopped to strap the load onto my ane back afore I'd chased him, for we'd twa o' us hae to come back to the station and pick up the load, only to have to ging a' the wye back doon to Main Street!

But he's definitely improvin'," Donald continued with a wink to Betty. "He has already bolted today. And we're both back in time for this next train - so we winna fa' behind wi' oor work the day!" He was shouting by the time he'd finished, for the train had rolled up to the station and the screeching of its brakes had almost drowned out his words.

Betty acknowledged Donald's humour with a smile while Sheila shouted innocently, "Is that nae your horse then?" and pointed to an animal, that looked very similar to Donald's, who was galloping across the Haugh at breakneck speed towards the village. "Dash it!" roared Donald the Horse, and took tearing after it.

Betty almost hurt herself laughing, and the engine driver, guard and porter, who were well acquainted with this scenario, wasted no time in shouting words of encouragement, among other things, to Donald whose fast-receding figure could scarcely have heard them

The train wasn't busy and Betty and Sheila got a compartment to themselves, which was fine, and no sooner had the train set out on its journey than the questions started up again. "Why are there two doors here mama? What's the other door for?" Why are there pictures on the walls? Why is there writing over them? What does it say? What's that rack for? Why is there a belt on the door?" Sheila's curiosity about her world was endless, and Betty's explanations were becoming more concise with all the practice she was getting. Eventually, though, she reached her limit, and encouraged Sheila to look out the window quietly instead.

Betty's main reason for going in to Aberdeen was to visit Milne's the Auctioneer's again. According to last Friday's Press and Journal, there was a Morris chair coming up for auction that she was interested in buying.

Over the last few years Betty had become quite experienced in buying at auction, and now had her own check-list of conditions to be satisfied before she bid for anything. First, she had to inspect it closely to make sure it wasn't broken or had woodworm in it. She wasn't too proud to buy something second-hand, but it had to be in perfect condition. Then she had to find out if she could buy a better or cheaper one new. Sometimes she spent almost the same amount of money on a second-hand one, because it was better made, and finished off in expensive wood like ebony, mahogany or cedar, that she could never afford to buy new. And once she'd decided to bid for something, she had to set a limit on how much she was prepared to pay for it. This had been extremely difficult for her in the beginning, when she'd got caught up in the excitement of bidding against other people, and had been reluctant to opt out when her ceiling price was passed. She was more sanguine about the whole process these days, and merely shrugged her shoulders if she missed out on a sale. A bargain's not a bargain if you overpay to get it.

And here Betty lapsed into a little daydream of auctions past, when she'd come home triumphant - like with the canteen of silver cutlery and the little oak bedside cabinet. And she smiled as she remembered retelling their stories to her dad later on. She was fair lost among her memories when Sheila's insistent voice penetrated her reverie and jerked her back into the present.

"Mama, I really do need the toilet," wailed the child plaintively. Guiltily, Betty wondered how long the bairn had been trying to get her attention, and at the same time she cast her eyes desperately around the compartment. She needed to find a solution - fast!

So this was how it came about, that mother and daughter shared their very first secret together. And it was by pure mischance that, with her daughter's attention being elsewhere at the time, the little girl misunderstood what her mother meant by 'a secret.' And Betty was going to have a red face about it later on!

It was chilly when they stepped off the train at Bucksburn an hour later, so they hurried through the streets to Grandma's.

Mr Cormack had lived long enough to know that his two sons had survived the war and was thankful for it. Bill, who had lived in Africa before it started, had elected to stay on there, and unfortunately had been unable to attend his father's funeral. Edwin had returned emaciated and in poor health. He stayed with his parents long enough to get fattened up by his mother's wholesome cooking, then he moved into lodgings and took up his apprenticeship with Stephen and Smith Advocates in Aberdeen again.

Sandy had finally moved out into a house in Stoneywood, which he was preparing for when he got married to Jessie the following year, 1923. Aunt Chat was living in Rickmansworth in the south of England, nowadays, with her husband David Mann, who hailed originally from Dundee.

All this meant that Mrs Cormack had moved alone into the downstairs flat of 16 Gilbert Road, not very far from her old house, where she had surrounded herself with her choice pieces of furniture. She had made many friends in Bucksburn over the years, who all helped to stave off any loneliness. Mr and Mrs Wright and their family who lived in the flat above, were good neighbours and kept a kindly eye out for her, thus allaying Betty's fears for her mother's safety. And of course Isabella adored visits from her daughter, especially when she now had her grandchild with her. To Betty's delight her mother had taken the Tiger rug with her when she moved, and it now graced the parlour where Sheila could play with it too.

Upon seeing her mother's wan face, for a second time that day Betty had thought about cancelling her auction plans. Isabella hadn't quite recovered from a bad cold that had kept her indoors for most of the previous week, but she insisted that she was feeling well enough now, even if she didn't look it. So, after an early lunch, and after having been assured for the umpteenth time that Sheila would be no trouble, Betty took herself off to the auction.

While she made her way to North Silver Street, Isabella and her granddaughter proceeded to spend a fairly busy afternoon together. Mrs Cormack was always happy to entertain the child in various ways, so first they took a short walk, and stopped to eat the small sandwiches they had prepared. Then, on their return, they baked some pancakes together. And all the time the bairn prattled on undisturbed by her indulgent grandmother.

*   *   *

"Oh mother I'm so happy I could dance a jig on the table!" beamed Betty when she burst through the door some hours later.

"I doubt that your jig would last very long with your knee in that state," observed her mother drily. She had noted with concern that her daughter was limping quite badly. "You've been told by the doctor, by Jim and by me that you have got to rest it more often you know."

Betty's face started to redden as she tried to defend herself. "You're right, mother. But I always see something that needs doing, and then I can't wait to get on with it. There never seems to be enough time."

"Then you've got to make the time," reprimanded her mother sharply. But when she saw her daughter looking so crestfallen, she relented. "Well now," she continued on a brighter note, "what have you been up to that's made you so happy, lass?"

"Oh mother!" responded Betty brightening at once. "I had a feeling that I was going to be lucky at the auction today, and I was right! I'm so glad you encouraged me to go after all."

"You and your 'feelings,'" smiled Isabella fondly. "Still, they've turned out to be more often right than wrong. Tell me about it then."

"You know how I've been looking out for a sewing machine since the bairn came along?" began Betty. She put her cup of steaming hot tea down on the table, and lifted Sheila onto her knee. "Well, when I got to Milne's, I had a quick scout around and found the Morris chair I was looking for. It was made of oak and upholstered in a plush velvet material. Its wooden arms and legs were well polished and it had obviously been well looked after. I knew at once that I wanted it, so I was definitely going to have to stay for the sale.

So I sat myself down on the chair and was ready to wait, and that's when I noticed what was next to it! 'It' was a square-looking cabinet that I think was finished in satinwood. It looked practically brand new, and I got off 'my' chair and examined it closely. It was a lovely piece of furniture and I kept running my hands over it, feeling that beautiful wood. But, tempting though it was, I couldn't justify buying another cabinet.

Then again, I was very reluctant to leave it. It kept pulling me back! Eventually, just out of interest you understand, I bent down and opened the door for a quick look inside. And when I peeped in, I saw that it was - of all things - a spanking new sewing machine! I knew I had to have it!

I took a chance and didn't open it any further in case someone else saw me and did the same. I didn't want the others to find out that it was a sewing machine, because I knew that that would put up the price. I really wanted it, mother, so ...I sat on it - and kept a sleekit eye on the oak Morris chair at the same time!

I had to wait ages, but it was time well spent because I was resting my knee," she grinned cheekily at her mother who responded with a smile. She'd always enjoyed her daughter's company, and even more so since William's death. Betty could always be relied upon to raise her spirits.

"It was just as well that I had a seat, because it took ages for my pieces to come up for sale. Then they both came one after the other. My heart was still thumping from buying the chair, when they moved on to the 'cabinet.' It was a bit obvious that I wanted it, seeing that I was sitting on it while I was bidding. But luck was with me and I got it at a very decent price, since no-one else had twigged that it was a sewing machine - even the auctioneer described it as 'a cabinet' which was luckier still for me. I got it for an unbelievably low price! Jim'll be so pleased!

Then I started to worry in case something was wrong with the sewing machine, and that I might have bought myself 'a pig in a poke.' I hadn't had a proper look at it because it had seemed more important at the time not to let the other buyers know what it really was. Me and my instincts!

But do you know what?" Betty asked with sparkling eyes. "After I'd paid for it, and was arranging for the carriage of both my pieces, a member of Milne's staff approached me. He told me that I'd made an exceptionally good buy with my sewing machine. It's an American model called "The Governor" and it had belonged to a bride who had died suddenly. The machine is in excellent working order and all the instructions and additional attachments are intact!

Just think of it mother. From now on I'll be able to make all my own dresses, overalls, aprons, petticoats, skirts, blouses - you name it. Then there are all the things that the bairn needs - she won't have to wear so many knitted clothes now that I've a sewing machine. There's new curtains and ...."

"And you'll be sitting down while you do them all!" smiled Isabella with satisfaction.

"Yes," replied Betty barely hearing her mother because her mind was still on all the future possibilities of her new sewing machine. " And I want to try my hand at making shirts for Jim. It shouldn't be too difficult, I was thinking. With the starched collars being detached I'll only have to make the body of the shirt. And I can make his left sleeve to fit him properly, instead of cutting off a perfectly good sleeve and finishing it off by hand. The collars are the most difficult part, but since we buy them separately, I'll only have to make the openings for the studs that keep the collars in place."

"What's this Sheila was telling me about toilets on trains now?" asked Isabella changing the subject unexpectedly.

"I've always thought that those detached starched collars must be the most uncomfortable things that..." continued Betty still in her world of endless possibilities afforded by her new purchase. "What did you say?" she asked sharply and now very alert to what her mother was saying.

"It was something Sheila was telling me," smiled Isabella. "She mentioned the toilets and compartments, and no corridors on the trains. What was she on about?"

"There aren't any toilets on the trains," said Betty sharply. "Sheila! What's this nonsense you've been telling grandma? Now I've told you that there's a difference between a tall story and a lie. I hope my little girl hasn't told a lie?"

"No, mama!" declared the bairn stoutly. "I haven't told a lie! I told grandma about the secret toilet on the train."

"Where did you get that idea from?" demanded Betty, obviously trying to keep her annoyance under control. "No lies now."

"Wheesht lass," intervened Isabella placatingly. "There'll be a logical explanation. Why, the lass is not yet three years old, Elizabeth. And three-year-olds don't understand the concept of lying."

"Mine does I assure you, mother!" answered Betty acidly. "Sheila! What's this about a secret toilet?"

"You know, mama," replied her daughter. She was puzzled at her mother's reaction. "You told me about it when I needed to go! On the big train!" The bairn was feeling confused by now. She didn't think that she'd said anything wrong - but looking at her mother's reaction she wasn't sure. She wasn't sure at all.

Betty thought back quickly.

"Oh no, oh no, I don't believe it," she said eventually as, for the second time during her visit, her face started to redden.

"You believe me don't you, grandma?" wailed the bairn.

"Yes, yes I believe you, lassie," said Betty quickly, and looked at her mother with a mixture of contrition and embarrassment.

"I shouldn't have been so hasty in condemning you, Sheila. Let's tell grandma all about it." Betty put her hand in front of her mouth and coughed in an attempt to cover her laugh. "It's all a mistake, mother," she said in a voice filled with self-reproach, while her eyes danced in amusement at what had happened.

"It doesn't seem like it at the moment, but it's quite funny really," said Betty shamefacedly. Her mother hadn't returned the smile.

"I think another cup of tea might help me to see the funny side of this," remarked Isabella neutrally as she reached for the teapot.

While she refilled her cup, the atmosphere began to relax. And, cuddled in her mother's arms, Sheila went back to feeling warm and secure. Betty sat and worked out how best to explain it all to her mother. It was time they were going, and she wanted her mother to be smiling when they left. She knew that her mother still missed her father very much, and always looked forward to her visits. But it was always sad to go and leave her on her own, and the least that she, Betty, could do, was to leave her laughing.

When she had sipped the fine warm tea, and had complimented her mother, again, on her tasty pancakes, Betty had her descriptions of "the event" worked out in a manner that she knew her mother would enjoy - and could enjoy retelling to her closest friends after they'd gone.

"As I said," Betty began. "We had an eventful morning what with Jim's fall, and the decision being made on the naming of our house. These things, and the extra cup of tea I made, meant that we were running late, by my reckoning, when we set off for the station. We were walking up Station Road when I remembered that I hadn't sent Sheila to the toilet before we left, so I meant to do it when we got to the station.

Well, we told you about our hilarious encounter with Donald the Horse, and again, we were on the train before I'd taken Sheila to the toilet. The bairn was right, we did speak about compartments and things. And Sheila

Two New Additions to Longside

Proud parents.

Sheila, who wanted to keep the chair afterwards.

Major Hutchinson opening Longside Tennis court (c 1922).

The Bauds Croft (1922/23)

Annie.

Annie & Beatrice.

Sheila making friends with that cockerel!

Sheila's Happy Childhood

TOP LEFT: Sheila and Grandma Cormack.

TOP RIGHT: Happy as the day is long.

LEFT: A sign of things to come.

Bill Cormack's Life in Africa

ABOVE: Bill's hotel in Nyasaland.

LEFT: Bill with his native staff.

BELOW: His wife, Janet, holding her customary cigarette.

thought that it would be a great idea if there was a 'tunnel' or as I corrected her, a 'corridor,' going up through the middle of the train, in case we got stuck in a compartment with someone 'we didn't like'!

So you can understand why I felt that it was my fault when she told me that she needed the toilet. I had to come up with something quickly, so, when the train pulled up at Aughnagatt Station, and I couldn't see a soul on the opposite platform, I lifted up the big leather belt and lowered the window as far as it would go, while Sheila took down her knickers. She wasn't all that happy with my explanation about it being a kind of secret toilet for children. But she sat on the sill with her bum hanging out the window, and held on tightly with her arms around my neck almost strangling me, while she relieved herself!"

"What if a train had come the other way?" asked Isabella both appalled and amused at what her daughter had done.

"I'd worked out that I would have heard it in plenty time," laughed Betty. "Anyway, it was better than trying to do it while the train was moving, because then I'd never have heard the other train in time - and how could I ever have explained to Jim how his bairn had come back without a bottom!"

Laughter broke free at last. "Oh Betty, you never stick for a solution - no matter how unconventional!" Isabella took out her handkerchief. "And this was her new toilet?"

"Yes and no, mother," replied Betty, her eyes equally moist. "You see I told her that this was to be a secret between her and me. How did I know what she was going to make of it?"

And the room echoed to the laughter of three generations - for Sheila laughed too although she wasn't sure what she'd said or done that had been so funny.

Then it was time to go. It had been a long day, and Betty wanted to be on her way. She'd got everything that she could have wished for - and more -this day.

And she had another, private, reason for wanting to leave fairly early. She had been appalled at the number of ex-servicemen dressed in their old greatcoats, whom she had seen standing on the street corners with begging bowls - in Aberdeen! She knew that times were bad, and a lot of men were out of work, but she hadn't reckoned on that ever happening in this area. The mood on the city streets could be unpleasant and, naturally, Betty was not wont to linger.

They were both tired by the time they reached Longside. With the initial excitement now wearing off, Betty was uncomfortably aware of the throbbing in her knee. Her legs and feet ached. Sheila was also subdued. Tiredness had set in and it was hard work for her little feet to make the journey all the way home. But they got there, and although Jim was busy working out the back, he had thoughtfully built up the fire so that the two voyagers were at once enveloped in the warm and cosy atmosphere of their own home.

While Betty set about making them some tea, Jim came in, having been alerted by their voices. He was glad to see them and it showed plainly on his face. After he had washed his hands he sat down by the fire, and Betty and Sheila between them brought him up to date on the day's enjoyments. Supper that evening was a fairly informal affair as Betty was really too tired to go to any great lengths, and Jim was happy to go along with it. He had reassured his wife that no ill was going to come to him from having eaten out at the Bruce.

Sheila was normally tucked up into bed after this meal, but her parents had a lot to discuss that evening, and Betty was content to let her tired bones sit awhile longer at the table. The bairn on the other hand, seemed to have taken a second wind and was sitting up beside her bright as a button, seeming to take in every word they were saying!

Eventually, Betty was the first to rise from the table and she was wearily drying the dishes while Sheila sat on her father's lap and began newsing to him about how her day had gone. Jim was being indulgent about his daughter's bedtime, and she, in turn, was keen to make the best of it. Sheila had to tell her daddy all about her afternoon at grandma's. By now, she understood what "a secret" was and she didn't include that part in her story.

Then, as children often do, she went off at a tangent and said, "Daddy, when I sit on your knee I can tell that you have one hard leg and one soft leg. My friend Alice says that when she sits on her daddy's lap, both his knees are soft. She says that's what a daddy's lap should feel like, and that there's something wrong with yours. Is she right, daddy? Should you have two soft knees?" And at her father's seemingly annoyed nod of his head, she continued somewhat querulously, "Why have you only got one soft knee then?"

Although she'd been in a tired world of her own whilst automatically drying the dishes, Betty had become instantly alert when her daughter's words penetrated her consciousness.

"Now Sheila, that's enough for one day. It's time you went off to bed," she commanded briskly, hoping to stave off what could be an emotional answer for Jim.

She had seen his body stiffen and his face go white. Her first thought was to protect him.

Dr Simpson's advice was ringing in her ears as if it were only yesterday he had given her his unequivocal advice, "Never ask him what happened. If he wants to speak about it, then let him. Have patience and let him. But if he doesn't - under no circumstances push him to tell you about it. Some things are better left alone. Now be sure you understand. Never ask him - but listen to him if he wants to talk about it."

Betty and the rest of the family had taken this advice to heart and had never broached the subject with Jim, not even in a roundabout way. Sometimes it had cut her to the quick when she'd watched an odd evening snooze turn sour on him, and his face would become contorted with pain while he got more restless. And she would watch warily and helplessly until he would finally waken with a start. To hide her own painful uselessness in these situations, she would pretend to be on her way to make a cup of tea or something - anything - to keep her busy while the colour returned to her husband's face, and the ravaged look had disappeared.

And now here, out of nowhere, her precious precocious bairn was unknowingly flying in the face of definitive medical advice - and asking her father to speak about his horror!

The blood was hammering in her ears and her heart was beating nineteen to the dozen. She lifted a hand to her mouth. How could this be happening?

"Oh the innocence of bairns!" she wailed inwardly, and held her breath.

Chapter 12

Best Nae To Let Auld Wounds Fester

Jim had stiffened at his daughter's question, but as Betty watched he gradually relaxed, and Sheila nestled comfortably into his bosie.

He stared at the fire for a few moments in silence and then asked softly, "Do you know what a bully is, lass?"

"A bad boy, daddy," answered Sheila promptly.

"Aye. That's right," responded Jim gravely. "And this story is about a bad man called the Kaiser who lived in Germany.

Now the Kaiser was a bigsie kind of man who had a lot of power. But he was greedy and wanted more and more land, and more people to rule over. So he trained up a huge army, and started taking control over his neighbours. The poor people in these countries tried their best to stop him but were too weak and there weren't enough of them. So the Kaiser got his own way, and an awful lot of men were killed.

When the people in Britain found out what he had been doing, they were angry and said the Kaiser wasn't being fair to the little countries round about him. He was being a bully. Then, when the Kaiser invaded Belgium, a little neutral country that wanted nothing to do with his war, it was the last straw. Britain got together with France and Russia, and decided to put a stop to the Kaiser's carry-on."

Jim settled himself more comfortably, and said reflectively, "I used to own a builder's yard at Portessie then, and employed thirteen men. Aye, there was always plenty of work for us."

He paused and looked into the flames as if remembering his old life, with an expression that was unfathomable to Betty.

"Anyway," he continued eventually, straightening in his chair, "I wanted to help my country stop the Kaiser. You see lass, if the big countries hadn't stopped him, the Kaiser would have got stronger and stronger, and tried to bully all of us. He was getting bolder and talking about 'Germany's place in the sun.' He even said it was his 'mission' to make Germany strong. Did you ever hear such dirt?"

There was so much anger and contempt in his voice that Sheila sat bolt upright, but Jim soothed her back into his arm.

"So I signed up with the Royal Engineers, and had to go to Aberdeen to learn to be a soldier." He smiled across at his wife. "It was there I met your mother."

Betty started to relax and was as interested in his story as her daughter, although a part of her remained vigilant.

"Next, I had to go to Greenock to learn about poisonous gases," Jim continued. "The Germans were very bad, and had started bombing us with gas shells and that was a cruel way for our soldiers to die. The gas rotted their lungs and they choked to death - once they'd inhaled the awful stuff there was nothing anyone could do to stop that happening. Our government provided us with masks to protect us from the gas, but they only worked if we got them on before the poison was released into the air. I remember my mask had green glass in the front of it, and when I put it on it was like being in the sea. It covered my ears too, so all the sounds were muffled, and it was just like being underwater.

So, whenever anyone shouted 'Gas!' we were all in a panic to get our masks on as quickly as we could - but sometimes our hands and fingers were so numbed with the cold, we could hardly fit the straps into place. There was one young man, I remember, couldn't get his mask fitted on, and he panicked and... it was a terrible way to die. Those mustard gas bombs did a lot of harm - a lot of harm." Jim shook his head sorrowfully.

Eventually he roused himself once more. "We had aeroplanes and submarines; and later on, we had tanks. But most of the war was fought from the trenches. We dug a large long ditch called a trench, and looked over at the Germans who dug a trench parallel to us, so that we faced one another. The space in between was called 'no man's land,' and we each tried to win that land for our country. Day after day we lived in that muddy hole defying the Germans. Sometimes we used canons against them, and sometimes we had to fight against them man to man, with our rifles and bayonets. Hundreds of thousands of good men died in those trenches.

It was boring and yet frightening. Although nothing happened for most of the time, we knew the firing could start at any moment, so we lived in a perpetual state of fear. It could be very dangerous sometimes - but we never knew when to expect it.

We lived in a trough dug out of the earth, so it was very muddy and dirty and cold. There was precious little water to drink, although we were surrounded with the dirty stuff. In the summer of '17 it rained so much the trenches filled up with filthy water and mud and a lot of men suffered from 'foot rot.' This meant their feet were so wet for so long that gangrene set in - and that usually meant their feet had to be amputated - cut off," he added quickly anticipating his daughter's query.

"It was a queer thing that," Jim continued quietly. "I knew a man who got foot rot, and they bound his feet and legs with bandages and told him to continue to work. So he did. You see, he told me afterwards that he never felt any pain. His feet and legs, right up to his knees were numb. So he was never aware of the damage - not until he was taken away in a medical train without his left foot! He had been so traumatised by the hasty operation performed in the field hospital, he hadn't understood what the doctors had done, until it was too late to protest. But there was nothing else they could have done, poor man.

Then there was the vermin - you know what that means - dirty rats and things. They would eat any rotting meat that was lying around, and if there was any decaying flesh from soldiers' wounds - well- they ate into that as well.

We were covered with lice too, and no matter how hard we tried to keep clean, they multiplied and gave us no peace from the constant itching. And if we scratched ourselves we ran the risk of opening the skin, which meant that infection got in. You see lass, our doctors have nothing to fight infection with, and the conditions in the trenches were so unsanitary, that if you got an infection you most likely died of it. I have never lived in such terrible conditions."

Most of this discourse had gone over the little mite's head, but she was merely aware that her father had stopped talking, and that meant she would be sent to bed.

"Did you fight with Sergeant Darling, daddy?" she asked quickly, hoping to delay the inevitable.

Jim went quiet as if unsure whether to continue talking about his wartime experiences, and Betty, instantly protective of him was about to intervene when Jim nodded acknowledgement of his daughter's question.

"No lass," he replied. "Not every man went to war. Some were too young - you had to be seventeen years old. And some men were too old, like Sergeant Darling. Other men had to stay at home and work on their farms so that the nation and our troops could be fed. Others had to work in munitions factories - where they made bombs and grenades and things needed at the front. The men who worked in those factories got so fed up of people calling them cowards for not going to war, they finally got the government to issue them with special badges, so that people would stop miscalling them.

It wasn't just men who went to the war either. Nurses went too, and they were just as brave as the soldiers were. These women saved our lives, and gave hope and strength to many of the young lads. Without them many more soldiers would have died. The doctors could do the surgery - but it was the nurses who understood what the men were going through emotionally, and were a tower of strength. They had to live and work in terrible conditions too, but I never heard them complain. They did everything they could for us soldiers, and I've a lot of admiration for them.

We needed to have strong bodies - and strong minds as it turned out," he added quietly. "And there were people called Conscientious Objectors who needed to be strong, too."

"What's a 'conshuss jecter?" demanded Sheila sleepily, rubbing her heavy eyelids with little fists.

"They were called Conscientious Objectors," Jim said the words slowly, "because their consciences wouldn't let them kill men for any reason whatsoever. They are also known as Pacifists. It comes from the Latin 'pax' meaning peace. And these people believed in resolving problems by peaceful measures, and wouldn't condone taking another man's life."

Betty had to smile at her husband who had never subscribed to "baby talk" and here he was, using Latin to explain a word to a child!

"It was a brave man, indeed, that said he was a conscientious objector!" opined Jim strongly. "People could be very cruel to them." He paused as if marshalling his thoughts into some kind of order, and when he was satisfied, nodded his head and continued his narrative.

"When the war started we thought it would be straightforward to put a stop to the Kaiser's shenanigans, and all us able-bodied men were glad to down tools and fight. Thousands of us joined up and were cheered on by the folk back home. But Christmas came and went and we were no nearer to victory. So many of us were being killed that, naturally, the men back home grew reluctant to join us. The government started putting pressure on them to sign up, printing posters all over the place saying that their country needed them, and telling them that they had to protect their wives and girlfriends. In other words, the government tried to shame them into joining up.

That only worked for a little while, so Lord Kitchener introduced 'Conscription.' That means," he said immediately, forestalling his daughter's next query, "it was illegal for fit and healthy men NOT to join up. In other words, it was made compulsory for most men over seventeen to go to war - unless they had a good excuse not to. If they had a weak heart like your Uncle Sandy, or were needed on a farm to provide the nation with food, then they were allowed to stay at home."

Jim could have saved himself the explanation, because Sheila had lost her own little battle against sleep and was lying flushed and vulnerable in her father's lap. However, encouraged by a gentle smile from his wife, Jim continued to face his demons.

"It was also 'acceptable' for men to swear they were Conscientious Objectors, although this excuse was very unpopular," he continued with a frown. "But it certainly wasn't an easy way out of going to war, because after conscription started these men were hated even more. You see, everyone thought the 'conchies' were cowards and gave them white feathers as a sign of their shame. People heckled them in the streets and threw stones at them as well as insults. What most of them didn't realise, was that it took an exceptionally brave man to go against the herd and act on his principles.

The lucky Conchies were conscripted into the Ambulance Service where they had to stretcher the wounded soldiers from the battlefield to the First Aid posts. Remember, these men refused to carry rifles or bayonets, and hadn't any means of defending themselves if they were caught by the enemy.

Other Conscientious Objectors had to remain at home - but weren't allowed their freedom. They were locked up in places like prisons and made to suffer. Because of their beliefs, they couldn't help make ammunition or have anything to do with the war effort. So they were given horrible useless demeaning jobs to do, like cleaning out toilets with a toothbrush, or picking out stones from the sand in quarries. Many of them were forced to live in dirty miserable conditions supervised by men who hated and despised them. These warders openly displayed their contempt for the Conchies and were exceedingly cruel to them.

I remember someone telling me when I was in hospital, that their mother had sent them a copy of the "Manchester Guardian" containing an article written by a Conchie who was locked up in Shore Camp in Cleethorpes. This man, James Brightmore, wrote to his mother from what he called The Pit. He had been reported for not having saluted a soldier quickly enough - a trumped up charge - and was sentenced to 'detention' for twenty eight days.

Everything personal had been taken off him, except by chance, a small pencil, which he used to describe what was happening to him at Shore Camp. He found some paper and hid what he wrote, so the paper wasn't found until after his death, before the end of the war. He wrote that he was bullied all the time, and constantly put in to detention on the slightest excuse.

Now there was one time, which turned out to be his last, when they put him into solitary confinement - that means he was on his own - and gave him only raw rations.

He had to dig a pit that started off three feet long by two wide, on the surface, had to be ten feet deep, and taper off to two and a half feet by fifteen inches at the bottom. He struck water while digging this hole, but was ordered to carry on. He then had to put in two planks of wood just above the water line, and stand on them all day while the rain and wind and sun beat down on him. He couldn't move, or bend his knees or sit down or anything, couldn't even relieve himself. Rats ran round his feet and nibbled at his boots, then his laces, then his legs and feet and he couldn't even kick them away, or use his hands to shove them off. He was forced to stand there every day - but he didn't finish his detention of twenty eight days, because he died.

At nights he had written in secret about the brutality and senselessness of it all; and how he was being driven mad and to despair by men who could barely read or write but who, because they were in charge, abused their power over him and the other Conchies." Jim became quiet.

"Aye," he said sadly. "Man's inhumanity to man..." And he shook his head slowly.

"Back to our muttons, though," he said tersely, and Betty steeled herself. Jim's narrative was moving inexorably towards his awful accident, and she could hear his pain as he struggled to set the scene.

"We had special instruments for listening in to the Germans' telephone conversations to find out where and when they were going to attack our line next. But sometimes they sent pretend-messages to confuse us.

Every so often we were ordered to attack, and would rise up against them. When I say 'we' I mean us soldiers and our officers. We were told what to do by the commanders at home, who had never been near the trenches and didn't understand the conditions we were up against in France. Often, these commanders were working from information that was well out of date, and sometimes their orders were clearly suicidal for us. If they had been there and seen the situation for themselves, they would never have told us to charge. But we couldn't defy these commanders! The officers repeated their instructions to us - because they couldn't defy them either. We couldn't question them at all, and had to obey every command - whether we thought it was sensible or not. If we didn't obey the orders we were shot for desertion."

He shook his head sorrowfully.

"Imagine, Betty. Our own soldiers were forced to shoot the deserters in front of the rest of us as a warning, to show what would happen to us if we ever questioned orders 'from above.'"

He looked her in the eye, beseeching her compassion. "They weren't all deserters. In some cases the gas had ruined their minds, and they weren't responsible for their actions."

Then his voice became clipped and formal, as he returned abruptly to his narrative, "We had to be very careful in the trenches, because if our heads appeared above the parapet the Germans opened fire at us. And if we got hit, it was very difficult for the medical orderlies to get to us and take us to safety."

Betty listened aghast. This was nothing like the reports she'd read in the newspapers. She'd read about the honour and pride of the young men, and about their glorious deaths on Flanders fields - not about this filthy, mean drudgery in the trenches.

Jim carried on. "The army wanted to use my skills as a Master Builder to put up water tanks for our troops, so after some more specialised training near London, I was sent to France.

The Frenchmen were a right greedy lot," he said after a pause. "They tied up the pumps and made us soldiers pay for the water we needed. And the women were right bold hussies!" he added disapprovingly. "They used to come and watch while we washed ourselves in the sea. But a few of our lads were fearless enough to outstare them, and pelted the missies with sand and stones and chased them off!

I had some German prisoners working for me. Doctors, teachers, labourers - they all helped me to build the concrete water tanks. Jolly good workers some of them were too," he added musingly.

Then Jim's face set like a mask and Betty held her breath.

"One day, we were making our way up to the front when one of our lads let his head show above the parapet, trying to pass the others. Naturally, he was seen, and the Germans opened fire immediately." Jim paused remembering.

"I was badly wounded and had my left leg blown off. I was carried to a Field Station thirty miles from Wimereux in Northern France, but that was shelled before we could reach it. So I, with the other casualties, was loaded on to a train early in the morning, and sent to Wimereux itself.

However, because of troop movements, our train was pushed into a siding, and it wasn't until after ten o'clock that evening that we finally arrived at the Australian hospital there. By that time my left arm, which had also been wounded, had turned gangrenous and it too, had to be amputated - above the elbow. I was very ill...."

Here again Jim stopped talking and Betty wondered if perhaps she should intervene. But quietly Jim returned to exorcising his painful memories.

"I had this dream of walking through a dark wood and there was a fierce wind blowing all the time, so I had to struggle and struggle to get through. And finally, after what seemed like ages, and I had no strength left, I managed to get there - wherever there was. I suppose I'd been fighting for my life and was determined to win.

When I was really ill, I was told that I kept asking for a drink of milk, and one of the nurses, Nurse Pocock, sent someone to get some for me. Milk was in very short supply then, and it took ages before the nurse found some. When she got it, Nurse Pocock boiled it, to prevent infection, before giving it to me. And do you know, after all the trouble she had gone to, I wouldn't drink it, saying that it wasn't Betsy's milk. Betsy was the cow we used to have at home in the Bauds."

Jim was clearly upset at the memory of his refusal. However when he spoke next, his voice was firm and determined.

"I was lucky to have ended up in that Australian hospital, because it was far better equipped than any of the British ones in that part of France. The doctors told me that if I hadn't been such a 'good living' man - neither smoking nor drinking, I wouldn't have survived."

Again Jim became contemplative and sat in silence with his young daughter cuddled up asleep on his knee, having finally laid all his old ghosts to rest, and Betty fought hard to keep back her tears.

"Jim, I never guessed that things were so bad for you over there. We knew it was difficult - but no one told us what was really going on. 'The Evening Express' and 'Daily Journal' only reported the good news, and how well 'our boys' were doing, and how honourable you all were and..."

"I know. I know," interrupted Jim calmly.

But he said nothing else for a while and Betty could see that something was still troubling him.

At last he broke his silence and said, "When I got back to this country I read the papers and listened to folk speaking about the war, and I knew I couldn't tell them what really happened. Oh, I don't mean you personally, Betty. It was just that...well...it would have been like a betrayal of all the soldiers that had died, if I had started telling people what the war had really been like. It would have hurt so many mothers and widows and...and I couldn't bring myself to say anything. So I joined the conspiracy of silence, and held my tongue.

When I was in Stobhill Hospital in Glasgow, I heard about a poet called...now let me see...it was a foreign-sounding name...Sassy...Sass...Sassoon. Yes, that was it - Seigfried Sassoon. He was one of us, despite his name," Jim smiled but it didn't reach his eyes. "This Sassoon fellow was admitted into Craiglockart Hospital in Edinburgh at the same time I was in Stobhill, and he wrote about the war as it really was. But his poems didn't rhyme, and nobody wanted to hear what he was saying - he was locked up in an asylum after all - so they ignored him.

I thought if a talented man like that couldn't get people to recognise what was happening, then I'd be a fool to try."

After another lapse into silence he eventually roused himself and indicating the sleeping child on his knee, asked Betty to fetch his Bible.

She returned quickly with the small leather-bound missal, always kept in a pouch along with other slim booklets and old pieces of paper. Jim took it and thanked her perfunctorily, his mind obviously back in the past once more.

"It was a wise decision to build the Cenotaph," he announced at length. "Thousands upon thousands of soldiers didn't make it back, and all there is to show for each life lost over there, is a little patch of ground marked with a cross. I can picture all the simple crosses laid out in rows and rows in the fields with red poppies grow wild. It's only proper that we celebrate a 'Poppy Day,' you know." He nodded his approval.

" The choice of poppies is very suitable for remembrance, I think. There's their link with the crosses set up in the fields, and their colour, red, that'll remind us of the blood spilt over there. And because they're flowers, they will die. But then they'll grow again, being hardy specimens." Jim reflected on the scene. "They're like our indomitable spirit that can never be crushed."

But the memory wouldn't go away.

"Row upon row of crosses," he continued bitterly. "Some soldiers were so badly dismembered that only bits of them were buried. Sometimes the recovery of a soldier's 'Record of Pay' book was all they had to go on. If it wasn't handed in at the end of the week, the soldier was presumed dead and on the strength of that pathetic piece of evidence those dreaded black-edged telegrams were sent out to loved ones back home. The poor distraught people were told their sons or husbands or brothers had 'died bravely' - and nothing else. They couldn't be told how or where the deaths had occurred in case the letters fell into enemy hands. They were left with a single piece of typewritten paper as the only proof of their loved-ones' death. Few of them can afford to visit their grave so it's only right they should have a focal point for their grief now, in this country. And they have the consolation that it might be their loved-one lying in the Cenotaph - the tomb of the Unknown Soldier."

He shook his head as if chasing a thought away. "Perhaps Sassoon and his ilk were wrong to write about the harsh realities of the war, Betty. I've observed that people in general prefer poems that rhyme, and heroic pictures of a war that was noble and glorious. They don't want to be told the ugly details of what victory really cost us."

Jim proceeded to rifle through the pouch Betty had fetched for him, and retrieved a crumpled worn piece of paper. He carefully unfolded it and Betty saw that it was covered in neat handwriting.

"Now that the Cenotaph has been built, we'll always commemorate our dead by celebrating 'Poppy Day,'" he announced decisively, "and this is the poem it gets its quotation from. It's called 'In Flander's Fields,' and was written by John McRae, a Canadian Medical Officer who died just before the end of the war. Despite the horrors he was living through, the old principles were still intact and safe in his mind as ever."

Jim took a deep breath, then quietly and without emotion read the lines:

> "In Flander's fields the poppies blow
> Between the crosses, row on row,
> That marks our place; and in the sky
> The larks, still bravely singing, fly
> Scarce heard amid the guns below.
>
> We are the Dead. Short days ago
> We lived, felt dawn, saw sunset glow,
> Loved and were loved, and now we lie
> In Flander's fields.
>
> Take up our quarrel with the foe:
> To you from failing hands we throw
> The torch; be yours to hold it high.
> If ye break faith with us who die
> We shall not sleep, though poppies grow
> In Flander's fields."

The last words were enveloped in silence.

Then he broke the spell and said conversationally, "I used to think the government was wrong to publicise only the 'better' bits of the war - the successes and the medals won. I believed they ought to tell people how sordid and horrendous the war really was - and make it so awful they would never go to war again. But now I realise there can never be a limit to the price of freedom, and no matter how bad or dangerous the circumstances, we must 'pick up the torch' again and again.

You know, while I think Life is a very precious gift, I see Freedom as a human right, and we all have a duty to protect it. No one can be allowed to deny us our liberty - certainly not the Kaiser. And if the freedom of this little mite on my knee is ever threatened I'll go to war again, so help me. But, Betty, I truly hope I never have to!" The anguish in his voice was palpable.

"Now, it's time this little girl was in bed," he said briskly, as if shaking off the shadows of his past. So Betty lifted the recumbent bairn from his arm and made her ready for bed. Sheila slept throughout her mother's ministrations and was soon cosily tucked up in the land of nod. They had a last cup of tea together, and taking her cue from her husband, Betty discussed the day's news with him as if nothing out of the ordinary had happened that evening. Later, Jim made for the bedroom while Betty gave the room its last tidy-up.

Although she had managed to converse quite naturally with him, her head was spinning with these new and frightening images of Jim's war experiences. She had been horrified by it all, but thankful that he'd spoken about it at last. She knew now the damage was limited to his body, and thankfully, his mind was alright. That he managed to talk about it was proof to her that he was emotionally whole again. No wonder he'd been unable to talk when she'd gone down to Stobhill!

She was just about to turn down the light and go to bed when she came across the pouch she'd fetched for him. When she picked it up a small red cloth-bound parcel fell onto the floor. And since she was still reeling from his revelations about the war and couldn't settle anyway, she satisfied her curiosity by opening it there and then.

It was "THE PROPERTY OF THE WAR OFFICE," and gave instructions to the "men of the army reserve" on what to do when "Mobilisation" took place. It also contained Jim's discharge certificate.

It certified that:

"No. 40276 Sapper James Mair has served with the Colours in the Royal Engineers for 2 years and 89 days. His 'conduct' was 'very satisfactory.' An excellent Builder. Wounded 31.8.17.

Cause of Transfer or Discharge - Being no longer physically fit for war service.

Identification Marks :- Loss of left arm and left leg."

Betty held the certificates in her hand, her thoughts in turmoil. There was no mention of the pain and suffering he had endured. No mention of the high principles so valiantly fought for. Nothing....not even a thank you

She remembered the brave young builder who gave up more than £360 per year and the prestige of owning his own business, to fight for his country. She thought back to the shell of a man she had seen in Stobhill Hospital, who couldn't do the work he loved any more. She recalled his strong determination to find some kind of employment and his ill-fated attempt to retrain as a Sanitary Inspector. He had refused to give up, and instead knuckled down to learn about being an Inspector of Poor - a sedentary job that went against his active nature - and for an awful lot less than £360 a year. She smiled sadly at their plans for living on his salary plus his full pension - and the dreams they'd dreamed together.

Then her sorrow turned to outrage and her lips pursed in anger when she re-lived the day his battle against the government had been fought....and lost - and they had had to accept that for as long as he persisted in working, his pension would remain at the reduced flat rate of £2 per week, as if he was being punished. Despite everything he never lost heart and always retained his pride - so difficult at times. Even now he was determined that she and the bairn would want for nothing, and had the steel in him to build his own home!

Betty loved her husband and was fiercely proud of him, especially tonight after sharing his war experiences. Bitter tears threatened but she brushed them away with the back of her fist in a curious mimicry of her daughter's actions earlier that evening. Betty was seething with impotent fury against deity and government and knew she was further from sleep than ever. She started banging each piece of breakfast crockery onto the table one by one to let off steam. Then she plumped up her cushions with unnecessary vigour until finally, anger spent; she slumped into his chair and sobbed.

"This," she thought heavily, weighing the documents lightly in her hand. "This is a poor reward for our freedom."

Chapter 13

Guid Claes And Keys Let Ye In

Betty shielded her eyes against the pale yet penetrating rays of the November sun a few weeks later, and scrutinised her windows. 'There's no two ways about it - they're definitely in need of a clean,' was her clinical assessment.

As in the year of her marriage, autumn was being reluctant to relinquish its hold over the earth and hand over the reins to winter. And as a result the weather was unseasonably warm.

She could have being doing without the physical effort of washing her windows that morning since she had made arrangements to go out in the afternoon. However she set to work with a briskness that belied her humour, and hoped to get the steps washed too, before Jim came home for his dinner.

Everything went fine and it seemed that in no time at all she was on her knees with the bar of Preservine, scrubbing the steps. As she got on with the job in hand she thought about her proposed visit to Mrs Penny that afternoon. Mrs Penny, no relation to Joseph up at the Terrace, lived in the croft at Boglash and was a genial old woman who had befriended Betty. Up until last week she had always arranged her visits beforehand, so Betty had been quite surprised last Wednesday when Mrs Penny stopped outside, tied her sheltie to the gatepost, and knocked on Betty's door. Betty had recognised the old woman's discomfort immediately, and now she smiled at the memory as she wrung out the cloth because she never, ever, would have guessed its outcome.

"Come in, come in Mistress Penny," she had invited immediately. "Is everything all right?" Mrs Penny's face was red, whether from her exertions with the horse or for some other reason, Betty couldn't tell. She'd looked keenly at Mrs Penny who suddenly seemed to have been struck dumb. Her elderly friend was wearing her usual sealskin coat with its bare patches, and her usual flat boots. The only thing different about the woman that day was her manner. Usually, she was confident and hearty and would speak rather loudly. Her whole demeanour that day had been different.

"Would you like to sit down?" Betty had asked the woman, giving her a reassuring smile.

"It's the Bachelors' Ball, Mistress Mair!" the old woman had blurted out. "Yes?" Betty had replied, puzzled. She knew about the great annual affair attended by nearly all the local single young men dressed in their finery. The committee was comprised of the most prominent bachelor farmers in Buchan, and everybody who was anybody attended the lavish supper and dance. It was usually held near the end of the year and was followed in January by the Ladies' Ball for the farmers and their wives. She had also heard that the drammies at these affairs were very very frequent! But she couldn't see her connection with either of them, since Jim was neither a bachelor nor farmer.

All this time Mrs Penny had been agitatedly shuffling her feet and wringing her hands, and it eventually dawned on Betty that the woman was embarrassed about something.

"What is it, Mistress Penny?" Betty had prompted gently. "Is there anything I can do for you? You have only to ask," she had urged in an attempt to allay the other woman's discomfort.

Thankful of the younger woman's perspicacity Mrs Penny had finally come out with it.

"It's my son, Jock," she had begun eagerly. "He aye goes tae the Bachelors' Ball, but this year he hisna a fite sark. His last een's fair deen and I've cut it up intae dusters! I hid thocht I would hae managed tae get him anither een by noo, but I hivna been able. I was wondering if you could see your way to lending him ane o' your man's fite sarks. Jock's got a fite collar so it's just the sark I'm after."

Betty had thought quickly. She had been making her first attempt at a shirt on her sewing machine but it was nowhere near finished. All of Jim's bought shirts had been cut off at the elbow of the left sleeve, but luckily she'd then remembered that she had a new one waiting to be done, so she did have a "whole" one to lend her friend.

"Of course he can borrow one of Jim's shirts, Mistress Penny," she had smiled. "I'm sure Jim won't mind - and Jock must go to the Ball!" Both women had laughed: Mrs Penny because her son would be happy, and Betty because the problem could be solved so easily.

"Now, of course I dinna expect to get this favour for naething," Mrs Penny had asserted bluntly, returning easily to her usual frank style of conversation. "When I next tak' my 'sheepies' wool' to the 'Oo Mill' in Peterheid, to be made intae blankets you, Mistress Mair, must hae een - if you'd like."

Betty had realised she was being offered one of her friend's beautiful herringbone, feather-light blankets at a reduced price. They were far too expensive to give away for nothing, and farming wasn't doing well enough for Mrs Penny to be so generous. She also knew that Mrs Penny usually sold her blankets to the Kirkburn woollen mill for a bit of money to spend at the local roups.

"Why thank you, Mistress Penny," she had beamed, "that would be most suitable! But I must insist on paying £1, because I can't accept such an expensive blanket as a gift."

The two women nodded in complete understanding and the deal had been struck.

Betty worked the bristles into the far corner of the bottom step intent on dislodging a bit of mud she'd spied there, and thought with pleasure of the new herringbone blanket that would soon be hers. As well as being of the finest quality, it would be deliciously warm at night, and its light weight wouldn't aggravate the nerve endings in Jim's left arm, where the pain had been getting worse again. The surgeon had warned Jim this might happen after such a crude amputation, and if it did he would have to have the endings pulled out. Jim was stoical by nature and wouldn't complain, but the continual pain and sleepless nights were evident on his white face. Betty had finally persuaded him to see their doctor, who had arranged for Jim to be seen at Woolmanhill, and they were meantime waiting for an appointment.

Betty was so lost in her thoughts that she didn't hear him the first time. So Donald the Horse raised his voice and repeated his opening gambit, "Losh, Mistress Mair, ye canna tether your child to that gatepost as if she was a horsie!"

Jerked from her reverie, Betty stopped trying to push the bit of mud off the edge of the step and got stiffly to her feet. She looked from him to where Sheila was now standing with a rope tied around her waist, and the other end tied round the gatepost. Betty blushed a bit and shook her head.

"I have to, you know, otherwise she'd be out the gate and away."

They both looked down at the bonny leggy bairn who had stopped playing in the little plot of earth, and now stood, spoon in hand, "lugging in" shamelessly to their conversation. Sheila was wearing a drop-waisted dress cut down from an old one of her mother's. On her feet were the boots that she had been pressed into earlier that morning, and beside them lay her discarded knitted socks. The sun shone down on her short bobbed hair and was turning the tip of her freckled nose red and covering her skinny arms with freckles. It was obvious the young lass yearned with every fibre in her body to be unshackled and let loose in the village.

Betty smiled with a fond sigh. "My daughter's such a flibbertigibbet if I let her go I might never see her again until hunger drives her home, which could be any time knowing Sheila - and I've made arrangements for us to go out this afternoon."

"But, Mistress Mair," the carter responded gently, winking at Sheila, "she's a bairn and nae a horsie."

Sheila nodded her vigorous assent, and could see her mama weakening.

"Och, Mr Milne," said Betty ruefully as she absently rubbed her knee, "I wish I could."

Sheila looked at her mother pleadingly and made herself look like the frailest, most injured and miserable-looking waif that she could. Standing there, spoon in hand, she waited with pathetic mute longing showing clearly in her eyes.

She almost succeeded, because Betty was hesitating - then suddenly she made up her mind.

"But I can't!" she asserted quite firmly. "There's no ill coming over the lassie, and I need to go out this afternoon. If I let her go now, there's no telling when she'd turn up again, nor what kind of state she'd be in.

I thank you kindly for your concern, Mr Milne, but she's fine as she is." And bidding him a respectful good day Betty lowered herself back down on to her knees and disposed of the piece of mud with one resolute flick of her brush.

Sheila regretfully waved goodbye to the old horse who, like her, had stood patiently waiting throughout this exchange. And with a shrug of his shoulders and a broad wink to Sheila that made her laugh, man and horse went on their way.

After lunch, Betty washed up the dishes, smartened up her bairn, and with a light heart looked out the money to take to Mrs Penny. She plonked her captive child into the wooden pushchair and tucked Jim's white shirt underneath the top blanket. It was her opinion that you couldn't sneeze in the village without someone giving you a blessing, then half the village hearing that you had pneumonia, so Betty wondered idly what the gossips would make of her visit to Mrs Penny that afternoon.

She placed her hat securely on her head, and giving a final glance in the mirror to check that she looked respectable, she set out for her appointment. Before her lay a considerably long journey to Boglash, about two miles away at the end of a rough track leading off Drums Road.

As she turned up Cooper's Brae, Miss Strachan, her next door neighbour, was working in her garden. She happily put down her trowel and came over to greet Betty on this lovely afternoon.

"How are you, Mrs Mair?" she enquired with a smile.

There followed the usual exchange about the weather, and child rearing, and other such pleasantries.

"And are Mr and Mrs Hutchison coming back to your house next year?" asked Betty, referring to the young couple from Peterhead who had rented Miss Strachan's cottage for the summer.

"Yes," nodded Miss Strachan with a chuckle. "They enjoyed themselves so much they want to do it all again next year, - except for one experience they definitely don't want to repeat," she added mysteriously.

At Betty's inquisitive look Miss Strachan giggled again before giving her explanation.

"Mrs Hutchison gave me a good laugh before they left. She told me that during the first week of their holiday here, her husband had gone out shooting with friends, and had come back with a hen from one of them.

Well, of course it was up to Mrs Hutchison to see to it - you know - pluck it and prepare it for the oven. But they hadn't brought their cook, and she confessed to me that she hadn't had a clue how to go about it, but she hadn't liked to tell her husband.

'Now mind and see to that hennie the day,' her husband had advised her the following morning before he left.

'Aye, aye,' his wife had replied.

When her husband returned at lunchtime he had asked if she had 'seen to the hennie yet,' and she had had to say that 'no' she hadn't, but that she would.

When he left, she had forced herself to take a look inside the sack but had been so horrified by the sight of the dead chicken that she'd tied it up again with a shiver, and left it be.

That evening, when her husband returned he had expressed surprise that he couldn't smell the chicken cooking, and had asked her again if she had seen to it.

She had truthfully replied that 'alas, no, she hadn't quite got round to it.'

Well, the same happened the following day - her husband got the same answers to the same questions, and that night he pointed out to her that the hen would definitely have to be cooked the next day if it was to be any good.

And what do you think, Mrs Mair?" continued Miss Strachan with mounting excitement. "The following morning before he left, her husband had turned to her and said, 'Aboot that hennie....' And his wife had looked fearfully at him.

'Ach tae Hell - jist you beery the bugger!' he'd commanded firmly, to the immense relief of his wife."

And at this ending to the tale the two women fell about laughing.

"And they never ate chicken the whole time they were here!" Miss Strachan ended in a crescendo that had both women holding their sides with mirth.

And so Betty took her leave of her neighbour, and with a smile still playing on her lips she pushed the pram on up and across the road, and turned into Laburnum Lane. Most of the long low cottages here held two families, one at either end, each with its own front door.

Maggie Shepherd lived in the nearer part of the first house on the Lane, and being crippled, she spent most of her time sitting at the open window looking out with interest on to the road. Betty had to stifle a giggle when she remembered a tale, which was probably true, about how Maggie had worn drawers all her life, made by herself out of durable cotton. One Christmas a well-meaning friend had given her a present of a pair of knickers that had elasticated top and bottoms, and Maggie had been tickled pink by them. Sadly however, she had soon afterwards reverted to her former garb - drawers, the excuse being that "she was fair smored" wearing knickers!

"It's a fine day for a walk, Mrs Mair!" she shouted across. Then when Betty replied in the affirmative, Maggie continued, "You'll be away to Boglash aboot your blanket nae doot?" And she accompanied this enquiry with a knowing smile.

The depth of the woman's information fairly took Betty's breath away. Caught off guard, Betty gave her an astonished nod, and passed quickly on.

'Village life!' she fumed to herself. 'Will I ever get used to it?'

In Burnbrae, farther along the road, Bob McKenzie the painter was away at work, but Helen Massie his housekeeper was out cleaning dust off the windowsills and came across to say hello.

"Would the bairn like ane o' my farthing biscuits?" she asked kindly.

Betty had heard of these by chance from the children in the village, when they had discussed Mrs Massie's farthing biscuits whilst on the other side of her garden hedge, not knowing that Betty was there and could hear every word. According to them, Helen would spread her Whyte's Butter Biscuits liberally with jam, and then scrape most of it off with her knife, leaving only that jam which had lodged in the indented pattern of the biscuit. In discussing this skill the children had indulged in not a little griping about her dexterity with the knife, and both Betty and Jim had been vastly amused.

Much as she would have liked to witness this woman's particular skill, Betty had to decline her offer and explain that they had an engagement that afternoon.

"Some other time then," smiled Helen kindly, for despite Helen Massie's stinginess with the jam, she was good-hearted and the bairns recognised it. "Please tell Mrs Penny I was asking for her," were her parting words which left Betty speechless for a second time!

She bounced the pram on, up past Linshart and on by the new cemetery. The old cemetery lay through the Lych Gate outside the Old Kirk, and had been filled to capacity. So this piece of land on the outskirts of the village had been designated as a last resting place for current villagers.

Betty bumped the pushchair along the road. Being very basic the vehicle had no springs, and it bounced over the rough terrain constantly threatening to eject its occupant. Sheila clung on for dear life, clearly enjoying the challenge; laughing and screaming in a manner that belied her steely determination to stay put. Betty offered her the chance to walk with her for a while but the thrawn little creature gleefully shook her head and held on all the more tightly. Mother and daughter laughed together as they took the right fork in the road, and turned left down into the valley where Boglash lay. The croft was basic and busy. Mrs Penny kept her pony, some sheep cows and hens with help from her two sons: Jock who was going to the Ball, and Tam who was slightly simple but a hard worker for all that.

The inside of the house was usually in a bit of a shambles because the good woman hated housekeeping, and anything and everything came before clearing up the clutter. But the genuine warmth of her welcome averted any criticism of untidiness and Mrs Penny was always glad to stop what she was doing, so that she could sit down with her guests and have a cup of her well-brewed tea by the open peat fire. The light sprinkling of ashes at their feet by the fireside would be ignored by her visitors as they bit into her delicious sponges and cakes baked on the sway in a three-legged black pot (just like a witch's, thought Betty privately). Mrs Penny produced some of the finest baking in the village. In particular, she made ginger sponges, which were superb. She really was a good soul.

Betty was grateful to sit down after her long walk, and her daughter was equally relieved to be freed from the pushchair. Sheila settled down happily on the fender stool, and Betty mentally resigned herself to the extra washing of her child's clothes. The two women enjoyed their cup of tea and immersed themselves in conversation.

"What's that?" interrupted Sheila, pointing to the corner.

"That, dearie, is Jock's gramophone," answered Mrs Penny proudly. And to please the bairn, she opened the lid, wound up the handle at the side and lowered the needle onto an old 78 record.

Sheila skirled with delight at the noise. "But where's the mannie?" she demanded, clearly puzzled. And since no explanation suited her, she crawled behind the gramophone and went from side to side of it, listening to the amplifier. She even reached up and looked inside it, but complained that she still couldn't "find the mannie!" The two women joined in laughter at the child's attempts to make sense of it.

Eventually, having concluded their business and got up to date with each other's news, it was time for Betty and Sheila to depart, and the women took their leave of each other, each happy with the transaction that had taken place. Mrs Penny was already looking forward to the next roup and Betty was looking forward to seeing the new herringbone blanket on her bed. And, of course, Jock's attendance at the forthcoming Bachelor's Ball was now secured.

Mother and daughter took to the road again. Sheila resumed her battle with the pushchair; and Betty overcame her weariness by thinking about how best to describe this visit to her husband in order to bring out a laugh. They raced on homewards, stopping only for a short word with Mrs Mutch and accepting one of her pandrops, which she was famous for dispensing throughout the village.

When tiredness threatened they burst into song to keep them going, and this resulted in their arriving home in high spirits, despite Sheila's new bruises from her bumpy ride, and Betty's throbbing knee and foot. They couldn't wait to tell Jim all their news and cheer him up. He had been involved in a lot of extra work as Poor Inspector lately, and had been looking tired. Added to this, Betty knew his arm was troubling him more than he was letting on. So she was looking forward to getting a laugh out of her husband when she regaled him with their latest exploits.

They were somewhat taken aback therefore, when they met him and saw that he was smiling hugely. In fact, as they drew nearer to him, it became obvious that Jim was in a state of barely concealed excitement.

Between pain and changes at work, Jim had had little to smile about recently. The government had brought in The Poor Law Act that extended relief to able-bodied persons "who had exhausted their right to covenanted benefit," and this had added greatly to Jim's workload.

Nowadays, with this post-war depression, it had become necessary for a great many people to apply to Poor Inspectors to supplement their incomes. A lot of them complained bitterly to the government about the way that they were being treated under this Poor Law, for instance they were very angry at being given "food tickets" instead of money. These new applicants were unaccustomed to holding out their hands for subsistence, and claimed that it was the government's "duty" to supply them with a reasonable standard of living. Naturally, the money for these extra benefits had to come from somewhere, and so the industrial sector was mainly targeted. The result was that the "poor" and the "workers" both resented the government. And all the while, the stigma of having to ask for Poor Relief was intensifying people's hatred of the whole system. Some of them were taking their protests into the streets so it was just as well that The Emergency Powers Act was still in force, and the army was helping to enforce the laws on the streets, because these were desperate times for a lot of people.

Although it never got so bad in his parish that he had to request outside help, the atmosphere during some of the interviews could be intimidating - not that they ever got the better of Jim by their threats. But sometimes there existed pressures that Jim could have done without, seeing that he could never sway from the strict implementation of the regulations, regardless of where his sympathies lay. However, where a Christian interpretation of the rules was possible, Jim applied it, and conscientiously tried to help his fellow men.

The post-war depression continued to bite hard, and the big industrial cities were hurting. In Glasgow, many shipyards had been forced to close down, and parents who couldn't afford to feed their families any more, began to send their children up north into the countryside, where they would be looked after by the state. These children became known as "boarded-oot bairns," and it was the responsibility of Jim and the other Poor Inspectors to place them into local homes. The people who took these children in would either get a maintenance allowance in the form of food or clothes, or they could choose to take the money. Mostly, they chose the money and dressed the children in hand-me-downs from their own offspring. Inevitably, this arrangement suited some children better than others.

In Jim's parish, kind people from the Cuttyhill at Rora took in many of the boarded-oot bairns from Glasgow. After placing them with families, it was part of Jim's remit to visit these bairns and check up on their circumstances. He wasn't given any extra money for the travelling involved, so he'd no option but to take a piece with him and set off on his tricycle round Rora.

Rora comprised numerous small crofts and but-and-bens spread over a wide area five miles to the north east of Longside, and covering such a district on his tricycle was no mean feat. Very occasionally, if the weather was particularly inclement, Jim hired a local taxi from Dod Gunn and did the round at his own expense.

Betty didn't always agree with his placement of some of the children. "But that's an afa place to put a bairn in, Jim," she'd complained once, unimpressed by her husband's choice. "It's aye in a mess!"

"The child won't learn how to keep a house clean, Betty, but mark my words, she'll know what it is to be loved, and that's more important. That child will be very happy there," was her husband's sanguine reply.

The constant changing and updating of the 1921 Act resulted in Jim's having an ever-increasing workload, and for a while now he had been looking for some kind of physical outlet in his spare time. His house was built, with nothing more he could add to its interior, so he had been feeling restive without a building project in hand. The pain from the stump of his left arm was worsening and all he could do was wait for word from the hospital. He couldn't take refuge in the routine of his work when things were in such an upheaval, and the winter loomed long and wearisome ahead of him.

Then out of the blue, he had been visited at his work that day, by some folk from the village. They had announced themselves as "representatives of a group in the village who were interested in having a tennis court built." They had set up a committee for this purpose, and Mrs Hutchison of Cairngall had agreed to be president, with Miss Low as Vice President. The chairman would be Mr Wilson Thomson, and the post of Secretary and Treasurer had been accepted by Mr H.E. MacKenzie. They had suggested a piece of land beside the meal mill might be a suitable location and they wanted Jim to check it out. Then, if he thought it would do, they wanted Jim to build the tennis court for them.

Of course, Jim had accepted this new challenge with relish!

Understandably, at teatime that evening Mr and Mrs Mair had a lot of news to impart to each other, and many plans to discuss.

"I'm really pleased for you, Jim," smiled a delighted Betty. "It's a great honour to have been asked. But you don't think you might be taking on too much, do you?" she asked solicitously. "I mean, you're not keeping too well and..."

"The hospital will soon sort that out," interrupted Jim gruffly.

Betty could see that she was treading on thin ice here, but concern for her husband made her speak out.

"You haven't been keeping very well, Jim, and although I know fine that you could do it, wouldn't you be the better of a rest? After all, you don't know how you'll feel after you come out from hospital."

Now that he fully understood the reason for his wife's hesitation in supporting him taking on the project, Jim concentrated on setting her mind at ease.

"I understand your concern, Betty, but you see, of late I've been feeling a wee bit bored with not having something to build - especially in the evenings. Boredom makes the pain worse. And what with all the extra work as Poor Inspector I'm more than ever in need of some form of recreation at night when I can relax. You know I can't sit twiddling my thumbs."

Betty had to smile at this last bit, for she had yet to see her husband sitting doing nothing! "Oh, Jim, I shouldn't have doubted you," she smiled. "It's just that I've been a bit worried about you."

"Well, don't worry any more!" commanded Jim confidently and with a grin. "I've been given the best medicine tonight. Building this tennis court is just the tonic I need!"

Betty grinned back at him then checked suddenly, "Jim," she asked warily. "What do you know about building tennis courts?"

"Why - not a thing, my dear," her husband laughed. "But I'll soon remedy that!"

"I might have known," smiled Betty, happy to see Jim's animated face.

She had every confidence in him, and knew that the job would be done to the highest possible standard. In a queer way she had missed all the activity that surrounded a building project, and she found herself almost looking forward to the early mornings of cement mixing, followed by the sounds of men busily working out the back every evening. Jim's right, she thought to herself. This proposition probably couldn't have come at a better time for him, and it'll help him get through the long winter ahead.

It had been an eventful day for both of them and Betty was still thinking it over as she tidied up later. She was feeling bemused by it all, and fell to contemplating how Jim was going to get to grips with the building of a tennis court. It would be a sizeable project, and one that she wouldn't have a clue where to start. The longer she thought about it the more problems came to mind until she was overwhelmed by the responsibility of it all.

So, with a shrug of her shoulders she mentally put the whole thing into her husband's capable hands. And without realising it, she imitated her mother when she absent-mindedly shook her head from side to side, and muttered with a smile, "Whatever next?"

Chapter 14

Better To Face The De'il

The tennis court project was the fillip that Jim needed to boost his flagging spirits and get him through the winter. After he had inspected the corn yard near the meal mill, he agreed it was entirely suitable for this purpose. The benign old gentleman, Major Hutchison of Cairngall, had already expressed himself in favour of the project that was to be presided over by his wife, and now he offered to rent the ground to the villagers for 1/- per year. After these satisfactory arrangements were finalised, Jim settled down to work.

During the dark winter months he learned as much as he could from books, about building a tennis court. Naturally, cement was to play the largest part in the building of it. He learned that if the surface was to be playable during, or after, the rain, he would have to raise the centre slightly for the water to drain off. There was a knack to doing this that left the playing surface completely playable and still allowed the balls to bounce true. The double court was also to be surrounded by a high fence, which meant he would have to build cement blocks and pillars to hold the metal stanchions. Jim drew up the appropriate plans, which were passed without any problems, and then worked out the sizes and shapes of the moulds he would need. He decided on the best approach for laying such a large expanse of cement using his own tools and equipment. Meanwhile some of the members started to raise money for the materials by organising various fund-raising events. They were going to have a Whist Drive before

Christmas followed by a Fair in early spring - and that was just the beginning of it.

When winter was drawing to its close, Jim's appointment came through to attend Woolmanhill. His visit required him to undergo a general anaesthetic this time, when the specialist would remove what was left of his arm up to the socket. Although Jim didn't like hospitals, which was understandable, he submitted himself to the medical system once more, and immediately felt much better for it. By the time he was discharged the pain was back under control.

Then, with the lighter mornings and the evenings growing longer, their back garden was filled once more with the noises of labouring men. Jim had happily resumed his former pattern of working as soon as daylight appeared, going to his 'real' work all day and returning to his project all evening until the sun went down. He laid the surrounding walls himself then was pleasantly surprised when a group of local lads offered to help him. Jim worked them like professional builders, with no bad language allowed and only hard graft accepted, and he was loud in his praise of these young men. They willingly gave up their free time to help, followed Jim's instructions to the letter - and never asked to be paid for their efforts. A satisfying atmosphere prevailed during these working hours.

But just as life is never all bad, it is never all good either. Jim's mother died at the end of February the following year and he was deeply affected by her demise since she had been a strong influence throughout his life. To say that Betty was more than saddened by it would have been an exaggeration. The breakthrough that she'd hoped for had never happened. Old Mrs Mair had always kept Betty at arm's length and had steadfastly refused to relinquish her hold over her son. It was symbolic of Betty's decision never to make her man choose between his mother and his wife, that she never encouraged him to grow his moustache again, even though it had suited him and he'd been so proud of it.

His mother's death required the whole family to travel to the Bauds and attend her funeral, and whilst there, arrangements would have to be made with regard to Annie's future. For once, the office was closed while both Betty and Jim went to Findochty.

Here was another new experience for Sheila who had no idea of what death meant, but when she saw all the people at the croft dressed in solemn black clothes knew that something was wrong. Then, when she saw her Auntie Annie all upset and crying, Sheila shed tears too - although she didn't know what for. She was told her grandmother was dead and gone to Heaven, and, strangely, having a rest in Findochty cemetery. She was in awe of the sombre old men dressed in black wearing or carrying their black bowler hats, and felt oppressed by the morose atmosphere. Recognising intuitively that she should make herself inconspicuous, she spent her time exploring the Bauds as children do, searching every nook and cranny, except for the front parlour where she was forbidden to go by herself. During this visit, Sheila had her first run-in with the bold cockerel when she went to the dry lavatory. She fared no better than her mother and had to resign herself to scratched ankles.

Their stay didn't last long. After the funeral was over it was decided that Annie would remain at the Bauds with financial assistance from Jim and Bill. The Mairs then returned home to Longside after arranging for Sheila to return in the summer for a holiday.

The young lass didn't have long to dwell on the mysteries of death because that Easter, at the tender age of four and a half years, she took hold of Violet Souter's hand and started off for school full of excitement. Strictly speaking, this wasn't Sheila's first attendance at the school, because during one of her former meanderings through the village she had ventured on her own to the Little Schoolie on the outskirts. She had knocked on the door and told Granny Gray pertly that she had "come to school!" The smiling infant teacher had humoured the bairn by giving her a slate and letting her sit with the 'little ones' for a while, before sending her back home.

As it turned out, Sheila loved school, and at home would pretend to teach her dollies all kinds of nonsense. But, no matter how much a child enjoys her education, the highlight of the academic year must be the Summer Holidays - and in this Sheila was no exception.

It had been pre-arranged with her Auntie Annie that Sheila would spend a long part of the summer holiday up at the Bauds along with her older cousins, Dorothy and John Jack, who would also be there for the school holidays. Jim was going to take her up to Findochty, and her Uncle Sandy and her new Auntie Jessie were going to take her back as far as Aberdeen station. Betty had concluded that Jessie must have been "bent suitably to her brother's will" for he was going to marry her at last. Their wedding was to take place in Aberdeen, and then the honeymoon pair were bound for Elgin. After that, they had been persuaded to stay a few days, for free, at the Bauds, before seeing Sheila safely back to Aberdeen.

"Now eat up your porridge and let's have no more of your nonsense," said Betty briskly to her young daughter.

After several attempts at eating the stuff, Sheila had declared herself too excited to finish it all. But it was going to be a long journey up to Findochty and she needed the nourishment provided by a good breakfast, so her mother's common sense prevailed and she was made to clean her plate. It seemed like an age to Sheila before she climbed down from her chair and eagerly helped her mother to shut the suitcase.

Betty had long-since acknowledged Annie's poor washing skills and knew that she always spread her clothes to dry on the whins that surrounded the croft, thereby bleaching and snagging everything that passed through her washtub. As a consequence, she had decided to pack only one "good" frock for her daughter to wear on Sundays, and the rest of the items in the case were chosen for their future consignment to the rag pile without a qualm.

The clothes had been looked out for the last two days, and now all that remained was for Betty to put in a few basic toiletries. Two liberty bodices, two pairs of knickers, three pairs of socks, a cardigan, two frocks, a petticoat and a smock completed the list of clothes her bairn would require for the next five weeks. Sheila was then allowed to put in Bessie her doll, and a book of her own choosing. Naturally the choice of book changed continually until the lid was finally shut.

The Mairs all left the house together, giving themselves plenty of time to get to the station. Betty was coming to see them safely off, and carry the light case containing a few bits and pieces for Jim's overnight stay with his sister. There were also some sandwiches in it for the journey. Unless the circumstances were exceptional, Betty and Jim could never go away on outings like this together, because one of them always had to man the office. This was Jim's turn for a weekend off. He had been working hard and got the tennis court project off the ground and now he deserved a wee break.

The adults progressed along Main Street and up Station Road while Sheila ran back and forth, tripping over her little case, and chattering with excitement all the way. Jim and Betty smiled indulgently at their daughter's adventurous spirit. The railway's current rules were that Jim could take his tricycle with him on the train for nothing, and since the croft was a good two miles out of Findochty it was going to be very useful for getting there.

Once into the station they bought their tickets and stood waiting on the platform. While they were there, they heard the familiar clip clop of a horse and cart approaching, and sure enough Donald the Horse hove into view.

"I've a few things to pick up from the Peterheid train this morning," he announced. "And the Davidson's chairs have arrived at last, so they'll be glad o' a sit doon the nicht," he observed, as he made his way to the back of the station master's office.

"Are ye gaun far?" he speired on his return, eyeing the two tickets in Jim's hand.

"Yes," answered Jim abruptly.

Donald accepted without rancour that he'd get no further news out of Mr Mair. "Is it you fa's biding?" he addressed Betty. And when she nodded in affirmation he offered her " a lift doon the road."

Betty accepted it with alacrity. Apart from saving her the walk, she knew that Donald would make the journey interesting by imparting the latest village news to her. She also recognised that Donald's offer wasn't motivated purely by altruism either, because she knew he would do his very best to winkle out everything concerning Jim and Sheila's trip on the train!

She looked down at her daughter fidgeting quietly by her side. "Now Sheila," she said briskly. "You'd better go to the toilet before the train comes because you won't get another chance for a while. And I dare say your father won't accommodate you by letting down the window," she added with a sidelong peek at Jim while she grinned. She took Sheila's hand and led her into the toilet.

It was cold inside and smelt of damp. A constant draught caused an eerie whistling sound when they closed the door behind them. Sheila was much too excited to function properly but was equally keen not to suffer any ignominy whilst out in public with her father. Big girls didn't do that sort of thing. The lavatory was dark with a high grill-covered window as its only source of light, and Sheila was panicking lest the train came and left without her. However, duty eventually done, Sheila went back through and washed her hands under the cold water tap then dried them on the cold damp towel hanging from a screw on the wall. She took her mother's hand and hurried out into the bright sunshine on the platform.

As they started to climb the metal footbridge that would take them over to the other line, Donald rushed forward to take care of the tricycle. It was a bit awkward for Jim, but it didn't take long, and Donald was thanked profusely for his help. Jim didn't like being obliged to anyone, but was grateful nevertheless at times like these. There was a thin line between pride and stubbornness.

The delay wore down Sheila's nerves and she was very relieved when they'd all got to the other platform before the train came. But her respite was short-lived, because her mother proceeded to give her a new fear to worry about.

"Now, Sheila," her mother said sternly, "you be a good girl and do what Auntie Annie tells you. Do you hear me?"

Sheila nodded her head vigorously. "Yes mama," she agreed.

"Well you be sure you do now or...or...Annie'll give you a flea in your ear. So mind and do what she says!"

Betty looked across at Jim and gave him a conspiratorial wink while they both smiled at the thought of Annie trying to impose any kind of discipline! However, because they were so totally involved with sharing the joke, they failed to see the spasm of fear that flickered across their daughter's face at this threat. The train's strident whistle put paid to the question Sheila had been about to ask, and the moment passed in a flurry of noisy smoky anticipation.

Huge billows of steam issued from various parts beneath the engine and carriages, and loud cranking and hissing noises deafened the passengers as the train ground to a sedate stop. Donald quickly made his way to the guard's van at the back of the train to put in Jim's tricycle and retrieve his consignment, while the Mairs chose their carriage.

Everything happened very quickly after that. Their goodbyes were said, the doors were closed, the guard waved his flag and the train let out a hiss that grew to a whistle. Then, slowly and in a stately manner, it started cranking its way out of the station. It trundled along in a straight line for the first mile or more, quickly building up speed as it went, and was well on its way to Mintlaw station by the time Betty and Donald the Horse set off back down to the village.

Sheila sat back amidst her opulent surroundings and looked around their compartment. The seats on either side were well upholstered and covered with scratchy material that made her legs itch. She counted four number tags equally spaced above each bench that divided them into four seats, with a white antimacassar above each one. Sheila wasn't tall enough yet to avail herself of these, but simply noted their existence in the same way she observed the luggage racks above them and the radiator grills below them. The two big windowed doors had heavy leather belts with holes in them for letting down the windows. There were blinds above the door windows and the side windows too, and she saw wooden slats on each side for pulling the blinds down to different levels.

Most appealing to Sheila though, were the framed posters above each of the benches, and when he saw his daughter's obvious interest in them, Jim obliged by answering her questions. The one facing Jim urged him to go to Edinburgh, while Sheila sitting opposite her father, was invited to admire the attractions of Aberdeen. Having spelled out their names, Jim described where the two cities were situated on the map of Scotland. The old castle on top of the rock dominated the one poster, while in the other, the boats in the harbour claimed her attention for a while longer. The shapes in it were very simple and the huge letters above them called Aberdeen the Granite City. The posters were bright and bold, and even though she was young, they fascinated Sheila for a while.

Then she looked out the window at the lush countryside whizzing past. Soon they stopped at Mintlaw and shortly afterwards at Maud Station Junction. Sheila held her breath as an older boy threw open their compartment door, looked over his shoulder and shouted, "I've got one dad!"

But it turned out to be a false alarm because the boy disappeared when his father found a suitable compartment farther down the train. Sheila heaved a sigh of relief and turned her thoughts inward. How was she going to ask daddy her very important question? She really had to find out about the fleas and what to do with them. And she needed to know all about them before they arrived at Findochty!

But she never got the chance to enquire after the fleas, because her father chatted to her the whole time. He told her the names of the various stations they stopped at, such as Auchnagatt and Arnage. In between the stops, he described the farmlands they were passing through, and told her all about rotating crops. He pointed out barley fields and corn fields, and explained how the grain landed up at the meal mill. He also spoke to her about the Bauds and about the things he used to do there as a lad. Sheila felt very grown up and important getting all this attention from her father. She sat up straight and listened very carefully to all that he said. She didn't want to spoil things by asking what might turn out to be a very silly question although she was desperate to know the answer. What about those fleas!

It seemed that, in next to no time, they had arrived at their first destination. They alighted at Aberdeen and Jim collected his tricycle. They hadn't long to wait for the northbound train, and soon had left the two long black tunnels behind them.

When the train stopped at Kittybrewster an older man, obviously a farmer by his clothes and walking stick, joined them in their compartment. To Sheila, the white-haired man looked ancient, but he seemed so kind and friendly that she didn't mind his intrusion too much. He soon entered into conversation with her father and Sheila realised that apart from feeling troubled by the fleas, she was also feeling quite tired. She found herself leaning against the upholstered pad by the side of the window, and struggled to remain awake while listening to the soporific background repetitive beat of the wheels on the rails. The continual murmuring of the men added to her sleepiness.

The stranger confirmed that he was a farmer and said that he had just come from the mart. He had bought a bull that day and it was tied up in one of the cattle trucks. Sheila tried to imagine what it was like to travel in a cattle truck, and wondered how the bull was getting on with the movement of the train. With childish logic she eventually concluded that it was just as well the beast had four legs for balance - and promptly fell asleep.

After they had exhausted the state of local farming, the men's conversation turned towards politics. Lloyd George had led his country to victory in 1918 and made a lot of social changes. Now he was in Opposition sponsoring a programme of national reconstruction, and the two men debated this at length. Jim didn't think that Lloyd George would have much success with this idea, although he was in agreement with most of the social policies that the man wanted to implement should he win the next election. The current Prime Minister, the Right Honourable Stanley Baldwin was considered, and found to be fairly acceptable by both men.

The old farmer then introduced King George V into the discussion and went into some detail about the precarious state of that monarch's health. Then he changed the topic and asked Jim what he thought about the Bolsheviks in Russia? Taken by surprise, Jim meditated for some time before answering. But just as he started to give his opinion, the farmer interrupted him and explained that the train was slowing down for his stop. He apologised to Jim for the intrusion before thanking him profusely for having made the journey so interesting. At this point the train rolled into Inverurie station, and the old farmer pulled down the window, reached outside to open the door, and was off to the cattle truck to retrieve his bull. Jim sat back well pleased with his journey so far.

Just as the door was being closed again, a young man jumped aboard beside them. He was either very confident or very nervous, because he had no sooner sat down than he struck up a conversation with Jim. It turned out he was a university student at Aberdeen who was going home to Buckie. He was reading English, he said, and blushed as he pulled a paperback book from his pocket. The book was by Agatha Christie, and Jim observed with a dry smile that he hadn't been aware that the popular authoress had attained university status. It turned out the young man was very enthusiastic about murder mysteries, and had read most of her novels. Jim too had read a few and they ardently discussed her books for some time. Both men had read a good deal more than just crime novels and the journey passed quickly for them. Jim relished this second chance encounter.

Sheila had woken up as the train drew into Inverurie and been watching out the window since then. At first she'd been disappointed that someone else had replaced the old farmer, and was claiming her father's attention. But, by the time the train had passed through Inveramsay Junction Sheila had quite forgiven the young man, because she was mentally trying, again, to get to grips with the new fear in her life.

She knew all about fears. Sure, she had had to run the gamut of the cockerel snapping at her heels every time she went to the dry lavatory up at the Bauds. She scoffed at the idea of ghosts haunting people, although a little part of her was never absolutely sure about their non-existence. Every noise and scary thing about night time had turned out to be a false alarm. The noises had turned out to be sawdust settling in the lath behind the plaster in her bedroom. The dark shadows had been just those - dark shadows of something real. But on the other hand, she had been brought up to fear God who was a sort of a ghost that everyone believed in - so she kept an open mind on the subject. She feared doing something wrong at school but that was a different kind of fear because she could escape the tawse by doing what she was told. And of course everyone knew about the bogeyman!

But what happened when you got a flea in your ear? A flea was a little blood-sucking beastie that jumped about. To get it in your ear must be something horrible because it was a punishment of some kind. Did it drink your blood till you had none left? Was it tickly and did its tickling drive you mad? Did it bite? Or did it eat its way into your brain? What if it laid eggs?

At the very idea of this, Sheila shuddered violently and refused to follow that line of thought altogether. Instead, she decided that when she got to the Bauds, she would take the bull by the horns. She would find out where Auntie Annie kept her fleas, and then give them as wide a berth as possible!

Having solved the problem to her satisfaction, Sheila gave herself up to enjoying the passing countryside. Since she had wakened, her father had taken to interrupting his conversation in order to read out the names of the stations to her, so she knew that Oyne and Insch were behind them. Jim told her to look out for Leith Hall before they arrived at Huntly. She thought she caught a glimpse of it, but couldn't be sure, because by that time her eyes had gone funny through not allowing herself to blink. Then the train veered right at Haughs Junction and went up to Tillynaught Station, where it branched off left and made for the coast.

Sheila craned her neck eagerly for her first glimpse of the sea - and at last there it was - in all its sparkling wonder! It was vast. She could see it stretching far off to the horizon of soft fluffy clouds away in the distance. It seemed ever so warm and inviting. Her father remarked that to look at it today, it would never occur to you that it could be cruel and kill people. It was calm and bright and totally unlike the dark brooding menace that could whip up huge waves and overturn the little fishing boats dancing brightly on its surface today.

Portsoy was the first stop on the coastal route, and then the train made its way across the viaduct at Cullen, which was thrilling for Sheila. When they had come up for grandma's funeral, Betty had told her that her great grandfather had helped to build this viaduct, and today Sheila felt a burst of pride as well as excitement when they crossed it. The next stop was Portknockie, followed at last by Findochty.

Much to Jim's annoyance the station master rushed to help him down from the train, but he forestalled any awkwardness by asking him to fetch his tricycle from the guard's van instead. The man checked his movements, and after a moment's indecision sped away to the back of the train. Jim easily manoeuvred himself down on to the platform while Sheila jumped lightly to the ground beside him. By the time Jim had reached back inside the compartment to retrieve the cases, and taken his leave of the youth who had made the journey so shortsome, the station master had returned with his tricycle.

"I expect you've come home for a bit of a holiday then?" asked the station master affably. Jim smilingly agreed, then made a show of checking on Sheila's safety to avoid being pumped for gossip.

"There's Auntie Annie!" trilled Sheila, and lost her grown-up poise momentarily as she jumped up and down with childish glee.

Unfortunately for her aunt, living all her life in her mother's shadow had left her shy and awkward amongst people. She was mortified when various heads turned in her direction, and she rushed forward, picked up Jim's case, and instinctively held it up in front of her like a barrier against the world.

"It's good to see you again, James," she squawked, her eyes darting nervously hither and thither, desperate to escape attention. "You too, Sheila," she added, turning purposefully towards the station entrance. "Have you been a good girl?" And she set off without waiting for an answer. "Come away home. Come away."

Once out of the station and away from the unwelcome stares of strangers she gradually relaxed and slowed down, giving her guests the chance to catch up with her. And at a more leisurely rate, the threesome turned their backs on the village lying to their right, and instead took the track on their left, over the bridge. As they started on their long two-mile journey they heard the train doors being slammed shut, followed by a piercing whistle, and with a loud wheezing groan the train embarked on its steamy exit.

They followed a roughcast road; grateful that it hadn't been raining recently, for it would have been much harder work ploughing over the resulting slippery stones. Instead, today the road was dry and dusty and allowed them to make good progress with Sheila's small leggies stepping along in her button boots, her little hands clamped around the handle of her case, and now, Annie talking nineteen to the dozen. They took only a few stops, ostensibly to give Sheila a wee rest, but really for Jim to admire the sun setting over Bin Hill. And in this way they soldiered on until they faced Jim's old home.

The croft looked very solid and secure to Sheila, and although it had been a very sad place on her last visit, there was no sign of any unhappiness this time. Daddy and Auntie Annie had talked and laughed on the way from the station, and the house now held a smiling welcome for her.

Jim felt the tug of much older memories as his home welcomed him back. Yet, while he was grateful to be here, he couldn't help noticing numerous small differences around the place that hinted at a new more benign rule.

Perhaps the rows of vegetables weren't as straight as they once were, and the ruts in the road looked as if they should have been filled in more often. The grass had surely grown a sight longer than the family was used to, the windows could be doing with a wash, and many more criticisms could be levelled at Annie's husbandry. But the truth was, despite the loss of manpower, and the lack of money, Annie was managing to keep the place going in her own haphazard way.

Jim looked at the old croft with deep contentment and voiced his appreciation of his sister's efforts. Poor Annie almost burst into tears of gratitude, and only then did Jim realise how nervous she had been coming up from the station. She had prattled on about various changes she had made, and at times he had thought her voice had sounded almost hysterical, and her laugh a bit forced. Now that he knew she had been looking for his approbation, it all fell into place. Poor Annie had so little self-confidence.

To augment the weekly contributions from Jim and Bill, Annie had rented out some of the land. She had kept the hennies, and now sold their eggs to her neighbours and some folk from the village. She sold some of her tatties too, and had recounted other new little ways she had implemented to save money, and now she could relax because her brother was happy with all the changes.

They made their way steadily to the front door and Sheila was desperately hoping that Auntie Isie (or Isabella as she was christened) would not have time to put her teeth in before they arrived. Auntie Isie was a loveable dear who bought a new hat every year and wore it every day, indoors and outdoors too. She kept her false teeth on top of the sideboard where they were readily to hand should a visitor arrive unexpectedly. Betty had thought it best to prepare Sheila for these little idiosyncrasies so as to forestall any embarrassment.

The door opened as they approached, and there was Sheila's Auntie Isie standing in the wood-panelled porch beaming at them and saying, "Come awa' in. Come awa' in." Sheila noted with disappointment that she had her teeth in. Since her mother had told her about Auntie Isie's teeth Sheila had made up all kinds of fantastic images in her mind as to what her auntie would look like without them in. Oh well, Sheila was going to have to wait a little while longer before she witnessed the "toothless" vision.

Isabella Brown, as she had become when she married a minister twenty-five years her senior, had been a widow for some years now - as had been expected. Mr Brown's bachelor brother had left his sister-in-law a huge old house in Cullen called The Elms, and Isie was in the habit of letting out this house every summer to a shipping family from Glasgow who came up with their maid, nursemaids, and cook.

Isie and her youngest daughter, Marguerita, stayed at the Bauds during this time. Margueritta worked at the Gasworks office in Cullen, and had to cycle there and back to the croft every day. Isie's son, Jim, had recently emigrated to Canada and was working on a farm out there. Isie's other daughter, Annie, had been clever enough to go to University, and whilst there had fallen in love with Kenneth McIntosh from Drumnadrochit. After he had been ordained, they got married and went out to India. As Annie saw it, she was required to wear riding clothes and other stylish outfits that befitted her new station in life, and her Auntie E.J. (another of Jim's sisters) had willingly paid for all of them, as well as for most of her favourite niece's trousseau. The bills hadn't ended there, and E.J. was well used to her letters constantly asking for money, which she hadn't the heart to refuse.

Auntie Isie wasn't particularly proficient in money matters, but she recognised the importance of renting out her home every summer, so she and Margueritta shared a room at the Bauds. There was no doubt that both women enjoyed the extra company too, it made a fine change from rattling around their huge old draughty house in Cullen.

The row of colourful geraniums growing in various old pots and tureens, still sat in the front windows. And as she followed the grown-ups into the kitchen, Sheila noticed with satisfaction that the assortment of sepia postcards pinned on the wood-panelled walls of the porch were still there as she remembered them. Uncle Bill travelled all over the world and diligently sent home postcards. Consequently, sepia pictures of all kinds of exotic places covered every surface of the porch, making a unique and interesting entrance.

In the presence of adults, and especially if one of those adults was her father, Sheila was brought up to be "seen but not heard." So while the grown ups exchanged pleasantries and brought each other up to date with their current news, Sheila took to thinking about the fleas again. "Where could they be?" she wondered. "And why haven't I seen them before now?"

She cast her eyes round the room, intently looking for a potential storage place for them. She was so preoccupied that Auntie Annie had to ask her twice, "What are you looking for, Sheila? You've such a solemn face on you. Just you drink up your tea, dearie."

This was it! Never one to baulk from danger, Sheila squared her shoulders and took the bull by the horns. She asked boldly, "Where do you keep your fleas, Auntie Annie?"

Her artless question caused a lot of spluttering and clacking of teacups as they were rattled back into their saucers. All three grownups looked at Sheila, and Annie and Isie became more and more flustered while Jim looked appalled at his offspring.

"Where did you hear such a thing?" he demanded sternly of his daughter.

Totally unprepared for this electric reaction to her innocent question, Sheila could only whisper in a small voice, "Mama told me."

At this, Annie and Isie flushed with indignation and vehemently denied the existence of fleas in their home - and their voices had risen to a screech!

Jim by now was apoplectic. "She said no such thing!" He growled, firmly emphasising every word. "Sheila! How could you say such a wicked thing?"

Hot tears sprang to Sheila's eyes. Her white face reflected her panic - but it was desperately important for her to prove her innocence. She couldn't bear to be the source of her father's displeasure. Her voice wobbled, but she struggled on. "You heard her too, daddy," she persisted. "At the station."

Jim fairly glowered at his daughter but Sheila continued fearfully, "Remember, daddy?" she pleaded. "Mama said that if I didn't behave Auntie Annie would give me a flea in my ear." The child rushed on, "And I thought that if I knew where Auntie Annie kept her fleas I would stay clear of them. I hate fleas!" she wailed, before finally giving in to her tears.

The effect of this explanation on the adults was immediate. They blinked in surprise, then started to smile with comprehension. The tense atmosphere instantly turned to one of indulgent relief as they each tried to reassure Sheila, and explain the metaphor to her.

The bairn was plied with more scones, and her cup of tea which she had valiantly finished, was refilled with more black tar.

And so peace and tranquillity was restored to the afternoon tea party. But not before the two sisters had shared a knowing smile when Jim had shaken his head and muttered bemusedly, "Whatever next?" in an unconscious imitation of his wife!

Chapter 15

Sma' Pitchers Hae Big Ears

After a short while Sheila was given leave to absent herself from the table, and as she shut the door behind her almost fell over Auntie Annie's dog stretched out on the hall floor. He was a lovely black cross-labrador who could do lots of tricks including "playing dead" on command, and he followed Sheila as she started to search the house looking for her hidey-holes from last time.

She stood in the front hallway looking up at the steep stairway, and decided to climb its narrow steps later. First she went into the kitchen opposite the front parlour that she just vacated. It held an open range fire with an oven attached, where Auntie Annie baked her rice and tapioca in enamel dishes. These were nearly always served cold and solid and Sheila hated the stuff. A kettle was on the boil on top of the fire along with a steaming teapot. Auntie Annie loved her tea strong and black, just as her mother before her. Betty had remarked to Jim in Sheila's hearing, that the tea had probably been responsible for many of Grandma's illnesses, because she always drank it after it had been "boiled, boiled and yeah boiled!" She said it had probably "ruined Grandma's innards," and been the cause of her "aye sending to the Chemist's for medicines."

Off the kitchen was a little roomie with a paraffin stove. There were cupboards on one side, and a big dresser on the other, dividing that room from another that was parallel to the front door. It was a funny kind of arrangement, because off that room was the scullery, where not only were the dishes washed, but human bodies too. It was one of Sheila's secret ambitions to find out what Auntie Annie wore under her long dress, for Sheila had only ever seen her giving a quick dicht to the bits that showed.

Adjoining the scullery was an L shaped room with one bed opposite the door and another round the corner by the window. This was where the Browns slept when they stayed during the summer. This odd arrangement of rooms helped to make the house a fun place for bairns.

Now, it was time for Sheila to retrace her steps to the front hall and climb the narrow staircase. At the top of the stairs stood a table flanked by little windows on either side. The views from up here were beautiful. You looked down over the friendly chimney pots of the village and then out over the Moray Firth. Sometimes you could just make out the hills of Caithness in the distance. And the sunsets! Even at this tender age the bairn could be filled with wonderment at the beauty in her world.

Also on the landing were two cupboards filled with blankets and books. There were no libraries being run this far north, not even Boots', and so Jim and Bill had to buy their books, which made reading expensive for them, but did provide a delightful library for visitors.

On the left of the landing was the guest room where Sheila would sleep with her father tonight. This room was hardly ever used and didn't have any heating, so it always felt cold and damp. A 'pig,' or stone hot water bottle, had to suffice, but was never enough stop the dampness. There were long-haired sheepskin rugs on the floor at either side of the bed and a chamber pot underneath it. Her mama always suffered when she stayed at the Bauds because the damp would get into her bones, especially her knee. But the pain was never enough to deter her from visiting because her friendship with Annie more than made up for it.

At the other side of the landing were two similar bedrooms with a little roomie in the middle of them. This room had a skylight window and a funny bed. It wasn't "boxed" but it was built-in, and at the back of it was a small press whose top you could just see. There was a chest of drawers and a chair, and apart from a rug, nothing else in the room. This was where Auntie Annie slept when everyone came.

Satisfied that all was well in the house, and that no more disappearances had occurred since her grandmother's death, Sheila ran back to her father and was granted leave to explore outside.

She made straight for the charabanc, the wheel-less bus, and inspected it closely. Her imagination was boundless. Apart from being able to jump up and down on it, it had two long shiny seats that were perfect for sliding along. And of course, there was the driver's cab that had a steering wheel you could sit behind - and there were hundreds of long imaginary journeys just waiting to be travelled! Sheila sat behind the wheel and pondered her good luck. "All this," she thought, "and the croft, and her beloved Auntie Annie. And Dorothy and Johnny Jack coming too!"

Jim's sister, Beatrice, had married John Jack, and gone to live in a farm outside Keith where they produced two children called Dorothy and Johnny. Although they were five and six years respectively older than Sheila, they acknowledged her leadership. Johnny had been born with a shrunken left arm and hand but it didn't impede him in any obvious way. He was expected to inherit their farm and carry it on after his father. Sheila looked forward to their arrival.

Truth to tell, while the charabanc was exciting for the children, it was by no means the only attraction for them at the Bauds, as Sheila and her cousins were to learn in the years that followed. The main enticement of the croft was Auntie Annie herself. It was a pity that Annie had never married and had family of her own, because she was gifted where children were concerned. They all adored her and would have gone to the ends of the earth for their Auntie Annie. With her in charge, it seemed that every chore became a game of some kind and the children vied with each other for her approval. When Auntie Annie was in charge, the children enjoyed freedom as never before.

Consequently, they ran wild. They played on the moors and enjoyed "Hide and Seek" in the woods. The girls jumped with their skipping ropes while the boys climbed trees and everyone played "Tacky" together. Auntie Annie and her dog were easily persuaded to join them, and the children were happy to help her through her chores to allow her to be free. They had picnics up on Bin Hill that lasted a whole day at a time. On other days they would take the bus to Portknockie and visit Auntie E.J. who was Annie's sister.

E.J., or Elsie Jane, lived in 38 Admiralty Street and at the bottom of her road the North Sea crashed over and through Bow Fiddle Rock. The children would play on the adjacent promontory and Sheila once fell in here whilst playing among the stones. She got such a scare that forever after, she would be reluctant to play anywhere near the sea if there was a chance of her getting wet.

These visits had to be set up in advance because E.J. spent a large part of her school holidays with Auntie Polly. "Aunt" was the nominal title given to Mrs Polly Williams who had caused a family scandal by deserting her husband on their wedding day - after the marriage ceremony. Polly, who was the only daughter of Grandpa Mair's brother Joe, had been very spoilt. She hadn't been at all keen on the state of matrimony, but had envied its trappings. And nowadays, secure with her married name, but none of the marital encumbrances, she taught at Ordquhill Primary school in Cornhill. Then spent most of the summer holidays roaming Scotland with E.J. in her little car. She loved to follow fashion and especially enjoyed wearing outrageous hats. She liked a good gossip and was bountiful when entertaining family and friends. Her table overflowed with plates of fancy cakes and chocolate biscuits with lots of boiling tea, and Jim disapproved of her.

Elsie Jane was always kind to the children too, even to Dorothy and Johnny Jack, despite her not talking to their mother. John Jack had "walked out" with E.J. for ages before suddenly dropping her and declaring his love for her sister Beatrice - who had promptly accepted his offer and married him with unseemly haste - before he could change his mind again. Naturally, the two sisters had fallen out and had stopped talking. Betty had remarked to Jim that she couldn't see what all the fuss was about because John Jack was certainly nothing to look at.

Be that as it was, the two "aunts" brought their own type of excitement to the bairns' holidays and it was always an adventure to visit them.

As they grew older the cousins played with Marguerita's bicycle. What did it matter to them if they couldn't sit down on it? It was fast, and there was always plenty of fun to be had with it.

A variety of vans would roll up to the front door on different days of the week. There was the grocer from Buckie from whom Auntie Annie always bought the bairns a bag of sweets of some kind. More often than not these

194

were of a most unnatural colour and sticky-sweet. Especially popular were coconut squares, of a particularly virulent green that invariably made the children sick. Whether or not this was due to the strength of the food colouring, or due to the poor hygiene practised by the grocer, nobody knew. The fact remained that they were irresistible to the bairns and week after week they sicked them up and then scampered off to play in the woods again.

The fish van and the butcher's van also had their delivery days and there were visits from Ingin' Johnnies, and Tinkies who came to the door offering to swap brightly coloured balloons for their old clothes and rags. The bairns had the job of keeping the access to the croft passable by filling up the potholes with little stones.

Sometimes they would be sent into Findochty, to the Post Office run by Jim's brother, George. George had left the building trade after his father died and had married an English woman from Manchester and together they had taken over the combined Post Office and Grocer Shop. They had four sons, the last one being younger than Sheila. George's wife spoke "posh" and was very quiet. She had been a member of the Salvation Army and people thought that she was "afa' holy." But the bairns discovered that she sold drink round the back of the premises. George had "acquired" Jim's tools and piano after the war and Sheila had been well warned not to fraternise with him or his family. Mrs George Mair would sometimes walk up to the Bauds to buy Annie's eggs and would be met with politeness - but nothing more.

Providing they played on the moor and kept away from the main road, the bairns experienced unaccustomed freedom during their holidays. Year after year Sheila was to meet up with her cousins at the Bauds and propose all kinds of adventures. Although the youngest, she was the natural leader with a vivid imagination and ability to orchestrate all kinds of shenanigans.

As successive summers passed, Jim and Betty got into the routine of one of them taking Sheila up to Findochty at the start of her holidays, and the other taking her home again at the end. But after this, her first holiday, Sheila was accompanied back as far as Aberdeen Station by her Uncle Sandy and his new bride. Then, as had been agreed, they put her under the charge of a reliable-looking young man as far as Longside. A very quiet Sheila sat opposite this stranger and drew with her finger in the mist of condensation on the carriage windows. She bottled up her fears until she alighted on the platform at Longside, whereupon she threw her arms round her mother's neck and bawled like the overtired bairn that she was.

However, by the time they were walking down Station Road, Sheila had already embarked on a series of stories about what she'd been doing at the Bauds.

"You'll never guess what Johnny Jack said to me, mama," she said in a voice full of indignation.

"No I can't, " replied her mother. "So you'll just have to tell me," Betty continued in a voice that mimicked her daughter's indignant tone.

"He said, 'Sheila when I'm a man will you marry me?' so I said, 'Dinna be daft Johnny Jack. What would I do with you? I will not!'," said Sheila scornfully. "Then he said, 'But when I'm big I'll get my father's farm and you'll be rich.' Really mama! Did you ever hear sic rubbish?" The exasperation in her daughter's voice at the poor swane's proposal caused Betty to look away until she could safely keep a straight face.

Oh, but it felt good to have her daughter home again!

*   *   *

Sheila's return heralded the start of a new school year. By now she was no longer in the "baby class" but was being taught by Miss Anderson. Sheila adored her "new" teacher and worked very hard in order to be held highly in that good woman's esteem. Her classmates all wanted to please their teacher - but a certain innovative subject led, eventually, to awful ructions at home that needed to be sorted out.

"You told your class what?" asked Jim in a clipped voice as he set his cup down with a clatter. "Say that again, Sheila!"

The object of his wrath went very very white as she looked down into her lap. She was shocked at her father's response to her story. She knew without doubt that she had displeased him but didn't know why. Consequently she was reluctant to continue her tale.

"Come on! Come on!" urged her father peremptorily. "Repeat what you just said, please!"

Sheila hung her head and a strange squeaky voice quivered, "I said that my father was an important man and that Mr Donald came in last night and asked you for half a crown for his..."

"How dare you! How dare you repeat that conversation to your classmates! That was a confidential conversation. That was a ....How did you know who he was? Speak up now. No telling lies!"

"Because I heard him, papa," muttered Sheila in a very quiet voice.

"How could you have heard him?" demanded Jim. "You weren't there. I was alone with him."

"But I was there, papa," wailed the little mite. "I was under the table with Bessie and I heard him ask you for....."

"Under the table with who? Who are you talking about? Speak up! Speak up!"

"Bessie's her doll, Jim." Betty interrupted their inquisition. "Bessie is her doll. And they were playing under the table. Quietly," she added. "She must have overheard everything."

Betty took a deep breath and continued. "Miss Anderson, Sheila's teacher has instigated a 'Talking Time' into their curriculum. I expect she was hoping to expand her children's imagination," she added generously. "But it seems that all the children can talk about, with any confidence, is about what is happening in their homes. Naturally Miss Anderson helps them along a bit," she said neutrally, "and unfortunately in this way Miss Anderson and the whole class get to know a fair bit about what is going on in all our households. The mothers are worried sick." She looked straight at her husband. "It's not the bairn's fault, Jim." She looked at him meaningfully.

Jim prided himself on being fair and when it became clear to him that Sheila was not the one at fault here, he backed down straightaway - although that seemed to take an awful long time by his daughter's reckoning.

"Yes! Yes. You're right, Betty. The bairn's not to blame. We always tell her to keep quiet so I expect it was bound to backfire on us at some time... I suppose."

Betty nodded. "It was just bad luck that she was there."

"But what's all this about a 'Talking Time'?" queried Jim once more.

This time he was composed enough to take in his wife's explanation and he listened carefully.

"I see now," he said. He looked hard at his daughter as he thought it over. "Now, Sheila I'm sorry I was angry at you. But you're old enough to know that anything to do with my work has to be kept a secret, because people won't be able to trust me if you repeat any of our conversations. Do you understand me?"

Sheila nodded vigorously in affirmation, still too anxious to speak.

"And as for Miss Anderson," said Jim gravely. "Well - I know that a teacher once had her tongue cut out for asking personal questions of her innocent pupils. So I think she had better be very careful, don't you?"

Again Sheila nodded vigorously in assent, her eyes shining and bright as two large saucers.

"Off you go then. You mustn't be late for school."

With no more ado, Sheila leapt down from her chair and after kissing them both goodbye she raced off to school.

Her parents stared at each other across the table. "Well I never, Jim. That's the first time I've ever heard you tell a lie - and it's a whopper!"

"I know," replied her husband shamefacedly. "But I really don't want any more of our business paraded before the whole class. I think I might have a word with Miss Anderson."

"Oh I don't think you'll need to do that, Jim," replied his wife. "I doubt that 'Talking Time' will continue much after today," she added knowingly.

"What do you mean?" asked Jim.

"You wait and see," replied his wife mysteriously.

Sure enough Betty had to comfort her child when she came home from school that afternoon.

"...and Miss Anderson was very angry and told me that she didn't want to hear any more of my stories mama. I just wanted to warn her!" Sheila wailed. "And then she said that we weren't going to have any more 'Talking Times' and I had to sit down and she wasn't nice to me for the rest of the afternoon."

"Don't worry, pet," soothed Betty. "She'll be alright again tomorrow. You wait and see."

And she smiled inwardly at the story of the excision of the teacher's tongue becoming known in most of Longside's households by nightfall. And she positively grinned when she thought of the relief it would bring to the other mothers!

Time sped by and the routines of work and school gobbled up the days till Autumn burst on to the scene - and with it came the "tattie holiday." It was time for the potatoes to be lifted in the fields and women and children were both coerced into harvesting the crops without delay. The extra money made at this time either went into the household accounts or was stored away for Christmas. The bairns had a holiday from school especially for this.

Sheila was too young to go tattie picking and so was free to enjoy another holiday, even though it was only for a few days. The Bauds wasn't her only holiday option for she had relatives in Aberdeen too. There was her beloved Grandma in Bucksburn where she played out the back with Minty Orr and her older sister. Minty was the daughter of Sir Boyd Orr who rented "Aunt" Susan's house in Bucksburn. And its back garden stood back to back with Grandma's.

Isabella Cormack had grown up in Overton of Dyce with two sisters called Lizzie (Elizabeth) and Susan. Lizzie had been a very quick-tempered, fussy woman when she lived there. For instance, whenever she hired a hansom cab, she always stipulated that it had to be drawn by white horses. However, when her boyfriend gathered her up and plonked her in a hansom cab drawn by brown horses, and brooked no resistance from Lizzie, she finally acknowledged his suitability for her. They married and left the area to go to Capetown in South Africa, and after trekking round that vast land they finally settled in Johannesburg. Sadly, her husband was killed when a coping stone fell on him, and she was left to fend for herself in that strange country. She then showed her mettle by starting up a Boarding House that became profitable in a modest way. Her customers were mainly Boers.

Isabella's other sister, Susan, had stayed on with her father in Dyce until he died. Like Isabella, Susan had become an excellent seamstress, but instead of getting married and giving up work as her sister had done, she had set up in business on her own working from a room in her father's house. Wonderful expensive carriages bearing rich well-dressed women would roll up to the door where Susan's four assistants worked with her. She was a very particular woman, which was an asset in her work. Most of the dresses she made were high-necked with boned bodices, with leg-of-mutton sleeves made of black-ribbed moiré silk imported especially from Paris, and lined with ordinary silk. She was always in demand because she followed the latest patterns sent for from London. During the winter she would style fur into muffs and make woollen articles such as capes for her clients. But she never ventured into hat-making.

When their father died, Susan would have been homeless but for the fact that her brother, William, came home from Canada and bought her a house in Bucksburn, whose garden backed onto their sister's. William had set himself up in the Tobacco business in Calgary where he was quite successful and had married a half-caste who returned with him to Scotland. Most people hereabouts had never seen a coloured person in the flesh before - they were the stuff of melodramatic films and not real life. Although she survived the curious stares and the damp cold, she declined ever to come back to this country after that first visit.

By this time Susan was nearing sixty, and demand for her dresses had fallen off since more competitively-priced, ready-made articles were being produced. Consequently, she found herself unable to sustain the financial upkeep of the house so she rented it out to Boyd Orr and his family, and took a job as housekeeper for George Murray. He was a widower and former Headmaster of Dyce Academy. Susan had been friendly with George and his wife for years, and they knew each other well. George had been born at Rora and now, after a highly successful teaching career he was enjoying his retirement. Although almost seventy years old, he continued to mark external examination papers in Greek and Latin, for the students of Manchester University.

Susan had recently agreed to become his second wife and they were comfortably settled in house number 151 on Midstocket Road in Aberdeen. Susan had accepted his proposal on condition that their marriage must never be consummated!

It was a pity that Auntie Susan had never married when she was younger and had had children, for she turned out to be very good with them, and she adored Sheila. However, with their particular type of marriage they were more than a little surprised, when on Sheila's first visit the little pet rose early as usual, and as usual took Bessie with her while she padded through to their bedroom, and clambered into bed beside them! Her Auntie Susan made a lasting impression on Sheila that morning, for her aunt wore a lace cap over her red hair, and a crepe de chine nightdress that draped beautifully over her body. No lasting harm was done by the bairn's innocent act and the old couple encouraged her to holiday with them whenever possible.

Then, just as in the previous year, when things were going well, fate threw another spanner into their works.

Betty had slept badly on the previous night and it was with a horrible sense of foreboding that she answered the door that Saturday morning in the Spring of 1924. Dully, she registered that a young telegram boy was standing on her doorstep proffering an envelope. In her mind she was suddenly transported back to that fateful afternoon during the war, and for a moment she was rigid with horror.

"Here you are, mistress," said the lad pressing the telegram into Betty's hand.

She was dreading its contents. She had known that something was wrong last night when she couldn't sleep. Now she couldn't think at all - her mind was blank and staying that way. The possibility that it might contain glad tidings never entered her head. She knew with certainty that the contents of this telegram were going to change her life irrevocably and continued to stand like one in a trance.

The young lad was getting used to this reaction since he started this job a month ago, and now he knew how to deal with it.

He gave a discreet cough and asked deferentially, "Is there any reply, mistress?"

There was a short delay while these words penetrated Betty's consciousness and with a start she looked down at the unopened missive. She watched too, as strange hands - her own hands - tore the top off and extricated the message contained inside. "MOTHER STROKE COME HOME, Sandy".

Betty looked at the words and looked and looked. Unemotionally, she thought that it must be bad before Sandy had spent the extra money on a telegram. The words alarmed her but did not sink in. It was as if she was watching someone else going through all these actions and she stood mutely holding the telegram.

"Hm. Is there any message?" enquired the lad. He was bored by this response and wanted to be away.

Betty looked at him blankly, "What?"

"Message?" the lad repeated. "Is there an answer to be given?"

Betty looked at him, then looked at the telegram in her hand. 'My mother has had a stroke,' she thought, 'and this young man wants to know if I have an answer to it. What kind of answer is there? My whole life is about to change and he wants to know if there's an answer.'

Then she shook her head - and in the shaking of it, everything snapped back into focus.

"No. No there isn't," she replied briskly. "Thank you for asking - but no, there isn't any reply."

She was back in control now and starting to make arrangements in her mind. When things were bad, Betty always took rescue in doing something with her hands, and today was no different. Without more ado she fetched out the case and began packing clothes for herself and Sheila. Jim would have to stay at work of course, and he could take his dinner at the hotel. Sheila was too young to be left with him so she would write a note to Miss Anderson. She didn't know how long she would be away for, but it wouldn't matter because she could wash their things at her mother's.

She was busily folding clothes into the case when Jim and Sheila came in. Sheila had been "helping" her daddy out the back.

"Yes Sheila, that's just what you are - a good joiner spoilt!" Jim was saying as they entered. "Betty, I was telling Sheila that I'd be fair lost without her help. She's a good joiner....What's wrong?" he demanded, when he realised that his wife was packing their case, and that she was very white-faced.

Betty did not pause for even a second. She had to remain busy. "I've just had a telegram from Sandy that mother has taken a stroke and it must be bad before Sandy spent extra money on a telegram and I don't know how bad it is or what I can do when I get there. I might not get there in time but I have got to get to her straightaway and do all I can. I don't want to lose my mother Jim and I must get the next train. I thought that you could have your dinner at the hotel and Sheila would come with me and I'm packing ..."

While she was saying all this without pausing even for breath, Jim took in the situation and assessed his wife's reaction. Without a word, he stepped over and caught her hand as she was casting round for the next item to go in the case, and held it tightly. He then pulled her to his bosie and held her closely there. Betty finally stopped talking and her head went down. Soon after, her silence gave way to crying as she succumbed to her emotions. They stood there with Jim stroking his wife's hair, while their bewildered bairn held her mother's apron screwed tightly in her hand.

Once it was out of her system Betty started her explanation all over again. Jim agreed with all her plans and soon afterwards they set off for the station. Jim was to travel in with them and return the following day for his work, while Betty and Sheila stayed on to help her mother.

Less than five hours later, they approached Grandma Cormack's house in Bucksburn. Betty's face was set with grim determination as she knocked on the door and walked in, willing herself to cope with the situation - however bad it was.

Chapter 16

Relations Are A Wilful Lot

There was nothing reassuring in the sight that met Betty's eyes. The stroke had left her mother bed-ridden and unconscious, and on the few occasions when she awoke, Isabella was scarcely lucid and did not recognise anyone. She could not chew and had to have all her food strained for her. Her limbs were useless and her mouth was twisted into an awful grimace that remained on her face even as she slept. Mercifully, she was to be cocooned in Blessed sleep for most of her remaining time on earth.

Sandy's new wife had a sister, Nancy, who was a trained nurse, and she came to look after Mrs Cormack along with Betty. They were both needed day and night, because although Betty slept with her mother, it required the two of them to move her. There was only one moment's light relief in all the time they nursed the poor old woman. Nancy was a "big" lass who had a prodigious appetite. And one afternoon the two younger women were having a cup of tea by the fireside, with Mrs Cormack "asleep" in the bed that had been brought through.

Suddenly, Grandma's eyes opened and with asperity she said perfectly clearly, "Nancy Allan, you're aye eating. You'll never die!" Then she closed her eyes and resumed her "sleep."

Betty and Nancy jumped up at her words but before they could say anything to her she was unconscious again. The two looked at each other - and burst out laughing. What else could they do?

The incident made Betty wonder to what extent her mother was sleeping, and how much awareness she had of what was going on. Could her mother still hear? It seemed to Betty that her mother was comatose for most of the time, because while the old woman's eyes were closed she didn't respond to any noise at all. Even when Nancy dropped a tray of teacups and saucers that had hit the ground with an almighty clatter, her mother's eyes hadn't so much as flickered. But on the other hand, her recent outburst showed that she had recognised Nancy and hadn't been surprised to find her there. It also showed that she could speak. What level of consciousness did her mother then inhabit? What kind of world was she living in?

While Betty pondered these imponderables her daughter hung around the house bored to tears. She didn't understand what had happened to Grandma but was confident that her mother would soon make her better. Unfortunately, there was nothing for Sheila to do. She wasn't needed in the house where she had to be very quiet, and Minty was at school so she had no one to play with. They had left in such a hurry she had only taken Bessie with her. Her books and toys and skipping rope were all back at home and she was fed up.

One morning while she was sitting on the doorstep, the local headmistress stopped on her way to school. She had seen Sheila there on numerous occasions and had formulated a plan. "Would you like to come to school and help teach the babies?" she asked Sheila who nodded vigorously. "Good. I'll have a wee word with your mother." And that's all it took for Sheila to start going to the local Primary school at Bucksburn. To Sheila's joy, the 'babies' were more responsive than her dollies back home, and she loved "teaching" them. Thereafter the days sped by for her.

After five weeks of nursing her mother, Betty was forced to make a change in their plans when Nancy was offered a permanent position elsewhere. Jim had been very good about staying on his own, but it really wasn't fair to expect him to put up with it for much longer. The doctor had explained that Mrs Cormack could "pass on" the next day, or continue like this for a while yet - and Sandy was moaning about the depletion of his inheritance caused by Nancy's wages being deducted from his mother's estate. He clearly hadn't expected his mother to linger for as long as she had.

All these thoughts and others went through Betty's mind when she came to the conclusion that things could not go on as they were. Subsequently, she gambled that the journey to Longside would not be too much for her mother, and brought her home.

After four more long weeks, Grandma Cormack died at The Gables with Betty at her bedside. The young couple made arrangements for her to be buried at Newhills Cemetery beside her husband, and until the day of her funeral Grandma lay in the Mair's front room. Sheila still didn't understand what death was about, for time and time again she would announce to her mother that she "just had to tell Grandma something else!" and would scamper off into the good room, lift the veil from her grandmother's face, and whisper her secrets. Sometimes she would just go in "to say goodbye to Grandma."

Betty was bearing up well until the cortege left for the cemetery. She caught a glimpse of a future without her mother, and was filled with desolation. However, with childish instinct Sheila put her arms around her mother's neck and whispered, "Never mind, mama, I'll look after you." Betty was made acutely aware that now she was the older one in this relationship, and she wished with all her heart that Sheila and herself would enjoy as strong a bond as she had shared with her mother.

She never got time to mope, even if she had been so inclined, for before the funeral was over, Sandy was snapping at her heels to clear out their mother's effects so that he could sell the house and get his share of the money. He had already "assisted" his sister in this, because while their mother had lain dying at Longside, Sandy had acquired the best pieces of furniture.

But Mrs Cormack turned out to be a woman who knew her bairns well. She had itemised everything in her will and put their names beside the pieces they were to receive - and Sandy had to relinquish most of his acquisitions to Betty. He was spitting feathers by the end of the list!

"I'm sorry you didn't get as much as you expected, Bill," said Betty quietly to her older brother."

"It doesn't really matter," he replied. Then he laughed and said, "I'll just have to go and make myself another fortune!"

Bill Cormack, the oldest of the four children, had served his apprenticeship as a plumber then been lured overseas to South Africa shortly afterwards. He had worked in the tobacco plantations there and amassed a small fortune. However, the money had started to disappear too quickly for his liking when he bought a hotel in Nyasaland and called it "Ryalls Limbe Hotel" It was situated in Limbe, and it wasn't doing too badly. Bill had given the place a Scottish flavour that was going down well with a lot of ex pats. He advertised it as "A Hame Frae Hame," and he was in a hurry to see his investment grow.

A handsome, extrovert man, Bill had always been very fashion-conscious and could charm the birds off the trees. When he lived at Bucksburn, the women in the household had usually asked for his advice about their clothes because it was acknowledged that he had "the eye" for it. But despite having plenty of female interest shown in him all this time, Bill had remained a bachelor.

Five months after his mother's death he had come back to Aberdeen ostensibly for an operation on his nose to remedy his sinus problem - but he was really there to collect the money he had inherited. While he was in hospital, he was nursed by Janet Craig who was single, attractive, intensely kind and had absolutely no sense of humour that Betty could see. Her folks were Plymouth Brethren and hadn't encouraged her to view the world with levity. For all that, Bill fell in love with her and had made his marriage proposal before he was discharged from hospital. She had promptly accepted, and they had married quickly and quietly. Now, Bill was intending to return to Nyasaland alone, and Janet was going to follow him out after she had put together her trousseau - which had to include a Riding Outfit of all things!

* * *

When Bill had first arrived at his sister's house in Longside he had brought with him a beautiful blue coat with a grey fur collar and matching grey fur hat for Sheila. The bairn adored the outfit and she was proudly wearing it today as they sat in the Aberdeen café saying their goodbyes. Sheila was sitting very demurely with her hands in her lap, and her eyes taking in all the details of this new experience.

The siblings had arranged to meet at Kenoway's Café on Union Street and Sheila's eyes were shining at the grandeur of it all. They had a cubicle to themselves and were being waited on by a very attentive waitress who was dressed in black with a white starched apron and frilled cap. There was a crisp white cloth on their table and painted crockery was laid out for their afternoon tea. The cutlery was shining, large and ornate, on either side of their heavy damask napkins. There was a two-tiered plate that held scones on the bottom and fancy "pieces" on the top. Bill had noticed how Sheila's eyes had glowed at the selection of cakes and asked her which one she wanted. He casually spun the plate slowly so that when Sheila chose the one nearest to her, as she had been taught to do, he would be confident that his niece got her favourite one. He was successful in this and so he asked her, "Would you like another one, Sheila?" It was fairly obvious that she did, but she replied, "No thank you!" as she had been taught to say. So Bill leaned over and in a conspiratorial whisper said, "I know, let's put the others in this paper bag I've got, and you can eat them when you get home." His niece's eyes shone with delight at this plan. It had been very difficult for her to say "no," and this was indeed reward for her manners. She was delighted when Bill pretended to put the fancies surreptitiously into a plain paper bag and it never occurred to the bairn that he was going to have to pay for them all anyway!

"When will Janet be able to join you?" asked Betty. They had been sitting talking for a while now, exchanging memories of their shared childhood, and had more or less brought each other up to date with their personal histories. They had both corresponded regularly since Bill had flown the nest but, as usual, there was always more to be said now that they had got together in person. At this point, they each had an eye on the clock that was speeding them towards their separation. They were keenly aware that this could be the last time that they saw each other since Nyasaland was far away and passages to Africa didn't come cheaply.

"Och it'll take a few months before Janet's ready to come out to me. She'll get her clothes and stuff together and work out her resignation at the hospital. Then she'll sail out to Africa."

"Sail out to Africa," echoed Betty. "Have you any idea how romantic that sounds, Bill?"

"Well, I suppose there's that," replied Bill. "But there's precious little romance to be had when you're out there, just hard work. My staff at the hotel are all Blacks you know, and their culture is completely different from ours, and so is their whole way of life. You know, I've had the same staff for almost a year now and I still have to watch them. They can't get the hang of the idea that the stuff in the hotel belongs to me and not them. They'll take home sheets, knives and anything they think they can get away with. But I'm fit for them and "relieve" them of their spoils before they go home - and they come back the next day as if nothing had happened - and try again! They're not embarrassed at being caught and have no shame about it - it's just something that they're expected to do! They don't understand our ways - nor me theirs. I dread to think of how much has "walked" out of my hotel since I've been over here.

"I'm sorry mother didn't leave you more money, Bill," said Betty gently. "This doesn't mean that you'll have to sell your hotel will it?" she asked urgently as the horrible possibility occurred to her.

"Not at all! Not at all, Elizabeth!" Bill hastened to reassure his sister. He shook his head and explained further, "I'm just in a hurry to see it grow. I've grand ideas for my hotel...and perhaps I'm more like Aunt Susan than I'd supposed. Remember how quick she aye was when we were wee? The slightest thing would set her off like a rocket - her and her red hair!"

"I mind fine," smiled his sister. "Remember that day when Aunt Susan was speaking to mother and we were reading our comics on the floor? You were lying on your belly swinging your feet up and down wearing your boots and making a right old din every time your steel toes hit the floor. The noise annoyed Auntie Susan so much she finally shouted, 'Stop that!' And then she grabbed you and told you to go on out." Betty gave a laugh at the memory. "You stomped off all red-faced to the door, and as you were closing it behind you, you yelled...."

"I hope you get married and have six reid-heided loons!" Bill exploded with laughter. "Aye, she never liked her red hair did she? But isn't she doing well now though?" he asked more soberly.

Then his eyes lit up with merriment, "She's not taking any chances of having six red-headed sons even yet, with that signed provision to her marriage. 'There must be no consummation of this marriage!' How old is she now - must be about sixty? She's being afa' careful isn't she?"

Betty giggled. Bill was always like this, and always had her laughing. "Yes, she's doing well. She's very happy where she is - and Sheila likes going to her for a holiday, don't you pet?" she asked turning to her daughter.

"Yes, mama," nodded Sheila.

"I'm sure you're a good girl at Auntie Susan's aren't you, Sheila?" asked Bill smiling. As the bairn nodded, Bill continued, "Talking of happiness, Sandy seems real pleased with his new wife. But I expect he's as stingy as ever?"

"Yes to both," asserted Betty. "It took quite a wee while to 'bend her to his will' but that wasn't because Jessie wasn't willing. Our Sandy likes to be extra sure of anything he does. And yes, Bill, our brother's as mean as ever. Do you know..." and Bill could hear the indignation in his sister's voice. "Do you know that he even demanded that the cost of his telegram to me had to be deducted from mother's estate before it was divided up between the four of us! Edwin's fair scunnert of him."

"Is Sandy still at Robert Gordon's then?" asked Bill.

"No, no," replied Betty more calmly. "Dr Alex Cormack is the dominie at Rosemount Junior Secondary School these days. He's been there for the last three years and seems to have found his niche at last. I'm told he's very popular with his pupils and their parents. He still writes articles for various magazines, and he's writing another book too. It's entitled, wait for it: 'The Gothenburg Activities of Jacobite Exiles After The '45 Rebellion.' He's a very clever man is our Sandy," finished Betty blandly.

"He is that," agreed Bill. "And this clever man now speaks to me in public. As I recall, he was always too embarrassed to acknowledge my presence in the street if I was in my dungarees. But I've become suitable for his image now that I'm a hotel owner."

"I remember when you wouldn't give your girlfriends the time of day if they ignored you in your dungarees," smiled Betty impishly.

"And quite right too!" asserted Bill sharply. "If I wasn't good enough to speak to when I was dressed as a plumber I wanted nothing to do with them when I was smartened up! But what about Sandy and Jessie?" he returned to their former topic. "Are they intending having children? I mean, what's he saving all his money up for?"

"I've really no idea," mused Betty. "He salts it away in the bank. He doesn't spend it on Jessie, nor on his home - that's full of cheap furniture. You heard of course that he tried to take mother's best pieces? But she was fit for him and he had to give most of it back. They don't go on extravagant holidays." Betty thought for a while. "Do you want to know what I think? I think that he puts money in the bank to give him confidence."

"But he doesn't need to get his confidence from money!" protested Bill.

"I know that and you know that, but for all his intelligence I don't think Sandy knows that."

"Well, well," said Bill with a sigh. Then he cheered up at his next thought. "Edwin doesn't have any worries on that score. He's a real "pack" animal if ever I saw one. He's hardly ever on his own, and is either on his way to meet with someone, or he's waiting for someone to join him. He was always popular - and still is as far as I can make out."

"Mm you're right, Bill," acknowledged Betty with a fond smile. "He's got a right good way about him and people are attracted to him. He's always interested in folk and they like that. You would never think that both Edwin and Sandy come from the same stock, would you?"

"Ah well, they're both doing well for themselves and that's the main thing," replied Bill in a contemplative voice.

"So are you, Bill," his sister reminded him gently.

He started to blush. "Och perhaps. Perhaps," he mused. "Does running a hotel with bare-footed servants elevate my status enough to compare with a teacher or lawyer I wonder?"

"Of course it does!" exploded Betty. " What's all this about status? Dinna speak dirt, Bill. It's what we've achieved in life that matters - and in that you've done easily as much as the next man!" Then she caught her brother's eye. "You stop teasing me like that," she smiled.

"Poor old 'garrety windaes,'" laughed Bill. "You're still easy to wind up, little sister. I'm glad you haven't changed while I've been away. You've even produced a little replica," added Bill looking at Sheila. "And a right wee angel she is."

Betty suddenly asked earnestly, "Must you go back to Africa? Wouldn't you prefer to stay here?" and Bill was disconcerted to see that her eyes were moist.

He took his time in answering. "I'd like fine to stay here - but only for a little while longer - for I'd soon begin to feel trapped. You see, I love Africa. It's a vast, wild, dangerous and beautiful land. It's a land of promise - a land of dreams. And as long as you're prepared to work hard it's possible to realise those dreams still. There's no mountain of red tape to get through before you start to do anything. There's no army of inspectors always poking their noses into your business all the time. If you want a thing badly enough you can still work for it in that vast continent. You can travel for days, weeks, even months without seeing or meeting another human being - if that's what you want. The country is huge, Betty - and it has plenty of room for big ideas. I love it!"

Betty smiled and put her ominous tears away. "So you're going to stay with Aunt Chat for a few days before you go back to Africa?"

"There's no way I'd go back without having seen my favourite aunt," grinned Bill. "She's still singing in nightclubs I believe. I wonder if she still demands a Hansom cab to take her there?"

"She does still sing and yes, she does still request a Hansom cab - if she can't get a motor taxi to take her. You've a few surprises in store when you go to see her in London."

"But she doesn't live in London - she lives in Rickmansworth."

"That's right, Bill, but Rickmansworth is now in the suburbs of London. Our Aunt Chat lives in suburbia," Betty announced the last word cheerily. "The government started building housing estates on green land outside the cities, instead of rebuilding the war-damaged houses in inner London. Some of the houses on these new estates are for rent, and some are good value to buy, and some are fantastically expensive. Aunt Chat says that not everyone's happy there. Some of the council house tenants find it boring and lonely after their tenements, and there are stories about them keeping coal in their baths because they don't know what else to use them for.

Davey's engineering job means they can own their modest house. Well, Aunt Chat describes it as modest, but that's not what I would call it. She's got electricity and running water and an inside bathroom with a toilet and a bath. She has a washing machine and an electric cooker and a vacuum cleaner. That's an electrical machine that sweeps the floor for you," she explained at his questioning look. "The advertisements are all about 'mod cons' that's 'modern conveniences' that are labour-saving devices - and Aunt Chat has most of them. I once asked in my letters to her what she did with all that spare time - and she said I'd be surprised at how long it took to get all her 'mod cons' going! I'm sure she was exaggerating but knowing Aunt Chat there was probably more than a grain of truth in there as well.

In her last letter she also said that they were going to buy a car! Can you believe it? She said that a lot of people on the estate have one now that they have come down in price. A modest car costs about twice Davey's annual salary, and that brings one within their reach. She thought that they would probably get an Austen Seven, because a 'Tin Lizzie' or 'Model T' is too big and cumbersome for their use - and it would be handier for driving in London. It'll have to be black of course. She said that the last time she went up there the roads were chaotic. In Piccadilly Circus there were some old horse-drawn Hansom Cabs jostling against the new motor taxis and buses and electric trams and bicycles and private motor cars. It was bedlam!

Anyone over the age of sixteen can drive - or should I say - is eligible to drive a car. A lot of people haven't got the hang of it yet but that doesn't stop them from hiccuping round London in their fancy cars. Some rich people still pay to have a man walk in front of them with a white flag - Aunt Chat says that they should get danger money for doing that in London. Now the government is talking about putting up some kind of electric lights at busy junctions so that the traffic will have to take turn about at some of the busy crossroads. They're even speaking about painting a white line down the middle of the roads so that the traffic will keep to its own side."

It was obvious that Aunt Chat had sparked off her niece's interest in cars. And Betty's next words showed that she wasn't just a passive reader of her aunt's correspondence, but had given the current traffic situation some thought.

"They sound like good ideas, Bill, but I wonder if they'll work?" asked Betty, unaware that her brother wasn't really listening to her. Instead, he was fondly watching her mannerisms remembered from childhood, and committing them afresh to memory.

"They should have to pass a test or something," she continued. "There are too many people being killed by all the new motors you know. Aunt Chat says that she read somewhere that fourteen people a day are killed on the roads, so the government will have to do something about it. The car drivers are clamouring for better roads to be built. What a carry on! But I don't think that the car is going to go away. No," said Betty shaking her head emphatically, "I think the car is here to stay."

"Davey must be doing not too badly to be able to afford their lifestyle," said Bill without envy, and changing the topic easily.

"You've no idea the amount of changes there have been at work down there," enthused Betty. "Offices are open-plan now, and there are lots of telephones and tickertape and Gestetner duplicating machines. They use typewriters most of the time now and young women can work as secretaries, typists, telephonists and clerks. There are some good jobs available for young women - until they marry. Then they're expected to resign. But Aunt Chat says that isn't happening so often nowadays, and there are more than a few married women on her estate who continue to work. Some of them even say that they don't want children now that they have a choice. That used to be 'unacceptable' and still is in some places, but it doesn't stop them carrying on with their work after they're married. Some of the unemployed men cut up real nasty about it.

Davey says it might be stylish work for them as secretaries and such, but it's not easy. They're expected to put in hours of unpaid overtime over and above weekdays and Saturday mornings. They're not allowed to go home until all the work for the day is finished - and that can mean arriving home very late at night. But most of them seem to think that it's worth it, and certainly prefer it to being in service or serving in the shops. There are precious few servants to be had, so it's just as well that they all have their labour-saving devices."

Betty had become vaguely aware that she was "rabbitting" on, but subconsciously she was reluctant for this last meeting with her older brother to finish.

"The women who work in the city are very modern and stylish you know!" she laughed, having decided to indulge Bill's interest in fashion. "They don't wear Aunt Susan's boned corsets and bombazine any more. They like lots of bright colours, and their dresses hang from their hips - no more squeezing into tight-fitting waisted garments for them. Davey says they're trying to look like men with their short haircuts and flat chests. But the women wear makeup and dye their hair with henna or peroxide. They also paint their nails and wear lipstick and mascara - so there's no mix-up. Mercy! Grandma Mair would turn over in her grave at the sight of a painted lady! Only actresses and people in brothels decorated themselves like that! These modern women are called 'Flappers' you know, and they're trying to get the vote reduced to twenty one for women - same as the men, and they're not all hussies. Aunt Chat says that some of them look really attractive with makeup on, while others, well...they get it all wrong...and oh me...disaster!"

They all laughed together, including young Sheila who was trying to be a grown-up. And Betty knew that all the talking in the world couldn't slow the clock down.

"Have you seen Violet while you've been here?" she asked. Then when she saw no comprehension in her brother's face she went on, "Violet, you know, Davey's sister - Aunt Chat's sister-in-law."

"No, I don't believe I have," replied Bill. "Why? I thought she was living in Dundee still."

"No, no. You're way behind with the news here. I'm sorry, I thought that I'd written to you about it. Never mind," she said hurriedly, grasping her last chance to share a bit of news with her brother.

"You were right that Violet used to live in Dundee with her father. He was the ship's Captain and often went to Russia, delivering jute mainly, I think. Well, when she was older, Violet got a job in Russia, as governess to a cousin of the Tsar. After a while she married a Russian soldier, I forget his name...but it doesn't matter. They were very happy for a while - until the Russian Revolution came along and ruined their plans. She was lucky her husband managed to get her a passage safely to Finland, and then, eventually, she managed to get back here. But as for what happened to her husband.....He probably came to the same sticky end as the Tsar and his family. Violet was devastated for a while but in time she came to accept that there was nothing she could do about it. Anyway, she's been living here in Aberdeen for the last five years and Edwin is helping her to get a divorce. Don't look so shocked, Bill. More and more women are filing for divorce now that they have been given equal rights in a marriage. They usually cite adultery as the cause - although not in Violet's case, naturally. Divorce is still seen as a source of shame by some folks, but that's changing."

"Well, who'd have thought it?" responded Bill quietly. It was clear that his mind was on his imminent departure. "Have you any word you'd like me to pass on to Aunt Chat?"

"What? Oh yes!" said Betty crisply. Then "No, it doesn't matter. It's my turn to write to her anyway." She hated goodbyes and while she had spun this one out for as long as she could, she acknowledged that time had now defeated her and he needed to get on his way. And she had better get home so that she could shed her tears in private.

While Bill was paying the waitress, Betty helped Sheila into her coat and beloved fur hat, and then slipped on her own outerwear. That time was upon them and she stood irresolutely waiting for Bill to take the initiative.

"Well then, lass," he smiled sadly as they all stood at the door. "This is goodbye then." And he gave her a hug. Normally an undemonstrative family, this couthie act threatened to undo Betty's determination not to cry.

"Bye bye, Sheila," he smiled, lifting up his niece and plonking a kiss on her cheek. "Give my regards to Jim, and you take care of yourself and that knee of yours," he commanded, looking keenly at his sister.

"Of course I will," answered Betty more sharply than she had intended. "Good luck with Janet and your hotel. Come back and see me when you can, Bill." And she added lamely, "I'll......miss you."

"I'll miss you too, Betty," he replied quietly.

Then Betty turned away and took Sheila's hand. The child launched into her usual prattle almost immediately, as they made their way to the station - and she was too young and too involved with her own chatter to notice her mother's prolonged silence.

Bill Mair in The Merchant Navy.

LEFT: *Bill Mair, Chief Engineer.*

BELOW: *Bill's wife, Pat, and daughter, Patsy.*

The Gables

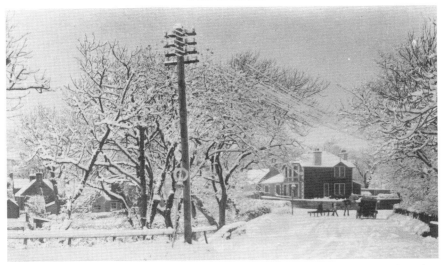

Winter in 1930's - Telephones but no electricity. (note the old street lamp).

COOPER'S BRAE, LONGSIDE.

1948 Longside has electricity.

Holidays

LEFT: *Sheila at 19 years old.*

BOTTOM LEFT: *First family car - the Lancaster 10.*

BELOW: *Sheila and her father returning from Norway on the 'Jupiter' in 1947.*

Mair Family Portraits

*TOP LEFT AND RIGHT: Portraits of Jim and Betty sketched by Sheila in 1950's
with the recently invented Biro pen.
BOTTOM: Photographic portrait of Sheila in 1950s.*

Chapter 17

Mak' Hay While The Sun Shines

When the excitement of Bill's visit was over, the Mair family settled back down into their familiar routine and four years rushed by before they knew it.

Jim finished the Tennis Court during the following spring, but was disappointed when his young helpers were unable to play on it because the cost of membership was set impossibly high for them. Jim tried to negotiate a reduction for them, but was refused. Everyone was very pleased with the courts he had built however, and the Tennis Club quickly became very popular.

Jim then turned towards planning the formal layout of his garden, and Sheila's little leggies flew on and helped him to mark out the paths with string. She would also "assist" her father to mix his beloved cement and make kerbs. Then she became his handyman when it came to pulling the raspberries, strawberries and blackcurrants that her mother made into jam for Jim to spread liberally onto his bread or bun. She loved working with her father and he often had cause indeed to repeat that his daughter was "a good joiner spoiled!"

And from 1925 onwards The Gables echoed with music, when Jim bought a very good second-hand piano and started teaching Sheila to play. It brought a new joy into the household, and reminded Jim of when he used to write Cantatas for the children at Buckie.

As winter drew near, that same year, the Reverend Carmichael approached Jim and asked him to conduct a mixed choir from the local churches. The minister was very keen to get his project off the ground, and had already persuaded his daughter Jessie to play the organ, while he himself would be its first choir member. His enthusiasm was infectious, and Jim happily agreed. But his enjoyment of it was short-lived though. People weren't keen to practise and didn't turn up regularly. The Reverend Carmichael and his daughter always attended, but while Jessie fulfilled her part of the bargain by playing the organ, her father never once sang a note! He thought himself such a bad singer that he would only mime the words. The choir gradually petered out - but not before Jim had acquired an awful lot of new grey hairs.

During the following year of 1926 - the year of the General Strike, Betty had a miscarriage. Doctor Wood attended to her in the small hours of the morning, but couldn't avert the death of their son. As he was leaving, he looked in to check on Sheila who should have been asleep in the adjoining room. She was sitting up in bed, quite the thing, reading a book which was usually forbidden at that time. When he smiled at her and asked what she was doing, the little imp replied, "I'm just taking the good of the light, doctor!" He chuckled as he left, and was reassured that the household would survive its sad loss.

Sheila had known nothing about the impending birth, and was unaffected by the deep disappointment felt by her parents. It was a double blow for them, because Doctor Wood had broken it to them gently that there would be no more children in the Mair household. And the strain of this pregnancy on her legs had caused Betty's knee problem to flare up again.

Pain was always to be a part of their lives, and by the end of '27 Jim had returned to his doctor with worsening pain in his left arm. The nerves had regenerated and gradually become exposed as predicted. Jim had grown paler and lost weight during the past few months and his prolonged silences were indications of a crisis looming. The surgeon in Aberdeen couldn't help him anymore and instead, arranged for him to attend the Ministry of Pensions Hospital in Erskine. There, they pulled the nerves and cut them, which gave Jim some relief from the pain when the site healed five weeks later. It wasn't a very satisfactory solution and he'd been warned it was only temporary, but at least it let him get on with his life normally for a while. During his visit to Erskine he met former soldiers who were destined to spend the rest of their lives there because their wives had deserted them. While disappointed with his treatment, Jim had come home with renewed gratitude and admiration for his wife whom he knew would never let him down. His five-yearly visits to hospital would have to continue, and he always hoped for some kind of breakthrough.

In the spring of 1928, Edwin surprised everyone by disappearing to Edinburgh for a few days - and coming home married! He had known his wife for a few years before this, and it wasn't as much of a surprise to Betty as it might have been to others who didn't know Edwin so well. Winifred Mutch was the eldest daughter of Robert Young Mutch, Master Butcher, whose premises were in George Street in Aberdeen. Her sister, Robina, was married to Doctor Walker from Fraserburgh and her brother, Robert, was training to take over the business from his father. Dorothy, or "Dolly," the youngest daughter was at school.

Edwin was still working for "Stephen and Smith Advocates," intending to become an Advocate with his own practice, and Winifred fully supported him in this goal.

Jim continued to work hard as Poor Inspector during the day, but was always on the lookout for projects to fill his evenings. The house had as many cupboards as it could hold, and his shed was packed with all kinds of tailor-made gadgets. However, when a party of men approached him for help to plan and construct a Golf Course out by Inverquhomery, Jim declined. He had not got over his disappointment with the tennis court committee who had excluded his young and unpaid, willing helpers. The injustice of the situation still rankled, and a new hurt had since been added. In August 1928, the Tennis Club celebrated the opening of their new Tennis Pavilion, and only Betty knew that Jim was deeply disappointed not to have been invited to the official opening.

But thanks to Edwin, he had been introduced to a new hobby to while away the long dark winter nights. As a relaxation, Jim would peruse the Financial Times of an evening to gauge the situation of the Stock Market, and he gradually acquired various stocks and bonds. He started in a very modest way using nothing more than what he could afford. "Slow but sure" was his motto. He got a lot of excitement from it as time went on and he grew in confidence and ability. The educational and intellectual exercises of this new hobby, whilst he coolly dragged on his Craven A cigarette - a practise also initiated by Edwin - filled in the dark evenings admirably.

Sheila loved to watch her father extract his packet of cigarettes from his pocket, expertly flick open the top, and extricate one cigarette - with only the one hand. He would likewise withdraw a match in much the same way. Then he would place the matchbox between his knees and strike the match - and proceed to light his cigarette all in one smooth movement. He would often then sit back and draw on his cigarette with his eyes closed as if savouring the moment. It was one of the very few times when Sheila saw her father fully relaxed. A smile would then cover his face and he would reach for his newspaper a contented man indeed.

Sheila knew that there would be no interrupting him for a good while - so engrossed would he become with his stocks and shares. Her mother called them a "Godsend" and Sheila had once tried reading the long columns with their difficult words and numbers, but she never saw any mention of "God" anywhere - not like in the Bible, and it remained a mystery to her where God came into it. But it did make daddy very happy!

By this time, Jim had been appointed Session Clerk of the Auld Kirk. The minister "Dickie" Henderson had known from their Parish meetings that, like himself, Jim Mair was a man who knew his own mind. So neither man was surprised to find that they were continually locking horns. The Reverend was a rotund, florid round-faced man with a quick temper who was a "go-ahead" type; "...and his ulcer wouldn't have troubled him so much if he had had the wisdom to surround himself with "yes men," instead of choosing Jim Mair who had integrity!" was Betty's 'impartial' comment.

While her parents dealt with the vicissitudes of village life, Sheila devoted herself to the important business of growing up. She passed from the hands of Miss Anderson and Miss Thomson in the Infant School, into the senior ranks ruled by Miss Riach and Miss Walker in the Upper School. Mr McKenzie, the headmaster, also taught them on Friday afternoons when he always gave his class the choice between learning grammar or listening to a story. And it was just as well that he took a book with him every Friday afternoon.

Education had been compulsory since the Education Act of 1918. Children had to learn the "three R's" - reading, writing and 'rithmetic, and were at least literate and numerate by fourteen years old, when they could leave school. If they chose to stay in Education after then, their parents had to pay their fares into Peterhead Academy and buy the books and jotters for their schoolwork. This meant that a substantial number of very bright pupils were forced to leave school because, either their parents couldn't afford the added expense, or they needed the extra money their children's employment would bring in.

Jim and Betty had long ago agreed that the door to education would be open for their daughter, and for as far as she wanted to go. Sheila was encouraged to do well at school, and knew that if she passed her Qualifying Examination in Primary 7, she would get to go to the Academy. Luckily she was bright and hard working, and was enjoying school.

She wasn't fussed for going to church, however, but she was prevailed upon to go anyway. Ever since her knee had worsened Betty had had to remain at home, and it fell to Sheila to accompany her father on Sundays, to the Auld Kirk at the top of the road. On Communion Sundays Betty was particularly proud of her husband when he left the house in his black morning coat, made from soft fine velour dutifully brushed for him, and his top hat set squarely on his head. She still thought him very handsome.

Completely unaware of the tensions between her father and the minister, Sheila had to sit in the pew beside him every Sunday and listen to, what was to a young lassie, a very long, very tedious and repetitive sermon. To relieve her boredom she would draw surreptitiously on scraps of paper, which she would later abandon in a hedge before she got home. Betty disapproved of her drawing in church and was sure to ask her sternly, "Sheila! Have you any paper in your pocket?" and this way Sheila would be able to answer, truthfully, that she hadn't. Inspired by the people around her, Sheila would draw caricatures of her fellow parishioners. When there was no paper she used the fly-leafs of the hymn books, which raised many a chuckle and cheered up a lot of people in the Kirk. Sheila meant no ill, although she ruined a good many hymn books in this way.

Meanwhile, her father was being driven round the bend by auld Mrs Cheyne in the pew in front of them. Mrs Cheyne thought herself very musical and so she belted out each hymn. Unfortunately, she sang slightly off key and tapped her foot loudly to the beat - which was always two beats behind everyone else in the Church - and it resulted in sounding as if a race was going on. Jim found this off-putting, but generally managed to laugh it off. Sheila had no such difficulties since she made no effort to join in the singing, and was more fascinated by the huge safety pin that Mrs Cheyne used to fasten her coat belt with.

On Sundays another of Sheila's talents came to light. After arriving home, she would gather her dollies in a row in front of her, and retell that day's sermon, unconsciously mimicking the dolorous voice used by the Minister. Betty and Jim would hurt themselves laughing behind their books. Their self-restraint would then be tested even further as Sheila livened things up by asking her 'pupils' General Knowledge questions to make sure they were paying attention. Her parents listened with aching sides while Sheila called out, "Bessie! What's the capital of Scotland? Longside? That's right. Go to the top of the class!"

On Sunday afternoons the whole family often took a walk out over the Ugie Bridge and on to the back road leading down to Bridge End. Usually, Sheila took delight in poking a stick through the wire netting at the chickens there, before they completed their circular tour by taking the main road back home again. Sheila would run on ahead while her parents followed together - Jim on his tricycle and Betty walking beside him. How they enjoyed these walks!

However fine it was to walk, Sheila was always keen to try out alternative modes of transport and sometimes this took the form of her father's tricycle. Sheila would be dispatched to the Smithy at Flushing to get her father's tools sharpened. She was safe enough on the road for there was very little traffic and she would be the envy of her pals as she set off for the smithy. When she got there, she would be sent to play on the swing while John Kane sharpened her father's tools, or sometimes he let her help him pump air into the furnace and make it glow red. These visits were always jam-packed with excitement.

Sheila also got to travel by car occasionally, when Jim would commission a taxi on a particular Saturday, and go round Rora, Kinmundy and Mintlaw collecting Rates from the householders there. He would set up his office in a classroom in the local school, and Sheila would happily draw on the blackboard, quietly, while her father got on with his work - on the understanding that she cleaned it all off when he finished. Betty would have prepared sandwiches and cake for them, and they made these into a picnic with their bottles of milk. Once in a while, Sheila would be given a whole penny to spend in the local sweetie shop. And the householders usually had a cheery word for the bairn, even though they were there to part with their hard-earned siller.

She also got to ride on the back of Mrs Penny's gig when the good lady set off for home after visiting Betty. Mrs Penny went everywhere in her gig which was pulled by a sheltie. At first, Sheila got to ride to the top of Cooper's Brae, and then as she grew older and bolder, was allowed to hang on until the outskirts of the village.

She learned to ride Marguerita's bike as well, while up at the Bauds, even though it was far too big for her. And she also had experience of riding a child-size tricycle when she visited her grandmother at Bucksburn. The trike belonged to Minty Orr, and she and Sheila loved to play on it. So did Minty's older sister - who once locked both younger children in the shed so that she could enjoy its pleasures all by herself.

On Friday nights during the winter, Sheila had a special treat. She would don her coat, hat and boots and wait while her mother wrapped a long scarf around her neck, cross it over at the front, and finally secure it with a safety pin at the back. Then she was ready to go up to the Church Hall and watch the silent films with her father. Felix the Cat and Charlie Chaplin were her favourites, and she got to stay up till nine thirty especially for these outings.

Sheila also enjoyed playing with the other village children. When she was older she went with Violet Souter to the Free Church Hall where they showed Magic Lantern Pictures to the children and arranged Kinderspiels. Local villagers and touring troupes used to put on children's shows for their amusement, and they were very popular.

It was safe enough for children to go around unaccompanied in those days. The streets were wide and although without pavements, the occasional traffic on the road made enough din to warn pedestrians in plenty time to seek safety.

There was no talk of child molesting or vandalism. Everyone knew everyone else, and grown ups were expected to clout any miscreants, and follow it up with a warning "to tell their parents!" whereupon punishment would be meted out twice to the hapless child. Children simply were not allowed to "affront" their parents, and indeed it seemed to the children at that time, that all the adults seemed to conspire against them getting up to much ill at all. Not that Sheila did get up to much ill. She was a willing child and eager to please her parents, and was always mindful of their orders.

One memorable Saturday evening in the late summer of 1928, Violet came round for Sheila as arranged, and they set off for the Kinderspiel at the Free Church Hall.

They went up Cooper's Brae and on round Armoury Lane where the ammunition used to be stored by the Territorial Army in the Great War. In the house adjoining it lived Mrs McKenzie, a Welsh woman and her husband. Quiet Mr Pratt lived with his family next door.

They ran past the house where Johnny Imray and his dog stayed, for he was so very ill-natured with children.

They crossed Inn Brae to Sharnie Lane, down the gable end of the Parish Church Hall, on past Mr Ritchie's house, then by Gardener Davidson's who tended the garden at Inverquhomery. Adjoining him was old Donald Gillies, who used to be the local carrier and coal merchant before Jimmy Milne took over from him.

Betty Harris was a big woman who lived on the corner between Sharnie Lane and Inverquhomery Road. The girls flew down through the Swan's Neck and up the road, then cut across the field to the top of Free Church Lane. They went down past Sandy Mair's place who worked at Meethill Farm for Fyfe the Slater. Then they turned to their left and climbed the steep Brae to the Free Church Hall.

A great evening was in store. The adults put on a super play for them which was all about the importance of friendships in life. Then they each got a drink of lemonade and a biscuit. Willie Cran, the son of the Chemist, was there handing out "sweeties" that he had taken from a jar in his father's shop, but Sheila and Violet along with most of the others declined to accept one. The last time Willie had done that, they had accepted his sweetie - and had had a sore tummy to show for it because they had turned out to be laxatives! They weren't taking any chances, although Willie swore to them that they were real sweeties this time.

The evening passed quickly for the girls and it seemed that in no time at all they were making their way home down Church Lane and along Main Street. As they turned into Cooper's Brae they met Charlie Ritchie, better known as "Leerie the Lamp" who went on his rounds night and morning with his little ladder to either light up or extinguish the stinking street lamps.

Sheila said goodbye to Violet and raced inside where she was immediately aware of excitement in the atmosphere.

"Sheila, you'll never guess what we've been discussing," smiled Betty, her face flushed with pleasure. She hadn't even opened the safety pin on her scarf, so Sheila knew at once that it must be something important.

"Daddy's going to make our house bigger!" Betty announced breathlessly, and waited for Sheila's reaction - and met with a blank stare from her daughter she rushed on, "We're going to have two storeys to our house extension and daddy's promised me that my kitchen window will overlook the road so that I can see what's going on. And he's going to build a lobby so that the doors will open off it and we won't have to go through each other's rooms to get to the one we want. There'll be a wonderful staircase with a stained glass window. We'll have lots of beautiful shiny wood and daddy will make special cement fireplaces and ornate ceilings. We'll have a separate dining room and kitchen and a lovely front parlour. Your new bedroom will be upstairs and you can help me to choose your curtains. Now what do you think of that, pet?" Betty's eyes were dancing with excitement as she put the question to her daughter, fully expecting her to join in with their celebrations.

They were therefore taken aback when their daughter stood and looked at them both for a while in silence.

Then, in a perfect mimicry of her mother and grandmother before her, Sheila put her hands on her hips and said in a voice that held just a touch of exasperation, "Well, well. Whatever next?"

At which they all fell about laughing.

*　　*　　*

Jim wasn't long in drawing up the plans for his new house, and managed to fit in all of Betty's requirements as well as his own. The front hall was to be made big enough to hold his older brother Bill's rug, which he had sent to them from India along with an elephant's foot that deputised as an umbrella stand. Jim had very decided ideas about the styles and colours of the fireplaces that he would make. The covings and architraves would be special too. He designed a beautiful stained-glass window for the stairs, and was very particular about the tiling of the porch floor.

Mr Chalmers of New Pitsligo was designated to do the masonry required. John Alexander Dickie of Peterhead, whose workyard was in King Street, did all the joinery. And Jim did all the interior and exterior cement craft himself.

Work on the huge extension started very quickly and soon tall scaffolding was erected against the staircase wall at the back of the house. A series of wooden ramps allowed the workmen access to the bedrooms, and Sheila flew up and down them while Betty covered her eyes. Her daughter had a whale of a time "helping" to build their house.

By the winter of 1929 the Mairs were snug in their new house with only minor interior details to be finished off. Betty was delighted with it all, including the view of the main road from her kitchen sink. She had been given everything she wanted for this house, and was now surrounded by quality fittings and furniture. Sandy had dismissed the whole project as "a waste of good money!" But Betty knew he was wrong.

The completion of their house heralded a new beginning for the family, and Betty started by having her hair cut for the first time, thinking it would be less bother. She had it styled into a "shingle" which suited her, but she found it was a lot colder that winter.

It had been an exciting and wearing year, but unfortunately, her knee had got a lot worse. Nevertheless Betty was extremely happy with their "new" house and was enjoying all its modern amenities.

*   *   *

But Fate hadn't finished with the family yet. Because, only three months later out of the blue, changes in government legislation meant that Jim no longer had a job as Poor Inspector in Longside.

Now he had to face a stark choice - stay in his beautiful new home and live off his pension: or sell up and move to Huntly as a Public Assistance Officer.

Chapter 18

The Tow Maun Gang Wi' The Bucket

Longside
30th May. 1930

Edwin J. Cormack
  Advocate
    Aberdeen

Dear Edd.,

I take up duty at Huntly on Monday first, and I propose to travel by train leaving Longside at 7.50 & arriving at Aberdeen about 9.25.

My train leaves Aberdeen for Huntly at 9.45, and as I won't have time to run up to your office could you come or send one of your girls to the Station for the Title Deeds, which I shall bring with me. Betty will be finished with the cleaning by the time that your advertisement will appear, and you can go ahead with the sale. I sincerely hope you will be successful.

Cheerio.
Jim

The unthinkable had really happened! Only three months after the new extension had been completed, Jim lost his position as Inspector of Poor and Registrar in Longside. If he wanted to continue exercising the Poor Law Codes he would have to do it as a Public Assistance Officer in some other town. As the effects of this new law began to materialise, it was inevitable that various areas would have to be amalgamated, and by the following year Jim's office in Longside was closed down and joined with Peterhead. The Poor Inspector there, was a relatively young man who was experienced enough to cope with this change, and Jim realised that it would be a long time before there was a vacancy in the Peterhead Office. His next choice was Fraserburgh, but that vacancy was already filled. So Jim then cast his eye farther afield and was offered a job at Huntly as a Public Assistance Officer.

The family went for a look round the area and liked what they saw. Betty and Jim discussed all the alternatives, such as Jim retraining for another job, or finding something else to do in the village, but concluded that if he was to work at all, he had better stick to what he was good at, and move to Huntly.

His intention, like when he first came to Longside, was to start work in Huntly while living in digs. Then he could cast around for suitable accommodation for his family to join him.

Once that decision was made, it was prudent to put the house up for sale as soon as possible. So they contacted Edwin and followed his advice.

Betty went along with these plans although her heart wasn't in it. She had grown to know and love Longside and was very reluctant to leave the friendly village. Also, although she had liked Huntly well enough, the decision to live there was causing her some anxiety. She couldn't put it into words - it just felt wrong somehow, and she wished she wasn't "fey." There was no practical reason why they shouldn't all move to Huntly, and she knew that her "feeling" about it wouldn't stand up to criticism.

She wrote to Bill in Nyasaland and explained her dilemma to him. He immediately wrote back by return of post urging her to follow her "feelings," and pointed out that they had all been "right" in the past. However, when it came to it, Betty could not find it within herself to undermine Jim's decision. She knew she had to go with her husband, so she placed her unresolved fear in God's hands and kept on praying.

In only one respect was Jim happy to be leaving Longside. Over the years his relationship with the Reverend Dickie Henderson had deteriorated and become increasingly acrimonious. The minister had started proceedings to oust Jim from his position as Session Clerk, and seemed to be succeeding mainly through the "old pals" network. Most of these old worthies had approached Jim privately and explained that while they supported him entirely, their hands were tied when it came to the vote. But they urged Jim to stay on for as long as he could. However the Reverend Dickie Henderson died of a heart attack shortly before Jim was due to leave the village.

Naturally, Jim tendered his resignation when he moved to Huntly. But he had been so thoroughly disillusioned by the internal politics of the church, that he decided to have nothing else to do with it - either here or in Huntly. It was a huge step for someone with his strong religious upbringing, but one that he never regretted.

Jim found excellent accommodation soon after his arrival in Huntly. Mr and Mrs George Smith and her sister Miss Gray ran "Deveron House" and were friendly and helpful people that made Jim very welcome and comfortable. The other boarders were Mr Farquhar, owner of a menswear shop, Eddie Anderson who worked in a bank, and an amiable travelling salesman who was only ever known by his nickname "Oxo." They all got on very well with each other.

Jim's new office was situated just off the square, through an arched doorway in a building at the back. This had been a very impressive house in its time and had five curved steps leading up to its front door. Jim's remit now covered an area large enough to support an assistant, and Charlie Simpson was his name.

The last government bill had radically changed Jim's workload. But although he approved of most of the changes, he was later quoted as saying that its weakness was that "Its rules were inflexible." Jim was now a Civil Servant - people whom he believed were "absolutely impartial and incorruptible," and "the finest in the world." But he thought this new scheme was like "a machine," and felt there was neither humanity nor common sense to be dispensed in the new system, and this was its Achilles Heel. Nevertheless, he followed its rules to the letter.

As well as being a much larger district, Huntly was a busy railway junction that also attracted a lot of vagrants who came to Jim for handouts. He deplored government money being spent on liquor, and dispensed bread and shoe tickets and any other tickets available, to the tramps instead of cash. This translation of the legislation was not widely appreciated by these men, and they showed their displeasure by slashing the tyres on his tricycle on many occasions.

However, Jim was kept busy implementing the latest changes in the bill, and on the whole liked Huntly well enough. His new friends invited him along to their local bowling club and Jim soon discovered that he had a talent for it. It was important that Jim found a new interest outside his work because he had a fair amount of leisure time to fill.

The main drawback to his working in Huntly was that he had to work all week and Saturday mornings too, and couldn't set out for home until Saturday afternoon. Added to this, the trains did not run on Sundays, making it almost impossible for Jim to come home at weekends. Also, he soon found out that winter conditions settled inland much earlier than on the coast, which added to his problems of getting home. However, being happy in his work, and having good friends made it easier for him to settle down there and accept his lot.

The same could not be said about his wife. In contrast, these became the loneliest years of Betty's life when she missed her husband dreadfully and hated spending so much time on her own. Her daily routine had gone, with no one to make dinner for at midday and no one to share a bit of news with and have a laugh.

Young Sheila was attending Peterhead Academy by this time and was thoroughly enjoying herself. She was proving to be very artistic and her parents were happy to encourage this gift. She was also old enough to join the Guides and Jim had built a large cupboard for their bits and pieces in Saint John's Hall where they had their meetings.

Sheila still enjoyed occasional weekends in Aberdeen with Aunt Susan and Uncle George. Now that she was older, she was allowed to go out with their young maid who was only fourteen years old herself, and hailed from Stuartfield. Their favourite outing was to The Picture House on Union Street. They would walk down Gordondale Road to the top of Fountainhall Road and catch a tram to Union Street that either went down by Albyn Place or Rosemount. Sheila enjoyed her short holidays with her "aunt" and "uncle" and was getting acquainted with the layout of Aberdeen as well.

During the week though, Sheila would catch the bus early in the morning to go to school. This bus route had only recently been set up, and before that the school children had had to go by train. But it was quite a distance for them to get to the station and they had had to leave very early in the morning. Then, because of the scheduled train timetable, the country children had had to be dismissed from school earlier than the others, causing them to miss a fair bit of their education over the years. So the parents welcomed this new bus route although the pupils didn't care much for it.

Once she had seen Sheila safely onto the bus in the morning, Betty was left with most of the day to fill in on her own. Twice a week, Mrs Wells came in to help her clean the house. Jim had insisted on this after he built the house extension, and now Betty was very glad of the friendly woman's company though it still left her with many long hours to fill in.

About once every two or three months Betty took the train into Aberdeen to the Co-op in Loch Street. Since 1918 it was called the Northern Co-operative Society Ltd. and its membership had more than doubled to 87,000. Each person who shopped there was given a number that was debited every time he or she spent money in that shop. Twice a year, in May and November, these members were entitled to their "divie" or dividend, and since the Co-op's prices were always competitive with neighbouring stores, it made sound economic sense to buy goods from them and get a share of the profits.

Betty preferred to buy in bulk there, and save even more money. If her goods came to over £2 in value, they would be packed into a wooden tea box and delivered by Mr Hardie a local carrier. It was an excellent arrangement that saved Betty money and more wear and tear on her worsening knee.

These monthly lists hardly varied. They were all written into her notebook, and as the assistant packed each item he would write down the price opposite, so that Betty could check the final total.

An example of one of her lists was the one bought in April 1934. It listed: 2sts. sugar = 6/5, 2lbs. castor sugar = 7d, 2lbs. brown sugar = 5d, 3lbs. tea = 7/-, 2 cakes Pear soap = 9d, 1lb. yellow soap = 6d, 1pkt. Lux = 6d, 1pkt Rinso = 6d, 1doz. boxes Puck matches = 1/-, 1doz. boxes Swan Vestas = 1/6, 2bottles coffee = 3/-, 3-2lb.tins syrup = 2/3, 1lb. semolina = 2d, 1pkt.

Creamola = 6d, 1tin Black Nugget (shoe polish) = 6d, 1tin lavatory pine cream = 1/-, 1tin Vim = 10d, 2tins pineapple cubes = 10d, 1tin pears = 1/-, box cheese Kraftlet = 1/-, 1lb. prunes = 10d, 1box dates = 8d, 2pkts McVitie's Abernethy (biscuits) = 6d, 1lb. tea = 2/4, 1lb. apple rings = 10d, 2lbs.water glass (preservative) = 6d, 2lbs.broken rice = 5d, 1strawberry and 1raspberry jelly = 9d, 2lbs.Imperial split peas = 8d, bottle of coffee = 1/6, 1lb.biscuits = 1/-. Total = 40/4 (£2.0.4d.)

The economy had settled down since the Depression and these prices seldom varied during the 1930s. But Betty's circumstances had changed and nowadays she was very aware that she had no parents in Bucksburn to pop in and see.

It was important that she kept busy, and she managed to economise on the housekeeping at the same time by making as much of her own jam as she could every year. Jim's garden was well established by now and yielded a lot of fruit, so with time on her hands Betty took a pride in documenting the annual results.

Between June and July of 1934 she made 12lbs of rhubarb jam, 13lbs of blackcurrant jam, 13lbs of strawberry jam, 17lbs of raspberry jam, 12lbs of raspberry jelly and 5lbs of apple jelly. Then in October of that year she added 14lbs of apple jam. This entailed a prodigious amount of work on her part but she thought it was well worth it when she looked in her store cupboard. This frenzy of jam- making also helped to stave off the loneliness that was never far away.

There was almost an acre of intense cultivation in the back garden by now and Alex Innes came and did the hard work including digging, hedge-cutting and planting. It was filled with apple and plum trees, blackcurrants, redcurrants, gooseberries, strawberries and raspberries. And during the holidays it fell to Sheila to pick most of the fruit, tie up the raspberry canes and cover the strawberries with netting, which she was happy to do when she wasn't enjoying herself at the tennis courts.

Despite her worsening knee, Betty insisted that Sheila accompany her for an evening walk whenever possible. She believed in the medicinal benefits of fresh air, for Sheila after a day cooped up in school, and tried to ensure that she got lots of good fresh air into her lungs every evening weather permitting, and despite the cold northeast climate. Their favourite walk was to the other end of the village as far as Whyte's Hygienic Bakery, and back again.

And so, although she was often lonely during the day, Betty was reminded almost every evening why she loved being in the village, and why she wanted to stay here.

There had been very little response to their advert to sell the house and Betty was still content to leave it at that. They had not raised the subject between themselves for a good while now, and Betty was daring to hope that that was the end of it.

But the constant pain in her knee sapped her energy and whittled away at her spirit. Both Sheila and Jim had tried to persuade her to see a doctor but Betty insisted that it would be a waste of money. Her own doctor at Bucksburn had convinced her years ago that nothing else could be done to help, so she was determined to carry on as best as she could. She found that if she got engrossed in some kind of project she could distract herself from the continual pain, and so she did this as often as possible. But it was very hard to do on her own.

*   *   *

The year was 1935, and everyone was saying that this was the warmest June they could remember. Betty had finished her morning chores and was waiting for Jim to come home. Her heart was not at peace though.

Six weeks ago Jim had gone down to a different hospital in Musselburgh to try out a new treatment on his arm. Instead of cutting the nerves, this time they were going to give him various injections followed by a special massage technique and according to Jim's letter from the hospital it had been more successful than anything he'd gone through before.

Betty had tried to persuade him to come home after this last session, but he had elected to go straight back to Huntly instead. She did her best to hide the hurt she had felt at his decision, and explained to Sheila that it was probably better for her father to go back to work and keep his mind off his pain.

Then Jim had written to her once a week for the following three weeks, saying that he was going to stay in Huntly for each of the three weekends "to help him get on." Part of Betty understood this, but the larger part of her was disappointed because she had always thought that she was the best person to help her husband recover. She hadn't seen him for eight weeks and was hurt that he hadn't come home to her sooner.

Then, this last week, Jim had written to say that he would be home on Saturday - which was today. But she wondered why he hadn't said which train he was arriving on, knowing that she and Sheila would have met him at the station.

Betty was at a loss. What was happening between them? Why had he stayed away for so long? She wondered if they were growing apart or ...she shuddered at the memory of her fey experience. Perhaps she was going to lose him...Jim was happy in Huntly, his work was fulfilling and his social life was thriving, while her own world was getting smaller and smaller, as more and more often she was unable to get out and about.

"When's daddy coming home, mama?" asked Sheila petulantly. She looked forward to her father's homecoming as only a child does. At fifteen years old Sheila was emerging as a young woman. She was at that stage in adolescence where she would show a mature outlook one minute, and revert to childishness the next. She had risen early this morning in happy anticipation of her father's homecoming, but that had been hours ago and now she had begun fretting.

"I don't really know, Sheila," her mother replied in as neutral a voice as she could manage. Betty was feeling nervous about Jim's arrival and was having difficulty keeping her doubts at bay. "He didn't say."

"Well, what time does his train come in?" persisted Sheila although she already knew the answer.

"Now, Sheila," answered Betty with a touch of sharpness. She collected herself quickly, and continued in her normal patient manner, "We don't know which train daddy's coming on because he forgot to say."

"That's because I didn't catch the train," said a quiet voice behind them.

"Jim!" breathed Betty. She whirled round and saw her husband framed in the doorway, smiling at them both. Betty looked directly at him, and to her immense relief saw that his smile reached his eyes, and all her half-baked fears dropped away. He still loved her.

Sheila threw herself at her father. "Daddy! You're home!"

"Where else would I be on this special Saturday?" he grinned.

"Where else indeed!" retorted Betty laughing. "But tell me, Jim. How did you get here? The next train isn't due for ages yet."

"You'll never guess," teased her husband, "so I'm going to tell you. No. Better still. I'm going to show you!" And his grin increased even more. "Come outside, you two!" he commanded. Then, "Whatever's happened to your leg, Betty?" he asked in concern as he watched his wife hobble towards him.

"Never mind," replied Betty briskly. "I'll tell you later. Now what do you want us outside for?"

"You'll see," said Jim enigmatically.

The bairn bounded out first but her step was arrested on the threshold. "Daddy!" she shrieked. "Is it ours? Is it?"

And Betty got to the doorway as Sheila flew down the path, opened the gate and screeched to a halt in front of a shining black Lanchester 10 car that was parked outside.

Betty gasped. "Is it ours?" she asked in wonder.

"It is indeed," nodded Jim. "I've had it for the last four weeks since I came out of hospital. I didn't come home these last weekends because I've been taking driving lessons. You don't mind do you?" he searched his wife's face closely.

"I've hated being away from you, Betty, and had to do something about it. Oxo convinced me that I would manage the pre-selected gears on this machine, and assured me that I would get used to using the clutch with practise. I was missing you so much, and that gave me the incentive to learn to drive."

He chuckled then added, "The examiner was non too pleased when I almost sent him through the windscreen at the 'emergency stop,' but he said that he passed me because I never took my hand off the steering wheel during the whole of the test. Thank goodness for my one big hand," he smiled. "You don't mind me buying the car do you, Betty?" he asked again earnestly.

"Mind?" echoed Betty. "Oh, Jim, what a wonderful surprise! And for the best reason in the world! I've missed you too," she added quietly. Then she laughed and added; "Now I couldn't be happier!"

"That's fine then," nodded Jim. "Now what do you say to a cup of tea, then I'll take you both for a spin? And while we're at it," he added grimly, "you can tell me what's been happening to that knee of yours."

The Ministry of Transport had issued their first Highway Code in April of 1931 in an effort to calm the chaos on Britain's roads. They had followed this up in 1934 with the Road Traffic Bill which made driving tests compulsory for all new drivers. Jim hadn't needed to alter his new car in any way, and he turned out to be the first disabled driver to pass his test in the north east. He was a canny man and promised himself never to drive above 35mph, just to be on the safe side.

With a car at their disposal Huntly didn't seem nearly so far away to the Mairs. The journey only took a few hours by road, so Jim drove home on Saturday afternoons and left early on Monday mornings. He was a careful and competent driver and Betty never knew a moment's fear with her husband at the wheel.

Then, as if that wasn't happiness enough, autumn of 1935 saw another upturn in the Mair family's fortunes when the position of Public Assistance Officer and Registrar in Fraserburgh became available. Jim applied for, and won the post. And to minimise the strain on him, he found very satisfactory lodgings in that coastal town with Mrs Leask at Grattan Place.

The Mairs lives were then set to carry on as before, except for one important difference. Because the journey home was so much shorter, Jim had more energy and could now come home every weekend. It was also much easier for everyone in the household, knowing that he was only a short distance away in case of emergency.

But no one could have predicted the way that Betty's loneliest years were to come to an end soon after her husband moved to Fraserburgh.

Chapter 19

East Or West, Hame's Best

There was no escaping politics during the next few years. So much was happening in the world, and it was being brought into British homes via the media. As well as newspapers and the radio, Pathe News Broadcasts shown in halls and picture houses all over the country were "windows to the world," and it seemed that the rest of the world had as little to celebrate as they themselves.

Three years earlier Paul von Hindenburg was elected German President. But most alarming, was that Adolf Hitler and his National Socialist Party had come second. Stories started to circulate about this young anti-Jewish man with fanatical eyes leading the fascist party and encouraging violence with his stirring rhetoric. Leaders around the world shuddered at his tactics but left him alone because they were too busy with their own problems.

Hitler's power grew until he was appointed Chancellor of Germany. And when the Reichstag in Berlin was burned down the following month, he blamed the communists in his country and clamped down on their civil liberties, and at the same time put an end to freedom of the press. Then he began whipping up national pride and unity by pointing at the Jews, branding them the enemy and ordering a boycott of all Jewish businesses in Germany.

In the "night of the long knives" in 1934, Hitler rid his Nazi Party of suspected traitors by organising a series of assassinations and arrests. Three months later he passed laws legitimising the persecution of the Jews, and made the Swastika his official flag.

Although the rest of the world found these acts abhorrent, they were still reluctant to get involved in anything that might lead to another war, and Britain was too deeply immersed in its own problems to consider taking on anyone else's.

Despite their victory in the Great War, the British people were still recovering from its devastation. Cities had been ruined and were still in the laborious process of being rebuilt. Machines were taking over much of the repetitive work in factories and putting workers out of jobs. The male population had been decimated by the war and their widows were struggling to survive on miserly pensions. The new middle classes were fighting their own battle to be accepted, and rise even farther up the echelons of the new class structure, while the working classes were battling daily against desperate poverty that threatened to take away their pride.

If people in other countries needed help it was their own look out, for the British had none to spare. They wanted peace now, and time to get back on their feet. But peace was elusive.

Problems continued to mount in Europe and in March Hitler re-occupied the Rhineland, in direct defiance of the Treaty of Versailles. Civil War erupted in Spain and the army mutinied against the republican government.

Britain could not intervene, because its own problems were escalating. Oswald Mosley had founded the "British Union of Fascists" at the end of 1932, and his followers wore black shirts bought for 5/- each. Their aim, through violent means, was to foster and promote patriotic ideals, and "purify the nation's blood." Mosley's instruments of persuasion were "rousing oratory, boot and fist" and people learned quickly to fear his Blackshirts. The parallels between Hitler's ideals and those of Mosley's were obvious, and the violence both used did not go unnoticed. But no effort was made in the beginning to stop either of the two men, so great was the desire for peace.

The year 1936 began with Stanley Baldwin as Prime Minister, and GeorgeV11 on the throne - but only just - for he died that January and his oldest son, Edward V11, succeeded him. However, the new king was immediately thrown into confrontation with the government because of political difficulties surrounding his future wife.

He had fallen in love with Mrs Wallis Simpson, an American who had already been divorced once, before she met Edward, and was still legally married to her second husband when the king began courting her. They were currently waiting for this second divorce to come through in order to marry, and Edward hoped the government would allow him to marry his American divorcee if she never took the position of queen. Along with this proviso the couple proposed that none of their children should accede to the throne. But the government refused to allow this marriage on any terms and would not budge.

So Edward abdicated on December 10th and added to the feeling of unrest in the country. Four months later his younger brother was crowned King George V1 at Westminster Cathedral but there was little time for celebrating.

During February the following year people saw and heard, courtesy of the Pathe News Broadcasts, that German planes had bombed the Basque city of Guernica. But although they were horrified and outraged at the loss of civilian life, they still did not intercede. Neville Chamberlain succeeded Stanley Baldwin as Prime Minister in May, and insisted he would continue to maintain peace for as long as he could.

A few weeks later Edward, now the Duke of Windsor, married Wallis Simpson in Paris, and because of his highly publicised dealings with Hitler, instantly became an outcast and embarrassment to the British Government.

Folks' understandable inclination was for peace, but those who were interested in politics could smell war in the wind that blew from the continent. Jim took stock of the situation and decided that seaside towns would be in more danger during a war, than Longside would be. And with this logic he proceeded to take his house off the market - much to Betty's relief. Then he made arrangements to paint the whole of its exterior red, walls windows and all - much to Betty's consternation.

She was right to be concerned, because Jim's plans were to erect scaffolding and enlist Sheila's help for painting the highest parts. Betty could not watch while her daughter, now seventeen years old and showing latent tomboy characteristics, climbed up ladders to paint the tall chimneys with a pail of red paint in one hand, and a huge paintbrush in the other. Sheila was in her element! She was working with her father again and being ascribed grown-up responsibilities. She laughed at her dangerous situations but was also careful not to get over-confident. She finished every day covered in red spots just as if she had the measles. Throughout this painting exercise Betty's pride in her family was tempered with concern for them. The frightening picture of Jim working up a ladder with only one arm and one leg simply didn't bear thinking about.

However, all things come to pass and the house was finished. Although the red was not particularly bright, the whole effect was eye-catching and well worth it.

Sheila had every reason to feel pleased with herself that year. She passed all her examinations at Peterhead Academy and was set to study for four years at Gray's School of Art in Aberdeen after the summer holidays. God had given her a talent and she was going to explore and improve her artistic ability before hopefully, making a living from it. She was especially good at "design" and had discussed with her parents the possibility of becoming a dress designer. When she looked into this, she had discovered that she would have to study in London, and knew this would have been a serious drain on the family's finances, although Jim and Betty would have agreed to it. However, the city was too far away for Sheila's comfort, and with war looming decided it was far too dangerous a place for her to consider moving to. Instead, she was looking forward to going into digs in Aberdeen.

She thought she had chosen wisely when she first settled in with a woman who came originally from Peterhead. It had been agreed that Sheila would be allowed to use the landlady's piano to practise on. But Sheila had come back one day soon afterwards to find the piano locked, and when she asked for the key, the woman had declined, saying that Sheila was "ca'ing a' the notes deen."

So Sheila cast around for alternative accommodation, and was lucky in that she found very suitable lodgings quite quickly. Mrs McDonald a widow, and her daughter Flora, opened their guesthouse to students, workers and soldiers who all got along exceptionally well together. Their lodgings were situated above the Henderson's Clock in Union Street, where they occupied the second, third and fourth floors. On the first floor was the premises of Mr Farquharson, a tailor. The English Army officers who lived there addressed him as Mr Fark-uar-son, much to his and the other guests' amusement.

Sheila shared a room with Vera Mercer, also an Art student, who was "walking out" with Alberto Morrocco who came visiting regularly. There was also Jan Gunn, a telephonist in the town and Archie Alexander, a maestro of the piano and the band-leader at the "Palais" dance hall in Diamond Street. Others came for a short time and left again, but these were the core lodgers. They were a jovial bunch and there was certainly no problem with regard to Sheila continuing her piano lessons. For £1 a week Sheila was given full board from Mondays to Fridays and she went home at the weekends. She was thoroughly enjoying being at Art School and working hard.

There was no respite for her at the weekends because by this time her mother was dependent on her. Betty's knee had twisted so far as to stop her walking, and she was spending the weekdays in lodgings with Mrs Leask along with Jim, who brought her home with him in the car at the weekends. This meant that there was lots for Sheila to do when she went home, but it never occurred to her to complain.

Finally, in April of the following year Betty went into Foresterhill Hospital for a long-overdue operation on her knee. "Septic Sandy" Anderson inserted two pins across her knee making it straight, and put a cast onto Betty's leg that went from her ankle to her hip. She had to keep this on for eighteen long months, which was an awful ordeal, but she looked forward to an improvement and eventually being pain-free. In the meantime the pain was dreadful, and Betty was fighting her own war.

Jim and Sheila grew very close, and one time when they were in Aberdeen together during her first year at college, they were walking past Claude Hamilton's Garage on Union Row where a grey Lanchester 14 was for sale. They both fell in love with it and Jim bought it on the spot! Sheila was one of only two women in Longside to have passed her driving test, and it was agreed that she should drive it out of the garage down Union Street and safely homewards.

It was so powerful that the first time Jim drove it, he abandoned his former vow never to drive faster than 35mph - saying that he and the car were happier to cruise at much higher speeds. And he later admitted to

Sheila that had he had two sound limbs he would have loved a career as a racing driver!

Just before Christmas in that year of 1937 the government voted to build air raid shelters in all major cities - the threat of war had moved significantly closer.

*   *   *

"Stop! Stop the tram! Now!" screamed Sheila. "Stop it!"

The bus conductor looked at her blankly. He didn't say a word, and more importantly for Sheila, he didn't move a muscle either.

"I said stop it! Now!" yelled Sheila again, and reached for the bell-pull. As her arm went up, the conductor was suddenly galvanised into action and pulled it for her.

The tram screeched to a halt and Sheila jumped off as quickly as she could.

"Father!" she asked anxiously, "Are you all right? Have you hurt yourself? Have you broken anything?"

Jim raised himself up to his full height and rested his arm on his daughter's shoulder. "I'm fine lass," he said shakily, and hauled himself onto the platform of the tram. "There's no bones broken and no harm done."

"No harm done?" spat Sheila as she rounded on the conductor. "How could you be so silly as to ring your bell before father had got on? He could have been killed!" This was a gross exaggeration although a true reflection of Sheila's rage.

"I'm sorry, hen," muttered the young chap whose face by now was burning red, and in his embarrassment he pushed his cap askew. He was young and acutely aware of being the centre of unwanted attention from his passengers.

"Sorry!" retorted Sheila. "I'll say you're sorry, but that doesn't help father! You saw him starting to get on the tram. What possessed you to ring the bell? He can't go any quicker than that you know. He's only got the one leg. And you never gave him a chance! I've a good mind to report you!"

242

Sheila had been taken totally unawares by the incident, but now that she knew that no permanent harm had come to her father she was flooded with relief. In the backlash of her emotions she was now giving vent to her fury at the hapless conductor who could do nothing other than stand there and take it.

And Sheila's tirade against him went on, for what seemed to him, to be an unnecessarily long time, while the passengers enjoyed the spectacle. They were adding their various comments on the subject, "That puir lassie's had a richt fleg," ventured one woman. "That yin's got a tongue on her that would clip cloots," remarked another. "He's only got the one leg," said another, while her friend noted that "he disna look as if he's only the one leg - and him so tall an' all." "Mercy he's an arm missing as well," commented another, while the man beside him surmised that, "He must hae been a sojer!" This latter was said unintentionally loudly, and it led to remarks of "brave man" and such, said in a tone of finality that seemed to draw an end to the whole business.

Sheila had eventually shouted herself to a standstill and so she led her father to a seat. He was affronted by all the commotion, and was very glad to sit down at last.

The conductor approached them gingerly. He hadn't enjoyed the rumpus and was relieved that things were getting back on an even keel.

"I'm sorry, hen," he apologised to Sheila for the umpteenth time. "I'll no take yer fare for this journey and I'll see yous off masel'."

"I am not a hen," began Sheila indignantly, "and don't think that you can....ouch!" she ended ignominiously when her father poked her in the side.

"That's very kind of you I'm sure," interceded Jim quietly. Then when the conductor had shot him a look of pure gratitude and self-consciously moved on, he turned to his daughter and whispered, "Ca' canny Sheila. You've hardly left him with a name to himself. You've got him so subdued that he'd throw himself off the tram if you told him to."

Sheila's face began to redden at her father's words. "Perhaps I was a bit hard on him - but I got an awful scare."

"I know you did, pet," her father replied in low tones. "But I'm fine now, and I think we should concentrate from here on, on getting you that hat you've had your eye on since we got here."

"How do you know about my hat?" asked Sheila in surprise.

"Aha," responded Jim. "Do you think I don't know my own daughter after all this time?"

So they shared a conspiratorial smile and each determined to enjoy what was left of their short holiday.

Sheila had mentioned in passing that her father was interested in going to the 1938 Empire Exhibition in Glasgow and Vera, her flatmate, had arranged for the pair of them to stay with her aunt in Cardonald for a few days.

She lived within walking distance of the exhibition, and everything had gone very smoothly up till then. Father and daughter had travelled down on the train and taken the tricycle with them. They had either walked or cycled to the exhibition each day of their holiday up till yesterday. As a war veteran, Jim had been allowed in for nothing, and as his assistant Sheila was given free entrance too.

They had thoroughly enjoyed themselves, and the icing on the cake had been when they met Nurse Pocock - the nurse who had been kind enough to get milk for Jim while in the hospital at Wimereux. Jim had been delighted to get it off his chest to her at last, that he hadn't meant to be so ungrateful as to refuse the milk that she had so carefully boiled up for him. The nurse quickly put Jim's mind at rest, and they had gone on to catch up with each other's news. Jim had been in high spirits ever since.

On this their last day, they had decided to take the tram into the centre of Paisley. Sheila had noticed a hat in one of the shop windows when they had arrived, and it had been at the back of her mind that they might visit the shop if they had time. She had been unaware of her father's perspicacity until he had brought up the subject of her hat whilst on the tram.

For a long time afterwards, Sheila was filled with self-recrimination whenever she thought back to that morning. If only she had made sure that her father had gone on the tram before her, the incident need never have happened. But, she made certain from then on, that her father preceded her safely on to any vehicle before she stepped onto it herself. However, the Empire Exhibition was voted a huge success by everyone who attended, and Sheila couldn't wait to describe it all to her mother.

*   *   *

But the war that threatened for so long could not be postponed forever. And when Germany occupied the rest of Czechoslovakia in March 1939, and followed it by invading Poland in September, the writing was finally on the wall. Hitler was asked to give an undertaking to withdraw from Poland, and when no such undertaking was given, for a second time in Jim's life Britain was plunged into war.

Jim felt sad as he watched his wife and daughter trying on their new gas masks and laughingly pretending to make a fashion statement of them. As he watched, he couldn't help feeling a kind of impotence that the government had been unable to prevent another unwanted war. But when he fitted on his own gas mask, he was filled with an unexpected determination to win. To make sure that this one would be the last.

He immediately offered his limited services, and was asked to be in charge of the Mortuary in Fraserburgh, which was in an old hall commandeered by the War Office. He began by arranging volunteers, mainly women, to be on duty if there was an air raid. Then he had to find tables and sheets and extra stationery.

One awful night a local store caught fire, and the flames alerted German bombers where to drop their remaining bombs, before returning to base. Unfortunately, a bomb landed directly on a local public bar filled with airmen from nearby Crimond. Jim set out in the dark to investigate the carnage, and had to clamber over debris and hoses to attend to his duties. More than thirty airmen were killed and Jim had the unenviable duty of identifying the bodies. This had to be done mainly through their identity discs, or "dog tags" as they came to be called when the Americans joined the war. Many bodies had been blown up beyond recognition, and their wives had to be called in for the sad identification process. Often, because they had been married so quickly, these women were unable to furnish appropriate details of their loved ones, and Jim had to wait until he found their Registration Books.

Marriages and Births were a large part of his remit at this time, and these pleasant duties helped fortify him against the horrors of the war. Once while he was conducting a marriage ceremony, a bomb landed close to his office, and before he could react, the couple threw themselves under the table. What good that was going to do them if another bomb fell, was anybody's guess, but Sheila's remark that at least they would have something funny to tell their grand children, brought a wry smile from her father. Both bride and groom were over sixty years old!

The war was going badly for Britain. German tentacles spread through Belgium and France, forcing the allied armies to withdraw. The last of the British troops were evacuated from Dunkirk in June 1940, and by then Germany had also overpowered Denmark and Norway. People at home in Britain expected a German invasion of their island at any moment, and had started fortifying themselves against it. In August that same year, the airforce launched the Battle of Britain, and Churchill broadcasted his famous words: "Never was so much owed by so many to so few."

Happiness could have been in short supply during these war years, but the British folk proved to be resilient.

Sheila's twenty-first birthday occurred at the end of 1940, in October, and everyone rallied round to give her a party. Her mother gave her two hens to take back to Aberdeen along with various vegetables; and all her fellow lodgers were invited to join in the celebration. Sheila's guest list included Captain and Mrs MacFyden. The Captain was in charge of a vessel that was currently berthed in Aberdeen Harbour, and he and his wife were temporarily residing with Mrs MacDonald and Flora.

They all enjoyed what was a veritable feast in the current circumstances, and by the time they started playing party games Archie Alexander had finished working at the Palais, and offered to play the piano for them. A little later there was a knock at the door. Vera went to answer it and returned to tell Sheila that two unknown young naval officers had come to join her party! When she investigated, Sheila discovered that when Captain and Mrs MacFyden realised they'd be unable to attend, they had deputised these two young naval lads in their stead. Naturally they were invited in, and they all had a whale of a time.

During the course of the evening the party played "Forfeits," and the hapless Archie was prevailed upon to go out into Union Street then and there and shout "Lost!" This was wartime Aberdeen and there were no streetlights on, no horses and carts clip-clopping past, and no vehicular traffic or tramcars going about. The place was deserted. The houses were all blacked out and it was a very spooky place to be! Archie survived to tell the tale, and they went on to enjoy Musical Chairs and other such children's games. It was hilarious!

When eventually the two Naval Officers were about to leave, they shamefacedly withdrew a bottle of whisky from one of their outdoor coats. They explained that they had brought it as a present and had been surprised when nobody was drinking at the party. However, they were agreed that with such fun as they'd had, there had been no need for spirits to keep the party going. And they thanked Sheila profusely once again for having invited them.

Of course Sheila accepted the whisky and eventually sold it to one of her fellow lodgers.

The war continued, but it wasn't all going Hitler's way any more. The British forces had pushed back the Italian army in North Africa, and Rommel had launched a Counter-offensive in mainland Africa. Soviet forces drove the German army back from the gates of Moscow, albeit with huge losses of life, and in December of 1941, Japan bombed Pearl Harbour which brought America into the war.

That same December, Sheila had a personal triumph to celebrate. She successfully completed her course at Gray's Art College, and was now half way through a six-months' course at Teacher Training College in Aberdeen. The position for an Assistant Art Teacher had come up at Peterhead Academy, and in a desperate attempt to move back home again, Sheila had applied for it. The competition consisted of three male teachers who all had more teaching experience than she had. However, the then Principal Teacher of Art, Miss Tough, chose Sheila, despite the fact that she would have to wait until her teaching course had finished. Sheila was overjoyed and began counting the days until she could go home to stay.

Although Betty's cast had been removed the previous year she was still in considerable pain with osteomyelitis. She needed help to run the house meanwhile and fortunately, Elsie Baxter agreed to be their live-in maid. A firm friendship was quickly established and Betty was enjoying teaching her to sew.

The war rumbled inexorably on, and as time went by, the tide of success gradually swung in favour of Britain and its allies. It took another three years to come to its conclusion, and by that time food and clothes were rationed and so was petrol. But, incredibly, there was still an abundant supply of optimism and camaraderie that kept the country going.

Again the British people were having to put up with the privations of war. Women took over various jobs in the factories, and food was always in short supply. Fashion went by the board, and a new generation of women learned to "make do and mend." Nothing was ever thrown out that wasn't absolutely worthless, and clothes were cut down and mended more than once in their lifetime. Silken parachutes were cut up for clothes. And because they had to do without nylon stockings, the women would cover their bare legs with "Sunburn" makeup, and draw a pencil line right up the backs of their legs so that it looked as if they were wearing seamed stockings. Utility furniture came on the market, and people were encouraged to buy the cheap simply designed pieces.

Life went on under the continual threat of being bombed, especially for those people in the cities. Doodlebugs were the worst, because they were quiet, and did not explode until a few seconds after they landed. The centres of cities could be reduced to bomb sites overnight, and everyone dreaded hearing the wail of sirens.

When America dropped atomic bombs on Hiroshima and Nagasaki, the Japanese surrendered, and by the 15th August in 1945 it was all over.

*   *   *

The British government declared it VJ Day, and it seemed to Jim and Sheila that everyone else in the world was celebrating while they stalked the corridors of their local hospital. They feared for Betty who was in the operating theatre.

Betty's cast had been on for a whole year before it was removed, and during that time her knee was suppurating and causing dreadful pain. She had lost a lot of weight and become a frail and pitiful semblance of her former self. Sleep eluded her most nights resulting in her looking pale and drawn, and she was forced to lie in bed almost all the time. Sheila did what she could to ply her mother with wholesome food to help fight off the infection, but Betty needed more than good food to get the better of this poison.

When she was first admitted to the cottage hospital at Peterhead in April the doctor pronounced her too ill to withstand the operation. So she had to lie there for four months - until VJ Day - before she was well enough to have her leg amputated. Generous local farmers and fishermen supplied the hospital with fish and eggs for the patients, that gradually helped Betty to put on weight. And the matron earned her eternal gratitude by introducing her to sleeping tablets.

Once her leg had been amputated, Betty was amazed at how much better she felt. The nurses were marvellous and soon had her fit enough to return home with crutches. By now she had more than made up for her weight-loss and all that healthy hospital food combined with no exercise meant that her muscles had turned to fat. She wanted to get back to her old active life again, but she soon found out how impossible that was going to be.

She needed her artificial leg, but the heavy strap that went round her waist was wide and thick and it chafed her skin with every move she made. Being a woman she didn't have a shoulder strap, like Jim's, to help keep the leg in place, and as a result she didn't have as much leverage either. Her stump too had to be fitted into a bucket, but it was much larger and heavier than Jim's, whose stump had been worn down to quite a small size by comparison. The construction was heavy and clumsy and caused her a lot of pain when she put her weight on it.

The difference between a healthy young man having his leg amputated and his much older wife having it done, soon became apparent, and Betty often wanted to scream with frustration. Now that she felt so much better she wanted to get cracking and make up for lost time but this was physically impossible. She progressed from relying on her crutches, to using two sticks, and then to the one stick that she'd use for the rest of her life. The chronic infection had left its mark and Betty would never feel fully fit again but she was determined to count her Blessings - which was easier said than done! However as time went by she gradually adjusted to her disability, just as Jim had done all those years ago, and although she coped in different ways from her husband, her strategies were just as successful.

That Christmas was one of the happiest Sheila could remember. Her father had retired in April and shortly afterwards her dearest wish had been granted. The whole family returned to living together under the one roof, Jim having accepted his retirement with equanimity.

He had worked hard during the war and as well as organising the mortuary, he had placed an assortment of child evacuees with various local families. He had also arranged for these Glasgow "keelies" as they were called; to have their education continued. Their numbers were so large that simple integration with the local pupils was impossible, and the outcome had been that the local children went to school in the mornings, and the evacuees attended in the afternoons with their own teachers. Most of these children had come from Glasgow, a prime target for German bombers on account of its huge shipyards. Thankfully, the children didn't have to stay long, and soon afterwards they returned to their parents whom they had missed dreadfully.

Jim hadn't minded his retirement in the least. As Inspector of Poor he had regarded himself as being in the service of his fellow man, and whilst in that position he had helped people to the best of his ability, within the rules of his office. He saw that the writing was on the wall for the rest of his colleagues, but had no regrets about it. For a while now, he had felt strongly that the time had come for the government to accept responsibility for its poor, and stop depending on an assortment of haphazard private agencies to somehow keep the existing system afloat. He knew that the stigma of being labelled "poor" did a lot of harm, and he thought that the government had a duty to care for these people without taking away their pride. And, after watching his wife's experience with illness, he also looked at the wider picture and thought it would be no bad thing if the government took responsibility for its people's health too. He would have liked them to set up a free Health Service that would care for the medical needs of everyone - rich and poor without exception. But his friends thought that this was taking things a bit too far.

Jim looked on his retirement as the start of a new and different adventure. One of the first things he did was to notify the government of his changed circumstances, and ask for his Pension to be reinstated. The government refused, so Jim contacted the British Legion again, and its lawyers argued his case until, eventually, Jim's pension was returned to £5. He wasn't surprised that he had to fight for it, because he now had had almost a lifetime's experience of working for the government, and he knew how "tight" they could be.

During all the time when he worked as Poor Inspector, he nearly always had a personal project for his spare time. His hobbies or "jobbies" as he called them, were as important to his well-being as his main employment. A few months before his retirement, he had been visiting an old couple in Lonmay and spied an old decrepit grandfather clock lying on their rubbish heap. He showed an interest in it, and eventually left the croft with the clock in pieces in the back of his car. He had taken it into one of the back rooms at his work and had reduced it to its component parts. Then he found a book on clocks, and began to study it.

When he left Fraserburgh he took all the bits of clock home with him, but Betty refused to have it in the house. He was content to take it into his shed out the back where he lavished it with care and attention. Jim was fascinated by its movement and concentrated on mending this mechanism first before turning his attention to the woodwork. He had collected various bits and pieces of matching wood that he cut to size and used to reconstruct a casement, and gradually, with the application of his new knowledge it began to resemble a clock again. When he finally completed it - he had the satisfaction of seeing his grandfather clock standing on the landing half way up the stairs, where Betty had given it pride of place!

He was inordinately proud of the finished article, and it never occurred to him that his achievement was all the greater for his having been self taught. And as for having done it all with only the one arm, he saw his disability as merely requiring a certain amount of ingenuity and an ability to adapt whatever was to hand.

Then, just when it seemed to Sheila that they were all settling nicely into a new and pleasant routine, Jim surprised them all one Saturday morning.

"I thought that you and I could have a wee holiday in Norway this summer," he said to his daughter as she poured the tea. "Let's go into Peterhead this afternoon and look into it. What do you say, Sheila?"

"Say...!" spluttered Sheila taken totally unawares by her father's proposition. ""What....?"

"Your father and I are agreed that you need a break, Sheila," her mother added smiling. "You should get away and see something of the world while you're young, and while we're not such a burden to you. The day'll come when you won't have a choice, so make the most of it now while you can."

Sheila was totally bemused at the turn their breakfast conversation had taken. She looked from one parent's face to the other and saw them smiling at her. And while her mind struggled to accept their offer, her voice took refuge in what was now the family's stock reaction to surprises.

"Well, well! Whatever ...?" she asked faintly.

"Before you ask," interrupted Betty crisply, "the next thing you're going to do is drink up your tea, then go into Peterhead with your father and book your tickets for Norway!"

And Sheila sat in stunned silence while her mother filled up her cup with tea, which is good for shock.

Chapter 20

Think Twice On A' Thing

"Mama! We've had the most wonderful time!" laughed Sheila as she entered the front door, addressing her mother by her old childhood title in her excitement. "It was absolutely marvellous!" she enthused.

Betty took in her daughter's flushed face and shining eyes and thought how bonny she looked. "So you enjoyed yourselves did you?"

"Oh yes, mother," replied Sheila smiling. But her mother's next words chased her smile away.

"That's a new coat you've got on your back surely!" remarked Betty eyeing her daughter critically.

Sheila looked troubled as she nodded her head in agreement. Her father had encouraged the spontaneous purchase of her fur coat while on holiday, but Sheila knew her mother's approval of such a luxury item would not come so easily.

"It was a bargain, mama," she replied softly, willing her mother to sanction her latest acquisition.

"Hmph! You and your coats," smiled Betty at length. "Still, this seems a good one you've chosen. And it suits you very well."

Sheila positively glowed at her mother's compliment. "Thank you, mama," she replied, mightily relieved.

She hung it up on the hallstand and both of them went into the front room where Sheila threw herself into one of the fireside chairs, eager to tell her mother all about their holiday in Norway.

"I wore it going through Customs, hoping I wouldn't have to pay duty on it! As you can imagine, mama, I was very nervous when our turn came. The young man looked at me very sternly and asked, 'Have you any Schnapps?'

And I answered innocently, 'No, I haven't got a camera.'

He roared with laughter and drew two crosses on our suitcases. I was so relieved!

Apart from that, everything in our holiday went very smoothly and not one thing went wrong," she continued happily.

"Except when it came to my bath," interrupted Jim laughing as he came in from his tour of the garden that he just had to see before settling down.

"Yes," giggled Sheila. "That could have been really embarrassing if the maid hadn't cottoned on so quickly that daddy wasn't a dirty old man." Father and daughter exchanged a significant look and burst out laughing!

"What's this all about?" asked Betty sharply. "Sheila! That's no way to talk about your father. And Jim! I'm surprised that you should find something funny about someone even thinking that you could be..."

"Dinna fret, Betty. You'll understand the joke when we explain it all," smiled Jim who had begun to look a little bit self-conscious.

"Well, tell me then!" demanded Betty crisply, and she looked keenly at the pair of them.

"It was like this mother," began Sheila. "We were in our rooms at Geilo when daddy decided that he would like a bath...."

"Start at the beginning!" commanded Jim. "Or we'll get your mother all mixed up." He looked directly at Sheila who nodded in agreement.

"Right," she said and sat up straighter in the armchair.

"After we parked the car in the long-term car park in Aberdeen, we took the train to Edinburgh as you know. Then we changed trains for Newcastle and arrived there more or less on time. The 'Stella Polaris' was waiting for us in the harbour. It was huge and beautiful. To think that it used to be the ex-Kaiser's own private yacht! It was far too big for only one person - much better for it to be shared with us!

It was very comfortable and the food was good - or so I'm told. I have never been so seasick in my life!"

"You were seasick for the first time in your life," interrupted Betty prosaically.

"Well, it felt as if I was sick for days," said her daughter ruefully. " It's hard to believe it only lasted for one night. It's true what they say, mama. At first you're scared that you're going to die - then you're scared in case you won't! Just about everybody was seasick and I hated that North Sea. Daddy was one of the very few people left standing - literally! Most of us took to our beds, but he strolled about the ship like an old sea dog!

We landed in Bergen very early next morning, and father had a shave in one of their barbershops. I was amazed at the amount of paper that the man wrapped around daddy's shoulders before he began. He tore it off from a huge roll that I just itched to get my hands on, I can tell you. That roll of paper would have lasted a whole week in my Art room!

Then we booked into our hotel, and it was huge and modern and completely luxurious to our eyes. We unpacked what little we needed for our overnight stay, and then we set out for a ride in the cable car up Floen.

We got in along with a Norwegian Army Officer, and you'll never believe it mama, but when he realised that we were Scottish, he asked us if we knew a town called - Fraserburgh! Can you imagine our surprise? Of course that got us talking. He told us how he had been stationed there during the war; and we told him how beautiful his city was. And all this while, the cable car was bearing us higher and higher up the mountain. The scenery was absolutely breathtaking! It was even colder at the top of that mountain, but I wouldn't have missed it for anything. The views were spectacular!

Once we were back down on terra firma we went for a walk. Everything is so different over there. Daddy had a good look at the structure of their buildings. We went to so many places, but I'll save that for later.

We had our evening meal in the hotel dining room and daddy ordered a whale steak!"

"Brave old you," said Betty looking at her husband.

"It wasn't too bad," came his contemplative reply. "It had a mild fishy taste and was rubbery. Eating it was a most peculiar sensation. It's supposed to be very good for you so I ate quite a few during our holiday, but, put it this way, I won't miss it now we're home," he ended with a smile.

"We were up early again the following day so that we could catch our train to Geilo," continued Sheila. "The journey passed quickly because we couldn't take our eyes off the magnificent scenery, especially at Myrdal which was so high up.

Geilo, where we stayed, was a small village, so there wasn't a huge amount we could do except admire the views, and go for walks and smell the beautiful clean fresh air. We looked in at the little local church when we were out on one of our walks."

"The air wasn't always fresh though, pet," smiled Jim. "You haven't forgotten the fox farm have you?"

"Yeugh!" said Sheila as her nose wrinkled up with distaste at the memory. "What an awful stink, and it lingered on our clothes for ages afterwards. I don't think I'll ever forget that smell!"

"It didn't put you off buying a fur coat though," teased Betty.

Sheila laughed, "I can assure you that my fur coat has a lovely smell that is nothing like the pong in that place!"

She sat back in her chair and looked into the middle distance, remembering some part of their holiday. Watching her, Betty saw that her daughter's face was pale with tell-tale dark circles under her eyes, and detected that beneath all the excitement, Sheila was very tired. She decided to make a cup of tea for them all, but was stopped short by her husband's next words.

"I didn't like their poufs one bit!" he announced.

"What?" asked Betty startled.

"Their poufs, you know what I mean. They're like our feather bedspreads, only they were encased in material, and went on top of you when you slept - instead of blankets," he persisted as his wife continued to look blank.

"Oh those!" she said with relief. "I've read about them, and aren't they called duvets? I'd have thought that with their being so light and warm, you would have got on better with them than with our woollen blankets. I take it you haven't brought one home with you then," she finished drily.

"Certainly not," confirmed Jim shaking his head. "I'll stick to cotton sheets and Mrs Penny's herringbone blankets, thank you very much!"

Sheila had revived a little, and entered the conversation again. "Shall we tell mama about your bath now?" she asked with a grin.

"Go on then," nodded her father with an answering smile.

"Well," began Sheila. "While we were in Geilo daddy decided to have a bath, and I went and got everything ready for him. And after he'd gone into the bathroom I went downstairs to see if anything was happening.

I can see that you've guessed already - I hadn't thought of everything. Poor dad had taken off his artificial leg and had got as far as trying to take off his shirt before he realised what I'd forgotten to do for him."

"His cufflink," interjected Betty, for whom this service had been automatic for years.

"Exactly, " nodded Sheila. "I wish I'd thought of it before..."

"It wasn't just your fault, I hadn't thought of it either," interrupted Jim taking over the story. "You understand, Betty, I couldn't get my cufflink off myself, could I? So I tried yelling for Sheila in case she was hovering nearby. She's very protective of me you know," he winked at his wife.

"As that poor tram conductor in Paisley found out to his cost," said Betty with a grin.

"When she didn't answer," continued Jim, "I pressed the bell for service - and it was my bad luck that a pink fresh-faced young lassie answered the call!

She appeared at the door, and when she saw me in my shirt, and sitting on the stool without my trousers, she went even pinker. She stood poised for flight while I tried to explain to her about my cufflink. But she didn't understand English and I certainly couldn't tell her about it in Norwegian.

You can imagine how it looked! But then I took the cufflink up to my teeth and held it out to her, and at last the penny dropped and she got the message. I think it was relief that made her giggle so much when she finally did the necessary - and I can only guess at what she said about it to her friends."

"Ah well," said Betty philosophically, "it's incidents like these that you'll remember all your life."

"I'll never forget this holiday, mama," replied Sheila sombrely. "Thank you so much for persuading me to go. And to make sure that you'll never forget it either," she added brightly, "I've written down every single detail of our holiday for you to enjoy at your leisure!"

"Thank you, pet," smiled Betty. "And what was your journey home like?"

"The sea was as smooth as a mill pond," said her husband. "All the seats in the dining room were filled on the way back."

"Yes," agreed Sheila. "And I finally ate a whale steak on the boat, and in answer to your next question, I wasn't particularly fussed for it either."

"Well, well, at least you can say now that you've tried it," laughed her mother. "Although I must admit from your description, it doesn't appeal to me in the least."

"Did anything interesting happen while we were away?" asked Jim.

"Nothing very much. The usual Hatches, Matches and Dispatches - that sort of thing," replied Betty in a deliberately nonchalant tone. "Except that I had a visit from Edwin."

She got their attention immediately, as she knew she would.

"When was this?"

"What did he want?"

"There's nothing wrong I hope," they both asked, instantly curious. A visit from Edwin was an almost unknown occurrence, and one she knew would generate a great deal of interest.

"No, there was nothing wrong," Betty shook her head. "He had to come up to Peterhead on business, and simply decided to come round past, since he was in the area.

It was right fine to see him again. He hasn't changed, although I don't think that he has ever looked well since he came back from the first war. Being torpedoed three times has clearly taken its toll. But he's always on the go. His work takes up a lot of his time of course, but he's also involved in a few local projects to help the poorer folk in Aberdeen. He has a quick sense of humour that makes everybody like him.

He and Winnie, who's doing fine by the way, are living at 30 Kingsgate in Aberdeen, and their sons Robert and James are at boarding school - Melville College in Edinburgh, where they're getting on fine. The boys come home for their mid-term holidays and you'll never guess what their favourite sport is! They love going to watch the wrestling at the Music Hall!

Edwin was so funny when he described it. Their favourite wrestlers are 'Ali the Wicked' and 'Abdul the Turk'- and they're both as Scottish as we are! Evidently, Ali stains his skin brown, and comes into the ring with a compass and prayer mat to get his direction right for a quick prayer to Allah. He shaves his head bald so that his opponents can't pull his hair, and pretends he's foreign and doesn't understand when the referee tells him to 'break.' But everyone knows that Ali understands just fine - because he comes from Fife and used to be a coal miner!

Edwin had me in stitches, and explained that the audience was part of the entertainment for him, because they would shout things like, "Tak' the hair oot o' yer een an' get on an' fecht!" He was so funny!

He was telling me as well, that when he goes to the kirk at Craigiebuckler Kirk, the minister Reverend Harry Ricketts, always seems to change his sermon to "the Rich having to give to the Poor." And this gets Edwin's back up, since he's always involved in good causes, and he takes exception to these veiled threats by the minister. It's to his credit that he doesn't let it stop him going to church altogether."

"Edwin was, and always will be, his own man," ventured Jim. "It'll take a lot more than petty badgering from a man of the cloth to make him leave the church."

They all nodded in agreement.

"Did he say anything about his work?" Jim asked.

"Only to say that it was going fine and that he has always plenty of work on his plate," answered Betty. "He was also saying that James is of a mind to study law at Aberdeen University. And Edwin's already made it clear that he won't employ his son while he's studying, because he doesn't think it would be healthy for him to be following quite so closely in his father's footsteps."

"Very wise," nodded Jim. "It seems that he's not looking to make it a family firm then, but you never know. And what about Robert, has he decided what he wants to do when he's older?"

"Yes, Jim," nodded Betty in response to his question. "Robert's going to study Animal Husbandry at Aberdeen University."

Again Jim nodded. "That's another wise choice. There'll be plenty of opportunities open to him with that diploma."

"Edwin was saying that Robert has itchy feet and intends to travel, " added Betty.

To which Jim replied, "Aye, he's got two bright boys there by the sounds of it. With their father's influence they'll not go far wrong in this world, and I'm pleased for him."

"It was wonderful to see him again," Betty smiled. "I'm right glad he came in past

"Well, Sheila," she turned to her daughter who was by now curled up in the armchair, "I think you should go upstairs for a little lie-down, pet. You look worn out."

"I'll not argue with you, mother," replied Sheila as she tried to stifle a yawn.

"And you too, Jim," added Betty. "I think that you'd be the better for a wee break as well."

"Na, na," said Jim briskly. "I've been wondering about building a greenhouse for a while now, and I think I'll just go out and get some measurements. I've decided that the best place for it will be at the far right-hand corner of the garden - opposite my sheddie."

Betty quickly smothered her surprise at his plans and merely said, "That's fine then. Just you do that."

"Right then," grinned Jim. "I'll away and change my clothes."

Left on her own, Betty pondered on their reactions to the holiday and concluded that she'd been right encourage them to take a break together, and was determined that they would get away as often as possible before Jim grew too old. She felt wistful that she would never be able to keep up with them now that she had her artificial leg. But on the other hand, she thought cheerfully as her natural optimism returned, at least she would never have that awful pain to cope with ever again.

This holiday set a precedent, and the pair enjoyed at least one holiday together every year for fifteen years, before they were overtaken by events.

Sheila was also sensitive to her mother's needs, and was determined that she too should get away for a short break. As it turned out, these long-weekend family holidays were so successful that they celebrated them at least twice every year - during the spring and autumn school breaks. They were short by necessity, but even so, the family got to know various Scottish towns fairly intimately. They went all over Scotland including Banchory, Ballater, Forres, Grantown and Strathpeffer. The latter wasn't one of their more successful holidays, being far too hilly for both parents with their walking disabilities. However, it always did them good to get away.

Sometimes Jim and Betty were persuaded to go on their own; with Jim doing the driving. Naturally, as time went by, and they could do less for themselves, they grew to depend on having Sheila with them. Now and again Jim would have a short holiday with his niece, Marguerita, up in Cullen. Marguerita's mother, Isie, had long since died and left The Elms to her and her husband, and they ran the big old place as a successful Boarding House. Marguerita loved to make a fuss of Jim, who loved having her fuss over him. So Betty and Sheila would leave them to it, and take off for a holiday together.

In each other's company their holidays were anything other than quiet, for they both shared the same sense of humour. And they loved to "people-watch" and speculate about their backgrounds and personalities as well as discuss their fashion sense. While Betty and Sheila were happy together, they were also well disposed to making new friends, and were so welcoming towards them that they soon had correspondents the length and breadth of the country. Hotels and Guest Houses rang with their laughter and these short holidays were never dull.

As the years went by, Sheila became more and more responsible for her parents' well-being and there was hardly a week passed when she didn't have to serve meals to one or both parents who were in bed. Sheila had thoroughly enjoyed her freedom whilst lodging in Aberdeen, and had made many friends, some of whom had offered their hands in matrimony. She enjoyed male company and really loved dancing. But she had discovered that she was truly happiest when all three members of her family were together, and so she looked on it as a blessing that she had never married, for it meant that she was free to look after her parents.

Sheila had chosen her career wisely, and was enjoying teaching art at Peterhead Academy so much, that she also conducted Evening Classes there for ten years. Miss Tough, her Head of Department, had Sheila's respect and friendship, and they got on well together.

Working in the Art Department meant that Sheila taught a high percentage of the school's pupils, and consequently became well known locally. She was strict but approachable, and had a never-ending fund of stories to bring home to her parents.

A circus was coming to Peterhead one time, and Sheila told her pupils to paint elements from the forthcoming attraction. Most students chose to paint a circus parade, except for one lad who painted a row of houses.

"Where's the circus, John?" Sheila enquired.

"Dash it," the lad replied. "It's jist gone roon the corner, so I doot you've missed it, Miss Mair!"

The boy was reprimanded for his insolence but his unique interpretation of Sheila's instructions raised many a chuckle inside the school and out!

However, while her job gave immense satisfaction, it was also tiring. And with the passing of the years Jim and Betty's dependence on her increased until the time came when the strain and pressure became too much for Sheila. Her doctor diagnosed "nervous exhaustion" and signed her off work. Sheila knew that she had arrived at a crossroads in her life, and with her parents' encouragement went away for a short holiday by herself.

She did a lot of thinking in Braemar, and even explored the possibility of leaving the area. To her ultimate relief her application for a promoted post in Edinburgh fell through, because after her interview in the city she admitted to herself that she didn't really want to go.

Still feeling fragile and vulnerable Sheila returned to her pupils in Peterhead and was caught unawares by the events there. "Toughie," or Miss Tough, Principal of the Art Department had accepted a proposal of marriage from "Middie," or Mr Middleton, a French teacher at the Academy, and immediately tendered her resignation. They had been courting for the last thirty years and the recent death of his mother had prompted him to pop the question. Toughie's answer had been a resounding "yes!" and then she had turned to Sheila and urged her to take over the running of the department. Encouraged by her art colleagues and with the blessing of her parents, Sheila applied for the promotion to Principal of the Art Department. She got onto the leet and was invited for interview the following Monday. But although she was back doing the job she loved, her usual assertiveness and optimism hadn't returned yet and she was worried that everything was happening too soon.

So to cheer herself up she caught the train to Aberdeen that Saturday morning and bought a new coat and hat.

"Well! What do you think mother?" asked Sheila, and turned round slowly to let her mother see the whole effect of her new grey coat.

"Well?" she asked when no answer was forthcoming. "What do you think of it?"

Betty scrutinised her daughter and thought what a sicht she was. The grey did absolutely nothing for her, and the old-fashioned style made her look drab. There had been a time when Betty would have spoken her mind without giving it a second thought, but looking at Sheila in that depressing coat Betty knew that she couldn't put her thoughts into words yet. Her daughter wasn't fully recovered, and although Sheila was smiling, her eyes were still guarded. Betty realised that Sheila didn't have complete confidence in herself, and longed to comfort her.

She couldn't give her honest opinion of the coat, in case she dented her daughter's confidence even further. Betty had no experience in dealing with this situation, for she had never had a problem with speaking her mind.

"You and your coats," she smiled, hoping to distract her while she thought of something more suitable to say.

It worked.

"I know," smiled Sheila. "I'm so fussy about my coats."

"Of course, I blame your Uncle Bill," grinned Betty, matching her daughter's humour. "He started you off with thon blue coat with the grey fur when you were little."

"I loved that coat," said Sheila softly and a faraway look crept into her eyes and a smile hovered on her lips. But then she glanced up and caught sight of herself in the mirror above the fireplace and abruptly, her mood changed. "But nowadays I've got to be practical and choose something that'll last."

"Do you remember the one you bought when you were a student?" laughed Betty persuasively, hoping to avoid commenting on the hideous new coat for a bit longer. And was rewarded when her daughter laughed with her.

"How could I forget it?" she chuckled. " I passed that shop every day, four times a day at least, going back and fore to the college. How I coveted that coat in the window! I tried and tried to save enough money to buy it - and then you gave me the money for my birthday present. I was so happy when I went into the shop with my £18 - and then she asked me for £21! I was devastated, and practically begged her to sell it to me for £18. I used every ruse I could think of - I told her I was a student and couldn't afford any more money. I said I would do without my dinner every day but the cost was included in my board and lodgings, and I couldn't save on bus fares because I was already using my bike. I was almost in tears before she finally agreed to sell it to me for £18. And hasn't it lasted well? It has done me for years, and it'll last a few more now that I've dyed it to that wine colour."

"Right enough," agreed Betty nodding, "It's very warm and cosy, and good for another winter at least. It has turned out to be a real bargain at £18 and I don't suppose your new one costs as little as that."

"No, but it was a bargain," asserted Sheila, as she smoothed down her coat yet again.

No it wasn't, thought Betty. I don't think you'll wear it very often because it'll get you down just as it's getting me down already. What a horrible colour. What's going on in my daughter's brain I wonder, that she could choose something so dull? I'd better have a word with Jim in case he puts his foot in it.

"You're not listening, mother," complained Sheila jolting Betty out of her reverie. "I said that my fur coat was a bargain too. I'll never forget how scared I was when I wore it to go through customs. It was worth it though, because I still adore my fur coat - even though it makes me itch!"

"Remember when you bought your waterproof?" asked Betty with a smile, again trying to postpone any criticism of the hapless new coat.

"Of course I do," replied Sheila. "What a good holiday that was. Certainly one of our best together."

There was a pause while each of them remembered their trip to Blairgowrie during one of Sheila's mid-term holidays.

They had stayed in the Glen Ericht Hotel on the edge of the Ericht River, and heard the water rushing over the weir immediately outside the windows. On the Saturday they had driven fifteen miles to Perth and Sheila had been disappointed not to find a suitable raincoat. But on their return to the hotel, Betty had remarked that there was a dress shop across the road, and suggested that her daughter have a look around it. Sheila had been delighted when she'd returned with a lovely navy blue trench coat with contrasting 'pebble dash' cuffs and collar - and a hat to match!

"Do you remember when I stopped off for a few days in London on my way back from Holland? I'd gone to Harrod's for a look at their millinery department, and I still smile when I think of that stranger approaching me," said Sheila reflectively.

"That's right," agreed Betty, happy as ever to keep away from the subject of Sheila's new coat. "You'd had a good holiday in Holland hadn't you? You did some of your best art work there."

"Yes, agreed Sheila. "and I was at the counter looking at scarves, when this total stranger came up and admired my coat, then asked me where I got it from."

"She never expected a geography lesson I'm sure," smiled Betty. "Now we know there's at least one Londoner who knows where Blairgowrie is situated."

They both chuckled at the memory

" But now I definitely need a new coat for my work," stated Sheila firmly, thus dispelling any further hopes that Betty had of prevarication. "And it has to be a good one that will last. So what do you think?" she finished, putting her mother on the spot for the second time. As Betty hesitated, Jim's firm voice was heard as he came in the back door.

"Is there any tea in the pot?" he shouted through. "I'm going to have a little break." There followed the sounds of his entry into the back hall and his slamming the door shut.

Shortly afterwards, he entered the sitting room where Sheila and Betty were having their conversation and Sheila was still standing with her new coat on. Jim checked his stride when he saw his daughter in her outerwear, and took a closer look at her.

"What a sicht!" he commented.

Betty's hand flew to her face in order to hide her concern. Oh dear, she thought sadly, I wish I could have warned him. Then she looked at her daughter with awe as Sheila immediately replied, "I know."

"What made you buy it then?" asked Jim puzzled. He was speaking for both parents.

"I don't know really," replied Sheila in a stilted voice. "I suppose it was such a good price, and the colour is serviceable and won't show the dirt. It's a bittie out of fashion, but it's good material and...."

As she searched for some other of its good points her father asked simply, "Wasn't there anything better in the shop?"

"Oh yes, daddy!" said Sheila eagerly. "There was a gorgeous pink one that was absolutely beautiful. It was very fashionable, and the material was out of this world!"

Betty was bemused by the change in her daughter whose eyes were now sparkling and whose speech was flowing easily.

"Why didn't you buy that one then?" asked Jim patiently.

Sheila's eyes became guarded again. "It wasn't really practical you know." And she lapsed into silence.

"What was wrong with it?" persisted Jim.

"Nothing," said Sheila keeping her head down in order to avoid meeting her father's eye.

"Well if there's nothing wrong with it, why didn't you buy it?" asked Jim pointedly.

There was a good deal of tension in the air by now, and Betty sensed that Jim was doing it deliberately. She felt really on edge now.

"Why didn't you buy it, pet?" repeated Jim gently.

Sheila hesitated then finally blurted out, "It was far too expensive!"

"How much is the difference?" asked her father.

Sheila thought quickly. "Twelve pounds," she said quietly. "But..."

"But nothing," said Jim affably, reaching into his pocket. "You get that other one." He glanced at the clock on the mantelpiece. "You can make the three o'clock train, and get into town before the shop closes. Go on now."

Betty watched while conflicting emotions crossed her daughter's face. Finally, Sheila turned and looked straight at her father, who smiled knowingly at her. Sheila's features cleared, and her own old grin that hadn't been seen of late, flooded her face. "Thank you, daddy!" she beamed. Then she quickly got everything ready and made a hasty exit.

"You took an awful chance there, Jim," said Betty reproachfully after they'd listened for her departure. She shook her head and didn't know whether to be amazed or angry. If it had all gone wrong and Sheila had buckled under the pressure of her father's questioning, there could have been unthinkable repercussions. She couldn't believe that Jim had chanced endangering Sheila's fragile recovery. And deep down, Betty acknowledged that she was angry with him.

"Not really," said Jim blandly." And at his wife's indignant snort he hurried on. "You see, I met her in the garden before she came in, and got her talking. I soon realised that she wasn't sure about the coat. And I knew by the way she spoke about it, that she didn't really like that one. One glance at thon ugly grey thing and I would have paid anything to get rid of it. Wasn't it awful?"

Her annoyance turned to relief, and then to happiness, as Betty realised that Jim had orchestrated the whole thing, and he'd been helping Sheila to get back to normal.

She thought long and hard. Then at last she put her thoughts into words as she summed up the incident, "Thon grey coat was the ugliest thing she's ever bought, and it made her a richt sight as you said. And deep down I'm glad it's on its way back to the shop," she stated decisively. Then she giggled, " - for it certainly would have depressed me if I had had to watch her wear it!"

"I wouldn't go that far," said Jim very seriously. "I mean, you once said much the same thing about my grandfather clock - and you've survived that experience."

Indignation rose up in Betty's breast and she immediately countered her husband. "But that was differ... Hey! Stop laughing at me!"

"We've too much fun in our household to ever let depression get the better of any of us, Betty. We'll soon put Sheila to rights!" joked Jim. But there was a look of determination in his eyes that was familiar to Betty.

Suddenly, she saw this kind, wise old man looking back at her, and wondered how she would ever manage without him. But she couldn't voice such a daft question, so she picked up the kettle and smiled at him,

"Tea for just us two then, is it?" And showed her love in a more practical way.

Chapter 21

Follow His Path And Ken The Man

The ferocious crackling fire had roared aggressively up the chimney for the last hour and now lay defeated among its ashes. From the grate came a muted glow in keeping with the contemplative atmosphere that had descended on the two women seated on either side of it. Polly Williams was making one of her rare visits to the Gables and Betty was enjoying her role as hostess. They had stuck rigidly to the demands of protocol and enquired after each other's health, and they had spoken in general terms about mutual family members and friends. Betty had served tea from her finest china tea service, and encouraged Polly to partake of her home-bakes.

Now, with tea over, Betty removed the trolley, and by unspoken consent the two women were ready to abandon propriety and indulge in more intimate revelations. It was late afternoon and the weather had turned colder. Rain was on its way if the dark scudding clouds were anything to go by as Betty drew the curtains closed. She switched on the standard lamp, which emitted a suffused glow that she preferred to the bright clinical strip light on the ceiling. The room felt cosy, and the comfortable mood invited confidences.

"Sheila shouldn't be long now," smiled Betty. "She visits her father every day after school. The matron arranged it for her, you know."

"Which hospital did you say Jim was in?" asked Polly. "Was it Maud?" "Not any more," came the reply. "When it first happened he was taken to

Peterhead Cottage Hospital, then after a while they put him into Woodend Hospital in Aberdeen for assessment. After that he was put back to Peterhead, then transferred to Maud for a while before getting a bed at the Ugie Hospital. They were very kind to him in Maud Hospital, and he was very well looked after - but he just couldn't settle in there." Betty shook her head.

"What was wrong with it?" asked Polly.

"There was nothing at all wrong with the hospital or the staff. In fact, Jim went to great lengths to explain that they were excellent. It was just that throughout his working life Maud Hospital had been the Poor House, and he had had to place people there. And although it's now completely different, he couldn't get over his continually associating it with the Poor House. Well, he couldn't use that as an excuse to change to another hospital, could he? But our Sheila found the answer."

Betty settled more comfortably in her chair, and her face was animated as she explained, "She always went to visit her father after school and usually read to him. She soon realised that the other men were always listening in, so she gave up any pretence of reading solely for her father, and read to the whole ward instead!" Betty smiled at the memory.

She came back to the present and gave Polly a rueful look, "'Back to our muttons though,' as Jim would say.

Sheila pointed out to the hospital director that driving to Maud Hospital late every afternoon after school was tiring her out unnecessarily - especially when there was a vacancy in the Ugie Hospital in Peterhead. It wasn't as if she got the rest of the evenings to herself either, since she had to come home and look after me. Well, you know how persistent our Sheila can be, and she finally got her way. Jim was so relieved I can't tell you! But it was nothing to do with Maud Hospital itself, because they were extremely good to him - it was just its association in his mind with the Poor House.

Anyway, he's happy in the Ugie Hospital. And he hasn't lost his sense of humour by all accounts. Yesterday he spotted a new young nurse, so he asked her to go into his locker for something. Of course when she opened the door, his artificial leg fell out and the lassie skirled out of her! She took the joke in good heart and has warned Jim that she's planning some kind of "revenge." They're really very good to him, and it is a lot handier for Sheila. She was getting very tired with all the running around."

"Is she still teaching Art?" asked Polly.

"Oh yes, she loves teaching," smiled Betty. "There's a lot of extra work involved with being a Principal Teacher but she's well used to it by now. She only applied once for promotion, and got it. Poor Toughie, her predecessor, left to get married in 1954 and do you know, her husband died the following spring! What a shame she never returned to teaching.

I think that Sheila would run a tight ship, but she seems to be popular with her pupils and her staff for all that.

She swears by her staff, and says there's none better. I feel as if I know them all personally; she's talked so much about them. There's Jim Barritson, Nan Cunningham and Edi Swan who work full time, and a quiet woman, Miss Cow, who works part time. The pupils call them 'the menagerie' because they have a Cow, a Swan and a 'Mair' in the department. Nan and Sheila are especially good friends. I met her once and she struck me as a warm and very elegant woman. Edi Swan's a character who has everyone laughing. He's got lots of energy and is always bringing in new ideas. Sheila knows she's lucky with her staff, and though I say so myself, I think her staff are lucky to have Sheila!

But there, you'll know all about staffing problems and such like yourself, Polly. How did you enjoy being a headmistress before you retired?"

"Very much, Betty," nodded Polly. "I liked teaching at Ordiquhill. It's such a pretty little place up by Cornhill, and the children were lovely. Everyone knew each other so there were no discipline problems - certainly nothing like what was going on with my colleagues in Glasgow, that's for sure! Yes, I had a lovely time up there.

But when they were looking for a headmistress at Saint Katherine's I thought I could take on the job. And I felt it was time for a change - it would have been very easy to stagnate where I was. Anyway, with nothing to lose, I threw my name into the hat, and the rest, they say, is history."

"Your father would have been right proud," asserted Betty.

"Mm," agreed Polly nodding, too long in the tooth for false modesty. "I haven't done badly. And my promotion gave the gossips something new to talk about and get all wrong," she smiled.

Betty grinned at her. "You've fairly kept the gossips busy!"

"I know," laughed Polly, but then her face darkened as she added, "I never thought my desertion would cause such an unholy scandal. It hurt papa terribly, and I regret that."

"What?" asked Betty sharply. Then she asked more kindly, "Are you saying you should've tried harder at your marriage?"

"Good Heavens no!" exploded Polly. "There was no way on earth that would have worked! Not at all!" And she laughed aloud while shaking her head.

Then, with all trace of hilarity gone, she continued soberly, "I mean that it hurt papa - not only my leaving my husband - but all the horrible rumours the gossips put about afterwards."

"He was a good man, your father," said Betty quietly.

"I know," agreed Polly. "Some people thought he went round doors selling Bibles because he wasn't much good for anything else, but they were wrong. My father was a very astute man and could have had a good job. But he truly believed he had a calling, and that was that. He travelled all round the north east, and was often soaked through and hungry, but always went back out again next day. He was deeply religious and didn't deserve to be hurt so much by my divorce," she ended bitterly.

"Couldn't you have prevented it?" asked Betty gently.

"If I could have, I would have," said Polly sadly, and Betty's heart went out to her cousin. Polly had caused a huge scandal when she'd left her husband on the night of their wedding, and some of the family had stopped talking to her long ago.

Then the sober atmosphere in the room changed completely as it rang with Polly's laughter. "I did enjoy all the trappings of marriage though, Betty! I'd never had it so good! I could wear all kinds of clothes without censure, come and go as I pleased, and of course - papa bought me my little car. Once I got married I was free of all kinds of silly restrictions. My 'marriage' gave me respectability and lots of advantages - without any drawbacks!"

"Some of us enjoy the 'drawbacks,'" laughed Betty with a knowing wink.

When their giggles had subsided, Polly continued, "One of the nicest things about staying in Fyvie now, is that I've got to know the buyer at Maitlands of Turriff."

"You always were interested in clothes," remarked Betty. "You're tall and have a lovely figure. No wonder you've always followed fashion. And you're certainly enjoying your retirement by the look of things."

"Oh yes," returned Polly. "I've always plenty to keep me busy, and of course I still love entertaining. But it's sad to think of how many family and friends are gone now."

"I know what you mean," nodded Betty. "I never saw myself growing old, but when I count how few of us there are left, I realise that the years have taken their toll." She paused. "There's only Sandy and myself left of the Cormacks now."

"He'll be retired by now, I suppose?" asked Polly sitting back comfortably in her chair. "Did he teach at Robert Gordon's all his life?"

"Yes, he's retired now," affirmed Betty, "But he was Headmaster at Rosemount School before then, and I believe he was well liked and respected by both pupils and parents. There's a funny story about that," she smiled impishly, and at a nod from Polly she continued. "Sandy took great pride in knowing every single one of his pupils by name, and one morning when he was on his way back to school from a meeting, he came across one of his pupils loitering on the pavement. Without more ado, he marched the boy back to school and straight into his office where he asked him what he'd been doing - and the boy answered, 'Delivering sausages to a customer, sir. I left school last year, sir.' And then Sandy noticed the brown paper parcel in the boy's hand!"

When their mirth had subsided Polly got back to the Cormacks.

"You used to have three brothers didn't you?" she asked.

"That's right," assented Betty. "Bill went out to Nyasaland where he tried his hand at farming. Then he took to converting the local fish into 'smoked haddies' but that never really caught on. Then he bought Ryans Hotel and was doing very nicely when he came home for a sinus operation. He married his nurse, Janet, and took her back to Africa with him. They were doing fine with the hotel until the war broke out and Bill went to help at the Military Training School for Drivers at Fort Johnson. Meanwhile, Janet got a job running the Military Hospital in Kenya as Matron. After the war was over, they tried growing tobacco in both Nyasaland and Northern Rhodesia, but they grew it at the wrong time and the crops failed. They were always so optimistic and were all set to try something else, when Bill died. By then Janet loved the country too much to come back here. And, in fact, she's so well liked in Lusaka where she lives now, that the local males take their intended brides to her for inspection first, before their own mothers." Betty's light laugh gave way to a more thoughtful expression as she added, "She's a real character is Janet, but not an ounce of humour in her and always a cigarette in her hand. It's a pity they didn't have any children."

Then she shook her head and continued her narrative. "Poor Edwin my youngest brother was never the same after the war. It destroyed his health, but not his spirit! He was genuinely Christian and had a terrific sense of humour. He was taken at just fifty two. It wasn't fair.

His family have all ended up in Africa, you know. His wife, Winnie, is in Rhodesia and his sons are in Nyasaland and Salisbury, with their wives Beryl and Babs.

His eldest son, Robert, got his diploma in Animal and Dairy Husbandry at Aberdeen, and then contacted the Colonial Development Corporation because he wanted to work abroad. He chose Bechuanaland, to the north-west of South Africa, and had to help clear 10,000 acres of African bush, then plant crops - unfortunately, the seedlings were all eaten up by the lions, elephants, baboons and all manner of wild animals out there!

So he moved to Southern Rhodesia and got a job driving a truck for Coca-Cola. He must be a good worker because they keep promoting him. It's on the cards that he's going to have to move to Malawi as their Chief Executive Officer of 'The Southern Bottlers Limited.' That shows how far he's come. He's well known there, I believe. You see, Polly, it's the same the world over; with ability and hard work there's no limit to what you can achieve - and Robert's already proved himself able!

His wife, Beryl, was born in Bloemfontein in the Orange Free State. Her father came from Belfast and was a doctor in the First World War. But Beryl told me that he witnessed so many atrocious things on the battlefield that he couldn't bring himself to practice medicine again after the war ended. So he became a dentist instead. His wife was Scottish and they met and married in Pretoria, then went on to have a son and a daughter. Shortly afterwards, the family moved to Johannesburg where Beryl grew up. She went on to study Agriculture there, then decided to move to Rhodesia when she got her first job. Her employer put her up in the 'Sydney House Hotel' which was a common stopover place for new employees and immigrants and such. Strangers were often asked to share a room because the hotel was in such demand. And because it made their stay so much cheaper, and it was only for a few nights, most people were only too happy to share. Of course, it was a "whites only" hotel so they all felt that they had at least something in common. Strange system that..." added Betty with a puzzled shake of her head. "Well, Polly, I believe it was fate that put Beryl and Winnie in the same room!" she continued with a twinkle in her eye. "Because then, it was only a matter of minutes before Beryl was introduced to Winnie's sons - Robert and James. Cupid's aim was true, as they say, and Robert and Beryl got married soon afterwards. Now they have two young children, Barbara Jane and Robert James, and they're all happily settled out there." Betty sat back in her chair with a satisfied smile. "Isn't fate a wonderful thing?"

She didn't wait for Polly's assent or otherwise before introducing her to Edwin's second son.

" Now, Robert's younger brother James, studied Law at Aberdeen. He began his degree in 1950, after completing two years National Service in the British Army. James needed to find a law firm that would take him in 'to serve articles' while he attended university, and Edwin had always said he wouldn't have his son working with him in Crown Street. Edwin was adamant that James was to stand on his own two feet, and told him knock on the doors of as many firms of solicitors as it took, until he was accepted as an apprentice. James confided in me later, that he walked round and round Golden Square in Aberdeen for over an hour, and was literally shaking with nerves when he approached Morrice and Wilson at number

15. It was his first attempt, and thankfully, his last, because he was accepted straightaway.

You know, Polly, I really believe that fate again had a hand in Edwin's refusal to have his son working for him. You see, James had only been with Morice and Wilson for five months when Edwin died suddenly of a cerebral haemorrhage. James would have had a lot more problems to deal with if he had been working for his father. Nobody could have foreseen that future. You see, although Edwin had never been particularly strong since the war, nevertheless he had been an active man who hadn't had a day off work through illness. His sudden death shocked everyone and it was especially sad that he didn't see his younger son graduate." Betty paused, and then smiled as she remembered the occasion.

"James was made a Bachelor of Law in 1954 and invited Sheila to the graduation ceremony along with his mother and cousin Sheena. Sheila was full of it at the time because it turned out that they were seated behind Sir John Hunt and Edmund Hilary who were being given honorary degrees. What excitement!" For a moment it seemed that Betty was about to expand on that thrilling occasion, but checked herself as she realised these reminiscences would be of little interest to her cousin.

"Where was I? Oh yes, South Africa!" She looked keenly across at Polly again, and was encouraged by the interest she saw on her face.

"James was newly qualified when he accompanied his mother, Winnie, then a widow of three years, and went out to join his brother in Southern Rhodesia. They set sail from Southampton on the 18th of November and spent five weeks at sea before disembarking at Beira in Mozambique. From there they travelled by train, and arrived at Salisbury on Christmas Day where Robert met them. I had a hilarious letter from James about that. He said that on the train journey most of the crew had 'over indulged,' including the driver, and as a result the train jolted in and out of all the small stations along the line. After it took a particularly violent leap leaving one of the stations, a suitcase plummeted from the luggage rack above her, and almost landed on Winnie's head! At about the same time, the drunken guard staggered along the corridor outside their compartment, and Winnie had had enough! So she summoned the guard, and demanded that he tell the driver to go slower and avoid all the jolting. 'Madam,' the guard had slurred in reply, 'You want the train to go slower. The people at the front want the train to go faster. And I don't want the bloody thing to go at all!'"

Betty and Polly shared a good laugh together, before Betty continued, "What a journey that must have been! And to arrive on Christmas Day of all days - it's just as well Winnie had a sense of humour."

"Did James have a job to go to?" asked Polly, caught up this family history.

"Surprisingly - no," answered Betty. "But you're forgetting, Polly. He had gone to 'the land of dreams' as my brother Bill called Africa. James had his qualifications and a positive attitude, and in no time at all he got a job with 'FB d'Enis and Associates.' They were a firm of Patent and Trade Mark practitioners, and James signed up with them for three years."

"Did he enjoy working there?" asked Polly.

"Not really, no," was the honest reply. "He soon discovered he would never be happy in that firm, but felt obliged to stick it out for the three years that he'd promised. The main thing was that during this time he was admitted as a Patent and Trademark practitioner in the Federation of Rhodesia and Nyasaland. So in 1959, after his three years were up, he entered into partnership with two South African attorneys, and the firm practised as 'Fisher, Cormack and Botha' with James as the sole resident partner. Then, when the Federation was dissolved two years ago, in 1963, James remained in Salisbury and opened branch offices in Lusaka and Blantyre."

However, all work and no play makes Jack, or in this case James, a dull boy. And with his impish smile and quick sense of humour James is anything but dull - and he likes to play. Don't look so shocked, Polly," laughed Betty. "He didn't get up to any ill. I just meant that he was too like his father and too gregarious, to go through life with just his mother for company."

"You mean he got married," smiled Polly.

"Just so," agreed Betty. "I got a lovely letter from him at the time. Did I tell you that he writes a good letter? He's informative and funny, and I always enjoy his letters!

Well, last Christmas he went to a 'do' at the O'Briens, a lovely family, and Irish as their name suggests. He met Kathleen Margaret Ann Gale, and it was 'love at first sight' for both of them. Her nickname is 'Babs,' which is what her grandmother used to call the family cat. Well, James always says that it was her sense of humour that he fell in love with, and not her legs — although there's not a thing wrong with them either! They were married in the Presbyterian Kirk in Salisbury soon afterwards.

Babs is third generation Rhodesian and her father, of Scottish descent, is a journalist who writes Rhodesian history books as a hobby. Babs is an Infant School Teacher, like you. She trained at Grahamstown Teaching College in Eastern Cape and was shortly appointed headmistress of, what was it called... Tombo...Tumba... no, it was 'Vumba Heights School' in Rhodesia. She was one of the youngest women in the country to obtain a headship. This school, which was attached to a nearby hostel, served the local village children and included certain 'disadvantaged children' whom the authorities thought would benefit from the healthy mountain air up in that area. Babs had always wanted to live in a beautiful and healthy spot high in the mountains, and all her colleagues encouraged her to apply for the post so they could join her during the school holidays.

"My goodness!" interrupted Polly. "Talk about jumping in at the deep end. These children must have been a handful - and her on her own too!"

"And that wasn't all of it," laughed Betty. "The school was supposed to be haunted as well!"

"No!" shrieked Polly. "Did she see any ghosts?"

"I doubt if any ghost would have stayed around there for long," smiled Betty. "According to Babs, the place was in such a dilapidated state, she invited the Director of Education up to inspect the place so that he would agree to get it all renovated.

Not only that, but there was a thick forest between the hostel and the school that she had to walk through every day, where monkeys swung and chattered on the high branches and threw things down on her!"

"Oh dear, thank goodness Scotland isn't like that. She must have been very brave," opined Polly.

"Babs didn't see it like that at all. She said she really enjoyed being in the wilds. Of course, when you're young you don't see the dangers do you? You think you're going to live forever."

Polly nodded sagely. "That's so true," she smiled. "You see horrible things happening to other people and you think you're immune."

"Quite so," agreed Betty. "But you haven't heard the worst of it yet. By the time the Director came up to inspect her school terrorist activity had been getting more and more frequent in that area. When the man saw how isolated the school was, and how vulnerable Babs was as a woman on her own, he decided it would be better for a man to run the school - and better still for that man to be married! I don't think the Director was being chauvinist in his decision, Polly, he just thought it made more sense - but it left Babs spitting feathers I can tell you.

The school was repaired but a couple of years later it was closed down - following a shocking massacre at a nearby school! So Babs' headship lasted just six months!"

Polly hesitated. She didn't want to appear ignorant, but on the other hand she recognised a good opportunity to satisfy her curiosity. "So what about this 'apartheid' business Betty? What does it mean to Jim and Babs? I mean...have you asked them how it works......or anything?" her voice trailed away.

"I was interested too," smiled Betty. "James said although 'separateness' or 'apartheid' hasn't been legalised in Southern Rhodesia, there's very little intermingling of the races. Blacks don't have a vote and have to carry 'situpas,' identification documents; while white people don't need any identity papers at all. There are hardly any black men in senior positions in government or business. And in railway stations and banks and other public buildings, they have separate entrances. For instance, the Post Office has a sign saying 'Whites Only' at one door, and 'Blacks Only' on the other. In general, the blacks are employed as farm labourers, cleaners, messengers and for other menial jobs and have a reputation for being lazy.

James explained that it has being going on for years, at least since 1948. Everyone is used to it, and there's no animosity between them as far as he's aware. He sees relations between blacks and whites as being friendly, as far as I can tell.

But then, Jim and Babs live in Rhodesia. When people think of apartheid they're usually thinking about South Africa where there's a lot of friction between the two races. Some of the white Afrikaaners are afa coorse to the blacks! They treat them as if they were animals and beat them and starve them and.....Oh it's too terrible to think about, Polly. Not all Afrikaaners are guilty - but there seem to be enough of them to provoke all the different black tribes into organised rebellion. The whites can't kill or imprison all the leaders of the ANC, - that's the African National Congress, so it goes on and on. This is a bad business in South Africa, Polly. There are an awful lot more blacks than whites, and if the blacks ever do get together - well; this is what the whites are scared of. And if the blacks take over it'll need a miracle to save their white skins. They say the best solution would be for blacks and whites to live in harmony with each other, but if anyone can achieve that, and without a massacre, ...Well, I'll take my hat off to him!" Betty had become fairly knowledgeable about the situation, and felt quite passionately about it.

Polly let her cousin's last words evaporate into the warm room. There was another question on her mind but she didn't want to cause Betty any embarrassment, since it concerned her African connections. However, this was too good a chance to miss, and Polly finally decided her curiosity just had to be satisfied.

"Er...is Babs white?" she asked uncertainly. Then she plunged in, "I mean, she's a Rhodesian didn't you say? Are they black or white, I'm afraid I'm not too sure."

"Babs is definitely white," beamed Betty, glad that she hadn't been asked anything too intimate. "With a gorgeous suntan from living in that lovely climate! Mind you, they've all got to be careful of the sun out there. It can get very hot, and white skins burn quickly. Poor James doesn't like the sun - and it doesn't like his nose so he tries to keep himself covered up. They're both early risers though, and it's safe to go out before the sun gets too high. Then they try and stay indoors during the hottest part of the day.

They're a lovely couple."

Another silence descended on the pair as one woman thought fondly about the love match, and the other one of the implications of teaching in a lawless land.

Polly resumed their conversation first. "Isn't it sad how so many of our family and friends are now dead? Even ones that survived the war have gone."

"I know what you mean," agreed Betty conversationally. "I still don't feel old enough to start preparing for death yet. But the fact is that at our age we should be - according to our family statistics. Look at the Mairs for example. There aren't many of them left, despite the prolific number that grandma Mair produced.

Annie's been dead for a while now. She was a dear soul, but only lived to fifty seven before she died of natural causes. Of course, I always blamed thon afa tea she and grandma drank. It was aye boiled, and yea boiled! It must have ruined their innards. I used to get up to all sorts of tricks to avoid drinking it - and the geraniums usually copped it."

"Was that her secret?" asked a surprised Polly.

"It wasn't so much her secret, as mine - and a few other people's too I suspect," smiled Betty. "Did you never notice how much darker the soil was in the pots in the good room?"

"No," laughed Polly, "and I don't think Annie ever guessed either. I asked her how she managed to get such lovely flower heads, because mine never looked as good. Poor Annie, she just thought she had naturally green fingers!"

Polly shook her head and smiled. "I might as well give up growing geraniums then, because I never have enough tea left over to give to my flowers. I drink it by the pot and not the cup, so there'd be lean pickings for my flowers."

Both women sat back in their chairs and quietly remembered Annie in her own way till Polly broke the silence again.

" Jim's brother, Bill, the one who joined the Merchant Navy then settled in South Africa. Did you manage to see him after he came home?"

"Yes we did," answered Betty promptly. "We met him up at Cullen just after they moved back. His wife and daughter were with him, little Patsy was only six years old as I remember," said Betty with a fond smile. "You know what young children are like. Before we met up, she was told about my artificial leg, and warned not to mention it. Well! Of course the warning made her really curious and it was only a matter of time before the bairn asked me about my 'bad' leg. Jim split his sides laughing, and said it wasn't the bairn's question he found so funny - it was the shocked faces of her parents! And, he blamed them for Patsy's inquisitiveness, because the innocent little mite hadn't noticed that he was sitting beside me, wearing an artificial leg and arm!

I remember we took Patsy back with us to Longside for a wee holiday and Sheila amused her and took her to play tennis. She was a charming girl and easily made friends in the village. It was a shame she was so young when her father died."

"Aye," assented Polly. "There are surprisingly few Mairs left considering Grandma gave birth to twelve. There's just Jim and E.J. now, since the others either died when they were young or were killed in the war - except for Isie. She died in '52, when she was eighty one. I think she had a good life, or perhaps I should say she had a quiet life that lasted a long time.

Then there's E.J. She was aye sending money to young Annie for something or other. And there she is now, my poor E.J. lying in Seafield Hospital longing for a visit from her niece." Polly's voice wavered and she surreptitiously wiped a tear that had slowly made its way down her cheek at the memory of her cousin.

"I do miss Elsie Jane you know," she smiled self-consciously. "We had some really good holidays away in my little car. When there was all that rumpus after my 'wedding,' E.J. defended me - and never once asked me why I had done it. She was a friend in a million,"

"You know it was while he was up in Cullen Jim had the first accident that led him to where he is now," said Betty sadly, breaking the stillness that had descended into the room. "When he was staying at The Elms," she added in response to Polly's inquisitive frown.

And with a deep sigh, she expanded, "You remember, after Isie died, according to the terms of the will The Elms had to go to the next male in the family, and that would have been Jim, Marguerita's brother. But the Browns got together and 'prevailed upon' him to give the house to his sister Marguerita. It was just as well, I suppose, because that boy was a lazy article and would never have made the effort to keep the old house in good condition. Well, Marguerita got married, and she and her husband turned the place into a boarding house, and they're still doing fairly well out of it.

Now, my Jim always had a soft spot for Marguerita, and she for him. So every now and then, we - Sheila and I, would drop daddy off for a wee holiday with her, and go away somewhere else ourselves two, then pick him up on our way back home. The arrangement suited everybody: because we weren't much fussed for Marguerita's company, and this way left her free to coddle him as much as she wanted. And Jim really liked her - and loved getting spoiled by her. So, as I said, it suited all of us to separate for our holidays every once in a while.

Until his fall at The Elms, Jim hadn't had many problems with his health. Apart from going into hospital every five years or so to have the nerves in his arm treated, he was only in hospital twice. One was for a varicose vein operation on his right leg - as you can imagine, it had to take an awful lot of extra strain throughout the years. And the other time was when he sprained his thumb. He had a lot of tumbles during his life, but nothing serious ever came of these.

But when he was up in Cullen staying with Marguerita, he had a particularly nasty fall, and thought he had bruised his stump. The local doctor looked at it and confirmed there was nothing more to it than that, and told Jim to rest it. That meant he would have to lie in bed until it mended, so Sheila made all the arrangements, then went up to Cullen and brought him back to the cottage hospital in Peterhead."

"Why did he have to go there if it was only a bruise?" asked Polly.

"He would have been totally dependent on Sheila, that's why," answered Betty a trifle sharply. Then checked her tongue and explained more gently, "You see, it meant that Jim needed to stay in bed all the time. I was in no condition to help him to the toilet, or turn him in bed, or sit him up or any of the hundred and one things that an infirm man needs done for him in that situation. And Sheila was working all day. Even if she had been at home, she didn't have the physical strength to lift him or do anything on her own. Jim required the assistance of at least two nurses, and to get that he had to go into hospital. He wasn't happy about it, but made the best of it."

A few days afterwards he asked Sheila to bring him in his artificial leg to try on, but when he put any weight on it he was in excruciating pain. Well, that showed the doctor that something a bit more serious than a bruise was causing the pain. It was only then that they sent him for an x-ray, and it showed the bone in his stump was broken. Not only that, Polly, but the two broken parts of the bone weren't properly aligned and had already started to join. Poor Jim! There was nothing else for it but to stay in bed until the two parts of bone fused fully. They couldn't put a cast on it, you see.

So, Jim lay there for weeks, and during that time his muscles began to waste away. When he did finally manage to come home he was painfully stiff and slow, but determined to get upstairs and back into his own bed - which he did eventually."

"Was it fine to have him back beside you?" asked Polly full of sympathy for their plight.

"Oh, no!" exclaimed Betty as if shocked by the very idea. "Jim and I had separate bedrooms long before then, he's always been an afa snorer. Mercy! He snores away like a steam engine!" She laughed aloud and continued mischievously, "I often wonder how the other patients are getting on with that racket every night. He fairly makes the rafters ring!"

She laughed and laughed but when she caught her breath suddenly, Polly realised that her cousin was on the verge of crying.

And Betty's eyes were still suspiciously bright when she went on to ask, "When did we turn old, Polly? It seemed to happen overnight, and I wasn't ready for it. I'm still not ready yet, but old age has come uninvited anyway."

She looked into the dying fire and her eyes gradually dimmed as she became contemplative. Her voice sounded sad and wistful when she eventually added softly, "We had such fun!"

However, Betty could never give in to self-pity, so automatically reached into her store of memories for a funny story.

" I remember when the time came that Jim couldn't have a bath on his own," she began, prompting Polly to sit up attentively - her cousin was never indiscreet but things might have changed with time!

"Sheila and I set the tub in front of the fire and supported him at different angles in order to wash him, and really, we all became contortionists to get to his different bits. I would wash him from the top down, as far as possible. Then Sheila started with his feet and worked her way up, as far as possible. And then, to preserve his decency, Jim would always take the sponge and insist that he would 'see to possible' himself!

It was all fun!" Betty's voice threatened to crack with emotion; but she took a deep breath and continued, "Jim's walking ability deteriorated badly after the bone was broken, and he was continually having to visit Hangars to have his bucket reduced, or changed or replaced. He was never as confident on his feet after that accident but loved to potter, and was always going to and from his sheddie working on his various 'jobbies' as he called them..." She stopped to collect herself again.

Polly's concern for her cousin prompted her to reach over and place her hand on Betty's knee and whisper softly, "I can see how hard this is for you. Leave it for now if you'd rather."

"No," said Betty shaking her head as if fortifying herself. "You're family, and it'll help me to talk about it."

Polly nodded sagely, "I know what you mean, Betty. Just you carry on."

Betty stared into the middle-distance and struggled to relive the nightmare event.

"He was pottering in the sheddie doing one of his 'jobbies' and when he didn't come in for his dinner, we just thought he'd lost track of time, so Sheila went out for him." She paused as the memory flooded back. "Sheila found him lying unconscious on the floor of the sheddie ...where he had collapsed.

Sheila couldn't lift him or anything, so she ran for Nattie and Kenny Anderson and Mr Craib from across the road. And they came and carried him upstairs, then the doctor arrived and said that Jim had had a cerebral haemorrhage.

The ambulance took him to Peterhead Cottage Hospital, and as I said before, they put him out to Woodend Hospital in Aberdeen for assessment. Back he came to Peterhead, then into Maud Hospital, and finally they moved him to the Ugie Hospital where he is now," she finished dully.

"I'm sorry, Betty," said Polly quietly. "How long ago did this happen?"

"Saturday the 23rd May 1964," replied Betty automatically. "Sixteen and a half months ago."

With no more words of comfort for her cousin Polly remained silent and gently rubbed her cousin's knee in sympathy.

"Well, there's nothing can be done about it now," said Betty with a touch of her old firmness. Polly took the hint and withdrew her hand, and colluded in the search for a happier topic. However, it was Betty who came up with something first.

"What a lot of changes we've seen in our lifetime, haven't we, Polly?" she asked. "I was discussing them with Sheila only the other day."

Polly nodded encouragingly.

"I can remember when I was young, running outside to watch a man go past on a bicycle. Then years later I'll never forget the Saturday Jim came home from Huntly with our first car. I hadn't seen him for weeks and was scared we'd grown apart - but he'd bought it and learned to drive so that he could come home more often and I was so relieved! Even Donald the Horse and the others had to give way eventually to the motor car.

Then buses came along and we had a choice of travelling either by train or bus - and now Doctor Beeching is going to close down our railway station! Why we can't have both is beyond me. They say the day will come when everyone has a car but I can't see where they'll put them all!" Betty sounded sceptical.

"Goodness knows," Polly chipped in. "I must admit I preferred driving when E.J. and I had practically all roads to ourselves. And the cars go so fast now!

Travelling has changed so much! Ordinary people like us can go on cruises now, and not just the rich and famous!"

"Who would have thought a man could buy his own yacht and sail it on his own across the Atlantic?" asked Betty.

"Imagine a man wanting to do that!" laughed Polly and was relieved to see her cousin more relaxed.

"Then there's the aeroplane," she added. "Fares are coming down all the time. Aye, we've come a long way since bicycles!"

"And who would have believed we would put a man into space?" asked Betty with awe. "That was the stuff of science fiction and children's comics. But Yuri Gagarin has gone round the world twice - and come back down again. It's amazing!"

"Hmph! And they still can't cure the common cold!" grumbled Polly, certainly not in awe of man's scientific achievement. "They would have done better, in my view, if they'd spent the money getting rid of our problems down here on earth, before careering off into space!"

"They've done wonders in the field of medicine, though," suggested Betty with a hint of her old asperity. "Take the anti-biotics they've got now, for instance. Sheila had awful trouble with a mastoid two years ago. In my day that meant putting up with dreadful pain for ages, hoping you were healthy enough to overcome it - and not everyone did," she added darkly. "Instead, Sheila was taken into the Cottage Hospital and given two anti-biotic injections a day for a week. They were afa sore - but she was home again seven days later and almost right as rain! It was like a miracle."

"I wish they'd discovered anti-biotics before the war, Betty," said Polly soberly. "Too many of our men didn't survive."

"And others wouldn't have been mutilated," added Betty earnestly. "And, people like me need not have feared Septic Sandy. Why! He'd have lost his nickname!" she joked, although her laugh didn't quite disguise her bitterness.

She tried again, "What would our parents think of all the changes?" she asked and pursed her lips in mock censure.

"They would disapprove of the time I spend watching television for a start," asserted Polly. "But I can't help it. I watch Grampian Television for the news every night, and I like 'Points North' when it's on, and I watch all their documentaries. I can't resist 'Bothy Nichts' or 'Country Focus.' I'm so hooked, I even watch children's programmes like 'Romper Room' before tea if I've time."

"We've never had a television set," remarked Betty with perhaps a hint of censure. "Jim never liked the idea, and Sheila and I have never thought about it."

"It's got lots of good points - if used in moderation," said Polly defensively, then seemed eager to change the subject. "What do you think of women's fashions today?"

Betty considered the question fully before answering, "I remember when women were given the vote at twenty eight, no one ever thought then that it would lead to 'Women's Liberation!'" Then she smiled and added, "I couldn't bring myself to burn my bra - most uncomfortable! As for navy blue 'jeans' both men and women are wearing! They're not healthy! And the short skirts in fashion these days! They'll have trouble with their kidneys - you mark my words!" she insisted with a grin as she waggled her finger at Polly who joined in laughing.

"We certainly sound old!" she giggled. "I don't think it is 'hip' to be sensible, Betty. We're definitely showing our age!"

"Do you remember when we got electricity?" asked Polly brightly.

"Indeed I do," asserted Betty. "1945 when it came to Longside. And I stood in the kitchen and flicked the switch up and down and thought it was a miracle," she chuckled.

"So did I!" grinned Polly. "And I took great delight in throwing out all those nasty smelly tilley lamps! Who'd have thought we'd end up cooking with electricity? Not that I mind because I was never friendly with the range myself."

"I remember great big black dollops of soot landing on top of my baking and making me hopping mad," laughed Betty. "And Jim would say..." Betty stopped abruptly, and a sigh escaped her, "I can't help it, Polly," she apologised, and her shoulders sagged. "Now that I've been talking about Jim, it's as if I can't stop.

I hate to think of him lying in that hospital bed!

He was a man who thrived on work and couldn't ever sit and twiddle his thumbs. He had to be doing something all the time. He would come in and say, 'I've been thinking that you could do with a.... five-sided cupboard to fit into a space in the kitchen. Or a high stool that I could sit on at the sink and look out the window, or a little stool for my feet when I sat down. He made lots of things for me. He'd had no training so he'd get a book and learn. The words 'I can't' didn't seem to be in his vocabulary. He never stuck. And never let his disabilities get in the way of anything he wanted to do."

"He was a good man." nodded Polly. Then she encouraged Betty to talk about Jim by asking, "Did he enjoy being an Inspector of Poor?"

"I don't think that 'enjoy' would be the right word," said Betty meditatively. She thought a while longer. "No, he didn't 'enjoy' his work. You must remember he came from a family of builders, and was happiest working with his hands. It was an effort for him to get on with people. He tried his hardest - and succeeded in the main. But no. In his heart of hearts he was denied working at his first love. But in all these years I've never heard him complain. I know he did his best. He would have wanted to do more for some of the people he dealt with, but had to stay within the rules. Mind you, Polly, he'd no time for wasters or drunkards. And he despised men who didn't treat their wives and children properly. It used to make him boiling mad.

He was a strict man, strict with himself, and with Sheila - and it doesn't seem to have done her any harm."

"She's a lovely young woman," stated Polly.

"But as for 'enjoying' his work," continued Betty as if she'd never heard her, "his real 'enjoyment' was in making things with his hands.

At work he drove himself very hard, and did all he could for his 'clients.' It sometimes brought him a feeling of success, like when he prevented a family being sent to the Poor House at Maud. Or when he saw a child was happy with the family he had placed him or her with.

No, I wouldn't say he 'enjoyed' his work, because communicating with people didn't come naturally to him. He worked very hard at his job, and put in extra hours and things to get a good result for someone he thought deserved it, in which case nothing was too much trouble. He earned the trust and respect of an awful lot of people and always lived up to his position within the community.

He served people all his life, and did all he could to make life better for as many of them as he could. He never turned down any reasonable request; he built the tennis court, and started a choral society. He gave talks about his work and would oblige people by writing 'professional' letters for them, which usually brought results. Or he was happy to advise them on any aspect of building, from planning on paper to actually making moulds and things. When Sheila started the Guides, and Jim heard they needed a cupboard he built them one. It's still there in Saint John's Hall.

He was never slow to put his hand in his pocket for a good cause in the village...

What was that?" Betty jumped involuntarily as she heard a sound from outside. And relaxed when she realised what is was.

"It'll be Sheila! Oh that's fine, I'm glad you'll meet her."

They listened while Sheila entered the front door, and were surprised when she burst straight in on them in the semi-darkness. She hadn't even stopped to take off her coat and hat.

"Mother, you'll never guess what daddy has planned!" Sheila said excitedly as she burst through the door. "Goodness, it's like a morgue in here," she stated breathlessly as she flicked on the stronger light.

"Oh, I'm sorry!" she cried, startled at the sight of Aunt Polly sitting by the fireside.

"Not at all, not at all," reassured her 'aunt.' "You're excited about something," she smiled.

Sheila looked uncertainly from her to her mother, who nodded and said, "Polly and I have shared so many intimacies this afternoon, one more won't go astray."

"Are you sure, mother?" asked Sheila doubtfully. "It's about father."

"Is anything wrong?" asked Betty sharply.

"No, no, he isn't any worse or anything bad, don't fret on that score," Sheila reassured her mother.

"Well, what is it then, pet," asked Betty briskly.

Sheila hesitated only slightly, then announced, "It's daddy, mother. He's going to leave his body to Medical Research. He's been told they'll be interested in the changes caused by having only one arm and leg. And he says that he's 'glad to be able to do this last service for his fellow men.'"

Both women were stunned at her piece of news.

"What did I tell you?" pronounced Betty almost instantly. She hadn't expected her words to Polly to be confirmed quite so soon - and so explicitly - as this. Really! she was in a state of shock.

She thought about it while Polly and Sheila engaged in smalltalk. Then, ever true to the family's traditional response when taken by surprise, Betty shook her head and clasped her hands together on her knee. And with a touch of vexation in her voice asked of no one in particular, "Whatever next?"

References

Personal letters and documented speeches of James Mair

The Parish of Longside - Rev. Alfred S. Barron

Statistical Account of Longside 1856

The Hendersons of Caskieben - Dr Alexander Cormack

Yesterday's Britain - Reader's Digest

Jamie Fleeman The Laird Of Udny's Fool - JB Pratt

The Clyack Sheaf - David Toulmin

Skinner's Poems and Songs - Rev. John Skinner

Letter from Robert Lunan to Enos Downie

The New Book of Knowledge - Waverly Book Company

Longside and its People - AH Duncan

The Imperial Gazetteer of Scotland approx. 1867

The Village Roupie and Other Poems - JR Imray

First Daily - Norman Harper

Goodbye To All That - Robert Graves

Leopard Magazine October 1999

The Oxford Book of War Poetry

The Manchester Guardian June 30th 1917

Burns Complete Poetical Works (Kilmarnock Edition)

Discovering Aberdeenshire - Robert Smith